1980

A Very Small Remnant

A Very Small Remnant

Michael Straight

Introduction by Don Graham

A Zia Book

UNIVERSITY OF NEW MEXICO PRESS
Albuquerque

Library of Congress Cataloging in Publication Data

Straight, Michael Whitney.
A very small remnant.

(A Zia book)
Reprint of the 1st ed. published by Knopf, New York.
1. Sand Creek, Battle of, 1864—Fiction. 2. Wynkoop, Edward Wanshear, b. 1836—Fiction. 3. Chivington, John Milton, 1821–1894—Fiction. I. Title.
[PZ4.S896Ve8] [PS3569.T678] 813'.5'4 76-21507
ISBN 0-8263-0433-8

University of New Mexico Press paperback edition reprinted 1976 by arrangement with Alfred A. Knopf, Inc. Manufactured in the United States of America. Library of Congress Catalog Card Number 76-21507. International Standard Book Number 0-8263-0433-8.

INTRODUCTION

In 1960, after a period of over twenty years in public affairs and two works of nonfiction, Michael Straight published a novel. *Carrington* dealt with a little-known incident, the Custer-like defeat of eighty-three men under the command of Lieutenant Colonel William Judd Fetterman, in Wyoming, 1866. Three years later came a second novel about the U.S. Cavalry in the West, *A Very Small Remnant,* this time re-creating the much-debated episode of the Sand Creek Massacre. Both are remarkable pieces of historical fiction. Based upon painstaking research among military records and a wealth of primary documents, *Carrington* and *A Very Small Remnant* convey an authentic sense of felt history, of lives and events wrought into formal clarity and invested with themes, as Straight says, "that were known to Homer."

Given his background and training, Straight's ventures

into writing fiction about the American West may come as something of a surprise. He was born in 1916, on Long Island, New York, into a distinguished family. His father, Willard Straight (1880–1918), served in China as a State Department officer; was later a Far Eastern expert for J. P. Morgan and Company; helped found two noteworthy journals, the *New Republic* and *Asia;* and held significant U.S. government administrative posts in Europe during World War I. His mother, Dorothy Whitney, was the daughter of William C. Whitney, the famous Wall Street financier.

Straight's education prepared him for a career of public service much like that of his father. At the London School of Economics, Straight studied under Harold J. Laski. He took an M.A. at Trinity College, Cambridge, in 1937, where he was a special student of John Maynard Keynes. Straight's many years of public service include service in the Air Force and positions as economic adviser in the U.S. State Department, writer for the Department of the Interior, and chairman of the American Veterans Committee. This is by no means a complete list of his accomplishments. From 1948 to 1956 he was an editor of the *New Republic.* Currently he is Deputy Chairman of the National Endowment for the Arts.

Before *Carrington* and *A Very Small Remnant,* Straight's writing had consisted almost entirely of reportage and two polemical public-affairs books, *Make This the Last War* (1943) and *Trial by Television* (1954). The first was a challenging and controversial liberal document, buttressed by some four hundred pages of closely argued factual data, which advocated an international policy of peace overseen by the U.N. and the building in America and abroad of "affirmative societies" or "social service states." Straight's second book was a character-oriented study of the principal figures in the televised Army-McCarthy hearings. The historical novels are not as incongruent with these earlier writings as one might think. In an interview Straight has pointed to a continuity of interests between his nonfiction and fiction: "I'd tried to recapitulate my thoughts on liberalism in *Carrington,* and I hoped to treat the problem of fanaticism in a deeper way in a study of Chivington."

Still, it is intriguing to ask why Straight turned to fiction and why, in particular, to the nineteenth-century American West for his materials. The preface to *Carrington* suggests an answer to the first question. Straight quotes Henry James on the historian's necessary adherence to facts, and Joseph Conrad on the novelist's liberation from the merely factual: "Fiction is nearer truth." As for the second question, Straight has said that when he spent a summer in Wyoming the landscape and history of the West "took hold" of him.

A Very Small Remnant presents the severest test of Straight's commitment to fiction as a means of expressing truth. The reason is that for historians themselves Sand Creek remains a controversial subject. The irreducible outlines are quite simple: on November 29, 1864, at Sand Creek, Colorado Territory, approximately one hundred and sixty Cheyenne and Arapaho Indians, a large majority of whom were women and children, were slain—and in some cases their bodies mutilated—by Colorado militia under the command of Colonel John Milton Chivington. But nearly every fact or inference bearing upon that day, before, during, and after November 29, has been subject to conflicting interpretations. Depending upon one's viewpoint, what happened at Sand Creek was either a successful military attack upon hostile Indians or a senseless slaughter of peaceful Indians who had been promised government protection. A historical marker at the site reflects the controversy perfectly: "Sand Creek 'Battle' or 'Massacre.' "

With so many conflicting opinions still swirling around the Sand Creek affair, Straight's fictional version was almost certain to provoke discussion, and it did. At a meeting of the Denver Posse of Westerners in 1963, Straight presented an essay laying out his understanding of the Sand Creek Massacre, and afterward debated his chief critic, Professor Raymond G. Carey of the University of Denver. Though this material is too lengthy to go into here, it is worth noting that the sum of the case against the novel is three rather minor errors in fact or misinterpretations of fact (all three are denigrations of Chivington's character), and, more important, the charge of "unrealistic simplicity" in the presentation of Chivington as "absolute devil" and Wynkoop as "pure saint." These labels, however, are themselves oversimplifications. Straight's Chivington is an ambitious, self-righteous fanatic, but no devil; and Wynkoop, while decent, generous, and courageous, lacks the foresight to realize that an optimistic belief in good intentions does not automatically assure the maintenance of objective good in the world.

Professor Carey himself has attested to the difficulty of getting at the truth of Sand Creek. Surveying the conflicting evidence on whether the Indians were hostile or not, he writes: "The conclusions arrived at differ widely, as in all matters connected with Sand Creek, since different writers with different predilections have given different weight to the divergent statements of different participants." Precisely. Any attempt to set down a narrative of what happened at Sand Creek involves the writer, whether historian or novelist, in judgments about the participants. Thus a pro-Chivington biographer (and there have been several) will emphasize the unrealistic, childlike faith of officers such as Major Wynkoop who trusted and believed the Cheyenne leaders to be honorable men when, according to this view, they were in fact only cunning savages.

Because the novelist is obliged to explore what Straight calls the "shadow world of character and motivation," moral questions are brought into the forefront, and imagination must perforce assume a major role in bringing these questions to life. Straight's narrative strategy well illustrates the blending of research and imagination in order to dramatize what is not found in surviving records. In 1876 Major Edward Wynkoop, the key figure in negotiating peace with Black Kettle, began an autobiography which he never completed. It is this fragment that Straight uses as a model for his fictional narrative. For purposes of dramatic economy, the date is moved up to 1868, four years after Sand Creek and immediately preceding the next "Sand Creek," Custer's attack upon Black Kettle's encampment on the Washita River. The change is effective for at least two reasons. Custer, who accused Wynkoop of being a corrupt Indian agent (he was not), was, like Chivington, bent on furthering his own national political ambitions and relentless in his determination to destroy Indians. The novel's single allusion to Washita thus foreshadows another tragedy to come, one which makes Wynkoop's dejection at the end even more compelling.

Another revision of Wynkoop's fragment shows Straight's concern with language. At the turning point of his life, Wynkoop received at Fort Lyon three Cheyennes led by One Eye and experienced a profound conversion from being one of Chivington's Exterminators to recognizing the rights and humanity of the Indians. In the fragment Wynkoop wrote:

> I was bewildered with an exhibition of such patriotism on the part of the two savages and felt myself in the presence of Superior beings; and these were the representatives of a race I theretofore looked upon without exception as being cruel, treacherous, and blood-thirsty without feeling or affection for friend or kindred.

In the novel Wynkoop's conversion is portrayed with less expository summary:

> I looked up at them, bewildered. Four years later, as I look back on the scene, I see the Indians with unaltered clarity. My own feelings, I am still at a loss to describe. A newborn animal struggles to stand up; a boat slips its moorings in the night and moves off in the current—no analogy serves me. I felt as if I had been lifted out of myself. . . .

Here imagery supplants the somewhat didactic abstractions of Wynkoop's account. Straight's invention is faithful to the spirit of the original while achieving more success as drama.

Wynkoop does not carry the whole moral burden of the novel. His friend Silas S. Soule sees further and displays courage at least as impressive as Wynkoop's. Through his refusal to lead his command against the Indians at Sand Creek, Soule demonstrates that such events are not the result of irresistible tides of historical force. He chooses not to be the victim of Chivington's passion and military power. Later, he expresses his rare courage again (in the novel as in life) when he chooses in the face of threats against his life to be the first witness against Chivington.

Other participants share various degrees of moral responsibility for the massacre. Wynkoop's replacement at Fort Lyon, Major Anthony, is perhaps the most baffling figure of all, because of his many inconsistencies. Another, Governor Evans, seems to have betrayed his best impulses, controverting his first proclamation for peaceful solutions to white-Indian conflicts with a second proclamation of open warfare. Ironically Chivington alone, the man most responsible for Sand Creek, is absolved of guilt: "Beyond the narrow realm of his own immediate desires he was without feeling." Standing against the weak, the temporizing, the fanatical are Wynkoop and Soule. Their examples assert a confidence in noble conduct, but it is a bleak confidence when we consider the cost. Still, this is the meaning of the moral reprise in the verse from Isaiah from which the novel's title is drawn. It is also a portent of American democracy as personified in the volume of poetry which Soule indirectly bequeaths to Wynkoop, *Leaves of Grass.*

A Very Small Remnant strives for a timeless statement about the human condition. This is the province of art. At the same time the novel adheres closely to the known facts about Sand Creek. This is the province of history. Whether Straight succeeds equally in both aims is for each reader to decide. In my judgment *A Very Small Remnant* will prove to be the best permanent legacy of Sand Creek.

Don Graham
The University of Texas at Austin

AUTHOR'S NOTE

Route 50, a broad highway, hurries you over the plains of Southern Colorado. But if, near the town of Lamar, you break out of the traffic, a dirt lane, cut by wagon wheels, leads you into an ancient valley. You pass broken wire and the wrecks of cast-off machines. You come to a field stretched out along the bluffs that rim the Arkansas River. Standing there, you see little but the pale earth and the flowering cactus. You hear only the cries of the killdeer—or else the dry warning of a rattlesnake curled in the mound of rubble at your feet. Stepping back, you see that all the field is bordered by these whitened mounds.

They are the ruins of Fort Lyon, a cavalry post that once guarded the Santa Fe Trail.

At Lyon there occurred, a century ago, a memorable incident, one that altered the lives of all who played a part in it. One of the participants was a young American of Dutch ancestry, Major Edward Wynkoop. He was born in Philadelphia in 1836, the youngest of eight children of a prosperous ironmaster. He set out for the Rockies as a young man. He helped to found a settlement on Cherry Creek and named it, Denver. In wartime he joined the Union Army; he led a cavalry charge at Glorieta, the "Gettysburg of the West."

Wynkoop was Commanding Officer of Lyon in 1864. He was well known as an Indian Fighter. Two years later, as the result of his experiences, Wynkoop resigned from the Army and became the Agent of the Indians against whom he had fought.

It was while he was an Indian Agent, the reader is asked to imagine, that Wynkoop wrote the pages that follow.

They are fictional, in that Wynkoop did not write them. But this story is not fiction that stands in opposition to fact. The characters who appear in these pages were living a century ago; the events occurred, and were described in sworn testimony taken by a Commssion of Inquiry, and published by the United States Senate in 1867.

I have followed this testimony closely. In addition, I have drawn upon many published and unpublished records, including Wynkoop's own scrapbooks and manuscripts, now in the State Historical Society in Denver and the Museum of Anthropology in Santa Fe.

I have followed the record, but I have not tried to construct a scale model of a past age. My interest centers, not in the details of the story, but in the themes which it suggests—themes that were known to Homer, and that, to me, are meaningful today.

PART ONE

1

The blows of a distant hammer broke my sleep. I awoke with an effort, wondering: where am I?

I had spent many nights out on the plains, hunting the enemy; I had awoken to many alarms. I felt now the softness of a bed; I sensed the heat of the day. I saw the room around me: the rough plaster, the narrow window, the roof of sod. I heard Louisa's calm voice as she read to our son: "*Q is Quintus, armed with a lance; R is Rachel, learning to dance . . .*"

I am back at Lyon, I told myself; I am with my family.

It is an early afternoon in September, and, following lunch, I must have fallen asleep. The first good sleep . . .

The hammering sounded again, close by, against the door; and a man's voice: "Major? Major?"

A trooper, standing in the fierce sunlight. "Indians, sir," he explained, as I stood blinking. "We struck them five miles out."

"You caught them?"

He nodded.

"And killed them?"

"No, sir"—he stroked his hat—"we're bringing them in."

"Wounded? You know we . . ."

"Unharmed, sir; as prisoners."

"We take no prisoners; you know that! This fort's in danger; the whole valley is under attack. And you bring a band of them in. . . ." I turned to call out the guard.

"There are three of them," the trooper said, "a one-eyed man, a squaw, and a boy."

"No matter, you kill them before they kill you. . . . Well, why didn't you kill them?" I demanded when he failed to answer.

He looked up at me. He said simply: "I didn't have to, Major, I'm not a part of your command any more."

I stood for a moment in an empty space. I looked at him. I remembered that he and his companions had completed their army service. They had been on their way to Denver and civilian life when they came upon the Indians. They had acted as I might have acted, had I been free.

Bound as I was, I felt resentment. "You're still in uniform," I told the trooper, "and as long as you're in uniform you'll obey orders!"

He nodded, staring westward. He said: "Here they come."

The specks in the distance were too small for me to distinguish. I went for my field glasses; in their narrow range, I made out four cavalrymen on the horizon; and behind them, on ponies, the woman, the boy, the old man.

I watched them in silence. The trooper beside me persisted in his effort to make me understand.

"Major . . ."

"What is it?"

"We were about to fire on them, Major. Then the one-eyed man held up a paper."

"That trick!"

"It was a message, sir. I'd have brought it to you myself, but he wouldn't let it out of his hands."

"Of course not! You would have seen that it was a fraud. I swear, that if there is any room left in the guardhouse . . ."

"Major," he said, "the message is for you."

2

The troopers rode into the fort and dismounted. The three Indians sat on their ponies, looking around.

They were looking for the gallows from which they expected to be hanged. But I did not know that. I assumed that they were spying, and my anger swelled.

"Get them off those ponies!" I shouted. "Search them, then bring them to me."

Still raging, I went to my headquarters and took my place at the Commanding Officer's desk.

There, on the top of my papers, was the Order governing our relations with the Indians of the Arkansas Valley: . . .

The Cheyennes will have to be soundly whipped before they will be quiet. If any of them are caught in your vicinity, kill them, as that is the only way.

It was from Colonel Chivington, the Commander of the Military District of Colorado. Beneath it was a copy of my reply: . . . *My intention is to kill all Indians I come across . . .*

I cannot today recapture the spirit in which I wrote those words. I see now that they were contrary to my whole upbringing and to all my inclinations. Yet they were in compliance with army policy, and I was certain, when I wrote them that my highest duty was to carry out that policy.

We were at that moment in a war to save the Union. We thought little of taking the lives of white men who were enemies, and still less of killing Indians. We hunted them down as you would hunt wild beasts. They set out in turn to destroy our scattered settlements. Week by week our situation became more desperate. Yet it never occurred to me that we had any alternative but to fight on.

Once, in the days before the war, I had undertaken, in the dead of winter, to carry a message from Denver to Leavenworth. I was snowbound and half frozen when a band of Cheyennes found me and took me in. I had been happy then to share their food and shelter. I was on my own in those days, a man without enemies. Now, as a soldier, I saw all Indians as one enemy, faceless and nameless; deserving no sympathy, capable of any treachery.

As the captives approached, I laid my papers away in a

drawer; I drew my revolver from its holster and set it out on my desk.

John Smith, the post interpreter, stepped into the room. A sergeant followed, leading the three Indians. The squaw crouched by the door; the boy paused in the center of the room; the old man advanced to the front of my desk. He stood there, silent and grave. His hair was gray and braided; his face was gaunt and deeply lined. It was one of the saddest faces I had ever seen.

Smith took up his position at my shoulder. I leaned back and asked: "Who is he?"

"One Eye. He was famous in his day."

"He looks as though he'd done his share of fighting against us."

"You mean his eye? He lost it defending a white man against the Kiowas."

"No matter." I leaned forward. "You understand that you are not prisoners of war," I said. "You are enemy captives, entitled to no protection."

The old man listened as Smith translated my words; he looked down at me and nodded.

"You know what I should do," I told him. "I should have the three of you taken out and hung."

Smith spoke again and ended with a gesture—a gasp as an invisible rope tightened around his neck. It was a death feared by all Indians, yet the old man showed no anxiety. Either he knows that I cannot kill him in cold blood, I thought, or else he is ready to die. I sensed that I had lost my advantage; I regretted all that I had said.

I started over. "Well," I demanded, "why are you here?"

The old man held out his hands; they were bound together. I untied the rope; his glance shifted to my revolver. I made no move to put it away.

He reached inside his blanket. He drew out a grubby piece of paper and handed it to me. It was an old receipt for buffalo hides; on the back was a message scrawled in the hand of some half-breed and signed with a crude cross. I could make nothing of it, but Smith leaned over my shoulder.

"I should be able to read it," he murmured. "It's written by my son."

The message was a reply to the proclamation sent out from Denver by John Evans, the newly appointed Governor of the Territory of Colorado. The Governor had called upon all friendly Indians to come in and to make peace. Now, Black Kettle, the chief of the Southern Cheyennes, answered that his council had met and had accepted the offer. They had never wanted war, so Black Kettle said. They had been driven to it by the whites. And so on. I began to lose interest, and then: "*We have some prisoners of yours*," Smith read, "*which we are willing to give up providing . . .*"

I broke in: "How many prisoners?"

The old man looked steadily at me. He nodded as Smith spoke. Then, by way of answering, he stroked his braids, he drew a line across his chest, he folded his arms in a cradle and rocked them gently.

"They hold four prisoners," Smith said. "A young woman, two boys, and one small girl."

"They admit that they took them captive?"

The old man nodded again, as if he had expected my question. "They were taken far away on the Little Blue. Black Kettle bought them, with many ponies."

"To ransom them."

The old man shook his head: "To give them back to you."

He could not make a fool of me. "Nonetheless," I said, "you admit that you have attacked our settlements."

"It is we who were attacked. The Black Beard led . . . "

"You stole a herd of cattle! The lieutenant you speak of was sent out by Colonel Chivington to recover it."

The old man waited. He gestured at the same unhurried pace. "The cattle had run off. Our young men came across them. They were returning the cattle when the Black Beard attacked."

I tried to shake his story; I failed. "Well," I said, "you had at least one war party, raiding the settlements along the river. The troops surprised you by the Cimarron Crossing and you charged them."

His expression of sadness and resignation never changed. "Our young men were out hunting the buffalo. The white soldiers chased them. Starving Bear, the great warrior of the Cheyennes, rode out alone to meet the white soldiers. He held his hand high in the peace sign. The white soldiers shot him. Then they charged."

"That's not their story," I said, but I didn't press the

point. Even if the old man's version were true, the soldiers had simply followed orders.

The old man sensed that his words were wasted on me. He spoke directly to Smith, and Smith answered, until I broke in: "What's going on?"

Smith spoke hesitantly: "One Eye wants me to convince you that his people need peace. He says I should understand, since I am married to a squaw, and my son lives with them."

"And fights with them! You tell One Eye that he's my captive; if he wishes to speak, then he must speak to me!"

The old man listened and was not disconcerted. "If you see the village of the Cheyennes, then even you will understand," he said. "There is hunger, and there is mourning. The message that I bring is the truth."

I doubted it. "You call this message a reply to the Governor's proclamation. Why didn't you answer the Governor in the summer, when you do your fighting? Why did you wait until the approach of winter?"

"We tried many times to answer the Governor. We sent many messengers."

"They never came to me."

"You would not let them. One month ago our messengers tried to reach you. They rode toward the fort. They held up the paper. They signaled that they came in peace. Your soldiers fired on them."

I remembered, now, Cramer's report of an encounter in which the Indians had tried some new trickery and he had responded with a volley of rifle fire.

"The Indians fled," I remarked.

"They were told not to fire back."

I nodded. Cramer had reported wounding four of the Indians. I had commended him, and, in my report to Chivington, had claimed a success.

I looked up at the old man; he stood without stirring. I had been striking at him with every accusation at hand, and he was unscathed. It was I who was weary. I stared at my desk, confused. I became aware of the revolver lying beside me. It looked incongruous lying there. I opened a drawer in my desk and laid it away. In the same drawer, I saw Chivington's order. I had enforced it, until this afternoon and this old man. Too late now; yet I resented him, the cause of my weakness.

"You knew our orders," I said. "You knew that an Indian coming within range of this post was certain to be killed."

"I knew it."

"Then how did you dare to approach?"

He folded his arms; as he spoke, I felt the ground shift from beneath me, as it had shifted once in the Platte, leaving me beyond my depth.

"I have been a warrior," he said. "I was not afraid to die when I was young. Should I be afraid now, when I am old? . . . Our chiefs sent out the young warriors with this message of peace. They were driven back by your soldiers. Then, some cried out in the Council that the Cheyennes had no choice but war. Our Great Spirit whispered to me: 'It is for you to try to save your people.' I went to the Council and told them. I said: 'Give me true news, such as is written, to carry to the chief at the fort.' " He gestured: "So I am here."

"You did not fear you would be killed when you tried to reach the fort?"

"I thought I would be killed. I hoped that the paper would be found on my dead body. I hoped it might be brought to you, and you might read it."

"And the boy?"

"Min-im-ie?" He turned to the boy and smiled. "He would not let One Eye go alone."

The boy nodded as the old man spoke. He stepped forward, and took his place at the old man's side.

I looked up at them, bewildered. Four years later, as I look back on the scene, I see the two Indians with unaltered clarity. My own feelings, I am still at a loss to describe. A newborn animal struggles to stand up; a boat slips its moorings in the night and moves off in the current—no analogy serves me. I felt as if I had been lifted out of myself; as if invisible hands had untied cords that bound me, as I had untied the ropes that bound the wrists of the old man.

I asked: "What do you want me to do?"

One Eye was unprepared for my question; his gestures were tentative: "If you come to the camp of the Cheyennes," Smith translated, "then you may return with the white captives."

"How far away is your camp?"

"Four days on a horse."

"What assurance can you give me that we won't be attacked?"

"The word of the Cheyennes."

"You understand that we will take you along as a hostage; and that we will kill you if they break their word."

"If the Cheyennes break their word, I will not want to live."

"How many warriors are in the camp?"

A fluttering gesture—"As many as the leaves on a tree," Smith translated. He added: "That means more than five hundred; I'd guess there are a thousand or more."

I could take one hundred and thirty men at most; I needed no more. I sent the Indians off to the guardhouse, with orders that they were to be fed and made comfortable. I called for the officers of the post to come to my office in one hour. I sat alone.

After a time I took out my maps and began to mark off distances and days. I wrote out a brief report to Chivington, to be sent if we failed to return. But that possibility did not trouble me. It was only when my work was done, and I was waiting for the officers to join me, that doubts stole into the darkening room. Was I acting once again on a rash impulse? Had I the right, as a commander of troops, to lead them into the camp of an acknowledged enemy, simply because I accepted the word of one old man? I knew all that I needed to know of him; his people were still unknown to me. His Council might not share his longing for peace; his chief, Black Kettle, might repudiate him, finding a small band of whites within his grasp.

I read the message from Black Kettle over many times for reassurance. I took out the copy of the Governor's proclamation that I had filed away. It was all that I could ask for. *The Great Father*, Governor Evans declared, *does not want to injure those who remain friendly to the whites. He desires to protect and take care of them.* And then the passage that Black Kettle had noted: *Friendly Arapahoes and Cheyennes belonging on the Arkansas River will go to Major Colley, United States Agent, who will give them provisions and show them a place of safety.*

A place of safety—I repeated those words with a sense of satisfaction on that September afternoon; and with a terrible bitterness in time to come.

3

All unsuspecting, the officers of the post gathered around my desk. They were men of my own age and inclination—Easterners by birth, gold miners by choice, patriots in a crisis, but adventurers at heart. They were ready for any foray; they were accustomed to unequal odds. But when I told them of my plan, to lead a band of volunteers into the stronghold of the Cheyennes, they looked at me in disbelief. It took some time to convince them that I was in earnest; then, glancing at each other, they grappled with me. They failed to weaken my determination; I failed to convey my new-found trust to them. So we confronted each other, inseparable once, and now, separated by a divide that they could not understand and I could not explain. We were, none of us, respecters of rank; we argued with the violence of brothers. They were angry, being loyal to me; I was sensitive, knowing that I needed them.

I had hoped that all of them would volunteer; at the end of an hour it was plain that my hope was forlorn. So I closed the council, swearing that I would go alone.

It was a low blow; I waited for the counterblows.

Once again I was mistaken. It was the idea of going alone that took Soule's fancy. His face brightened. "Provided no one else goes," he said, "I'll keep you company."

Then Cramer, in his dour way, sighed. "The Army will need one survivor to write the report," he said. "I'll follow along at a safe distance."

In the last light of the day, the men assembled on the parade ground for the ceremony of retreat. I stood before them, with Soule and Cramer on either side of me.

"Word has come to me today," I shouted, "that the Cheyennes are holding four captives in the Big Timbers. . . . Four white captives: a woman, two boys, and a young girl."

The men stood at parade rest, waiting.

"I am going for them tomorrow! I am going to bring them back!"

"Without a fight," Soule murmured. He alone shared my conviction that it could be done.

"Without a fight," I shouted, "unless we have to fight. I want a hundred and thirty volunteers."

I waited; not one trooper moved. Then Mulkey, the blacksmith, spat on the ground. He stepped forward, and no man dared hold back.

I rejected the married men and those whom wounds had weakened; I took the rest. So our column was formed: one hundred and twenty-seven men, all mounted; ten horses to spare; four wagons with food, tents, and ammunition; two howitzers in case of an argument, and an empty ambulance to bring back the captives. For hostages, we took the three Indians—no, we took four. A Cheyenne known as the Fool lived in a hovel near the fort, eating scraps of food that the soldiers threw to him. He was harmless, and hopelessly insane. He clung to the men, making urgent noises as they saddled up their horses, and, on an impulse, I took him along. I had heard that the Cheyennes were awed by madmen, and besides, as Cramer remarked, he was no crazier than the rest of us.

4

We rode out before dawn. I could still feel the pressure of Louisa's head against my chest; I could hear her low reproach: if you loved me, would you still go?

We mounted slowly onto the high prairie. The sun rose on our right; before long, the day was burning. The buffalo grass was pale in the late summer; the horizon reached out for miles around us without a landmark; the dust from our column drifted off on a dry wind. We were like sailors on a trackless ocean, and I for one was content.

We crossed Sand Creek at noon. We halted for the night in the whitened ruins of a cottonwood grove. It proved to be the site of an ancient Indian village; bits of earthenware and old bones turned up in the dust. The horses rolled on the turf and fell to grazing; the cooks worked over their cauldrons; the men broke off the dead limbs of the cottonwoods and lit their fires. They crouched around the low flames, heating coffee. I wandered among them, listening. We had spent many such nights together, surrounded by the war parties of the enemy. Then, no risk or hardship could deaden the good humor of the men. On this night, in contrast, we had nothing to hide and little to fear. Yet the men were silent, each in his own cell. They were more like condemned prisoners than cavalrymen, and I knew why: each man believed that we were riding into an ambush.

I walked to where Soule lay, ruddy-faced by his fire. "Damned Jayhawker," I said, "move over."

I stretched out beside him. "The men are uneasy," I told him. "In three or four days they may be hard to handle."

His dark eyes glinted in the firelight. "I told you we should have gone alone!"

And he meant it. He had joined the Army as a Scout for Kit Carson. Before that he had worked for the Abolitionists in Kansas, Bleeding Kansas. It was Soule who rode with a handful of men into St. Joseph and rescued Dr. Doy from the slaveowners' scaffold. And it was Soule who led the rescue party for John Brown. He disguised himself as an Irish laborer; he played the part well. Seeing the flask lodged in one of his hip pockets, you would not guess that the other contained a volume of verses inscribed by a friend of his, a poet named Whitman.

We set out again before dawn; we rode through another cloudless day. Buffalo grazed in the far distance; antelope lifted their heads as we passed, and stalked away; once, a wolf sprang up from a bush and loped off, glancing over his shoulder to see if we were pursuing him; the grasshoppers kept up their metallic note all day long. We moved through sage country; its shades of gray and blue were restful after the glare of the dry grass. But water was scarce. The horses were weary at the day's end; so were the men.

One Eye had said four days. He rode at the head of the column, his eyes fixed upon some invisible point on the bare horizon. There was no trail to follow; I wondered if he were leading us to nowhere. Many times I gripped my reins, ready to turn back; but One Eye, swaying slightly on his pony, drew me on.

At sunrise on the fourth day, I sent Min-im-ie on ahead to tell Black Kettle we were coming. It was a little like Noah sending forth the dove. The boy cantered off to the northeast and we followed. We saw no sign of the Cheyennes. We rode through the fiery day; when the sun was low, we moved down a long slope to the Smoky Hill River.

We halted there. The horses sucked up the shallow water; the men dismounted and knelt, filling their canteens. It was a moment to be thankful for. Then One Eye gestured. We looked up, and saw the pennons and spears above the northern horizon; then the horses, and, at last, the riders. They paused on the crest of the hill and confronted us: a thousand warriors, drawn up in line of battle, all streaked in white and ocher and vermilion, their war paint.

We churned up sand and water. On the north bank of the river we formed our battle line. The Cheyennes watched us and did not move.

I sent One Eye out to tell them that we came in peace. He rode without haste across the half mile that separated us, and was lost in their line. With carbines drawn, we advanced at a walk up the slope.

The center of their line fell back as we approached; in classical style, their flanks closed in around us. Still moving forward, we re-formed as squadrons, with our wagons and howitzers in the center. They completed the maneuver and enclosed us in a square. So we rode the four miles to their village. Outwardly, as Cramer later testified, we kept up an air of "reckless indifference." Inwardly, we waited for the shot that would set off a hopeless fight.

Two shots were fired. A sparrow hawk flew over us, beating to windward with a mouse in its talons; a warrior raised his rifle and fired; the sparrow hawk tumbled from the sky. A terrier that had trotted beside us all the way from Lyon darted out to meet one of their mongrels. A second warrior fired and our terrier somersaulted, yelping. I heard the cursing and cried: "Easy!" The men understood.

We rode on in silence; we sighted, at last, the Big Timbers—a grove of ancient trees where the Cheyennes were camped. We rode on past the grove in our involuntary formation. We halted by a stream, fringed by green willows. "They want us to camp here," Smith said. The men began to dismount, but I led them on, up to a bare hill, where, if need be, we could make a stand. I set up my howitzers and posted a heavy guard. Then, for the first time in two hours, I felt able to breathe.

I had, without authorization, led my troops into hostile territory. In the presence of the enemy, I had deprived them of every advantage they possessed. I had placed them at the mercy of a people who were believed to be merciless. No worse disaster could overtake me than the one I had been spared. I had never seen Black Kettle, but already I was in his debt.

5

At daybreak, Smith stood outside my tent. In his frock coat and wing collar, the old scoundrel looked more like a wandering preacher than a mountain man.

"Major," he said, "I've been through the night with my son."

"What does he say?"

"He says you have little chance of getting out of here alive."

I shook my head. "Black Kettle had his opportunity yesterday. He didn't take it."

"I'm not speaking about Black Kettle; I'm speaking about his young men."

"You mean he has his problems too?"

"Major, these young warriors mean to kill you. Their leader is the brother of the chief your soldiers shot down."

Not mine, but white soldiers; for the first time I wondered: are all white men responsible for one white man's folly?

The chiefs were waiting. I left the camp in the hands of an uneasy lieutenant. I told him that if he heard shots, never to come for us, but to hold out on the hill. I set out with the men I wanted near me: Soule, Cramer, Smith, one or two more.

We crossed the stream and rode into the shade of the cottonwoods where the tepees stood. Black ribbons of buffalo meat hung there; fires smoldered; old men and women, sightless, strained to hear the sounds of our horses as we passed.

In a clearing at the center of the village the chiefs were seated. A crowd of a thousand or more stood in a circle and closed behind us as we rode in. We dismounted and took our places on hides that had been set out for us.

The chiefs confronted us unsmiling. Black Kettle was the most inscrutable of them. His forehead was high, his nose prominent, his mouth thin and wide and drawn down. He regarded us through half-closed eyes.

I scanned the crowd: the silent children, the sullen women, the warriors, gripping their weapons. Their hostility was impenetrable; I felt as if I were being choked.

I stared at the ground before me; the Indians made no move. Only a dog detached itself from the crowd. It approached, and sniffed at us, and slumped down on our hide. It was half-starved and hairless; still, it accepted us. It lay beside us, panting.

Black Kettle motioned at last; Smith and I stood up. I held out the paper, and asked if the chiefs had sent it.

They nodded. I explained that, because of the paper, I had come, in peace.

"If you come in peace," Black Kettle said, "why have you brought so many soldiers?"

"I have brought few soldiers, but enough to fight, if I am forced to fight."

I waited. In all the assembly, no one stirred.

I read aloud the message that One Eye had given me. I spoke a few phrases about peace. I grasped the nettle: "You say you are holding four white captives. I have come to take them back."

A murmur started up in the crowd, and mounted. I could not say today how great the din was; at the time it seemed deafening.

In a low voice, Smith spoke beside me: "You are talking for your life now; go on."

"You want me to promise peace in return for the captives," I said. "I cannot do that. But if you will give me the captives I . . ." I faltered and turned to Smith. At his translation, the noise billowed again; the crowd pressed in upon us. In the midst of it all, Black Kettle sat, the one clear image to me, in a blurred setting. He saw my desperation;

his mouth lifted in a faint smile that, to me, was worth a thousand bayonets.

"If you will give me the captives," I cried, "I will take them to our Governor in Denver. I will tell him: 'Here is proof that the Cheyennes and their allies, the Arapahoes, are friendly.' If you wish, I will take your chiefs to Denver with me. I will pledge my own life, to see that they go and return without harm. . . . You have seen the Governor's message," I cried. "The one that offers you a place of safety. If you will come in, with us, then I will make my post, Fort Lyon, that place."

I took my place on the hide, watching Black Kettle. I have done all that I can, I thought; it is his turn.

He sat like a boulder. Close by him, a young chief stood up. He shambled over the ground, his arms arched out. He stood over me and, with a brusque gesture, motioned me to rise again. I stood, and he glared up at me with a dull malevolence.

He was Bull Bear, brother of Starving Bear; he spoke of the death of the young chief in a voice hoarse with hatred. As he spoke, his followers pushed to the front ranks of the crowd.

Soule and Cramer stood up beside me, gripping their holsters; Black Kettle sat motionless. From the crowd, One Eye broke through. He pointed to Bull Bear and his followers. "Where were they," he demanded, "when I carried the paper to the fort?"

"The white soldier took me in," he cried. "He trusted the words of the Council. So now, the Council must decide if they are dogs or men." He turned to the crowd. "The white soldier asked me: 'What if the chiefs do not keep their word?' I told him I would not want to go on living. I will go down fighting beside him. And there are those who will fight with me, to keep the word of the Cheyennes."

As he spoke, Min-im-ie and a dozen young men slipped out of the crowd and formed a ring around us. In their bright belts they wore butcher knives.

The crowd was hushed; One Eye spoke again. "Bull Bear says we should not give away our captives. He wants to trade them. I say that is shameful. To spare our people the shame, I will trade with him. He may have my horses if he will let the captives go."

He waited. After a moment Bull Bear muttered: "I will take the horses." He returned to his place.

Other members of the Council spoke in turn. When they had finished, Black Kettle stood up. He embraced me and led me to the center of the Council. He spoke with his hand on my shoulder.

"This white man is not here to laugh at us," he said. "He was supposed to kill our messenger, but he took him in. He believed in the word of an Indian although his people brand us as unworthy of belief. It was like coming through a fire for a white man to follow an Indian; but he followed our warrior.

"He could not give us peace. If he had promised peace in return for the captives, I would have asked him if he took us for fools. I listened, ready to despise him for lying; I heard only the truth. And I embrace the truth."

He turned to me. "Take your soldiers back on the trail. Make your camp at sunset and stay there until sunset tomorrow. We will spend the night in council, and by tomorrow night, you will have some word from us. Whatever it may be, you and your soldiers may return to your fort, unharmed."

He embraced me again; the other chiefs came in turn to shake my hand. With Cramer and Soule at my side, I stood in the clearing, sustained.

6

We rode twelve miles toward the fort. At sundown we went into camp in a cottonwood grove.

The men were jittery. Some had been drinking through the day; all of them, including Cramer, believed that the Indians meant to attack us. Only Soule was untroubled.

I did what I could to calm the men; I kept the horses in, tied to picket ropes; I doubled the sentries. It was no use. Our outriders reported that Indian scouts had shadowed us; a ring of wolves closed around us in the night. The horses reared and tore at their halters; the Fool wandered through the camp plucking at the soldiers and pointing. The men understood his incoherent pleading: the Cheyennes used the wolf call as a war signal.

No one slept. The men drew together and argued in low voices. I knew what was coming. There was nothing to do but let it come.

Soule, Cramer, and I waited around my fire. We feigned indifference as the mutiny mounted against us; we considered what we should do.

"They'll try to disarm us," I said, "but we won't give them a chance. We'll move first."

"No," Cramer said. "They'll try to persuade us, being our own men. Let them try. We can cite what they say as evidence, if it comes to a trial."

Beyond the small circle of our firelight the arguments swelled and subsided. Then, toward midnight, they ceased. The men moved off silently into the darkness.

"They're going for their rifles," Cramer said. In his detached way he asked: "Are you ready to shoot them?"

"If I have to," I said. We checked our revolvers. "If we don't shoot them," I added, "Chivington will hang them."

"Or else he'll hang us," Cramer said, "for leading them here."

Soule protested: "We did what we had to do."

Cramer shook his head. "We didn't have to come. We could have stayed at Lyon, and let the captives die. That would have been the safe course."

"We didn't choose the safe course," Soule said.

"Neither did the Confederate raiders Chivington caught."

"They were bushwhackers," Soule said. "In any case, they were killed trying to escape."

Cramer nodded. "So Chivington said."

"You don't trust him?"

"I'm not a trusting man."

"Well, you can trust Chivington," Soule said. He turned to me. "Do you remember the mutiny on the way to Glorieta?"

I nodded. "Colonel Slough was commanding our regiment," I told Cramer, "and a company of Germans defied him. He called in my company and ordered us to shoot the Germans down."

"And Chivington saved the situation," Soule said.

"They stood up to us," I told Cramer, "but they were cowed by him."

"The Fighting Parson," Cramer said. He was staring out into the darkness. "They are gathering out there," he said. "It won't be long."

Soule laughed. "Are you afraid?" he asked.

"Of our own men?" Cramer shook his head.

"Of what then?"

Cramer squinted down the sights of his revolver. He asked: "Will we ever get out of this place?"

"Of course!" Soule said.

Cramer glanced at me. "Will we get to Denver, with the captives and the chiefs?"

"I think so," I said.

Cramer nodded. "That's what I'm afraid of."

He laid a few dead limbs on the fire and stirred the ashes.

We waited, watching as the fire gained against the darkness. The flames were pale and high when Cramer murmured: "Here they come."

A band of men moved into the firelight. Some carried rifles, but surreptitiously.

Mulkey and three of his companions stepped forward. "Major," Mulkey began.

"Stand at attention when you speak to me."

He stiffened; I motioned to Soule and Cramer, and we stood up.

"Major," Mulkey repeated, "we're going back."

I nodded. "When we get the captives."

"At sunrise, Major. We don't even know if there are any captives. We figure the redskins are lying. Even if they're telling the truth, it's four captives against a hundred and thirty odd of us."

"We're staying, Mulkey."

"You can stay, Major, the men are going. If you don't want to lead us, then Lieutenant . . ."

We moved quickly. Soule and I covered the men; Cramer took their rifles. I called for a wagon and had the four ringleaders bound to the wagon wheels. They hung, spread-eagled, through the night, twisting and groaning as the ropes bit into their wrists. Mulkey talked, or tried to talk, to me. "We meant no harm, Major. . . . We never would have harmed you." And later: "Major? . . . I could do with a cup of water, Major. . . ."

All four of the men had followed me, at Glorieta, into the smoke and fire of the Texas brigades. And Mulkey had been the first to follow me in this adventure. I was bitterly sorry; but I knew where mutiny could end.

Struggling against sleep, as I kept the night watch, I thought again of the Germans, standing proudly while we fumbled with our rifles. With a gesture, Chivington had humbled them; with another gesture, of contempt, he handed them back to Slough. But not for long. Slough soon departed for the States, to fight a gentleman's war against Lee. John Milton Chivington, the preacher turned soldier, took the regiment. No matter what the men felt or suffered, there was no whisper of mutiny from then on.

7

I cut Mulkey and his companions loose at sunrise. I stumbled through the camp, telling the rest of the mutineers to come and claim their rifles. They turned away as I passed.

There was nothing to do but wait. The sun arched over us; I lay with my eyes closed until the alert sounded. Soldiers hurried past me; a team of horses pounded up with a howitzer. Cramer led me to the rim of the camp. "It may be the attack," he said, "in which case we're ten per cent better off dead."

We saw dust in the distance; then four or five Indians riding in from the north. Around the copper chest of one brave, two pale arms were braced; a head of black hair bobbed behind his head: a white girl, straddling his pony.

The Indians signaled; they came in at a walk through our lines and into our circle of armed men. They halted. We stared at the girl, still clinging to the Indian; none of us moved to help her. One of the Indians slid from his pony and lifted her to the ground. She stood ashen and mute. An Indian shawl covered her tattered dress.

She was tall and flat-chested; there was no use in giving her the dress that Louisa had sent. I offered her my jacket, but she clutched the shawl, shivering in the heat of the day.

I led her to a tent and brought her coffee. I tried to talk to her. Once I had drawn a fistful of porcupine quills from the nose of a thoroughbred. It took the same patience to draw words from this girl.

Her name, I learned, was Laura Roper; her parents were settlers on the Little Blue. One Sunday in August, she had walked a mile up the river to visit her neighbors, a family named Eubanks. Since the day was fine, they had walked back with her; Mrs. Eubanks carrying her baby; her husband leading their three-year-old, Isabella.

They were picking wild flowers in a cottonwood grove when they heard yelling. They ran into the brush and crouched there; Eubanks stuffed a handkerchief into his daughter's mouth to stifle her cries. The Indians rode past them, but the girl was choking; the father pulled out the handkerchief, too soon.

The child screamed; the Indians turned back. They killed

Eubanks and scalped him. They tied the women onto the ponies and led them away.

Near by there lived a simple-minded woman. The Indians caught her ten-year-old son and another boy hiding in a shed. That brought the woman out of her own hiding place. She clawed and bit, trying to get the boys back. The Indians took her scalp and left her for dead. "But she wasn't dead," Laura added, "not when my horse trod over her. I saw her pass one leg over the other."

The Indians traveled westward for many days. At night they camped on the open plain. Before long, the baby died. The warriors sold the mother to a band of north-riding Sioux.

"And what about Isabella and the boys?" I asked. I waited, but Laura turned from me to the tent wall, plucking at the shreds of her dress.

I left her, for the leader of the Cheyennes was waiting with a message from Black Kettle. The Council had met through the night, so he reported; it had accepted my proposal. Black Kettle had guessed that my soldiers would grow restless, so he had sent Laura ahead with an escort as evidence of his good faith. Black Kettle himself would deliver Isabella and the two boys to me on the following day. He and six of his chiefs would ride with me to Lyon, and then on to Denver to meet with Governor Evans and to sign a treaty of peace.

You brace yourself to smash down a door; it opens before you; you stand in disbelief. The men listened to the message from Black Kettle; they went about the odd jobs of camp life, shaking their heads. But the girl was with us, standing beside the cooks and stirring our supper in her listless way.

I kept the Indians as hostages, just in case. I counted the hours. Cramer kept up his self-appointed vigil, protecting me from my own folly. Soule kept me company. Soule, of course, was in the best of spirits. He joked and sang and, after dark, brought out his flask, which was fashioned in the shape of a book and titled *Paradise Regained*. We read a stanza or two in the course of the night.

Some time after noon on the next day, a lone Indian rode into our camp bearing the news that Black Kettle and his party were a few miles away.

I went out alone, with the Indian as my guide. I rode with a wildly throbbing heart. It was a brilliant day; the wind in the grass urged us on as we cantered over the plains; larks rose around us, singing; thousands of sunflowers seemed to have burst from the earth. When, at last, we came in sight of the party, I was filled with a happiness such as I had never before experienced and do not expect to know again in this world.

We rode toward the party. A white boy on a dappled pony broke from its ranks and galloped toward me. He reined in beside me and reached up for my hand.

"My name's Dan," he said. "What's yours?"

"Ned Wynkoop."

"Are you the soldier who has come to get me?"

"I am."

"Well, hurray for you!" he cried. "You know," he added proudly, "I was a prisoner."

"Are you glad to be free?"

"Of course. But will they let me keep my pony?"

"Why don't you ask them?"

He kicked the pony and galloped off. By then the second boy had joined us. He clung to my side. So we came to the Indians. I should have paused to greet the chiefs, but I rode past them, searching for the child that was close to the age of my son. In a squaw's bent arm, I saw at last a bundle, wrapped in an Indian blanket. I approached in fear, remembering Laura's story. I saw, above the blanket, a tuft of golden hair and blue, imploring eyes. I reached forward, and, from the blanket, her arms stretched out to me. I lifted her into my saddle; she clasped my neck and pressed her head against my shoulder. Between her sobs she whispered: "I want my mother!" I smoothed her hair, knowing she would never see her mother again. I rode far ahead with her, not wanting the chiefs to see me unmanned.

So, alone and bereaved, we led the triumphal procession to the camp. All the men were gathered there to greet us. As we rode in, they broke into wild cheers. Isabella clung to me, frightened; the men crowded around us. Still stiff from the punishment, Mulkey elbowed his way to my horse and reached for her. "For God's sake, Major," he cried, "forgive me!" He took the child in his arms and bore her off to my tent; a hundred men swarmed after him, arguing over what she should be fed.

At the day's end I took her to Laura's tent. But Laura

showed no interest, and Isabella would not let me go. So we lay, side by side in my tent, in the dusk. She was worn out by then, but she would not give in to sleep. She lifted her head many times; she opened one eye to be sure I was beside her. She sang snatches of songs, she shuddered, she whimpered a little, at last she breathed evenly; she never relinquished her grip upon my fingers. I thought for a time of slipping away, to make certain that all was in order in the camp. I decided there was nothing that could not wait until morning. I could not stir without waking Isabella, and besides, there was something comforting, after days of bearing so much responsibility, in having my actions determined for me by a three-year-old. I listened to the familiar sounds as the men settled down for the evening. I stared at the small form beside me, and the gray walls overhead. Gradually the sounds outside faded; I was aware only of the grip of the child's hand. For the first time since Lyon, I sank into fathoms of sleep.

PART TWO

8

We paused long enough at Lyon to rest the children. The boys, to be sure, were healthy; they had been well treated. Laura, I realized, would never recover. Isabella stayed in my room; she clung to Louisa and to me. She cried continually—at times Frank, our son, could not stand her crying, and ran from the house. Each night, she woke screaming. She was haunted by her father's death and her mother's suffering, and that was not all. Her small body, Louisa discovered, was covered with red marks. We took them at first to be a rash; Louisa learned at last that they were the scars of arrows, thrust into the child by jealous squaws.

When the time came for leaving, Louisa begged to be allowed to keep Isabella. She would have adopted her, but I could not give in. I had to take all of the captive children with me to Denver. How else could I convince Governor Evans that Black Kettle was sincere in seeking peace?

I packed the children in one wagon and the chiefs in another. I set out with Soule and Cramer and thirty men. We traveled light, intending to eat and sleep at ranch houses and stage coach stations along the way.

Throughout the first day that seemed a sound decision; settlers waved as we approached, and made us welcome.

On the second day, all was changed.

We rode through the wide and shallow valley of the Arkansas. All that rich country was brightened by the first traces of autumn. The aspen were turning along the river; the rabbit brush covered the lowlands with its golden flowers. Everything wild was fruitful; but where the land had been cleared by settlers, all had failed. The hay that should have been cut was still standing; the corn that should have been harvested was spoiling on the stalk; the potatoes that should have been pulled were rotting in the ground.

We came to a sod house. No smoke curled upward from its chimney pipe; no dog ran out barking as I rode into the yard. The gate of the corral hung open; a white shirt struggled on a clothesline as if, once freed, it would flap away after its owner. There was no sign of life. I pushed the door of the house open; the stove was cold in the abandoned room. The drawers were open and empty in the painted chest; a pail hanging from the roof was half filled with water. Jars stood in rows along the mud walls; a blanket lay askew on the rope bed; a bottle of pills was open on a chair. I thought for one moment: cholera.

Four miles up the river we came to a second ranch. Weeds were multiplying where the ground should have been cultivated. The house was deserted. A pair of wolf traps dangled by the open door; a pair of boots stood in a dark corner. A Bible lay by a candle on the table. I stood there, baffled; I heard a faint thumping on the dirt floor. A starved hound crawled out from beneath the stove and licked my heel.

Throughout the day we passed abandoned settlements. We came at last to the Indian Agency at Point of Rocks. Horses were corralled there; wagons were drawn up in a circle to form battlements; from earthworks, dug around the wagons, rifles covered our approach.

I halted the column, and rode in alone. A rancher, Haynes, rose from the earthworks and, with his rifle, waved me in.

"What took you so long?" he called out. "You think we can hold out forever?"

A score of haggard men stood up beside him, stretching, sighing, talking all at once. "Thought you were never coming, Major." "Those wagons filled with ammunition?" "You going to take us back to Lyon or are we going to make a stand here?" They pointed to the earthworks and the wagons. "Not what you'd call a fort, Major, but we can hold them off for a while."

I looked at the battlements, and beyond them to the

building. I saw the faces of women and children, pressed against the windowpanes. A door opened as I looked on; Sam Colley, the Indian Agent, stumbled out; drunk again.

I asked: "What's going on?"

The men crowded around me. "You mean you don't know?"

"I know there were ranches burned and settlers killed at Fillmore. But that's no reason . . ."

"Fillmore! The whole territory is under attack. . . ." "Denver's starving!" "Three thousand . . ."

Haynes silenced them. "It's a general war," he said. "Three thousand Indians are ready to strike us—they're going to wipe out every settlement from Denver to Leavenworth."

"They're going to try, you mean," a settler said. He patted his long hunting rifle.

"That's right," another man cried. "We may not last long, but we'll take some of the red devils with us."

I glanced back at the chiefs, who were sitting impassively in the wagon. They were wearing black hats and shabby cloaks. They looked more like missionaries than devils.

I asked: "What three thousand Indians?"

Haynes was impatient. "What does it matter?" he asked. "Sioux, Cheyennes, Comanches . . ."

"Cheyennes?"

"Satanta, Roman Nose, Black Kettle—they're all out with their war parties."

I nodded toward the wagon. "Black Kettle is here, with me."

The settlers looked for the first time at my companions. They turned back to me. "You mean you've fought already?" "You've beaten Black Kettle?" The news rushed outward. "Major's captured Black Kettle; taking him to Denver to hang."

"Not to hang, to make peace," I said. "There's not going to be an attack," I added. "And I have not beaten Black Kettle. He and his chiefs are coming of their own free will."

The settlers stared at me in silence. My patience gave out. "There's not going to be an attack," I repeated, "so get out of those trenches and let us in! I've children to care for, and horses to water, and men to feed and settle in before dark."

I waved to the column. The troopers rode up and dismounted; the wagons creaked into the yard. The women and children came out of the house and stood behind the men, looking on. I opened the tailgate, and the chiefs stepped down.

The settlers held back. Colley forced a crazy way between them. He lurched up to the wagon, wiping his mouth and swaying; he upbraided the chiefs for going to a bluecoat when they should have gone to Sam Colley, their tried and trusted friend.

The chiefs listened and did not answer. They knew how Colley had swindled them. The settlers knew it too, and they were ashamed. They came forward and, without ceremony, led the chiefs indoors.

That night, when supper was over and the children were asleep, I spoke of the meeting in the Big Timbers. I trusted the men and women who sat around me in the lamplight; I knew that they wanted to believe me. They had staked their lives and all that they owned on this valley; they wanted to stay.

They whispered among themselves when I had finished. Then Haynes spoke for them: "You say Black Kettle's people will keep the peace while you're in Denver?"

"He promised me that they would."

"What if they break his promise?"

"He and his chiefs are my hostages."

"We know that. But we've seen homesteads burned five miles from here. We've seen women and children killed."

"I remember."

"Do you? Or have you forgotten? You were an Exterminator when we last saw you, Major. You were one of Chivington's men."

"I still am."

The settlers stared at me for a moment. Then they turned to one another. The whispers went their rounds again and converged upon Haynes.

"Major, we're agreed. Our homes are out there, untended; our crops are spoiling; once they're gone we've no way of getting through the winter."

"I know that."

"It's the winter that we're worried about. With your permission, Major, we'd like to return to our homesteads and save what we can.

"You have my permission," I said.

9

Colley sat alone beyond the lamplight. When the last of the settlers had left the room, he came forward. He took a bottle of whiskey from his desk and poured out two drinks.

"You despise me," he said.

He was right. To the soldier, there is nothing lower in the community of white men than an Indian Agent. And Sam Colley was the lowest of his kind.

"You despise me," he repeated, "but you don't pity me." He swallowed his whiskey and doubled over in a spasm of coughing. I waited. After a time he sat up and poured himself a second drink. He gasped: "I pity you!"

"Save your pity. I don't need it."

"You will, Major." He stared at me. "You're out alone, where no man should be."

"I'm acting on orders, Colley. Governor Evans sent out orders for the Cheyennes to come in."

"Governor Evans! Who do you think spread the rumors that brought these settlers rushing in to my Agency? Who do you suppose . . ."

"All guesswork," I said. "I've got it in writing." I had carried the Governor's proclamation in my chest pocket since the day I met One Eye. I laid it on the desk.

Colley glanced at the proclamation and shoved it aside. He said: "That was in June, boy; this is late September."

He drank and coughed; he laid his head on his desk. "I'm sick, boy, sick."

I looked at him in disgust. You're not sick, I thought; you're drunk, Drunk and dishonest; crooked like all your kind.

I started to go, but Colley gripped my arm. After a time he raised his head from the table. "Evans," he muttered. "Evans . . . He talked peace in June. But now . . ." He glanced up. "You think I'm drunk; you think I don't know what I'm saying. Here!" He fumbled among his papers. "You've got it in writing; well, so have I!"

He thrust a telegram across the desk. "Read it!"

It was from Evans to Edwin Stanton, the Secretary of War. It began: *Extensive depredations with murder of families occurred yesterday thirty miles south of Denver....*

"A lie!" Colley interrupted. "Only one family was killed: the Hungates." He motioned and I read on.

Our lines of communication are cut, and our crops, our sole dependence, are all in exposed localities and cannot be gathered by our scattered population. Large bodies of Indians are undoubtedly near to Denver and we are in danger of destruction from both attack of Indians and starvation. It is impossible to exaggerate our danger.

I looked up. "He'll be glad to see me then."

Colley laughed in an ugly way. "Oh, delighted!"

"Well, Chivington will support me," I said.

Colley looked at me sidelong. He asked: "What makes you so sure?"

"He's a Union soldier as I am; his enemy is the Confederacy. He has no troops to spare, not while the . . ."

"No troops?" Colley leaned back in his chair, enjoying his superiority. "You've been out of touch, boy," he said. "You don't know what's going on. They've armed the rabble in Denver. . . . Yes," he went on, seeing my chagrin, "they've cleaned off the street corners and emptied the saloons. They've put a thousand men into uniform, for one hundred days. They call them the Third Regiment."

The taste in my mouth was sour. "They'll join the Union armies in Missouri," I said. "They'll go after the graybacks."

"For one hundred days?" Colley laughed. "They'll hunt Indians," he said. "And they'd better find them! Your friend Chivington is in trouble, boy. His term in the Army runs out this autumn. He's heading for the Senate. The pressure is on, boy, and he knows it. He needs a victory."

"I'll give him a victory," I said. "I'll bring in the chiefs, and let him take credit for the peace."

"Ah!" Colley leaned forward and reached out for the bottle. He tipped it clumsily into his mouth, so that the whiskey sloshed over his chin. He looked at me, his eyes blurred and dim.

"Don't you see, boy?" he said. "Don't you see?"

He wiped his mouth on his sleeve and set the bottle down. "Evans," he said, "and Chivington, your hero; they're men of great ambition; they're very ambitious men. They don't want to ship any more boys out of the Territory. So, they work up their own war. They stir up the mob in every saloon. They run crying to Stanton, and Stanton gives in. They hand out a rifle to every tramp in Denver. They say: 'Here! Shoot yourself a red man!' "

He waved the empty bottle in my face. "And then, you come along," he said. "When every tramp is armed and every rifle is loaded, you come out of the Big Timbers with Black Kettle! You send the warriors back to their villages and the settlers back to their farms. And you expect Evans to be grateful!"

"I'm carrying out the Governor's orders," I said.

"You fool!" He pounded on the desk. "You've made a liar out of Evans, don't you see! You've made a laughing stock out of Chivington. They'll take you in turn and break every bone in your body. They'll . . ."

"That's enough!" I said, rising. Colley was an Indian Agent and a thief; they were fine men; my superiors, and my friends.

10

We rode on through the valley, up the slow rise toward the Rocky Mountains. Late on the third day, as we came to the crest of a ridge, I saw, faint in the far distance, the Spanish Peaks.

I paused while the wagon train plodded past me. I remembered the moment, six years before, when I had come to this same place on the trail. I was then one of a party of pioneers, sent out from Kansas by Governor Denver to claim the land in the lee of the Rockies; the unknown land where, by repute, every stream flowed over a bed of gold.

We were thirty-five days out of Lecompton, I remembered, when we came to this crest and saw the Peaks, shining on the western horizon. We cheered as if no white men had ever seen them before.

To the left of the trail, the Arkansas wound off toward the lowering sun. It lit a reach in the river that I remembered well. We had pitched our tents there in 1858; we were at rest when the cries of one man led us bounding through the willows and into the shallow water. There, all the brilliance of the sun was reflected by thousands of gold flakes. They were mica, of course, but we did not know that. Shouting, we scraped them up, each man with his vision of life as he wished it to be.

My own vision was simple enough. I saw, in the glitter around my knees, a palace on Fifth Avenue, a villa in Newport, a yacht riding at anchor. I heard the applause of the crowds as I led my thoroughbreds into the winner's circle. I led a hundred guests into my banqueting hall where footmen waited behind chairs of embossed leather and gold plate shone beneath the chandeliers.

I looked back now from the river to the wagon train plodding along the trail: the troops that I commanded; the children I had recovered; the chiefs who had placed themselves in my hands. A far cry, I thought, from my early ambitions; but if I bring back a settlement from Denver, I'll be content.

We moved slowly up the valley, sending the settlers home from each fortified point. At Pueblo, we left the

Arkansas and rode north, beneath the Sangre de Cristo range. The wind that flowed from those heights was chilling; the storms that piled up over them broke upon us, drenching us. When the sun shone, the peaks were brilliant, covered as they were by the early snow.

The ground was stony at the base of the mountains; the soil was poor. We met few travelers. Most of the sod houses were boarded up; the few settlers who had not fled to Denver regarded us in silence as we passed. But there was one place where we were assured of a welcome.

The way station two days south of Denver was a ranch, owned by Charles Coberly. It was known as the Half Way House, and for the soldiers of the Second Battalion, it was a favorite resting place. The creek was clean there; the pasture was green; the timber was plentiful. The main lodging, between a roof of sod and a dirt floor, was warm and dry. The food was spiced with plums and chokecherries gathered by Coberly's two daughters.

I rode on ahead of the wagons, to tell the Coberlys that we were coming. To get to the Half Way House, I had to work my way through a barricade.

Coberly watched me from the door. He recognized me and laid his rifle aside.

"You too?" I said.

He nodded. "My wife's begging me to leave this place," he said. "The girls sleep in their clothes—if they sleep at all."

"I thought you got along with the Indians."

"I thought so too. So did Ward Hungate." He shook his head. "Never again!"

We moved inside. "I'm on my way to Denver," I began. "I . . ."

"You'll see Hungate's ranch then—all that the Indians left of it. They butchered the . . ."

"There are Indians in my party," I told him. "I'm taking them to see the Governor."

He waited.

"We're planning to stop over here," I said.

Coberly took a moment to reply. "You're welcome to stay, Ned; any soldier of the Second Battalion is welcome. But keep your Indians out of my house."

The wagon train drew in at the end of the day. We lodged the children in the house; we pitched a tent outside for the chiefs and carried supper out to them. As always, when supper was over, we moved the tables and benches back and set two chairs out on the floor of the main cabin. Coberly and his son sat down and tuned their fiddles. The elder of the girls joined them and sang an English air.

She was nineteen, and a favorite of ours. When she had finished, we sang a song of our own:

Eighteen pounds of meat a week,
Whiskey here to sell,
How can the boys stay at home
When the girls all look so well? . . .

Soule sang to Coberly's daughter in his bantering way; she watched him gravely. If, at the end of the song, he had stepped forward and asked for her hand, she would have chided him for tarrying so long.

He took her hand, but only to lead her in a country dance. Other couples joined in. I opened a bottle I had brought with me. I was well along when Mulkey found me and led me grumbling outside.

A group of men were crowded around the entrance to the Indians' tent. The chiefs were seated on the ground. A ranchhand swayed over them, calling on them to stand up and fight.

"Just stand up," he cried, "and we'll kill you, same as you killed Hungate."

I grabbed him and spun him around, while he was still talking: "Eighty bullets they fired into him. Scalped his kids and threw them down a well."

I shook him violently. "Not these Indians," I shouted. "Not these!"

He looked up at me, his face filled with misery. "It was Cheyennes that done it, Major! Same as these here."

I felt, in place of anger, my own uncertainty, my pent-up doubt. I turned to Black Kettle. "Close by here," I told him, "a white family was murdered by Indians. A man and his wife and his two daughters, all killed in cold blood."

The old chief looked at me intently.

"Don't tell me you never heard of it! Don't tell me it was the Indians who were attacked!"

He shook his head.

"This man says they were Cheyennes. He says they were from your band. Now tell us, who were they?"

"They were not Cheyennes."

"He's lying!" the ranchhand cried. "They were from his band, and he knows it!"

The crowd took up the cry. "He's right, Major!" "They all lie." "You know that, Major." "You should know that."

I turned on Black Kettle. "These men say you're lying; what's your answer?"

He looked at me calmly, and did not reply.

His stubborn calmness angered me. I moved close to him, still holding on to the ranchhand. "Maybe you are lying," I said. "This is still your territory, so maybe the killers were your men. By God, if they were . . ."

"They were not Cheyennes," he said.

I stood over him, and shouted down at him. "Then, damn it, who were they?"

He turned and whispered to the chiefs who sat beside him. He looked up at me. "Northern Arapahoes," he said, "young ones, from far to the North."

"From far to the north were they? Then what were they doing here?"

"They came against the Utes. They did a great wrong."

He looked up at me, waiting for my response. No one in the crowd could fail to see the pain in his face.

I let the ranchhand go. He and the rest of the men drifted off. I stood by the chiefs, shaking my head. After a time the roaring in my head died away; I became aware of familiar sounds: the laughter of the dancers; the violins scraping away indoors.

I turned back to Black Kettle. "There is a bad feeling," I said, "because of the killing."

He nodded.

"Well?" I asked, "do you still want to go on?"

He looked at me for a moment; he nodded again.

We rode on early the next morning. We passed the charred ruins of the Hungate ranch. We labored on, up the winding trail to the divide where six years before our Lecompton party had struggled in the snowdrifts. I thought: it was harder then.

At the start of the descent I turned the column over to Cramer. I fell back to the wagon in which the chiefs sat. *It was like going through a fire*, Black Kettle had said of my journey to the Big Timbers; this, I guessed, was like going through a fire for him. In the broken English that we had learned to use together, I told him that I was going on ahead to prepare the way with the Governor. He reached out and gripped my hand.

11

Soule and I pressed on down the divide and across the plain. At dusk we came to Denver.

The city had stretched out across the plains; then it had shrunk, leaving its borders dead. No lamps shone in the shacks that jutted up along the way. We saw nothing stir. We heard nothing, save the sound of our horses' hoofs striking the road.

Yet we were under scrutiny. From the roof of the first brick building, a gray flag rose on a mast, to signal our approach. A rifle poked out from a narrow battlement; it swung slowly, covering us as we passed.

We rode on. The streets were deserted, save for bands of drunken soldiers. The vacant lots were filled with cattle that had been driven into the city. Families who had fled from outlying ranches huddled around low fires. It was as if these people expected the Confederate ghosts of Sibley's army to issue out of the mountain passes and lay siege to the city.

We came at last to a log barrier that blocked the street. A sentry with a heavy rifle halted us. His uniform was outlandish; his manner was insolent. I was about to strike him when, from the shadows, an officer sauntered out, like an actor moving onstage to pick up his cue.

"We've been expecting you, Ned," he said.

He was Harry Richmond; in the days before the war we had been amateur actors together. He slapped my thigh, and spoke of the old days in the Apollo Theatre. He joked about his temporary status as a captain in the Third Regiment. He inquired, in passing, after Louisa. He looked up at me with that solemn air that actors assume in speaking of the dead.

"Too bad about Rose," he said.

I gathered in my reins, but Richmond held on, fondling the bridle. Casually he asked: "What happened to your red friends?"

"They'll be here tomorrow."

Richmond shook his head. "We were hoping you'd sent them back."

"Why should I?"

"This town is no place for them, Ned. It's been boiling ever since they put the Hungates on display."

"Who did?"

"The powers that be. They halted the burial. They laid the bodies out in the front window of a dry-goods store. They kept them there three days, for everyone to see."

"Arapahoes from the north killed the Hungates. I'm bringing in Cheyennes."

"No matter; they're Indians, and this town is crying for blood."

Richmond laid his hand on my arm. "Take the word of an old friend, Ned," he said. "Turn back."

We rode on into the city. We stabled our horses and took a room at the Tremont House. We went our ways. Soule headed for the saloons; I walked to the Governor's imposing mansion.

I rang the bell and stepped inside. The hallway of the mansion was rich with cigar smoke; from the parlor, the din of many voices reached me. I started forward; a servant barred my way. He took my card and vanished; the din died away. The servant returned bearing regrets: His Excellency was indisposed.

I strode off, and had nowhere to go. The saloons were crowded with my old companions; I could no longer trust them. In the mansions of Denver were many citizens who would listen to my story; I dared not approach them until I had seen the Governor. So I wandered through the darkening streets; an alien in the city I had helped to found.

I was known of course—my height alone gave me away. From the shadows, men I could not see called out my name.

As if to say: We know you, Wynkoop; and we're watching you. All friends of mine once, but no longer. I walked on, and all the time the ties that bound me to my own wild days were breaking.

I crossed the city block that I had staked out as my own. I had raised my cabin there in the winter of 1858. Now a row of grog shops lined the street.

I walked on, and came to a lumberyard stacked high with two-by-fours. It had served as a site for duels in our early days. I had seen more than one man stumble with a death wound on that site. I had gone there to practice for my own appointment with a Southerner who called himself Bold Thunder. My aim was accurate, and led to a visit from his seconds. "No need to show off," the spokesman said; "Thunder says to tell you he can shoot a lark on the wing." I was cocksure and carefree in those days. I laughed and said: "Not if the lark fires first."

I wandered on past the Louisiana and the Western Star. I came to the Criterion, whose proprietor, Charles Harrison, had held all my debts. Once, I remembered, he had killed a man in the Criterion who was threatening to kill me. Three years later, he met his own end, as a colonel in the Confederate Army. Now, I thought, he would be striding through hell in his Confederate uniform, hell being his choice after death. The Criterion, nonetheless, was noisy enough.

The Apollo, in contrast, was dark and deserted; where once Rose ruled. I leaned on the stair that led to the stage door. I felt my blood draining from an old wound.

It was in 1859 that Colonel Thorne and his Theatrical

Company arrived in Denver. The Colonel found his audiences more dramatic than his plays. He braved our audience of miners for five performances; then he fled, leaving stranded his leading ladies—three daughters of an improvident English aristocrat. Undaunted, the three formed their own company at the Apollo. Rose, brilliant and beautiful, was the star; Flora, the youngest, sang ballads in the intermissions; Louisa played supporting roles.

Every miner in the Territory worshipped Rose. They lost her to me. She took me with her when she played in Georgia Gulch and Central City. She would have married me, but I held back. So she left me. She fled from the Apollo with a gambler on the night before her last show was to open.

I was a sheriff in those days; I hunted the gambler down and brought him back to Denver; I turned him over to a miners' court on a charge of kidnapping. The miners lost no time in sentencing him to hang.

Rose married him on the same day to save his neck.

I went wild when Rose left me. I barely knew night from day, until Louisa moved into my cabin to care for me. She endured the scorn of respectable people. She named my address as her own when the census taker came around. I gave her nothing and she asked for nothing—until word reached Denver that a Confederate army was marching up the Rio Grande to capture our city. Then, knowing I would volunteer, Louisa pleaded with me to marry her for the sake of the child she was bearing. For the child's sake, I gave in.

Rose went to the States with her husband. Before long, she wrote to us. She was unhappy, as I knew she would be; she begged to be allowed to return. There was nowhere she could go in the Territory save to my house. If she had come to us, what might have happened? There was no forgiveness in me, and no love either. Yet I waited for her, and kept a part of myself only for her. Even in anger, I gave more of myself to Rose, two thousand miles away, than to Louisa, lying at my side.

But no longer. Rose was dead, somewhere in the States. And I was glad, being free of her.

12

In the morning I was summoned downstairs. There, waiting for me, was Governor Evans. He advanced, an imposing figure with his fine features, his morning coat and wing collar, his satin waistcoat and gold watch chain. I rubbed my shoes against my shabby trousers and snuffed out my cheap cigar.

He smiled, in his cold way. He steered me into a back parlor. There, his words of welcome tapered to an end.

"Now, Wynkoop," he said, "just what are you up to?"

"Didn't you receive my report?"

"I did."

"I tried to make it clear."

"You failed, sir."

"Governor, it was your own proclamation that started it. The Cheyennes replied to your proclamation and offered to return the captives if we . . ."

"You should have rescued them, by force of arms."

"We were one hundred and thirty, sir, against a thousand or more."

"Others have faced the odds."

"The children would have been killed."

"That, in itself, is proof that the Indians are savages."

I struggled to control myself. He waited with a trace of impatience.

"Governor," I said, "I took it to be obedience to your wishes that I should recover the captives, alive. I did so, and in turn . . ."

"I am gratified that you are obedient to my wishes. I wish you now to ride out; to halt your Indians and to escort them back where they came from. . . . Now!" he added, when I failed to answer. "Within the hour! I want none of them."

"Not even the white children?"

"Leave the children of course; take back the Indians. The time has passed when Indians are welcome in Denver."

"Governor, they have come four hundred . . ."

"You should have known better than to bring them! They are enemies, Wynkoop; we and they are at war."

"They don't want war, sir; that's why they . . ."

"They don't want to be punished, you mean. And rightly

punished for the outrages they have committed; They plunder and kill without mercy through the summer months. Then as winter approaches they come posing as peace lovers. They must be made to suffer, Wynkoop; they must be punished so that they may learn respect."

All the familiar arguments . . .

"Don't you see, Wynkoop?" he went on. "If we make peace with them now, before we punish them, the United States will be acknowledging itself whipped."

I was startled. "The United States whipped, by a band of Indians? Governor, you must be joking!"

"That's enough, Wynkoop! I want them turned back; now, before it's too late."

I felt my chest heave. I said: "It's already too late."

"You choose to disobey me? You willfully disregard . . ."

"Governor, by now every Indian on the plains knows that Black Kettle is on his way to talk with you. I couldn't turn him back now, even if I wanted to. It was in answer to your proclamation that he set out. He is coming to Denver because he has faith in you."

Evans looked at me keenly. For the first time, I could see anxiety and doubt in his eyes.

"If I could be sure of that," he began. He winced. "The matter is out of my hands," he said. "It is in the hands of the military. I cannot see Black Kettle while he is at war with the United States."

"Governor, you are the United States. You represent the President, and if I know Mr. . . ."

"Out of my hands," he repeated. "Besides, I am leaving

Denver tomorrow morning. I am going away, on urgent business. I shall be gone at least five days."

"Black Kettle will wait."

"Wynkoop"—he shivered—"you place me in a most difficult position."

"My own position is not easy, sir." I continued to talk, sensing that I had gained the initiative, and that he needed time in which to shift his ground. I spoke of the meeting in the Big Timbers. I pointed out that I had pledged my word as an officer that he would see the chiefs. "I think you must see them," I said.

He wavered. "Do you realize what you are asking of me?"

"I think so."

"Wynkoop, you cannot conceive of the pressure I am under! The settlers throughout the Territory have been driven from their ranches in terror. . . ."

"They have gone back now."

"Our contractors are close to bankruptcy thanks to the Indians; our manufacturers are without machinery; our merchants have no stocks left."

"If you reach settlement with the chiefs, then, sir, the supplies will move again."

"The people forbid it! When the bodies of the Hungates were brought in, the people were like beasts! They blamed me for permitting the Hungates to be murdered. And now"—he sank into a chair, shaking his head—"you force me to meet with their murderers!"

"I do not!"

He was not listening. "Horrible!" he murmured. "I'll never forget the sight! The youngest of the girls was just the age of my daughter!"

"Governor," I said, "Black Kettle and his band did not murder the Hungates!"

"No matter; they kill white men whenever they can."

"That's not true! They could have killed us in the Big Timbers; they spared us."

"They knew they could use you."

"Use me! Governor, I'd killed the best of their warriors. They'd killed my men. They spared me because they know that there's no end to killing. That's why they're here."

"If I thought that"—he pressed his fine hands against his forehead—"if I could be sure of that . . ."

"Governor, it's the truth!"

"If I could be sure! I've tried to make peace with the Indians, Wynkoop; I swear it! Even today, if I were free . . . But I'm not a free man, Wynkoop. I'm bound by my oath of office; I'm responsible for the lives of every man, woman, and child for hundreds of miles around. I must protect every little farmhouse. And yet," he sighed, "I have been stripped of my troops."

"You have them now."

"That's it, Wynkoop; that's just it! For months I've pleaded with Washington. I've been on my knees, begging them to let me raise troops to replace the ones they have taken from me. Now, at last, they have recognized our plight. We've raised the Third Regiment; we're spending thousands of dollars to equip it. . . ." His voice lapsed to a whisper. "Wynkoop, what will I do with the Third Regiment if I make peace?"

"Disband it," I said.

"And make a fool of myself?" He stood up. "What would Stanton think after all my cries for help? What would the President think of me?" He went to a window and stared out, his hands clasped behind his back. "The Third Regiment was raised to kill Indians," he said, "and kill Indians it must."

He stood there with his back toward me, hoping, I suppose, that I would leave.

"You asked me," I said, "what Mr. Lincoln would think of you if you made peace with the chiefs. I ask you: what will he think when he learns that you refused even to receive them, after they came four hundred miles to talk to you?"

He turned on me. "How will Lincoln learn that?"

"I'll tell him, if no one else will."

Evans paced back and forth across the room. He stopped short before me. "Wynkoop," he said, "I pray to God you know what you are doing!" He strode out, slamming the door.

13

In the morning Soule and I rode south to meet the chiefs. We intended to guide them unseen into Denver. It was no use. Down Fourteenth Street, a long and narrow gauntlet, men were gathered in knots, leaning against the buildings, straddling the porch rails, waiting. "Those revolvers of yours loaded, boy?" one man called out. "They'd better be."

Three miles south of the city, we saw our column approaching. The men were weary of course; but if Soule and I had been Lincoln and Grant in the reviewing stand of the White House, no body of troops could have looked finer. Cramer led the column; behind him three veterans of Glorieta bore the standard of the First Colorado Cavalry and the company guidons with all their battle stars. The troops rode in close order; the chiefs sat upright in their wagon. From white masts, held by Black Kettle and Bull Bear, there floated two American flags.

We saluted and took the salute; we rode on with the column. We were ready for the mob; instead, at the edge of the city, forty carriages were drawn up in line, waiting to escort us into Denver.

We rode down the line. The men seated in the carriages took off their hats as we passed; the ladies, in white dresses, bowed. I recognized a minister, a surgeon, a federal judge; an abolitionist or two; a family of Quakers; Hickory Rogers and Joe McCubbin from our Lecompton party; two ladies who had started the first school in the Territory, and —strangest of all—three other ladies who had once started up a Temperance League. Someone, I knew, had organized the welcome. I glanced at Soule; he grinned.

We did not pause, and no command was given; the carriages simply fell into line behind us. So we paraded down Fourteenth Street; past the crowd, sullen but subdued; past the Governor's Mansion, where, I trusted, Evans was standing behind a curtain, looking on. We crossed the whole city; we halted in the shadow of the Methodist church, where, two years before, Chivington had roared at his congregation about the tortures of hell. There, Soule and I turned, and stood at attention; the troops clattered by us; in the carriages, the ladies and gentlemen smiled.

Camp Weld was the site chosen by Governor Evans for his meeting with the chiefs. It was the training camp of the Third Regiment, the worst possible place to talk of peace.

We set out for Weld in the morning. I took all of our troops. For, by then, stories were coming in from all quarters: among the thousand soldiers of the Third Regiment, bands were forming, with the sworn purpose of waylaying and killing the chiefs.

We rode through the narrow gates of Weld. We halted and looked around. We saw all that you would expect to see in the camp of a regiment that was to exist for just one hundred days. All manner of equipment was littered around the square; no troops were being drilled; a single squad of cavalrymen humped around the parade ground on spavined horses; a sergeant shouted at them, they stared at us.

In the doors and windows of the barracks, more of the hundred-day men appeared. A few of them shouted obscenities at us. One picked up a rifle, aimed it at the chiefs, and made a loud *tock!* with his tongue. His companions laughed. There were protests from within the barracks and most of the men went back to their cards.

The men who tramped to Glorieta were, God knows, no cavaliers. They went cursing, brawling, thieving, and drinking into the mountains; they were more like pirates than soldiers when they fell upon the Texans.

These men were worse. They were the backwash of the Pikes Peak tide: too late to strike gold; too shiftless to work the land; too impoverished to move on west; too stubborn to head home. They were, most of them, bummers and drifters, haunting the fringes of legality, begging or stealing the price of a bottle, while their kids cried in dugouts along the river. They bore long grudges, and they chose easy victims. They were happiest when the odds were one hundred against one.

We started across the parade ground toward the Colonel's mansion. The Officer of the Day intercepted us and led us to an empty mess hall. Soule, Smith, and I went inside with the chiefs. A bench was set out there and, facing it, a table and four chairs. An orderly motioned to us to be seated on the bench; he fussed around the table, setting out a pitcher of water and four glasses. We eyed them, thirsting.

We waited, listening to the familiar sounds of camp life. A carriage creaked outside, and Cramer called our guard to attention. The Officer of the Day shouted to us to stand.

Evans stepped in, pulling off his gloves. For a moment the light from the entrance flooded the room. Then, all the doorway was filled by Chivington.

He was a giant. He wore the largest uniform in the Army, and it barely reached around his chest and shoulders. His neck, his arms, his wrists, were all immense; he could kill any man in the Territory with his bare hands.

He had been a purse fighter before he turned to the ministry, and purse fights continued until one man or the other surrendered. Chivington had never surrendered; he had left many opponents lying on the turf more dead than alive.

He entered the room as he might have entered the ring: his bald head arched back; his bearded chin thrust out; his eyes, small and fierce, appraising us.

We stood at attention, like poor boys awaiting his patronage. With no more than a nod in our direction he turned and hung his sword upon his chair.

After a moment I led the chiefs forward. Evans reached out to shake hands with Black Kettle as if he were offering a morsel of meat to a fanged animal. Chivington merely nodded. We took our places again on the bench. At once Evans motioned to Black Kettle to rise and to speak.

Instead, the old chief drew from within his blanket a long-stemmed pipe. To light it, and to pass it around, was for him a sacred ceremony, binding all who smoked the pipe to act honorably and to live as friends.

Black Kettle stuffed the pipe with tobacco that I had given to him. He lit it and passed it to his left. I took it in turn and carried it to Evans; he sipped it and passed it on to Chivington. In time, it returned to Black Kettle.

Evans was restless. He glanced at his watch; he motioned to Simon Whiteley, the recorder, to start writing; he cleared his throat.

"Well," he demanded of Black Kettle, "what have you got to say?"

Black Kettle rose. He praised the Governor's proclamation. He added that he had, at once, accepted its terms. He said nothing of his troubles in reaching us with his reply. Instead, he spoke with pride of my journey to the Big Timbers. He noted that the chiefs' journey to Denver was for them a risk. "We came with our eyes shut," he said, "following Major Wynkoop."

"You are our father," he told Evans. "All that we ask for is peace."

Evans stood up, shuffling his papers. He delivered the speech that he had prepared. He blamed Black Kettle for not responding at once to his proclamation. He complained of the discomforts he had suffered, a full year before this meeting, when he had journeyed to meet the chiefs. "You have gone into an alliance with the Sioux who are against us," he said. "While we have been spending thousands of dollars to protect you and to make you comfortable, you have smoked the war pipe with our enemies."

Ardently, the chiefs shook their heads. "They say you are mistaken," Smith told the Governor. "They have made no alliances. They have not smoked the war pipe, neither with the Sioux nor with anyone else."

"Well, I am speaking figuratively," Evans said. He fingered his notes; he moved on to his next point. "So far as making a treaty now is concerned," he said, "we are in no position to do it. Your young men are on the war path. My soldiers are preparing for the fight. You, so far, have had the advantage; but the time is coming when the plains will swarm with United States soldiers."

He paused and Smith echoed his words. The chiefs looked steadily at the Governor. He glanced at them. He was prepared, I think, to encounter fear or defiance in their faces. He saw nothing and he faltered. He began to plead with the chiefs, as if their acquiescence in the destruction of their people were necessary to his plan. He granted that the chiefs had always opposed war with the whites. He suggested that they had been unable to control their young warriors. "Is this not so?" he asked, and the chiefs answered: "It has been so."

It was as if the Governor and the chiefs were linked by a common handicap; for a moment, kinship flickered between them like a flame on a cold hearth.

Chivington looked on in silence. He wrote a brief message on a sheet of paper and thrust it along the table. The Governor read it; he nodded, sighing. "Another reason that I am not in a condition to make a treaty," he said, "is that war has begun and the power to make a treaty of peace has passed from me to the great war chief."

Smith carried the words across a great distance to the Indians. They sat with their hands in their laps. There was no sound, save for the scratching of Whiteley's quill pen. After a time, the scratching ceased; Whiteley stared at his pad.

Evans remained standing. He had made it plain that the hostile Indians could not escape punishment for their transgressions. But he knew in his heart that the men who faced him were not guilty and he wanted to be just. So he reverted to his summer struggle, to detach the friendly Indians from the hostiles. He conceded that the chiefs were not at war with the United States. "My advice to you," he told the chiefs, "is to turn on the side of the Government, and to show, by your acts, that friendly disposition you profess to me."

The chiefs bent forward. "What is meant by being on the side of the Government?"

"Keeping close to the soldiers. Having nothing to do with our enemies."

The chiefs conferred. They said: "We accept that."

Evans glanced at Chivington. He retreated a step.

"The only way you can show your friendship," he said, "is by making some arrangement with the soldiers; by helping them."

The chiefs asked: "What is meant by helping them?"

"Acting as scouts for them. Keeping them informed; telling them all you know. And fighting beside them, if need be, against their enemies."

The chiefs conferred again. Black Kettle rose, and spoke: "We will go on to our village and take to our young men every word that you say. I cannot answer for all of them, but I think there will be little difficulty in getting them to help the soldiers."

So the terms of agreement were reached.

The oldest of the chiefs, White Antelope, stood up. He held out a silver medal, one that Abraham Lincoln had placed around his neck. "Ever since I went to Washington and received this medal," he said, "I have called all white men my brothers." He asked: "Who are your enemies?"

"All the Indians who are fighting us," Evans said.

White Antelope nodded. He declared that the Cheyennes and the Arapahoes would never again fight against the whites. But, he added, the tribes to the south of the Arkansas, the Apaches, the Comanches, and the Kiowas, were all committed to war. So were the undefeated warriors to the north—the Sioux. Thirteen bands of Sioux had crossed the Platte to raid on the plains, so White Antelope said. They were aroused and well armed and constantly on the move.

So Chivington's task was defined.

It was no easy task, even for Chivington and his force of a thousand men. In all the years of Indian warfare, General Harney alone had managed to surround and to defeat a band of Sioux. Scores of ambitious officers had undertaken to repeat Harney's triumph. Riding out onto the plains with all flags flying, they had crawled back weeks later; their supplies exhausted; their horses lame; their men mutinous, their dreams of glory in shards.

Chivington listened intently as White Antelope spoke. Throughout the conference he had remained silent; yet I knew that he was agitated. Now, at the mention of the Sioux, his fists closed, his neck tightened: small signals, betraying the rage that he kept like a prisoner within himself.

On many occasions I had seen that rage burst forth, as the Reverend Chivington stormed through the streets of Denver, "battling for the Lord." Once, I remembered, he had come upon a wagon loaded with barrels of whiskey, outside the Criterion. He seized an ax and climbed aboard the wagon; in no time, staves were flying and whiskey was flowing down the gutter. In the crowd that gathered around, some newcomer to Denver was rash enough to ask by what authority the Reverend was destroying other people's property. Chivington paused, with the ax high above his head. "By the authority of Almighty God!" he shouted; and down the ax crashed, as if the broken barrels were a horde of demons, swarming at his feet.

He sat in silence through the conference. Then, as it moved to its conclusion, the time approached when he had to speak.

The chiefs answered frankly all of the Governor's questions. They acknowledged their own acts of violence; they made no effort to voice their own grievances, saying that it was better to bury the past. Toward the end of the conference they offered to fight with the whites, against the Sioux. They added that their decision would expose their wives and their children to great danger of reprisal. They asked for some assurance that we would protect them.

"That," Evans answered, "is a matter for the great war chief to decide."

Chivington stood up and towered over us. He spoke with some difficulty, as if his main effort were directed inwards, to control himself.

"I am not a big war chief," he said, "but all the soldiers in this country are at my command. My rule of fighting, white men or Indians, is to fight them until they lay down their arms and submit to military authority. They are nearer Major Wynkoop than anyone else," he said to Evans, "and they can go to him when they get ready to do that."

The chiefs gestured in assent. They were reassured by all that Chivington said. For they were ready to submit, and they trusted wholly in me. They knew that for them safety lay in living close to Lyon. They stood smiling at the close of the conference. They embraced Evans and then myself. They moved to embrace Chivington, but he turned from them and left the room, buckling on his sword.

On the steps of the mess hall a photographer was waiting. The Governor ignored his pleas, and left with his party; I gave in. I led the chiefs back into the mess hall; I convinced them that the camera would do them no harm. We set the bench up at the end of the hall, between a coat rack and a slop bucket, with an army blanket for background. Then, solemn as stuffed owls, we drew deep breaths and glared at the camera's round eye. The photograph, frayed and faded, is here on my desk. Soule and I are squatting in front, he with his devil-take-you stare, I with my cavalry hat on at a rakish angle and my jaws clamped upon a half-smoked cigar. Seated behind us are Neva, White Antelope, Black Kettle, Bull Bear, and One Eye, all rigid and a little apprehensive. Standing behind them are a mixed lot: a young settler who volunteered to guard us; Dexter Colley, Sam's boy; Uncle John Smith in his melancholy mood; two Indians whose names I've forgotten; Whiteley, the recorder, with his hands thrust into his waistcoat pockets; and Mulkey, clutching his rifle, and ready to blow the head off the first man who might hurt the chiefs or me. One side of the photograph is blurred; a line of black dots bisects us, where acid must have fallen on the wet plate. But, looking at it closely, I can make out minor details: White Antelope's medal, for instance, and his fine earrings; Neva's top hat, resting where he laid it on the floor; Black Kettle's peace pipe, lying across his lap in such a way that it seems to be an arrow, piercing my chest and emerging from my back.

14

We stayed on for two days at Denver—time enough for all that I had to do.

I found good homes for the boys and for Laura. I left Isabella with a young couple who had lost their own child.

I went back to the Governor's Mansion—and Evans received me. He was preparing to leave for Washington; he promised to give the President a favorable report on all that we had done.

I rode out to Camp Weld to take my leave of Chivington. I felt unsure of him. I was convinced that I had eased his task of safeguarding the Territory by making allies of the Cheyennes. I feared, nonetheless, that he had taken the conference as an affront.

As I rode out to Weld I hardened myself for Chivington's reproaches. To my relief, I found his mood wholly changed.

He was seated with his staff on the porch of the Commanding Officer's Quarters. He was in high spirits, as if his burdens had been lightened. He greeted me with the warmth he had shown toward me in the past. He presented me to George Shoup, the young officer he had picked to lead the Third Regiment, and to Major Downing, a well-born attorney who had become his principal adviser.

On the parade ground, a captain of the Third Regiment was training his company in the School of the Saber. We stood watching the cavalrymen charge an invisible enemy, and slash the air and haul their mounts to a halt.

"Well," Chivington said to me, "what do you think of them?"

"What does any soldier think of the militia?"

"They'll do," Chivington said; "for men who have been in service for six weeks, they'll do."

"They've been in for six weeks? Then they have only eight weeks more to go."

"It's enough."

I was doubtful. I asked: "When will you take the field?"

Chivington grinned. "When I'm ready."

We moved down the steps of the porch and onto the parade ground. Downing began to point to details in the drill. He was anxious, I could see, to break off my questioning. I saw no reason to accommodate him.

"Will you be leading the regiment?" I asked Chivington.

He laughed. "That is something that only Shoup and I know!"

"Will you follow the Platte route?"

"Not even Shoup knows that!"

"That's where the Sioux are," I said, "between the South Platte and the Smoky Hill."

"So I understand."

"You think you can catch them?"

"We can catch one of them! And one is enough, eh, Downing?" He nudged my side. "I sent Downing after a band of savages last spring," he said. "He caught one of them, and soon found out where the rest were hiding!"

"Toasted his feet over a fire," Chivington added. "He talked soon enough!"

In one corner of the parade ground, a sergeant was drilling a squad of men on foot. They came to a halt, at present arms, as we approached.

Chivington strode down the line of dusty soldiers. He turned to face one of them and wrenched the rifle from his hands. He tossed it to me. "Austrian Mauser," he said, "made for the Imperial Guard."

It was heavy and a muzzle-loader. But it was finely built. I admired its workmanship, and then handed it back to Chivington.

"Knock down a buffalo at three hundred yards," he said. He raised the rifle and sighted it on a horse picketed on the far side of the parade ground. I waited for the explosion. But Chivington lowered the Mauser and thrust it against its owner's chest. "Filthy!" he said. "Your barrel is filthy! Take the man's name for punishment," he told Shoup.

We walked back to the porch, matching our strides with Chivington's. He issued a few orders that sent his staff officers scurrying off. When he and I were alone, he turned again to me.

"Those Indians of yours," he said. "How many men are there?"

"A thousand or so, when they're all in."

"What have they got for weapons?"

"Bows and arrows; a few old hunting rifles."

He nodded. "And they'll do just as you say?"

"I guarantee it."

"Bring them in close to the fort then. See that they stay there."

"I'll do my best," I said.

He glanced at me with a trace of suspicion. He said: "That's an order, Wynkoop!"

"I'll carry it out, Colonel."

"That's the spirit!" He laughed. "You know, you've got Major Downing worried! He can't figure you out! 'Don't worry, Downing!' I tell him. 'Wynkoop's my boy!' " He looked down on me. "Am I right?"

"Yes, sir."

"Of course I am! You know what I say to Downing? 'I was the one who promoted Wynkoop,' I say to him. 'I was the one who gave him the command at Lyon. Wynkoop's a good soldier,' I tell Downing. 'He was with me at Glorieta.' "

He turned to me with an air of affection. "Do you remember, Ned, how we came on the Texans, in the pass?"

"I'll never forget it," I said.

"I shouted 'Charge!' and gave my mule a kick. And you were the first to follow me! Across the canyon we went, and over the ditch—how wide would you say that ditch was?"

"Ten feet at least."

"You're right! Clear over the ditch we went, and into their fire! Right into their ranks with sabers drawn! As God is my witness," he cried, "there's nothing finer in the Old Testament!"

"We scattered them," I said.

"A whole day's fighting! And then in the night, over the mountains and down the cliffside to their base camp. We killed every mule and burned every wagon they had."

"They set out for Texas on foot," I said. "Most of them died of thirst on the way."

"It was a great moment," Chivington said, "the greatest moment of my life."

He laid a heavy hand on my shoulder. "Well, boy," he said, "we've got work to do. Good luck, if I don't see you again."

15

All the way home the country was healthy again. The crops were harvested; the fortifications were dismantled; smoke curled upward from the chimney of every sod house; many wagon trains passed us on the road. For the news had traveled before us—that in the conference at Camp Weld, the Governor and the chiefs had agreed on the terms of peace.

Pride filled my days. And desire—I had not missed Louisa in Denver, but, as we headed home, I found that I was reaching out in my sleep to draw her to me. In the crowd that awaited us at Lyon, I looked for her. I saw her at last, waiting in the background.

For the chiefs too, our return was a homecoming. They climbed down from their cart and trudged off to their lodges. Their squaws padded after them, without a word.

In the afternoon I sought out Black Kettle. I found him smoking, while his wife stirred a pot.

"I want you to bring all your people in," I said, "where I can watch over them."

He nodded. He picked up a blanket and some dried meat; he rode away. One week later, three hundred lodges were standing a mile or so to the west of the fort.

So we lived through the autumn, side by side. The young warriors set out with my permission to hunt buffalo. The women worked, tanning the few hides their men had taken in the course of the summer. The old people sat quietly in the autumnal sun. They knew that they were at our mercy; they showed no fear.

They asked for nothing, yet as I rode through their village, I could see many signs of distress. The blankets that the women wore were ragged; the pole frames bore few strips of meat; the children looked at me from lowered heads.

The Indians were, of course, forbidden to come into the fort. But, as the days grew shorter and colder, I noticed soldiers slipping away with sacks of potato peelings and scraps salvaged from our mess. For we were well fed, now that our supply lines were open again to the States.

I had no authorization to feed and to clothe the Indians—

I knew that. Cramer warned me; he advised me to wait. But I could not wait. Twice in the course of October, I issued rations for the Indians—bacon, flour, coffee, sugar, a little salt. Say what you will about my rashness—throughout the autumn, from Denver to Leavenworth, from the Arkansas to the Platte, there was not one instance of an Indian attacking a white.

And not by good chance—we left nothing to chance. Indian scouts spread over the plains at my direction and reported to me every morning. They led us to every place where trouble was stirring. If a trader crept into the Territory with a barrel of whiskey we arrested him. If a young malcontent slipped off to join the Sioux we hunted him down and brought him back. If a settler reported that a dozen cows were missing, we found them and drove them home. We never used the word "surrender," so dear to the War Department. But day by day, we moved far beyond surrender. The young warriors began to think of themselves as troopers. The chiefs held dances, and invited us to witness their secret and sacred ceremonies. A kind of serenity settled on the plains; we slept well.

In the north, to be sure, the Sioux were gathering. To the south the Kiowas, Comanches, and Apaches had yet to be subdued. But with the Cheyennes and Arapahoes, the holders of the middle ground, as allies, I was certain that we could end the Indian wars.

Only the authorization of the Army was lacking. And, by a twist of fortune, it was hard to obtain. Fort Lyon, the key to any settlement, was by law, by tradition, by the overriding factor of distance, a part of Colorado. Yet it was taken from the Military District of Colorado and given to a new district in Kansas, whose commander, General Curtis, was stationed four hundred miles away.

On the day after I returned to Lyon, I wrote out a full report for Curtis. I handed it to an officer and sent him off at a canter. In the closing days of October, I looked each day for the mail coach that would bring the General's reply.

The reply came on the second of November. The coach rolled down the stony descent from Bent's Fort. It was accompanied by a cavalry escort—an indication that some important personage was aboard.

The usual crowd gathered at Lyon to greet the coach. It came to a halt; the door opened; a banker climbed out and, turning, helped two ladies to the ground. The last passenger, the important personage, took his time in appearing. He was a soldier, Scott Anthony, a dandy in peacetime, and now, like myself, a major in the First Colorado Cavalry.

He looked around; he saw me; he waited for me to come to him. His orderly lowered two trunks from the coach as I approached.

"What brings you to Lyon?" I began. "I thought you . . . "

He cut me short. "Not here."

We walked across the parade ground, talking of inconsequential matters. He talked on, in my office. And all the time his eyes were roving over my furnishings: my desk, my chairs, my frayed curtains and carpet; my filing cabinet; my pen.

When his appraisal was completed he turned to me. He handed me an army order. "Rough luck, Wynkoop," he said.

The order was from General Curtis. Unofficial rumors had reached headquarters, so the order read, that I had issued supplies to hostile Indians, in direct violation of orders from the General Commanding the Department. I was, therefore, relieved of my command and ordered to Kansas to explain my unmilitary conduct. Major Scott Anthony was appointed Commanding Officer of Fort Lyon, in my place.

Rumors; unofficial rumors had reached Curtis—but no troops had gone from Lyon to Leavenworth in October. The traffic was all westward.

"Who spread the rumors?" I demanded. "How did they get to Leavenworth?"

Anthony shrugged his shoulders.

16

I took my papers from the desk that was no longer mine. Anthony watched me closely. "I gather," he said, "that there have been a number of irregularities in your command."

He might have added: "I expected as much." Anthony had been a leader of the Young Republicans in Denver. I had been a McClellan Democrat. He took it for granted that I and my ilk were of doubtful loyalty; we bore watching.

I emptied out the desk. I called in the officers of the

post. They came as they had come six weeks before—unsuspecting.

I presented them to their new Commanding Officer. Anthony informed them that they were to return on the following morning, at which time he would instruct them as to the changes that were to be made.

I chose not to attend Anthony's meeting with the officers. I was an exile within the fort; it was up to those who had followed me to assert the rightness of all that we had done.

And they asserted it—so Cramer told me.

Anthony opened the meeting in a forceful manner. His predecessor, he said, had acted irresponsibly; sound policies would be promptly restored. Indians of all tribes were enemies, and would once more be treated as enemies. They were to be driven from the vicinity of the fort. If they wished to fight, then we would give them the thrashing they deserved. And so on. When he had finished, Anthony asked if there were any questions.

"I have no questions," Soule said. "But I do have one comment: you are committing a breach of faith!"

Anthony demanded a retraction; Soule stood fast. The argument mounted until Anthony threatened to have Soule cashiered from the Army.

"The sooner the better," Soule answered. "I want no part of an organization that punishes men like Major Wynkoop and promotes men like you."

Anthony would have arrested Soule, but the other officers intervened. They spoke of the gains that we had made, and of the danger of an attack by the Sioux. They urged Anthony not to act precipitately, and they threatened to resign if he pressed charges against Soule.

Anthony shifted his ground. He dismissed his officers, and busied himself in administrative details. After two days, he asked me to go with him to meet the chiefs.

We rode to a trader's hut halfway to the Indian camp. The chiefs met us there. I expected to see reproach in their faces; I saw none. Black Kettle, in his patient way, lit his pipe and passed it on.

It traveled the circle and returned. Still no one spoke. So I asked Anthony for permission to say a few words. He granted my request.

I stood to speak, as I had stood in the Big Timbers. "I am no longer chief at Fort Lyon," I told the chiefs. "Major Anthony is in command now. I have been called away, to Kansas. There is nothing I can do for you any more."

The chiefs looked at Smith as he echoed my words. They turned back to me.

"You have always done as I asked," I told them. "I ask you now to do as Major Anthony says."

The chiefs conferred; one or two, I think, dissented. But, in the end, Black Kettle spoke for all of them.

"We trust Major Wynkoop. He knows what is best for us. We will do as he says."

I thanked them, and took my place.

Anthony had brought along a black book in which he kept his notes. He opened it and began: "First, I wish to know: by what authority are Indians camped near this fort?"

Black Kettle answered: "The Governor in Denver called us in. The Colonel in Denver told us to stay."

"Colonel Chivington had no authority to issue such instructions," Anthony said. He consulted his book.

"Secondly: for what purpose are the Indians camped near the fort?"

"For peace."

"I think not."

"We have given our word."

Anthony smiled. "For the present perhaps. In the spring you will make war upon the whites."

"Our word is given. You may take us out and kill us. You will still not induce us to fight."

Anthony glanced at his book. He declared: "No body of armed men may camp near an army post."

"We have but few arms."

"A few too many! You are forbidden to remain, unless it is understood that, in all respects, you are prisoners of war."

"It is understood."

"I doubt it. You realize that we alone will set the terms of your surrender?"

I could not look up; I heard Black Kettle's answer: "We are ready to accept whatever terms you may propose."

"Very well: all of your weapons must be surrendered, at once."

"We will surrender them."

"All of the stock which once belonged to the whites must be given up, forthwith."

"We will give up the stock."

"We shall see!" Anthony shut his book with a snap and returned to the fort.

At dawn on the next day Anthony rode out of the fort with two hundred armed troopers. He hid most of them in the canebrakes close by the Indian camp. He led some into the camp, with rifles drawn. He sent others to recover the stock. They rode among the Indian herds for an hour and returned with a few broken-down mules. The rest of the troopers were sent among the lodges to search for weapons. The Indians, without protesting, surrendered a score of ancient hunting rifles and many bows. Anthony rode back with his booty.

On that same day, winter reached the fort. The skies lowered; the wind was bitter; toward dusk snow fell, lightly at first and then in earnest. It continued to fall through the night; in the morning it lay heavy on the plains.

At the edge of the fort, a crowd of Indians assembled. They stood in silence, waiting.

Several times in the course of the morning, Anthony slipped out to look at them. At noon, he called the chiefs into the fort. When he spoke to them, his manner at least was altered.

"Many bad reports were given to me about you," he told the chiefs. "I came here expecting that we would have a fight. I see now that the reports were wrong and that you are ready to live as prisoners. But I have no authority as yet to give you prisoners' rations. So I want you to leave the fort.

"I want you to go out to Sand Creek. I want you to stay there. However, your young men may go out hunting buffalo. I will see to it that all the promises made to you by Major Wynkoop are kept. As soon as I receive word from Leavenworth, whether it is good or bad, I will let you know."

The chiefs conferred; Black Kettle spoke for them. "We had planned to winter by the Purgatory River," he said. "But since you wish it, we will go to Sand Creek."

The meeting ended. I was reassured. I told Black Kettle: "You can trust Major Anthony."

Black Kettle shook his head. "Major Anthony has red eyes."

"It's not his fault. They were made red by the scurvy."

"We do not like his eyes."

For the rest of the day, the Indians dismantled their lodges. They rolled up the hides; they hoisted the travois poles onto the bony shoulders of their ponies. They set out through the snow: warriors and women, children and old men. I rode out beside them for a mile or so. I dismounted and stood as they trudged past in the dusk. Neva and White Antelope broke from the column to clasp my hand; One Eye saluted me; I gripped Black Kettle in an awkward embrace. I said in his language: "I thank you for all things." He answered in English: "I cannot appreciate you enough."

From that moment on, I wanted to get away from Lyon. But Cramer pleaded with me to delay my departure. I did not know why, until my last night at the fort.

On that night, a knocking sounded at my door. The officers of the post stood outside. Soule carried a bottle, Cramer an armful of glasses. We celebrated as best we could.

At the end of the evening, Soule rose and called for silence. He gave, as a parody, the speech that Anthony might have given. Then, as a parting present, he handed me two dispatches, neatly bound.

The first dispatch was a letter, written in the terse style of Lieutenant Cramer, but signed by the settlers of the Arkansas Valley. The settlers thanked me for preventing bloodshed; they praised me for doing what was "right, politic and just."

The second dispatch was also in the form of a letter. It noted with regret that I had been relieved of my command and ordered to Leavenworth; it held that my course of action had been the only proper one, and that it had saved the lives of hundreds of men, women, and children. It added that Indians and whites in the valley were living peaceably side by side, "as if the bloody scenes of the past summer had never been enacted." It ended with the hope that my course would be approved by the Commander of the Department, and that I would soon be restored to my command.

It was signed: Joseph A. Cramer. It was undersigned by every officer on the post—with one exception. But Soule was smiling as I looked up, unable to smile. He held out a third dispatch, saying: "And now a special surprise for General Curtis."

It was an endorsement of the second letter, by Major Scott Anthony. The Major noted that it was the general opinion of officers, soldiers, and civilians that my course had saved the valley; he ended: "I think Major Wynkoop acted for the best in this matter."

There was little more to say, but, as the officers left, I drew Cramer aside. I held out the letter signed by the settlers; I asked: "Was this the reason you wanted me to delay my departure?"

"It was one of the reasons."

He glanced into the night, where Soule, in high spirits, was singing. "Tomorrow is the twenty-sixth of November," Cramer said, "and the danger is past. The hundred days of the Third Regiment are up."

"They may still be in the field."

"That's impossible. Anthony would have heard if they were approaching and there's been no whisper of them; nothing at all."

The east-bound coach was already at the fort. Early in the morning it was ready to leave. A crowd of troopers stood in silence as we left our house. Frank, of course, was bewildered; Louisa had no tears left. The troopers helped her into the dark interior of the coach. I mounted my horse; an escort of sixteen men swung into line behind me; we moved off.

We rode in silence; there was no reason to be alert. I slumped in my saddle, a captive of apathy and bitterness. I would do what I could for the Indians in Leavenworth; but I had little inclination to defend myself. I felt that my best days were over.

We were in no danger while we rode through the country of the Cheyennes. It was on the third day of our journey that we reined in, to the cry of "Indians!"

From the west, three warriors came pounding up on ponies that were near collapse. They were messengers, sent by Black Kettle. He warned me that two hundred Sioux were raiding along the road ahead of us. He begged me to return to Lyon, and to wait there for a larger escort.

I was under orders. I sent the warriors back with my thanks to Black Kettle. We rode on into the long, dun-colored horizons of Kansas.

17

Two weeks later I stood before General Curtis. He seemed half as tall as I was, and ten times as fierce.

I started on the well-worn story; Curtis cut me short. He peppered me with questions; I defended myself as best I could. Before long, his real reason for depriving me of my command at Lyon became clear. It was that I had taken the chiefs to Chivington and not to him.

The room seemed flat around me, and my own voice, another's. I might have damned Curtis, or laughed, or left the room. Instead, I crawled. I granted that I had made a mistake in going to Denver. I cited my reasons, good reasons, and Curtis seemed content. He seemed to feel that I had been punished enough.

I brought out the letters that Cramer had given me. I waited as Curtis read them. I knew that he might be angered by Cramer's effort to bring pressure to bear upon him.

He laid the letters in his desk; he looked up at me. He said: "You seem to have a great many friends."

Hope stirred in me. I blurted out all my plans for securing the peace that we had made. Curtis listened without interrupting, but he seemed far away. When I had finished, he reverted to our earlier exchange.

"You say it was Chivington who told Black Kettle to bring his people to Lyon?"

"Yes, sir."

"Who was it who sent them to Sand Creek?"

"Major Anthony, sir." The question struck me as odd, since I had not mentioned Sand Creek.

Curtis picked up a paper cutter that lay on his desk; he examined its blade.

"So Black Kettle was obedient," he said. "He and his people were reconciled to being prisoners of war."

"They still are, sir."

"They were truly peaceful? They would not have attacked us in the spring?"

"General, if you will give me back my command, I will answer personally for Black Kettle and every member of his band."

I was startled by the air of pity in Curtis's face. "You've been on the road," he said. "You haven't heard."

He searched among his papers. He found a telegram, one of many, and handed it to me.

It was headed: *In the field on Big Bend of Sand Creek, Colorado Territory, November 29, 1864:* It read:

Sir: I have not the time to give you a detailed history of our engagement of today, or to mention those officers and men who distinguished themselves in one of the most bloody Indian battles ever fought on these plains. You will find enclosed the report of my surgeon in charge, which will bring to many anxious friends the sad fate of loved ones who are, and have been, risking everything to avenge the horrid deeds of those savages we have so severely handled. We made a forced march of forty miles, and surprised, at break of day, one of the most powerful villages of the Cheyenne nation, and captured over five hundred animals, killing the celebrated chiefs One Eye, White Antelope, Knock Knee, Black Kettle, and Little Robe, with about five hundred of their people, destroying all their lodges and equipage, making almost an annihilation of the entire tribe.

I shall leave here, as soon as I can see our wounded safely on the way to the hospital at Fort Lyon, for the villages of the Sioux, which are reported about eighty miles from here, on the Smoky Hill, and three thousand strong; so look out for more fighting. I will state, for the consideration of gentlemen who are opposed to fighting these red scoundrels, that I was shown, by my chief surgeon, the scalp of a white man taken from the lodge of one of the chiefs, which could not have been more than two or three days taken; and I could mention many more things to show how these Indians, who have been drawing government rations at Fort Lyon, are and have been acting.

Very respectfully, your obedient servant,

J. M. Chivington

PART THREE

18

For a time, after my interview with General Curtis, I saw little but the dirt at my feet. I lived like a prisoner in the one room we were given at Leavenworth. I stalked around it, raging, while Frank crouched in a corner and Louisa wept. I raged on at Chivington until I was exhausted. I lay in a drunken stupor, cursing myself.

Cursing my blindness; cursing my simple faith. Cramer had warned me; Colley had warned me; even Chivington's actions were revealing, if only I had understood. I understood now his sullen anger and his sudden change of mood; his confident air when I last saw him at Weld; his casual questioning of me. I understood his feeling of affection for me: I had served him well. I had brought the Indians in and left them helpless. I had laid them like a sacrifice at his feet.

The only purpose left for me was to halt Chivington. It was a hopeless task. Only if the truth were known about Sand Creek could he be weakened. And the truth, I knew, would never be brought out. The War Department and the President would receive only the reports that Chivington wrote about Sand Creek. The people would read only the dispatches that he forwarded to the press. At Lyon there might be a handful of men willing to dispute Chivington. But they could not act alone, and I could not help them. Chivington had succeeded in running me out of the Territory. And he would never let me return.

He had betrayed me and beaten me; I was beaten as thoroughly as any man he had left lying in the ring.

In my own mind, I set out in pursuit of Chivington. I made my way to Denver and hunted him through the streets. I cornered him, and killed him, and trod on his dead face. I dragged his carcass across the plains behind my horse and left him at Sand Creek lying in the dirt among the Indians. All fantasies, save for the last; Chivington was enthroned in Denver; I was rotting in Kansas; Black Kettle and his band were at Sand Creek, dead because they had trusted in me. And nothing could bring them to life again.

I lingered on with no hope at Leavenworth. Then, one evening, as I lay in my room, I heard dimly the sound of knocking. Louisa went to the door and came back to me with a letter.

It was from Cramer; I had not the heart to open it. But I listened as Louisa read it aloud. She read it with difficulty, for Cramer made it plain that at Sand Creek, Chivington and his men had committed crimes as terrible as any ever committed by soldiers wearing the uniform of the United States.

Cramer had witnessed all that had happened. He conceded that he had obeyed orders and taken part in the fighting. He added that, at the risk of his own life, Soule had defied Chivington and forbidden his men to fight.

It was true, Cramer said, that Black Kettle and the other chiefs had been killed. It was for us to pay the debt owed to them. Speaking for the officers of the Second Battalion, Cramer promised that if I could bring about an investigation into Chivington's conduct, they would testify to the whole story. In his precise way, Cramer told me what to do.

Louisa laid down the letter. She looked at me for a moment. "Why are you waiting?" she said.

I stumbled to the washstand; she poured a jug of water over my head. She went next door to borrow some note paper while I held my hands against the stove, to steady them.

I copied out Cramer's letter many times that evening. I sent it to all the men in high places whose names Cramer had provided. One was Hiram Bennet, Delegate to the Congress from the Colorado Territory, and an old friend of mine. Another was Senator Harlan, chairman of the Joint Committee on Indian Affairs. I sent copies to Ben Wade and to James Doolittle. But my main hope lay in Slough. I had forgotten my first commander, driven from his own regiment by Chivington. Now, as Cramer reminded me, Slough was a brigadier, commanding the southern approaches to Washington and so within earshot of the White House and the War Department. If anyone in the States hated Chivington as I hated him, it was John Slough.

The mails moved swiftly to Washington; the year had not come to its end when an orderly hurried to my room with an order to report to Headquarters.

So, once again, I came before General Curtis. Without looking up, he handed me an envelope. "Your orders," he said.

The orders were signed by Curtis, but they came from Washington. I could have asked for no more. I was reassigned as Commanding Officer to Fort Lyon. And I was instructed to report to the War Department upon conditions among the Indians with particular reference to the recent conduct of Colonel Chivington.

"General," I began, "I can never . . ."

"Don't thank me," Curtis said.

I turned back to the paper in my hand. Beyond the stock phrases, I saw the report that I would write, damning Chivington; the court-martial that would follow; the sentence, branding him a criminal and casting him out of the Army.

From a distance I heard Curtis: "You have your orders, Wynkoop; now take my advice: some things are best forgotten."

"Not if I can help it," I said.

He held out a sheaf of newspapers. "Consider what

you're up against," he said. "Chivington is the great man of the Territory; he's a national hero."

"General, before this is over, he'll wish he was lying in the creek where he left Black Kettle."

I felt at that moment a harsh exaltation. I barely heard Curtis's last words as I turned and left; but I remember them now. "Be careful, Wynkoop," he said, "lest you place more lives in jeopardy."

I hurried off with the good news to Louisa. I swept her up in a way that left her startled.

"We're going back to Lyon!" I told her.

She looked at me, bewildered. I handed her my orders. She read them slowly and looked at me, trying to smile.

I took it for granted, at the time, that she was glad. Now, as I write, I see that the news came to her as a bitter disappointment. She had shared in my defeat and my humiliation. She had prayed that I might regain my self-respect. She had, at the same time, nourished a secret hope that, once my ties to Lyon and my regiment were broken, I would resign my commission and return to Pennsylvania, to the comfort of my father's house. There, she would regain all the things she had grown up with: silver on the table, sheets on the bed; heels on her shoes; clean bodices to change into, a dress with no buttons missing; a closet, a full-length mirror, a bath, a basin even, with soft water to wash her hair in; and more: friends who shared her interests; variety; days without worry and nights without fear; a carpet for her children to play on; a home of her own. She longed for these things; they were a part of her womanhood and her pride. But no torture would have forced her to confess her longing. She stood for a moment; she turned away, hiding her tears, and began to pack our few belongings.

In the depth of winter, we set out. The sky was leaden; the plains were lifeless. The coach that carried Louisa and Frank jolted over the frozen trail that crossed Kansas; the soldiers who rode beside me, as our escort, were masked against the wind and the cold. There was no time in the brief span of daylight to pause at the familiar ranches. The few settlers we met at the way stations were, once again, oppressed by dread. They knew, as I did, that to the north the Indians were arming for revenge. And they knew that the shrunken garrison at Lyon could provide them little or no protection. Once again they spoke of abandoning their homesteads, and this time I could not reassure them.

We rode for ten days; we came at last to Lyon. The troops were waiting; as we clattered in, a cheer rose on the chill air. I saw many men whom I knew, but Soule and Cramer were not among them.

Neither was Anthony; filled with loathing, I went to the office where he was waiting. I handed him my orders, as he had handed his orders to me.

Anthony did not look up. But, as he stared at the orders,

words spilled out of him. He cursed Chivington as a double-crosser and a coward. "We could have gone on to the Smoky Hill," he said. "We could have given the Sioux the same treatment we gave Black Kettle."

I said nothing. Anthony glanced at me, and I, in turn, avoided those red eyes. "Chivington promised me he would go on from Sand Creek," he said, rising. "Then he turned and ran. By God, if I see him again I'll . . ."

"You'll see him," I said, "in court." I moved past him, to my desk.

Anthony faced me; he rattled on. "You think you'll bring him to court? Well, I hope you do! But I warn you, Wynkoop, it won't be pleasant. He'll lie on a stack of Bibles about the so-called Battle of Sand Creek. He'll lie about you and Soule. He'll lie about me."

"He won't have to," I said. I pulled out my chair.

"He'll lie about the Indians. He'll swear that he found scalps, fresh scalps of white women in their tepees. First it was one scalp, then five; before he left for Denver the count was up to nineteen."

I sat at my desk. At once, One Eye was standing over me.

"All lies," Anthony was saying. "There wasn't a white scalp in all the village; not one."

His wrists, handcuffed and held out to me; the single eye regarding me; even the faint smell; my revolver lying on the desk beside me; my sense of bewilderment and of discovery; it all broke over me, like a dark comber, and left me half drowned.

19

One by one, the men who were left at Lyon came to my office to tell their stories. A clerk labored at my side, writing out each statement. I listened, sick with rage and dreaming of revenge.

Soule and Cramer, the two men I needed most, were no longer at Lyon. But John Smith was there, waiting to testify. He sat before me and whispered a long defense of my policy of conciliation. He described his own journey, late in November, to Black Kettle's village; he came to the morning of the massacre. "When the troops approached," he said, "I saw Black Kettle hoist the American flag over his lodge as well as a white flag. . . ."

Smith faltered there, and I did not press him. Others were waiting to pick up the story. In no time, I was able to reconstruct, hour by hour, all that had taken place after my departure from the fort.

Soule was the first man to encounter Chivington. On the day after I left Lyon, Soule led a scouting party out, in search of the Sioux. For the Sioux were concentrated, and committed to war. From their stronghold on the Smoky Hill, they had sent a challenge to Lyon, daring Anthony to come out and fight.

Soule rode in a wide arc from the north to the west. At the end of the day, he came to a high and wind-swept place on the road to Denver. From there the road descended into lowlands; five miles distant, it rose again, to the western horizon.

There, rimmed by the sunset, Soule saw a black thread in the snow; buffalo, or else mounted men.

Soule flogged his horse home to Lyon. He and Anthony agreed that the oncoming riders were Sioux. Anthony ordered the alarm to be sounded. He issued arms and ammunition to all the garrison. He sent Soule out again at midnight with twenty men.

Soule rode through the night. As the moon set, he came to the plateau. He found no trace there of the Sioux; nothing but a lone mule driver squatting by a fire. He dismounted and questioned the driver; his men huddled around the fire, heating coffee.

Then, up from the lowlands, came the thousand soldiers of the Third Regiment.

At the head of the long column, Chivington rode on a huge black mule. He ordered Soule's men to fall into line; he summoned Soule to his side. And Soule went gladly; he took it for granted that Chivington had come to lead a strike against the Sioux.

Chivington did not look at Soule; but he asked many questions. At last he was satisfied that neither Soule nor anyone at Lyon knew of his approach.

"Where are the hostiles?" he said.

"On the Smoky Hill, Colonel; we understand they . . ."

"I am speaking of the Cheyennes."

"Black Kettle's band? On Sand Creek, where we sent them."

"Where exactly on Sand Creek?"

"On the Big Bend, Colonel; but they . . ."

"You hear that, Beckwourth?" Chivington turned to the old man, Negro by birth and Indian by adoption, who was his guide. "You know the place?"

"Like I know my empty pockets," Beckwourth said.

"They are not hostiles, Colonel," Soule began; "they . . ."

"How many are there at this moment?"

"Nine hundred; women and children mostly. The men are out hunting; they went with our . . ."

"I think you said plundering, Captain. They are out plundering white men's property, are they not, Beckwourth? . . . Are they not, Beckwourth?" Chivington demanded.

The old man murmured: "If you say so, Colonel."

"They are hunting buffalo, with our permission," Soule said. "They are our prisoners of war."

"Prisoners, are they?" one of Chivington's officers murmured to another. "They won't be prisoners for long!"

At sunrise the column came to Caddoe, the ranch where John Prowers raised horses and cattle for the Army. It was the finest of the Arkansas Valley ranches, heavily stocked and well cared for. In the worst days of the summer, when all other settlers had fled, Prowers had stayed on at his home. But now, as the Third Regiment rode up, Caddoe seemed deserted. The stock was scattered; no men could be seen; the haystacks stood abandoned in the snow.

The ranchhouse was guarded by soldiers. One of them, a lieutenant, moved forward and saluted as Chivington rode up.

"You found your way, then?" Chivington said.

"Just followed the river like you told us."

"You caught them all?"

"Surprised them at supper."

"Let's take a look at them," Chivington said.

The troopers lifted the bars from the door of the house. Prowers and his seven ranchhands stumbled out. In the doorway behind them, Prowers's wife stood shielding a child: his Indian wife—she was One Eye's daughter.

Chivington looked the prisoners over. He spoke to the lieutenant. "You're certain none of them got away?"

"Not a one, Colonel."

"You've taken all their weapons?"

"All they had."

Prowers stepped forward. "Colonel Chivington! You know me, Colonel!"

"I do indeed."

"Why have they imprisoned us, Colonel? What have I done?"

"What have you done?" Chivington laughed. "Look behind you!" The laughter spread along the column.

Prowers looked back from his wife to the Colonel. "I'm a citizen!" he cried. "Major Anthony knows me! Governor Evans will vouch for me! The Governor . . ."

"Shut your mouth, squaw man," a sergeant said.

Chivington assigned the sergeant and four troopers to guard the house. He warned the sergeant to let no one out. "Three days should do it," he added. "You can let them out in three days."

As he was hustled indoors, Prowers caught sight of Soule. "Captain!" he cried. "Captain Soule, for God's sake! My milk cows will die if I don't get to them! My foals will be killed by wolves. My . . ."

The troopers thrust him into the house. They bolted the door and took up their positions, on guard.

Soule drove his horse up beside Chivington. "You have no right to arrest them," he said.

Chivington kicked his mule into motion. He waved for the column to follow. He said nothing, but Major Downing rode over to Soule. "Do not provoke him further!" Downing said.

Soule ignored the warning. "You've no cause to arrest him!" he shouted to Chivington. "You've . . ."

Downing grabbed Soule by the shoulder. "Quiet!" he cried. "Be quiet if you know what's good for you!"

Soule wrenched himself free. "You're going to attack the Cheyennes!" he shouted. "That's why you arrested Prowers! You're afraid his wife will warn them, and you want to catch them by surprise! But you can't do it! They're our prisoners of war, unarmed and . . ."

Chivington turned at last. "No captain gives orders to Colonel Chivington! No Indian lover tells Chivington what he may do!"

He summoned Downing to his side; they spoke in undertones. Then Chivington called for fifty men. "We're riding ahead," he told Shoup. "You can follow. Hold the captain until you reach the fort. If he tries to escape, place him in irons. Report to me in Major Anthony's office!" Lashing his mule, he cantered off toward Lyon.

20

When Soule reached Fort Lyon it was ringed by a cordon of Chivington's men. No one was allowed out of the fort.

Soule had been in the saddle for twenty-seven hours. He dismounted and ran to Anthony's quarters.

Anthony was instructing his officers on the expedition to come: Soule's and Cramer's companies and one other would form a battalion under Anthony; company commanders were to draw three days' cooked rations and twenty days' uncooked rations; commissary would issue fifty thousand rounds of ammunition; troops would assemble, mounted, at eight, for an all-night ride. Nothing was to be said to the troops about the purpose of the expedition, but the officers could be told: the challenge of the hostiles had been accepted; Colonel Chivington had come to lead a combined force against the Sioux.

"You are lying," Soule told Anthony, "or else you are deceived."

The officers closed around Soule. He forced his way through them, to Anthony's desk.

"If we're going to the Smoky Hill," he said, "then why is Prowers locked up in his house at Caddoe? Why is this fort surrounded by Chivington's men? You are going to attack Sand Creek!" Soule cried.

And Anthony said calmly: "Yes; we shall clean up Sand Creek on the way."

An uproar followed; it was some time before Cramer could be heard. "First," he said, "Colonel Chivington's term of service has expired. Unless he has re-enlisted, he has no authority to command troops."

"He has orders from Leavenworth," Anthony answered. "What is good enough for General Curtis is good enough for me."

"Second, Fort Lyon is not in Chivington's district. He has no right to take command here, except with your consent."

"He has my consent."

"To attack Black Kettle? His band are prisoners of war, under your protection."

"They are Indians; they deserve whatever they get."

Cramer held Soule back; he made himself heard again. "One hundred and thirty men in your command," he told

Anthony, "owe their lives to Black Kettle. In turn, every one of us is bound by the commitment Major Wynkoop made. If you order us to attack Black Kettle, you will dishonor us."

Anthony smiled. "You can come under protest," he said. "Oh, I grant you," he continued, "that some foolish statements were made by Major Wynkoop. He acted without authorization, and the Army punished him for it. I am certainly not responsible for what Wynkoop may have said."

"Oh yes you are! You told the chiefs you would carry on his policy!"

"Only until word came from the Department."

"Has it come?"

"I made no promise. I simply told Black Kettle I would pass along such information as I might receive."

No one spoke.

"I was acting under pressure," Anthony said. "I lacked the troops to take the military action that I considered appropriate. I had to keep Black Kettle's band close at hand until reinforcements came."

There was a long silence.

"I made no pledges that I consider binding," Anthony said. "I did nothing that restricts my freedom of action now."

Still no one spoke.

"A pledge given to a savage," Anthony said at last, "is not the same as one given between civilized men."

"Murder," Soule said. "You are ordering us to murder men who saved our lives."

"Yes, ordering! I am ordering you to be ready with your company at eight. And now"—Anthony stood up—"this meeting is ended. . . . Well," he demanded, "what are you waiting for?"

"We want to talk to Colonel Chivington," Cramer said.

Anthony looked at all the officers. He gave in. "Those of you who wish to see Colonel Chivington," he said, "may report here at seven. But you"—he turned to Soule—"you stay away!"

The officers protested; Anthony was firm. "I'm acting for his safety," he said. "Colonel Chivington was enraged by his insolence. He swore many times in my hearing that it would not go unpunished. Even I," Anthony added, "even I was shocked by the Colonel's threats."

At seven, the officers of Lyon returned to Anthony's office. They varied, of course, in their resolution. Minton would have stood against the devil himself, in defense of Cramer and Soule; Baldwin was more concerned with his promotion. Cossitt, the quartermaster, had his own reason for being outraged—Chivington's quartermaster had confessed to him that they would have to sack an Indian village in order to make up for all the stores that the Third Regiment had lost or stolen.

Anthony was working at his desk when the officers returned. Downing was seated at his side. Behind them, Chivington stood, marking each face as the officers entered the room.

Anthony made certain that all preparations were completed for the expedition. Then his manner shifted. "I have spoken to Colonel Chivington," he told the officers. "I have advised him of the doubts which some of you may feel, thanks to Major Wynkoop. I now repeat what I first told you," he added. "Our objective is the Smoky Hill. We are going out there to thrash the Sioux."

There were murmurs of relief; Cramer alone was skeptical. "Do you mean," he said, "that we are not going to Sand Creek?"

"We are going by way of Sand Creek."

There was a long silence, so Cossitt told me. Anthony fondled the beard that hid his girlish face. Chivington stood motionless; only his black eyes shifted from man to man, daring them to say more.

"What will you do when you get to Sand Creek?" Cramer asked.

"We will surround the village," Anthony said. "We will call the chiefs out. We will kill a few criminals and hotheads. We will spare the rest. That is our purpose in going to Sand Creek," Anthony added, "to save the chiefs from their own enemies."

There were, once more, murmurs of relief. Again Cramer persisted. "You know that Uncle John Smith is there," he told Anthony, "and his boy; and Louderback."

"They are as safe there as they are here. . . . Well," Anthony continued, "if there are no more . . ."

"Which of the chiefs will you call out?" Cramer asked.

"Black Kettle, White Antelope, One Eye . . . they are all known to the Colonel."

"Yes," Chivington said, "I know them."

"And which of the hotheads do you intend to kill?"

"They are also known," Anthony said. "Now, since there are no more questions, this conference . . ."

"I have one more question," Cramer told Anthony. "When you went with Major Wynkoop to see Black Kettle . . ."

Chivington interrupted: "Wynkoop is a fool!"

"Major Wynkoop has done more . . ."

"Bringing red rebels into Denver! Forcing Evans to get down to them on bended knee! What madness possessed him, I shall never know."

At that, Cossitt and Minton spoke up, insisting that I had done my duty.

Chivington looked at them intently. "I see Wynkoop has infected more than one man with his poison," he said to Downing. "And you"—he turned to Anthony—"you let this poison spread!"

"I . . ." Anthony stammered. "My position was difficult, Colonel. Wynkoop turned them all against me; he . . . since there are no further questions, I . . ."

"I shall be watching," Chivington said. "If any officer hangs back tomorrow"—he picked up a volume of army regulations from the desk and shook it—"desertion in the face of the enemy; remember that! Major Downing can tell you what Chivington does with deserters."

"They understand," Anthony muttered. "No more need be said. Now, since there are no more questions, this conference . . ."

Cramer broke in. "I had one more question, Major; I was interrupted. When you and Major Wynkoop went to see the Indians," he continued, "you . . ."

"The Indians!" Chivington was striding back and forth behind the desk. "They crawl like vermin over this country! They are as cunning as serpents. They are as cowardly as coyotes. Yes, and as treacherous! They rape white women," he cried. "They scalp white children. Damn any man who takes their side!" He turned on Cramer. "You! If you and Wynkoop side with Indians, then get out of the Army! Get out of the uniform of the United States!"

Cramer waited until Chivington had finished. Then he spoke again, to Anthony. "When you and Major Wynkoop conferred with Black Kettle, you promised to keep him informed of all developments."

"I recall no such promise."

"But we do! Major, you're pledged to tell Black Kettle that the Third Regiment is on its way to Sand Creek!"

Anthony spoke in a low voice. "You're out of your mind; you don't know what you're saying."

"You're bound in God's name, Major; your oath . . ."

"In God's name!" Chivington's roar left every man stunned. "You invoke God's name, for them? They are godless savages; sons of Satan. And God Almighty justifies every means the white man can devise for wiping them from the face of the earth!" He stood, heaving. "I am in command here," he said at last. "All of you are under my orders. I order you now to assemble your companies! Come, Downing."

The door slammed shut behind them; but before any man in the room moved, it opened again.

"All companies will assemble," Downing repeated. "But you, Cramer," he said softly, "you and Soule may remain. Other officers can take your companies. You two will remain at the post."

Cramer shook his head.

"The Colonel gave you orders, is that it? Well, ignore them. I can arrange it."

Cramer roused himself. "You won't get out of our sight," he said.

21

The troops assembled in the darkness. Anthony called the roll by the light of a taper; Soule and Cramer answered for their companies. They wheeled and followed Anthony out of the fort and into line, behind the Third Regiment.

Chivington led the column north with Beckwourth at his side. The sky was clear and the moon full; the trail was plain that led to Sand Creek.

The troops rode in silence, numbed by the wind. Beckwourth, for one, became too stiff and weak to act as guide —or so he said. In his place, Chivington called up the guide of the Lyon battalion. He was a young half-breed, the son of William Bent and his Cheyenne wife. He did his best to get out of the assignment, for his own brother and his mother's family were with Black Kettle. But Chivington threatened to kill the boy and then eat him if he failed to lead the column to the village.

The boy believed Chivington. He made no mistakes. The column walked, trotted, and cantered in turn. At dawn it came to the long descent that ends at the Big Bend of Sand Creek.

The creek flows from the northwest into the bend. There, beneath high bluffs, it curves like a scythe to the northeast. Then, as the bluffs fall away, it winds south through groves of cottonwood.

Black Kettle's village lay within the bend, blind to the approach of the soldiers. In the lowlands to the east, the ponies of the Cheyennes grazed undisturbed.

Chivington sent a dozen troopers off to round up the herd. He sat, waiting.

The earth shuddered as the Indian ponies stampeded, so one man told me. In the village, a dog barked. Chivington raised himself up on his black mule; he drew his saber and roared out his command. He ordered his troops to surround the village and destroy it; to fire on everyone who moved within it, and to let no one escape. He ended with an incitement to massacre. "I am not ordering you to kill all ages and sexes," he shouted, "but, men, remember the women and children murdered on the Platte!"

The soldiers of the Lyon battalion crossed the creek to the south of the village. They dismounted and stood with rifles ready, but Anthony did not order them to open fire. "I don't want to start the ball," he said.

Chivington's men massed on both sides of the battalion. They fired over it and through it, wildly and without effect. In the village there were sounds of women wailing, and of a few warriors chanting their war songs. Black Kettle moved swiftly to raise the American flag and the white flag of surrender above his lodge: he was following my instructions, but to no avail. The shells of the howitzers began to crash into the village, and from the bluffs, Chivington drove his men on. Anthony, in turn, ordered the Lyon battalion to open fire. Cramer passed the order on to his company; Soule defied it. He thrust his revolver into its holster. And when his men edged forward, he motioned them back.

From the lodge where he had been sleeping, John Smith ran out. He gestured, trying to stop the fighting. At once, Chivington's men concentrated their fire upon him. He stood, unbelieving, as the bullets kicked up the dirt at his feet.

George Pierce was the bravest trooper in the Colorado Cavalry. At Glorieta on the first day of the battle he had charged through the ranks of a Texas regiment; he had shot their major and brought their captain back to me. Now, as Anthony waved ineffectually at Smith, Pierce cried: "Let me bring him out!" He rode alone into the village; he circled Smith, trying to lift him into the saddle.

The firing from the Third Regiment never slackened. Pierce was hit. He swayed, still clinging to Smith, and trying to lift him. Then the horse crumpled. Two Indians dragged Pierce from his saddle and clubbed him to the ground.

Smith stumbled back to his lodge and hid there. White Antelope took his place. He strode toward Chivington, holding his arm high in the peace sign and crying in English: "Stop!"

An officer shouted an order; his troops fired a ragged volley; the bullets kicked up the gravel at the old chief's feet. He paused; he folded his arms and chanted his death song: "*Nothing lives long Except the earth and the mountains. . . .*" The troopers knelt for the second volley and fired again. "I saw a medal bounce on the old man's chest," one trooper told me; "then he fell on his face."

From then on the women and children moved out of the village and up the creek. The troops shot them down as they fled. Some women lay in labor; some tore open their robes to prove their sex; they were not spared. One woman, dying, called her children to her and cut their throats.

A family fled from one lodge: it was Scott Anthony who told me the story in his emotionless way. "We were covering the entrance with our rifles," he said, "and out crept a child. He was perfectly naked, and just old enough to walk. He started off after his mother, across the sand. Then one of the troopers of the Third Regiment rode by. He dismounted and fired at the child from seventy-five yards away. He missed, and a second trooper reined in, shouting: 'Let me try the son of a bitch!' He dismounted and knelt and fired. We saw sand spurt by the child, but he stumbled on. Then a third trooper joined them, saying: 'Leave him to me!' He took his time in aiming, and when he fired, the child tumbled into the sand."

It was no battle. There were one hundred men at most in the village—men too young, too old, or too infirm to go buffalo hunting. Some strode unarmed into the concentrated fire of the Third Regiment; it was their day to die, and they died well. Others climbed up the bluffs; there they dug pits in the sand and with arrows, held a regiment back.

Chivington swore that they caused all his casualties; once again he was lying. The Cheyennes killed four soldiers in all; the rest of Chivington's casualties were caused by his own men, firing into one another as they encircled the village.

Anthony was not troubled by the wild firing of the Third Regiment. But when the grape and cannister of Chivington's howitzers fell upon his men, he took stock of his position. "It was then," he told me, "that I discovered that Soule had defied me, and forbidden his men to fight."

I said nothing. "Desertion in the face of the enemy," Anthony added. "That's an offense punishable by death."

"If the Cheyennes were an enemy," I said.

"You're trying to protect Soule; well, so am I. I risked my skin to protect him. I ignored his defiance of my order. It was to get him away that I ordered him to lead his men up the creek."

Soule led his men over the bluffs and on toward the northwest. There, for four miles along the creek, the killing continued as the Indians fled. The women and children paused in their flight to scrape pits in the earth; the men, following them, held the pits while the women and children moved on. The troops accompanied them, dismounting, firing, and mounting again. At last the Indians broke up and scattered, a mother going one way, her children another. The troops pursued them over the frozen plain.

Soule and his squadron rode beside the Indians, more as escorts than as enemies. They did not pause, but the time came when their horses would not go on. Then Soule and his men slid to the ground and, for an hour, lay dead to the world.

It was mid-afternoon when they started back. By then, the firing in the distance had lapsed to occasional shots as the officers wandered over the field finishing off the wounded Indians. By the time the squadron reached the scene the soldiers had started on a new assignment: they were looting the lodges, bearing off robes, trinkets, everything of value; they were working at the bodies of the Cheyennes.

On the bluffs, Chivington sat on his mule, so flushed with his victory that he had forgotten all that had gone before. He saw the squadron as it moved slowly past him. He summoned Soule to his side.

"Well?" he cried. He waited for Soule's praise.

Soule nodded toward the ruined village. "Call off your men," he said. "They are disfiguring the dead."

"Trophies," Chivington said. "They are taking trophies from the glorious field of Sand Creek."

Soule turned his horse and moved off.

Chivington called after him: "We gained a great victory! You are a part of it!"

"You committed a great crime," Soule answered, "and we are no part of it."

Chivington persisted: "You were in the fighting."

Soule shook his head. "I and my men have not fired a shot at the Indians all day; thank God."

It was Anthony who described the scene to me. "Chivington would have arrested Soule then and there," he said, "but I diverted his attention. I did everything I could to keep Soule out of his reach."

"I suppose that's why you sent him to Denver," I said.

"So you think I transferred Soule and Cramer to Denver! You blame me for that."

I nodded.

"The truth is," Anthony went on, "that they insisted on going, a week after Chivington left. Their companies were due to be mustered out, and Soule insisted that his men would never make it unless he was there to see them through. I warned him to stay away from Denver," he continued. "He wouldn't listen to me."

I glanced up and saw to my surprise that Anthony was in earnest.

"I did my best for Soule," he said.

22

On the night of the massacre, so one man told me, dogs roamed over the battleground of Sand Creek. There were three hundred or more dogs in the village; all night long they roamed, howling, among the dead.

There were no burials. Chivington wanted the Indian dead to lie forever where they had fallen, as proof to the living of the white man's mastery. He swore that any soldier who buried an Indian would be hanged.

Chivington and his men slept soundly on the bluffs above the creek. In the morning they moved down to the village and worked, robbing and mutilating the dead. One squad, as it rummaged among a pile of warriors lying in a trench, uncovered a boy of eight, alive and unhurt. A sergeant blew his head off. A little later, Jack Smith, Uncle John's half-breed son, was shot. He had been captured in the village and was suspected of past atrocities. The soldiers had taunted him through the night as dogs taunt a caged animal. In the morning, Uncle John and Scott Anthony went together to Chivington and pleaded for the young man's life. Chivington answered that his policy on prisoners was well known; he would not stir.

At noon, so the witnesses said, a report reached Chivington that the Sioux were moving against him from the northwest. Then Chivington stirred. He loaded his wagons with plunder; he ordered Cramer to raze the village; at the head of his fighting column, he rode off—to the southeast. He sent Soule and twenty troopers off in pursuit of a band of Arapahoes; he led his own men back to Lyon.

Chivington stayed on at Lyon for three days, writing his dispatches for the newspapers, while his men drank and his officers sold off the Indian ponies they had stolen. Then, on the night before they left for Denver, the officers of the Third Regiment held a victory celebration. They cleared out the commissary building, so Cossitt told me. They commandeered our stocks of whiskey. They gambled, and were entertained. Harry Richmond staged a dramatic appearance, clad in the headdress and robe he had stripped from the corpse of White Antelope. He feigned amazement on finding white men in command at Lyon. He asked to see his friend Ned Wynkoop, and was told that he would find me in hell. He declared that he knew the place well and would bring me back from there. He went out and returned, leading the one Indian who was left at Lyon—the Fool. The poor fellow stood in the center of the room, humping up and down and uttering his animal noises; Richmond pirouetted around him, patting his mouth with his palm, in the manner of the music-hall Indian, while the officers laughed and jeered.

At the end of the evening, Downing called for silence. He stood, glass in hand, before Chivington. He called Chivington "General" and "Senator from the state of Colorado." He raised his glass.

Chivington bowed, so Cossitt said. He thanked Almighty God for giving him the strength to crush his country's enemies. He predicted that they, and their friends, would never rise again. He prayed that the Union might prove worthy of the sacrifices of his men. He spoke of the regiment's hated nickname, the Bloodless Third. "From now on," he shouted, "no one can call it Bloodless!"

He paused there, but his officers cried: "More!" So Chivington followed Richmond's lead. He waved to an invisible figure. "Good morning, Kit Carson!" he cried. He thrust out his right hand. "How are you, General Harney!" He swept both images behind him, saying: "It don't take Chivington six months to find Indians!"

He walked in a circle, nodding to imaginary acquaintances. "Mr. Secretary . . . General Grant . . ." He listened to an unseen admirer. "Well, Mr. President," he said, "since you ask my advice . . ." He burst into laughter and struck

Downing with such force that the major staggered. "The little man's right!" Chivington cried. "This will put stars on my shoulders! This will take me to the Senate—and beyond the Senate!" He glared around the room, where a few of the officers of Lyon stood among the Third Regiment men. "No one," he cried out, "no one can stop Chivington now!"

At noon on the next day, the Third Regiment assembled, its plunder loaded, its banners flying. An eagle, disabled by a lucky shot, was tied to a pole and hoisted, flapping and screaming, at the head of the column. A squaw, the sole captive to survive, was led along in the rear, as the Romans led their slaves. So the Third Regiment rode off in triumph to Denver.

All this was told to me by the troopers of Lyon who came to my office to be questioned. Some were eager to help me; some were fearful and would not sign the statements they had dictated. A few were sullen and evasive. I guessed that they had joined the men of the Third Regiment in robbing the dead.

I had the testimony copied out for the use of the War Department. I felt, as I read it over, that nothing remained in doubt.

Then, early in January, a half-breed, Edmond Guerrier, slipped into Lyon from the north.

Guerrier told me that eighty Indian men and one hundred and twenty Indian women and children had died of wounds received at Sand Creek. He added that he had come to Lyon by way of the battlefield and that he had counted sixty-nine bodies, still lying beside the creek. "Most of the chiefs are lying there," he said, "but not all: Black Kettle is not there."

"His body must have been taken away, for burial," I said.

Guerrier shook his head. He insisted that Black Kettle had escaped and that, like Peter the Hermit, he was traveling over the plains, summoning all the Indian nations to war.

It was John Smith who had identified the dead at Sand Creek. Chivington's claim that he had killed Black Kettle was based upon Smith's report; and I had accepted it.

I called Smith back to my office and questioned him again. He conceded that he had based his findings upon uncertain clues—a peace medal, overlooked by the plunderers; an old body scar; a broken vest of eagle bones—there was nothing more to go on, he said.

I sent the evidence I had gathered to the War Department, together with my report. My action, I was certain, would make inevitable a full investigation of Sand Creek. Where and when it would take place, I did not know. I worked furiously to complete the defenses of Lyon in order that I might be free to leave the post. I waited impatiently, questioning every traveler who rode in from the west and siezing from the mail coach every copy of the *Rocky Mountain Daily News*.

The first copy of the *News* that I read was filled with Chivington's own account of his victory. In later issues, I read of the triumphant return of the Third Regiment; the parades and the speeches; the night-long celebrations. One dispatch in the *News* portrayed the solemn moment when the Territorial Legislature paid homage to Chivington. Another story described the hilarious occasion when Harry Richmond strutted across the stage of the Apollo in his Indian costume, followed by a line of troopers waving scalps.

No voice was raised in those days to challenge Chivington. His domination of the Territory seemed to be assured; his further rise in the nation was foreseen. Petitions were circulated to send him to the Senate, candidates for minor posts were canvassed, and handbills were posted on every street, corner—so the newspapers said.

In the midst of all this activity, an item no bigger than a thumb appeared in the *News*. It was from Washington, and it reported that, as a result of letters received from certain high officials in Colorado, there would shortly be commenced an investigation into the recent affair near Fort Lyon.

On that same evening, so I learned later, a mob gathered outside the frame building that housed the *News*. The veterans of the Third Regiment brought their rifles; their friends carried bull whips and lengths of rope. They stood in the chill evening shouting for William Byers, the editor of the *News*. When Byers appeared, they demanded the names of the "high officials" who wanted to investigate Sand Creek.

Byers liked to think of himself as a crusader. But his crusades were on behalf of the powerful. In addition, Evans held all his debts. So Byers gave in to the mob. He swore that he did not know who the "high officials" were. He promised to hunt them down, and to run them out of Denver. No traitor to Colorado, he said, and no friend of the Indians would henceforth draw an ounce of comfort from the *News*.

Byers kept his word. The next issue of the *News* revealed that the confessed murderers of the Hungates had been killed at Sand Creek. It declared that freshly taken scalps, of white men, women, and children, had been found hanging from the lodgepoles of Black Kettle's warriors; and that the saddle blankets of the Cheyennes were fringed with braids woven from white women's hair.

In the issues that followed, rewards were posted in the *News* for information leading to the exposure of the men behind the investigation of Sand Creek. Suspects were found, and hounded, and made to crawl. Then, almost as a footnote, a second small item appeared in the *News*. It announced that a Military Commission of Inquiry would shortly convene in Denver to investigate Sand Creek; and that its chairman would be Lieutenant Colonel Samuel Tappan.

I remembered Tappan as a journalist and a radical; a little twisted abolitionist who had helped to organize the First Colorado Cavalry, and whom we had cast aside, in Chivington's favor. He would be filled with hatred of Chivington, as I was, but he could not for a moment stand up against him.

I thought of leaving at once for Denver but decided against it—I remembered how I had been punished once before for acting without orders. I wrote to Tappan offering him my assistance; I hung on at Lyon, waiting, and scanning the *News*.

The *News*, of course, denounced the Commission of Inquiry. The thrashing of the savages at Sand Creek, the *News* declared, could mean untold wealth for every man in the Territory. The Inquiry would drive off new capital, and so condemn the Territory to poverty for generations to come.

It was a powerful argument in a new country. It was echoed by every newspaper that came across my desk, save one. The editors of the *Black Hawk Mining Journal* had no love for the Indians; but they had one firm principle: whatever the *News* was against, they were for.

It was in the *Journal* that I read, early in February, that Tappan had arrived in Denver to organize the Inquiry. And it was in the *Journal*, a week later, that I found an item about Soule. "Captain Soule," said the *Journal*, "is a witness who expects to testify before the Court of Inquiry, and his testimony is evidently feared. Hence he is shot at, at night, in the suburbs of Denver."

I knew then that I could not go on waiting at Lyon until Tappan summoned me. And I knew I could not count on many of the men whose affidavits I had taken. The main burden of the testimony would fall on Soule, on Cramer, and on myself. But, if I was to be a witness, I would first have to go to Sand Creek.

I set out, in the darkness, with twenty men. When the day came up at last, the light was dim. There was no color on the plains. And none in the sky, save shades of gray. A raw wind scraped the ridges; it rained fitfully. Low clouds swept over the landscape, bearing more rain from the mountains.

We saw nothing at all save hawks and an occasional wolf. At nightfall we came to the long descent that ended on the bluffs above Sand Creek. We camped there, among the debris left by Chivington's men.

It was too dark that night to see beyond the bluffs. But the next morning we could see clearly enough.

I had thought that the Indians would have returned to bury their dead; for the ceremony was sacred to them, and a matter of pride. Certainly they could not have stayed away out of fear. For their own reasons, they had chosen, with Chivington, to let the evidence stand. And it stood, preserved by the cold of the winter, and untouched by the wolves.

Nothing was altered. The ruins of the village were as Cramer had left them; the dead lay where they had fallen; some spread-eagled on the ground, some doubled over; some partly buried in trenches that they had been digging, some frozen in grotesque attitudes with knees or elbows raised, as if to ward off blows. On the edge of the settlement, two ponies grazed in the still morning. Among the charred lodgepoles and hides, I saw, moving feebly, the last of the dogs.

23

I set out for Denver in February with half a dozen men. We hurried over the plains, riding from the start to the finish of each day.

We paused to rest at the Point of Rocks Agency. I found Colley there, asleep at his desk with a bottle in his hand. I woke him and started to tell him about the Inquiry. He nodded for a few moments and then sank back into sleep. I pulled him up; I held him erect and told him the half-breed's story. "Guerrier swears that Black Kettle is alive. He swears that Black Kettle escaped, and that he's . . ." Colley hung in my grip; he shook his head.

We rode on, stopping at only a few way stations. One was the Half Way House.

It was dark when we clattered into the familiar yard. I left the troopers there to care for the horses. I walked alone to the house. I knocked on the front door; at once it was torn open. Coberly's daughter stood there, wild with delight, and, then, at the sight of me, crestfallen.

"I thought you were Captain Soule," she said.

She was a favorite of mine, but I moved past her saying: "He's in Denver."

"I know that"—she followed me to the fireplace—"but he's coming back for me. I thought he might come for me tonight. I was hoping . . ."

"Why would he come back for you?"

She looked at me in surprise. "We're to be married!"

"Soule, marrying? I doubt that!"

"Ask my father then!" Coberly had come into the room. He stood behind her, nodding.

"It's true that Captain Soule was never serious," Coberly said. "But he's changed. He came through here a few weeks ago and he seemed like another man."

"We'd be married by now," the girl said, "but for the Inquiry."

She had followed Soule to Denver; they had searched for lodgings together. Then, so she told me, Tappan sent for Soule. He spoke of the difficulties he faced in organizing the Inquiry. He asked Soule to be his first witness; and Soule agreed. He went to the girl and tried to break off the marriage; she refused. She had been named for a Greek nymph by her father, and raised on Greek legends of heroism. She agreed only to postpone the wedding until Soule completed his testimony. In turn, Soule promised that if she would return to the Half Way House and wait there, he would come for her as soon as he was free.

"So," she ended, "when you came to the door, I thought . . ."

"You mean that the Inquiry has been going on?"

"I hoped it had been called off."

"That's impossible! It has to . . ."

"Who knows?" Coberly said. He sent his daughter out to get our supper. He came back to the fireplace. "Who knows if there will be an inquiry?" he said. "Can you see Chivington obeying a summons from Sam Tappan? Can you see him submitting to questioning by Tappan?"

"He'd better," I said. "Tappan may not be much, but he represents the Government of the United States."

"The Government is two thousand miles away; fighting for its life in Virginia. You may have friends in Washington. But you're on your own in Denver if you testify against Chivington and the Third Regiment."

"The Government will protect its witnesses," I said.

"I hope so! You know," Coberly added, "that the Army held back the pay of the Third Regiment? The men have no work in Denver; they have no money. Five hundred dollars is a lot to them."

"It's a lot to anyone."

Coberly nodded. "Ten days ago," he said, "the officers of the Third Regiment called a rally to protest against the

Inquiry. Chivington was in the crowd. He told the crowd that he believed in action, not in speeches. He swore that there was five hundred dollars in his wallet for anyone who would bring in a dead Indian or else a dead white man who took the Indian side."

I left the Half Way House early in the morning. Coberly's daughter was waiting at the front door.

"Don't mistake me," I said as she moved toward me. "I'm not Soule."

"But you'll be seeing him! Tell him I'm waiting!"

"You think he's forgotten?"

"He may have forgotten! How long must I wait for him?"

"I don't know."

"You should know! You were the one who started it all!"

I nodded. In the dim light, I could see the troopers, leading the horses into the yard.

"You started it," she repeated; "why can't you take his place as the chief witness?"

"They wouldn't let me; I wasn't at Sand Creek."

"Would you take his place if you could?"

"That's not for me to say."

"Yet you worry about him! You think he's in danger, don't you!"

"He's been in far greater danger."

"That doesn't mean that he's safe. A traveler came

through from Denver last week. He said that shots were fired . . ."

"He was lying."

". . . that shots were fired from an ambush, and that Captain Soule barely escaped. Are you sure he was lying? Or are you trying to protect me? The only way I can tell is by going to Denver and finding out. . . ."

"He told you to stay here; so stay. It won't be long."

"Do you believe that? How do you know? You said you didn't know."

Beyond her head I could see the troopers waiting; I edged past her.

She held me back. "Tell him," she said, "that I can't live apart from him any longer! Tell him that if he cares for me at all he'll . . ." She broke off. "You're not going to tell him," she said. I shook my head.

24

We hurried on and came to Denver at the end of the day. I spoke to no one save to ask the way to the small boarding-house where Soule was staying. I found his room, and knocked, and called out my name. I heard the lock turn as he opened the door.

It was a small room, with a table in the center. Soule had been writing at the table; as I passed it, I caught sight of one line: . . . *when my just debts are settled I . . .*

My mind, at that moment, was on the Inquiry. I questioned Soule eagerly; I learned that the Inquiry was about to begin, and that he would be the first to testify. I mentioned my suspicion of Tappan, and he cut me short. "We were wrong about Tappan," he said.

He took his papers from the table and laid them away in his foot locker. From the same locker he brought out the *Paradise Regained*. We sat talking and drinking; it was some time before I remembered that I had a message to deliver.

"Coberly's daughter wants you to know that she's waiting for you," I said.

Soule looked at me, greatly troubled. He asked: "What am I to do?"

"Marry her, of course!" Soule's question sounded foolish.

It seemed less foolish when I learned, from Soule, from Tappan, and from Cramer, all that had taken place before my arrival in Denver.

It had been late in January when Tappan slipped into Denver. He took a small room in the Planters House. For two days, he worked alone. Then he sent word to Soule to visit him, under cover of night.

He questioned Soule closely on every aspect of his story. He took notes on Soule's answers and compared them with my transcripts. He showed no feeling until he closed his notebook. Then: " 'Let someone give me a sword, that I may kill this monster,' " he said.

Soule said nothing. Tappan was troubled by his silence —so he told me later. But he trusted Soule, and was determined to use him.

"We will convene in twelve days," he told Soule. "We will call up our witnesses. They will testify, and we will examine them; then we will turn them over to Colonel Chivington and his counsel for cross-examination. You understand that, don't you?" he asked.

Soule nodded, so Tappan told me, and did not speak.

"Chivington will do everything that he can to break down our witnesses," Tappan said. "Then he will present his side. He has any number of witnesses he can call on; we have only a few.

"That is why the first witness is all-important. If he tells the truth and stands on the truth, it can never be refuted. If he falters, then we are lost.

"Captain," he said, "you understand, of course, why I tell you this. You are to be the first witness."

"There are dangers . . ." Soule began.

Tappan interrupted: "Name them."

Soule spoke then of his act of defiance at Sand Creek. "It was desertion in the face of the enemy," he said, "and that's a crime, punishable by death."

Tappan shook his head. "The Cheyennes were prisoners of war," he said; "you committed no crime."

"There are others who would go first," Soule said.

"Who?"

"Wynkoop, for instance."

"He was not at Sand Creek."

"Cramer, then."

"He took part in the fighting; he bears some of the guilt."

"If there were a choice . . ." Soule said.

And Tappan answered: "There is none."

Soule said nothing more. He saluted and left the room.

Soule spoke to no man of his meeting with Tappan; but many men were watching him.

Two days after his meeting with Tappan, Soule was summoned to break up a gunfight in a cabin outside of Denver. Being Provost Marshal—for he had been assigned to duty in the city—he had to go.

He set out in the dusk with the man who had come for him. They rode to the ragged border of Denver. There, Soule's companion pointed ahead and left Soule to ride on alone.

Soule picked his way among the last of the shacks, but they were unfamiliar to him. He asked a group of people the way. They told him that the cabin he was seeking was deserted; as for a gunfight, they had heard no shots.

Soule came within sight of the cabin, leaning by itself on the plain. He saw no lights within it, no smoke, nothing but a black interior and an open window. He paused; his horse raised its head and neighed.

Soule turned off the road and approached the cabin from the rear. There he saw a horse, saddled and tied to a rail. He dismounted; as he walked forward the back door of the cabin burst open; a man darted out, fired wildly at Soule, and fled.

A marshal may have many enemies. Soule tried to persuade himself that the man who had waited in the cabin to kill him was not acting for Chivington. But his belief could not last long.

Three days later, Soule was called to Golden. He rode out alone across the snow, to the north of Denver. When he was a mile beyond the city, he looked back. Two horsemen were riding behind him on the trail. They rode without haste, but they kept pace with him; cantering when he cantered; pausing when he paused.

There was no place in that country where Soule could take shelter. There was no safety in racing over the crust and ice. Soule rode steadily for an hour; he crossed the wind-swept divide. He was in the valley, within sight of Golden, when his horse plunged, pitching him off. He heard the shots as he fell; from the ground he glanced back. In the distance the two men stood in silhouette. They stuffed their rifles back into their holsters, remounted, and rode off over the crest of the hill.

Soule said nothing about the efforts to kill him. But the story spread. It reached Cramer, who was stationed at Camp Weld. He went to Tappan with the story. He claimed the right to be called as first witness, in Soule's place.

Tappan sent for Soule. He questioned Soule on the two incidents. He was searching for evidence of a master hand; and Soule had evidence. But he said nothing.

Tappan waited. Then: "Captain," he said, "we need to

understand each other. I've placed my faith in you as a witness. But you place no faith in me. You still distrust me," he added. "Or is it that you still feel some loyalty to Chivington? You were close to him once. You believed in him."

"He was against slavery," Soule said.

"Was he?" Tappan asked. "Or does he wish to enslave all men? There are no free men in Chivington's world. You follow him, as a slave follows his master, or you are his enemy."

"You were always his enemy," Soule said.

"Do you know why?" Tappan asked.

"You wanted the colonelcy, at Glorieta."

"Yes, I wanted it," Tappan said. "And I surrendered it, to Chivington. But I held on to the lieutenant-colonelcy. He'd promised the position to Major Downing. He had to get me out of his way.

"He exiled me to Fort Garland," Tappan said. "He hoped I would resign. But I held on. So he set out to cashier me from the Army. Month after month, he and Downing sent in false reports about me to the War Department. They accused me of insubordination and of dereliction of duty. They accused me of disloyalty to President Lincoln and to the Union."

"You weren't cashiered," Soule said.

"Not quite. General Curtis sent a captain down from Denver to report on my administration. Chivington and Downing were waiting for him when he got back. They questioned him, and found that his report would support me. They gave him a choice: he could write a new report, calling for my removal, in which case they would make him a major; or he could write the truth as he saw it, in which case they would break him.

"He wrote the truth," Tappan added. "And they broke him. They carry out their threats."

Soule said nothing for a time, so Tappan told me. Then he said: "Breaking a man is one thing; killing a man is another."

"Is it?" Tappan asked. "You were with the First Colorado when we rode to Glorieta," he said. "Did you ever wonder what really happened to Colonel Slough?"

"The men turned against him."

"And who incited the men? You remember," Tappan added, "that Colonel Slough was called a coward because he kept clear of the flank where Chivington was fighting?"

Soule nodded. "I helped to spread the story," he said.

"And you remember that when Colonel Slough resigned his command, he gave as his reason the Army's refusal to back his plan for an advance? The reason was a false one, given out for the sake of the regiment. Slough resigned," Tappan said, "because if he had not resigned he would have been assassinated."

"You can never prove that," Soule said.

"I proved it to myself, when I was acting colonel of the regiment. Slough wrote out his resignation one night in March. I found out that on the same night the sentinels had been withdrawn from Slough's tent, on orders from a high-ranking officer. Half a dozen soldiers had surrounded Slough's tent in the darkness, with orders to kill him."

"They could have been the Germans," Soule said. "The Germans were angry enough."

"They were not the Germans. You must believe me," Tappan said. "I sent the evidence to Slough; with my interpretation. He wrote back to say that I was right. He had been warned, even before he left Denver, that he would be assassinated if he held on to his command. At the Battle of Pigeons Ranch a part of Chivington's command fired a volley at him, which was why he kept clear of them."

Soule said: "There were many men who hated Slough."

"But only one who would order his execution. Here—" Tappan took from his trunk a letter, which later on he showed to me. *I resigned the colonelcy*, Slough ended, *because I was satisfied that a further connection would result in my assassination. I am satisfied that men now high in rank and command were at the bottom of the thing. I am satisfied that today if a chance offered I would be murdered. I say this to you in confidence that you will keep it secret.*

"I've kept it secret," Tappan said. "I've lived with the secret for two years. I've known that a tyrant was rising among us in Colorado. I knew, long ago, that Sand Creek was coming, just as I know now that unless we stop him there will be many more Sand Creeks.

"I was given the chance to stop him," Tappan added, "when I was named as chairman of this Inquiry. I knew that the chance might never be given to us again. So I was determined to make the most of it.

"That is why I picked you," Tappan told Soule. "You were a hero in the Territory. And you defied Chivington. You saw his attack on Sand Creek for the crime that it was. And you alone refused to be a part of it. I was certain that your action in testifying could be the turning point.

"I acted blindly," Tappan said. "I called you here and I ordered you to be the first witness. Then, from the moment you left, my conscience troubled me. Now I know that I was wrong. I had no right to do what I did."

Soule protested: "I don't understand."

"I was commanding the regiment," Tappan said, "when I learned the truth about Chivington. Had I chosen to stay on, I could have stood in his path. I knew then that some brave man would have to stand against him. I had thought of myself as brave, but I was wrong. A few shots were fired in my direction, and I ran. I signed your petition to place Chivington in command."

"I was glad when you signed it," Soule said; "but that was long ago. It doesn't matter now."

"It matters to me," Tappan said. "I try to live by a sense of honor," he added. "I will not order you, I will not even ask you, to do something I could not do."

"You mean that I am not to be the first witness?" Soule asked.

"No," Tappan answered. "I mean only that I will not make the decision. It's for you to choose."

Soule shook his head, protesting, but Tappan led him

to the door. "Remember," he said, "that there are others who can testify first and who are not in danger. At least they are not in as much danger. We will build our story slowly around them. And we will come in time to you."

The next day, the hotel clerk handed Tappan a note, left early in the morning. It was from Soule; it read: *I choose to be first.*

25

On the morning of February 13, the Military Commission convened to hear the case of Colonel J. M. Chivington.

Three hundred men gathered outside the courthouse on that morning. Most of them were veterans of the Third Regiment; many were dressed in the ragged jackets they had worn on the way to Sand Creek. Standing closely together, they formed a barricade, so that anyone whom they distrusted had some difficulty in entering the courthouse. Only a few of them recognized me, but they knew Soule.

The courtroom was empty when we arrived. The floor of the room was lined with benches. At one end, in place of the judge's chair, two tables were set out, for the Commissioners and for Chivington. The side walls of the room were covered with recruiting posters and dusty guidons, captured from the Confederacy. On the end wall were hung two grim portraits of President Lincoln and General Grant.

We sat in the jury box, and waited. Before long, Tappan and his two fellow Commissioners entered the room through a side door and took their places. In their dress uniforms—their sashes and sabers and their long white gloves—they looked imposing enough. But the junior members of the Commission were captains, low in rank, and overawed by the occasion. And Sam Tappan, sitting between them, was no more impressive.

He was a small man, almost a runt. His uniform was too large for him; his hair was too long. His voice was high-pitched and his hands were nervous; he had a wild, haunted air.

He looked like a dreamer, incapable of acting. It was Soule who reminded me that Tappan had led counter-raids for the Abolitionists in Kansas, and that he had been Speaker of the Kansas Legislature in the state's worst days. I remembered then that at Glorieta he had cantered, calmly and coldly, into the fire of the Texas brigades.

For twenty minutes or more the Commissioners waited, glancing at their watches and reviewing their notes. Then a shout went up in the street. We heard cheering; the frame building shook under the tread of heavy boots. Chivington strode into the courtroom, surrounded by his bodyguard and followed by Downing. The crowd flooded in after him—filling up the benches, standing in the empty spaces, blocking the doorways and the halls, so that the Commissioners were surrounded at their table and seemed to be trapped.

The din was immense; the guards were powerless. Tappan seized his gavel and pounded upon the table; the crowd laughed.

Chivington sat at his place, in command. He looked around the room; he glanced at the notes that Downing handed to him. At last he held up his hand; then the crowd fell silent.

Tappan stood up, still gripping his gavel. In his high voice he read out the Order from the Army defining the purposes of the Commission and its powers.

The Commission was directed to determine who were the aggressors at Sand Creek, and whether the campaign was directed by Colonel Chivington in accordance with the recognized rules of civilized warfare. It was told to find out if the proper steps had been taken by the Colonel to prevent unnatural outrages by his command and to punish the transgressors if such there were. It was given the power to call witnesses and to compel attendance. It could meet in public or in private session, as its members deemed prudent and right.

Chivington listened as Tappan read the order. Then he rose and walked to the Commissioners' table. He stood there, so tall that the Commissioners had to tilt their heads far back to look at him.

He spoke in a voice a full octave below Tappan's. He

warned the Commissioners that they were acting illegally. He told them to take no further action until his formal protest had been filed.

The two captains nodded respectfully. They had served under Chivington, thriving in his shadow. They had not chosen to serve on the Commission; they would, no doubt, have given all that they possessed to be freed of the burden of responsibility that had been loaded upon them.

They leaned close to Tappan and gave in reluctantly to his arguments. They stared at the table when Tappan announced that Chivington's objections had been overruled.

Chivington returned in silence to his table. The Commission continued its work. The three members swore to uphold the honor and dignity of the court; the youngest of them, George Stilwell, was appointed recorder for the proceedings; the crowd listened, sullen but subdued.

Tappan made certain that the organization of the court was completed. Then he called for the first witness. Soule moved toward the stand, but Chivington barred the way. He challenged the Commission again, on the ground that Tappan was prejudiced. "The said Lieutenant Colonel S. F. Tappan," he declared, "is, and for a long time has been, my open and avowed enemy."

At that, all of Chivington's supporters stood up and shouted. They went on, shouting at Tappan, and when they stopped, Downing saw to it that they were stirred up again. He hoped, then and there, to bring the Inquiry to an end.

He failed. Tappan waited until, for one moment, the

shouting died away. Then he struck the table with his gavel and cried out that the session was adjourned.

Chivington and his supporters left, thinking that the day was theirs. The Commissioners watched them leave. Then the two captains turned on Tappan, saying: "We can't go on like this!"

"We don't have to," Tappan said. He read again the section of the Order granting the Commissioners the right to meet in private.

The captains were relieved. "Whoever wrote that Order had a good deal of foresight," Stilwell said.

Tappan nodded. He said: "I always try to look ahead."

The Commission reconvened on the following morning. The day was spent in legal wrangling. Tappan replied to Chivington's objections, and the captains upheld him. Chivington then presented six further objections. He might have won over the captains, but he pressed too hard. He denied the right of the Commission to search out the truth about Sand Creek; so he united the Commissioners. They considered his objections and dismissed them, one by one.

Then, at last, the way was cleared for the investigation. Soule was called to the stand without objection, and sworn in.

The Commission had no counsel. Glancing at the notes

he had taken, Tappan led Soule through the preliminary questions:

"Your full name, age, and rank in the Army?"

"Silas Soule; twenty-six years of age; Captain, Company D, Veteran Battalion, First Colorado Cavalry."

"How long have you been an officer in the First Regiment?"

"Since December 11, 1861."

"Were you on duty at Fort Lyon in August and September last year?"

"I was."

"Did you accompany Major Wynkoop's command to an Indian camp on the Smoky Hill about that time?"

"I did."

Tappan spoke in a thin monotone. George Stilwell took down the testimony in longhand. Downing listened intently, alert for any slip. Chivington watched Soule without moving; on the bald dome of his head, the sweat began to shine.

Tappan led Soule on, through the meeting in the Big Timbers, the journey to Denver, the council at Camp Weld. Soule spoke of the Governor's hesitation, and of the conditions which Chivington told the chiefs they must carry out, if they wanted peace.

Tappan asked: "Did the Indians in council manifest a desire for peace, and a willingness to comply with the conditions of Colonel Chivington?"

Soule started to answer, but Stilwell held up his hand. His quill pen scratched on across the yellow paper. It halted and Stilwell nodded.

Soule answered: "They did."

Tappan moved on to the weeks that followed at Lyon. Soule asserted that Black Kettle had complied fully with Chivington's order, bringing his people in to the fort and doing all that Anthony and I asked of him.

"What was the understanding with the Indians?" Tappan asked.

"They were to be protected by the troops," Soule answered, "until the messenger arrived from General Curtis."

"Did the messenger arrive prior to the first of December?"

"He did not."

Tappan moved on. "Were you at Fort Lyon on or about the twenty-seventh of November? If so, what happened on that day?"

"I was there," Soule answered. He described the night when he rode out to intercept the Sioux and, instead, encountered Chivington, leading his column up the road from Denver. He spoke of Chivington's insistence upon secrecy, and his questions concerning the whereabouts of the Cheyennes.

Tappan looked up from his notes. He asked: "What answer did you make?"

Soule spoke slowly for the recorder's sake: "I said that there were some Indians camped near the fort, but that they were not dangerous. I said that they were waiting to hear from General Curtis."

Soule paused there. For a moment perhaps, he longed to save himself. He glanced over his shoulder at Downing—

at those cold, intelligent eyes. He turned back to Tappan, who waited with an air of sadness.

"I told Colonel Chivington that the Indians were considered prisoners," Soule said. "And someone made the answer that they would not be prisoners for long."

By then the day was over; the light in the courtroom was dim. Soule stood without moving on the witness stand; Tappan leaned back in his chair and sighed; Stilwell's head all but touched the pad on which he wrote; beneath the scratches of the pen, I heard Chivington's heavy breathing.

On the following morning, Soule was called back to the stand. "State what was done," Tappan said, "after Colonel Chivington reached Fort Lyon."

Soule spoke of the posting of the guard around the fort; the night ride to Sand Creek; the day of fighting; the dead.

"Have you been at Sand Creek since that day?" Tappan asked. "If so, what did you see there?"

"I went to Sand Creek on the last of December," Soule testified. "I saw sixty-nine dead Indians and about one hundred live dogs and two live ponies and a few dead ones."

Chivington shuddered; above his tight collar, his neck swelled and darkened. A murmur stirred in the courtroom. For it was well known that, in his official reports to the War Department, and in his dispatches to the *News*, Chivington had stated that he had left between five hundred and six hundred dead Indians lying on the battlefield.

Tappan moved on. He asked what had become of the

Indian property taken at Sand Creek, and how the troopers who were killed there died. Soule testified that the Indian ponies were sold for profit by Chivington's officers, and that the dead, slain by the Indians according to Chivington, were, with few exceptions, killed by Chivington's own men.

At the end of the day, Tappan asked about the Indians.

"Did any of the Indians advance towards Colonel Chivington's command making signs that they were friends?"

"I saw them advance toward the line," Soule answered. "Some of them were holding their hands up."

"Was any demand made upon the Indians prior to the attack? Or any attention paid to their signs that they were friends?"

"Not to my knowledge."

Tappan glanced at Chivington. The Colonel was pressing his fingers beneath his bearded chin, as if a knot had formed within his throat.

Still looking at Chivington, Tappan asked: "Were the women and children shot while trying to escape, by Colonel Chivington's command?"

"They were," Soule answered, but his words were lost. Chivington struck the table before him with his fist. He turned upon Downing with such force that the Major shielded himself from a blow. "I've had enough of this!" Chivington cried. "I want it ended, now!"

Downing stood up. He mumbled a few legal phrases to the Commission. But there was no ground for protest, and Downing knew it. He sat down, shaking his head.

Tappan waited. When the courtroom was still, he asked

if the recorder had been able to hear the last response of the witness.

Stilwell was not sure.

"Then let me repeat it," Tappan said. Calmly, he asked: "Were the women and children followed while trying to escape, shot down, and scalped, and otherwise mutilated, by any of Colonel Chivington's command?"

"They were," Soule said.

Chivington thrust his chair back. He stood, heaving. "You want to destroy me!" he cried. "You want to nail me to a cross because a few men disregarded my efforts!"

Tappan was never more calm. He turned from Chivington to Soule. He asked: "Were any efforts made by the commanding officers, Colonels Chivington and Shoup, and Major Anthony, to prevent these mutilations?"

Soule waited until Stilwell was ready. "Not that I know of," he said.

Throughout the next morning, Tappan rounded off his questions. Soule in turn named the officers of Chivington's command who had stolen and sold the Indian ponies. He spoke of the killing of the prisoners. He testified that, on returning to Sand Creek, he had found all of the Indian dead, men, women, and children, scalped and mutilated.

At last, Tappan declared that he had finished. Soule was turned over to Chivington and Downing for cross-examination.

For three days Chivington questioned Soule. He went

over every line of Soule's testimony, probing for inconsistencies. He tried, through a hundred innocent-sounding questions, to draw Soule to his side. All the time, he was reading from slips of paper handed to him by Downing. And so, for three days, Soule stood alone against Downing's subtlety and Chivington's brute force.

At the end of each day, Soule was close to exhaustion. The tension in the courtroom was such that all of us who were there were worn out. We stepped into the street at each day's end as prisoners emerge from a dungeon: our eyes aching, our throats dry. I knew that, much as I wanted to help Soule, there was little I could say. I was drained of all my strength, and he wished to be alone; after a few words, we went our ways.

Chivington kept his rage down when he was in control of the questioning. Yet I think now that those days were harrowing, even for him. And not only because his whole being cried out against the restraints of the courtroom. Soule had admired Chivington in the days when he fought against the Confederacy. And, to the extent that Chivington could feel affection for another, he had been fond of Soule.

Chivington followed Tappan's course in tracing the background to Sand Creek. Through his questions, he gave his version of all that I had done. I had acted without authority in going to the Big Timbers; I had endangered the lives of my men; I had been drunk during the council with the chiefs; I had presented treacherous enemies as loyal friends. All this, Chivington read into the record; but he gained no support from Soule.

In time, Chivington came to the scene which followed his own arrival at Lyon. His purpose, I suppose, was to prove that the officers of Lyon had supported his attack at Sand Creek.

"State if you know," Chivington said, "whether any officer at Fort Lyon objected to joining Colonel Chivington's command; and if so, to whom such objection was made."

"Objection was made to Major Anthony," Soule answered. "I think objections were made to Colonel Chivington also, by officers."

"What are your means of knowledge," Chivington asked, "respecting objections having been made to Colonel Chivington personally?"

Soule hesitated. He said: "Lieutenant Cramer and someone else told me that day that they had objected to Colonel Chivington."

Soule paused there; he shook his head in an effort to clear his mind. In his weariness and his desperation, he spoke directly to Stilwell.

He said: "I was warned by Major Anthony, Lieutenant Cramer, and some others not to go to the camp where Colonel Chivington was. I was told that he had made threats against me, for language I had used on that day against Colonel Chivington's command going out to kill those Indians on Sand Creek."

Chivington moved on. Throughout the next day he questioned Soule about the fighting. Soule in turn held to his story. He conceded nothing, and, although Chivington traced Soule's actions hour by hour, he stopped short of Soule's refusal to fire on the Indians.

At the end of the day, Chivington conferred for a long time with Downing. He crumpled the paper slips that lay on his table; he motioned to Soule to leave the witness stand.

Soule stepped down and returned to his bench. Tappan read over his notes. Stilwell stretched and rubbed the stiffness from his fingers.

The sheafs of yellow paper—one hundred and seven pages of them—lay stacked on the table: the story of Sand Creek, for the President of the United States and his Cabinet to consider. Chivington had been given every opportunity in those pages to dismember Soule's story. He had failed to attack its core; he had not even chipped away its edges. Whatever happens to us, I thought, the truth is there, intact.

26

The rest of our testimony was all in support of Soule: Cramer filled out the story in his methodical way; Jim Beckwourth pictured White Antelope standing with arms folded at the moment of his death; John Prowers spoke of his imprisonment at Caddoe. I took up the argument in my turn and left the stand, as I thought, unscathed. I feared most for three young recruits whom Tappan called up to testify. They described the day at Sand Creek, and when Chivington challenged them, they did not retreat.

In the presence of resistance, Chivington seemed at a loss. He insisted that Black Kettle was a merciless enemy; we who had been at Black Kettle's mercy were there in the courtroom to prove him wrong. He moved to disqualify Jim Beckwourth, saying that he lacked religious faith. Solemnly the old reprobate reaffirmed his belief in God. To one young witness, Chivington suggested that the Indian dead had been scalped and mutilated by their own dogs, or else by wolves. The boy laughed in Chivington's face. "I don't hardly think," he said, "that dogs or wolves would chaw the scalp off and leave the body alone."

Chivington sought another way out. "On your second visit to Sand Creek," he said to a trooper, "did not Captain Soule send a number of his men ahead, with instructions to mutilate the dead?"

The trooper answered: "No."

Chivington was insistent: "Did not Captain Soule direct you to go ahead of his command, and tie up a squaw with your lariat in such a position that Captain Boothe, Inspector, would think she had been hung?"

These questions were, of course, preposterous. I welcomed them, hearing in them a note of desperation, and failing to hear the malignant bitterness aimed at Soule.

It seemed to me that for Soule the danger had passed. His testimony was taken and could not be erased. No end could be served by harming him, save vengeance. And venegance would be an act of madness—so I told Soule. He agreed, or he seemed to agree. He rode off across the plains to the Half Way House.

Soule and Miss Coberly were married on the first of April. Not in any church—we met in the house of Hickory

Rogers; it was one of the few houses in Denver where we were welcome. We met early in the morning in order to avoid attention.

We gathered in the sitting room, where the chairs had been pushed back against the walls. Soule stood by the fire; I was at his side, as his best man. Hickory's father-in-law, the Reverend Mr. Kehler, waited beside us, holding his Bible in his hand. Cramer was there, and Tappan, and a few other close friends. We turned as Coberly led his daughter down the stairs. She was dressed in her mother's wedding gown and veil; so she brought the church to us.

At the end of the ceremony, Soule and his wife knelt to receive the benediction. As they rose, Cramer uncorked a bottle of champagne he had brought in from Camp Weld. We gathered in a circle; I said the obvious things. I claimed free board and lodging at the Half Way House as chief promoter of the wedding; I swore that dragging Soule to the altar was as hard as flogging a mule train into action. I ended with an old line from the theater: *May heaven give you many, many merry days.*

Soule, in turn, accepted my comparison of the mule train. "Only," he added, "the mules are smarter than Ned supposes. They know there's a long day ahead when the bell mare sets out in the morning. But they're ready to be led.

"I was ready three months ago," he said. "Just as Cramer is ready now. The best of us have to surrender our independence sooner or later. Even Ned Wynkoop is going to give in to married life one day, although if his wife were here, she wouldn't believe it."

He turned to his wife. "The halter fits," he said. "I'll settle down. I'll even become a general, if you want to be a general's wife. I'll let the lieutenants sleep out on the plains from now on; I'll sit at a desk. I'll live to be ninety, and die in my bed."

Soule had no time in the weeks that followed for anything but his home. He and his wife worked together, hanging curtains and papering walls. They went out only once—to the memorial service that was held in mid-April for President Lincoln.

For a week after the assassination, the city mourned for the President. At the week's end, Mrs. Langrishe was ready with a new play. By then the Soules were settled; they invited all their friends to a housewarming after the theater.

They spent the day in making cakes and punch; they set out plates and glasses in advance, so that we might go from the theater to their home. We met at the play. It was a dull play, but we made the most of it. In high spirits, we moved with the crowd, out of the theater and into a night that was brilliant with stars.

We heard shots; dim at first, through the chatter of the crowd, and then, in the shocked silence, close and clear. A block from the theater, two men in soldiers' coats staggered into the street, as if they were drunk, and fired wildly. At the edge of the crowd, someone shouted: "Soule! Captain Soule!"

Soule started off, but his wife held on to him. He turned

and embraced her; he spoke to her, but what he said I do not know. Then he broke away from us and ran up the street. His wife started after him, but, for a moment, I held her back.

As he ran, Soule called to the two men to wait. They waited for him. He walked up to them and asked for their weapons. One of the men held out a revolver. Soule reached for it, and the man fired into his chest. Soule pitched forward onto the muddy road. It was only a moment before I reached him and turned him over; he coughed once and was dead.

I left him in the mud and rushed after his killers, down the street and around the first corner. There, two horses were tied, saddled and waiting. The men clambered onto the horses and pounded off beyond the last street light.

Soule lay in the street. The crowd kept its distance; his wife alone clung to him, wiping the mud from his face, trying to keep the warmth in his body. I lifted her from him at last and led her home. We put away the food and the dishes. There was little to say. After a time a woman, one of the neighbors, came in and took her to the bed she had shared with him.

I went back the next day; the house was crowded. The Coberlys had come to reclaim their daughter; the officers' wives had closed around her, to support her, as they always do. The county coroner was there, holding his hat in his hand. Officially, he said, he could make no comment on the unfortunate occurrence; unofficially and not for publication, he could tell us that the guilty parties were veterans and that they had not been apprehended; in fact, they had escaped, with the aid of persons unknown.

The service was to be held in St. John's, Episcopal. The Reverend Mr. Hitchings, whose church it was, sat beside Mrs. Soule, gathering material for his sermon. "Your late husband was from Maine then? . . . His father was sent to Kansas by the Emigrant Aid Society of Boston? . . . As a boy, your late husband helped his father rescue the slaves? . . . Captain Soule was a company commander in the Veteran Battalion, was he not? . . . And before that, a lieutenant in Colonel Carson's Scouts? . . . Yes indeed, the name of Kit Carson is known to all of us. . . ."

I sat at Soule's desk sorting out his papers: old messages, written in code; a reprint of a sermon by Theodore Parker; a will, written at the time of his marriage; a letter from his mother: *You say that you refused to fire on the Indians. Your father and your brother would have been proud of you, as I am proud. . . .* Half hidden beneath the papers I came upon two familiar volumes—the book of poems and the *Paradise Regained.* I kept them for myself.

I moved on to Soule's belongings; I filled out the army form: *Inventory of the effects of* Silas Soule; *late a* Captain; *died on the day of* April 23, 1865; *by reason of* killed while on duty. . . . There followed the list of effects: *forage caps* one; *trousers* three; *flannel shirts* four; *pairs boots* two. . . . There seemed to be nothing left of Soule at that moment but a small heap of old clothes.

The funeral was held on the following morning. I rode to St. John's on a stallion, pure white and high-strung. My purpose—it sounds foolish—was to be conspicuous. For Harry Richmond had come to my room, bearing regrets for Soule's death and expressions of concern for me that could be taken as threats.

I expected to find a small cluster of mourners at the church; I was mistaken. Around its walls were gathered all of the carriages that had met our column when we led the chiefs into Denver. And I saw other carriages belonging to high officials of the Territory.

The church was filled with silent people. Tappan was there of course, with the officers of the First Regiment; so were two generals, recently arrived in Denver. I saw many ranchers in their rough clothes, up from the country around the Half Way House. The teachers, the federal judges, all the good people who had stayed indoors after Sand Creek, had come to pay tribute to Soule and to protest his death. And there were some whose presence was ironical. Byers was there, with his staff; the cabinet of Governor Evans filled a prominent pew; I saw the Governor, kneeling alone. Only Chivington and his followers had stayed away.

Kehler led the gathering in the first prayers. Then he gave up his place to Hitchings—to my regret. Hitchings was one who moved with the majority in Denver. I expected him to cling to the commonplace; I wanted more.

Again, I was wrong. Hitchings spoke for a time of the war that was coming to an end. He said that he would not trespass upon the personal life and character of the dead man. He glanced at the coffin beneath him—a pine box covered with flags. He cleared his throat.

"I am told that Captain Soule was a good soldier," he said. "I ask you, what does that one, short adjective imply?

"It implies that he had no fear of work, of fatigue, of suffering, of danger, of death. And was it not so? Did he not, in the darkness of night, go to discharge his duty as Commander of the Provost Guard of this city? Did he not go when he had every reason to believe that the alarm which called him out was only to decoy him into danger? Did he not go feeling so certain that his doom was sealed that he took farewell of his young wife, telling her what she must do, in case he returned no more alive?

"He did; and there is the spirit of the good soldier. He did his duty in the face of death, and fell by the assassin's hand."

Hitchings paused there. He waited, as if to give every man present the opportunity to stand up and dispute his assertion. No one stirred.

"We come from mourning for the President of the United States," Hitchings continued. "We mourn now for one of our young men. That there is a bond in time between their deaths, all of us will affirm. That there is a further bond, none of us can deny. Just as slavery, in dying, took the life of Abraham Lincoln, so Sand Creek has taken the life of Silas Soule."

The service ended; the procession formed outside the church; first the regimental band; then the cavalry of Company D, led by its first lieutenant; then the hearse; then the rest of us, riding in a long column.

We moved off slowly, to the beat of the drums; down the bare road that led to the river. The wheels of the hearse grated on the crust of the earth. A barren wind sliced down upon us from the mountains. It stirred up eddies of dust on the street, and fragments of papers: old recruiting posters, and torn pages of the *News*.

We came to the river; we started across the flimsy bridge. I was halfway over when a sheet of white paper whirled across the column. My horse reared up and fell, crushing me. I felt a rib crack as the blackness closed out my sight. When I regained consciousness, I was upright, supported by two officers. A third man held my horse for me; I remounted and saw the ceremony to its end. But, four years later, the pain in my chest weakens me as I write, and breaks into my rest.

I went back to my room at the Tremont House. I tried to sleep. I lay on my bed, shifting from side to side as my ribs stiffened.

At dusk there was a knock on my door. A young officer, a stranger to me, stepped into the room. He introduced himself: "George Price, captain in the Second California Cavalry."

"I was at the service today," he said.

I waited.

"I went to the Reverend Hitchings when the service was over," Price continued. "I told him that I had some information which bore upon the death of Captain Soule, as he described it. He told me to come to you."

I nodded.

"I was assigned to Denver in March," Price said, "as District Inspector. I was new to the district, and Captain Soule took me in hand. He drove me one day up to Central City. It's a day's journey, as you know," Price added, "and we were alone. I asked him a good many questions about himself and he talked freely—as if there was no one else whom he could talk to."

"Go on," I said.

"He spoke of his defiance of Colonel Chivington, at Sand Creek and on the witness stand. He felt he had placed himself in jeopardy; a feeling, he said, that you and his other friends didn't share."

"Go on."

"He said that he was thinking of being married. He asked me if he were not doing the girl a great wrong. I replied that I could see nothing wrong in marrying, provided I loved the girl. And he said: 'Supposing you knew that you were going to be killed?'

"I told him that he must be mistaken," Price continued. "I said to him: 'No one could have any reason for killing you, least of all now.' He shook his head. He said: 'They are going to kill me. And after they have killed me, they will blacken my character before the Commission of Inquiry.' I asked: 'Why? Why would anyone want to blacken your character?' And he said: 'It is the only way to weaken my testimony; they cannot allow my testimony to stand.' "

I raised myself up. "Will you write that out?" I asked. "And will you swear to it?"

"Of course," Price said. "I told the story to the Coroner's Jury," he added as he sat down to write. "They paid no attention to me."

I thanked him; I signed his affidavit, as a witness, and locked it away. I asked: "Was there anything else that was said on the way to Central City?"

Price shook his head. "Only that I urged Soule to leave Denver," he said. "I saw that he was firm in his belief that he was to be killed, and so I shifted my ground. I urged him to marry and then to leave the city. I told him to go to California, or else back to the States."

"What did he say?"

"He said that if he left Denver, his testimony would be discredited; people would think that he had lied, and that he was fleeing from the truth."

"Was that all?"

"I told him he was wrong. I said that no one would think he was fleeing; and that in any case, his testimony was not that important. I told him that Sand Creek was over and done with; and that he was worth more alive than dead."

"What did he answer?"

"He didn't answer. All that he would say was: 'I might have agreed with you six years ago.' "

"That was all?"

Price nodded. "I didn't understand what he meant, and I didn't want to press him. So we turned to other things."

Six years is a long time in the West. I was baffled at first; then, after Price had left, I remembered a night on the plains when Soule spoke of his attempted rescue of John Brown.

It was in November 1859 that Brown was sentenced to be hanged for his raid on Harpers Ferry. He was held in a prison cell in Charleston, and a group of Boston abolitionists decided to rescue him. They sought out Soule, remembering that he and his band of Jayhawkers had rescued Dr. Doy from the scaffold in St. Joseph. They brought the band to the East, and equipped it with arms.

The band halted in the mountains outside of Charleston. Soule went into the city alone. He disguised himself as an Irish laborer. He pretended to be drunk and had himself locked up in the jail where Brown was held.

Through the rest of the night, Soule entertained the jailer and his family with Irish songs. He won them over, and so gained a passage to Brown's cell. He bent close to the old man; he whispered that eighty friends were near by, ready to save him.

Brown refused to be saved. He told Soule that he had given the jailer his word that he would not try to escape.

Soule argued with the old man. He promised that the escape would be so arranged that the jailer would bear no blame. He told Brown that the freeing of the slaves was more important than the jailer's good name.

Brown still refused. As for slavery, he said, his work in freeing the slaves would be rounded out on the gallows. He told Soule: "I am worth more to die than to live."

. . . So you knew all along, I thought. Even at the wedding, you were not deceived. I set a course and never weighed the cost. You knew what the cost would be, and you paid it, willingly.

The papers on my table lost their value; I felt, with Price, that one life was worth more than all the truths that the testimony contained. I blamed myself alone for a life cut short. I saw no way, in the years I had, to make up even a part of the loss.

I bore a heavy burden. It was lightened for me when I opened the volume of poetry I had taken from Soule's room. I read the inscription: *To my young comrade;* I turned over the pages, and came to lines that were underscored:

I bequeath myself to the dirt,
to grow from the grass I love,
If you want me again,
look for me under your boot-soles.

27

Chivington was apparently untouched by the killing of Soule. He broke an army tradition by staying away from the funeral. He did not comply with the bare formality of calling on Soule's widow; he did not even send her a message of condolence. Expressions of sadness were heard throughout Denver—they seemed to baffle Chivington. The only feeling he expressed was one of impatience, when the Commission adjourned for two days, out of respect for Soule.

Nonetheless, when the Commission reconvened, there were traces of a change in Chivington. There was a gray cast in his face, and a lack of vigor in his voice. Downing coursed over the courtroom like a hound, following a fading scent. Chivington, in contrast, sat at his desk without stirring; at times he seemed to be on the verge of sleep.

It was Chivington's turn to call his witnesses. The first was a lieutenant who had led a company at Sand Creek. He had little to offer save a few rumors that I had handed out whiskey and rifles to the Indians. His testimony was all hearsay, but Tappan let it pass. He asked a few questions and then motioned to the lieutenant to step down.

The Commissioners waited, but no one moved to the stand. Downing whispered to Chivington, and handed him a sheaf of papers. Chivington heaved himself up.

"Our second witness," he said, "cannot be present in person to testify. But we have his sworn evidence in a deposition we have taken. We propose to read it into the records of the Inquiry."

"For what purpose?" Tappan asked.

"It contains information vital to our case."

"What kind of information?"

"Information bearing upon the character and credibility of a witness who testified against us."

The deposition could not be questioned as a witness is questioned. Yet the Commissioners agreed that it should be heard. So Chivington read out his questions, and the answers of a man who was invisible and out of reach; whose face none of us had ever seen, and whose name none of us knew.

"State your name, age, and occupation."

"Lipman Meyer; age thirty-four years; freighter."

> "Where were you on or about the first day of December 1864?"
>
> "I was on the Arkansas, about thirty miles east of Fort Lyon."

On that day, Chivington was leading his column back from Sand Creek to Lyon. He had sent Soule out, scouting to the east of Lyon, with a force of twenty men.

Chivington read on:

> "Do you know a captain by the name of Silas Soule?"
>
> "I know an officer by the name of Soule. I have heard him styled Captain."

Meyer swore that he had met Soule on the Arkansas; and that he had persuaded Soule to ride to the rescue of his embattled wagon train. Soule led his column south, until he saw smoke rising from the train. Then he turned back—or so Meyer testified.

Why did Soule turn back? Chivington read Meyer's answer: ". . . he was afraid. . . ."

At those words, I was back on my bed in the Tremont, listening to George Price describe the journey into the mountains with Soule. "They will kill me," Soule had said, "and after they kill me they will blacken my character. . . ." Within two weeks of his death, the second part of Soule's prophecy had come true.

Of all the charges that could be brought against Soule, cowardice was the cruelest and the most unjust. There were murmurs of anger in the courtroom. Tappan for one was outraged. He started to intervene; he changed his mind and took notes in his swift, agitated way.

Chivington never looked up from his papers. He seemed insulated from the tension that was mounting around him. At his side, Downing sat, watching Tappan. I saw his face brighten in a thin smile.

Chivington read on:

> "In what condition was Captain Soule on this expedition; intoxicated or not?"
>
> "I should judge him to be drunk, judging from his actions."
>
> "In what condition was he when his command went into camp that night on the Arkansas?"
>
> "He was drunk."

"That night" was "about the fourth or fifth of December." At two in the morning, so Meyer testified, a great noise was heard and the alarm of "Indians!" was given. But:

> "Captain Soule remained sleeping. When he got awake, he did not know which was up or down the river. His program was to go up the river, but he was unable to tell which was up or down."

So, according to Meyer, Soule endangered the lives of his own men. The command was saved, so Meyer testified, by himself and the sergeant.

Most of us in the courtroom were too sickened to stir. Tappan alone covered his pad with furious strokes. Chivington read on in a dull monotone. As if cowardice, drunkenness, and dereliction of duty were not enough, he added a last charge, robbery, against Soule.

> "Did you have any blankets on that trip?"
>
> "I had blankets—two pair—and they were stolen from me."
>
> "By whom do you think they were taken?"
>
> ". . . by Captain Soule. . . ."

That was Meyer's story—doctored as it was by Downing. Chivington held out the transcript to Tappan. "You will want this for purposes of accuracy," he said.

Tappan looked with repugnance at the sheaf of papers. He said: "You propose to place *that* in the records of this Inquiry?"

"Of course."

Tappan stood up, reaching the level of Chivington's chest. "Well," he said, "I object! This Commission is charged with searching out the truth. And I object to having our record fouled by lies!"

Chivington stood, blinking. In the background, Downing called out: "Make him state his grounds for objecting!"

"Your grounds," Chivington said.

"First," Tappan said, "this deposition has nothing to do with Sand Creek. It is utterly irrelevant to the investigation."

Downing broke in: "It establishes that the witness was deficient in . . ."

"It establishes nothing! The witness was a brave officer, and an honest man! He testified under oath and he submitted himself to cross-examination. And because he testified before this Commission, he was assassinated.

"Yes, assassinated!" Tappan shouted. "Twice it was attempted; often it was threatened; at last it was successful in his being instantly killed!

"It is as he said it would be," Tappan added in a low voice. "First he would be killed, because of his testimony. Then his character would be blackened before this Commission."

An uproar followed in the courtroom. "Proof," Downing shouted. "You have no proof!"

"We have the proof," Tappan said. He took from his papers and read, into the record, the affidavit signed by George Price.

It was a moment I had waited for. I watched Chivington, looking for surprise, or indignation, or guilt, or fear in his face. I saw nothing.

At Downing's insistence, Chivington entered his protest. But it was a legal gesture, reflecting no emotion. Tappan's conduct was improper, Chivington said, and appeared to be directed by malice against himself. He hoped that such was not the case.

For the last time in my dealings with Chivington, I was surprised. I loathed him, God knows, yet I saw him as a man like the rest of us. But Chivington was no longer like the rest of us, if he had ever been. An innocent man would have been outraged by the accusation that he was responsible for Soule's death. A guilty man would have been shaken, if he had any conscience. But Chivington was untouched by the accusation. He had no conscience, no remorse, no sense of responsibility or of guilt. He had no capacity for sympathy or sorrow. Beyond the narrow realm of his own immediate desires he was without feeling; he had come to his Dunsinane.

Two weeks later the Inquiry came to an end. The volumes of testimony were sent off to Washington; the Commissioners returned to their posts.

Chivington walked out of the courtroom, a free man, but broken.

In time, the Congress and the War Department both condemned Chivington. Their words were welcome, but, by the time they were published, the issue was settled: Chivington had been defeated on his own ground.

Soule's death was the turning point; from then on, opinion shifted. Doors that had been flung open for Chivington were silently closed to him; men no longer crossed the streets of Denver to shake his hand. He could not leave public life to make a fortune, as Evans and Downing did. He could not rejoin the ministry—his church would not take him. He drifted north to Laramie, but no one was afraid of him any longer and he found no followers. He drifted on to Ohio; there, trying in a dim way to vindicate himself, he is running for Congress. And wherever he speaks, men stand up in the audience and shout: "Sand Creek!"

PART FOUR

28

From Sand Creek, the Indians of Black Kettle's village had stumbled north toward the Smoky Hill. Many froze to death or died of wounds on the way. The survivors were taken in and cared for by their hereditary enemies, the Sioux. The young braves of the village, back from their hunting, came upon the ruins of Sand Creek and followed the trails northward. With the Sioux, they plotted a war of revenge.

They did not lay siege to Denver; instead, a thousand warriors rode out in January and sacked Julesburg, a key point on the Platte. They whipped the garrison; they plundered the warehouses; they butchered the settlers; they fired the town. Then they fanned out, east and west, along the California Road. They tore down telegraph wires; they burned way stations; they ran off herds of cattle and horses; they scoured the plains. From January until October, if an Indian lost his way, he had only to climb the nearest hill. From there he could see the campfires of a dozen war parties; he could hear the throbbing of a hundred drums, beating out the rhythms of the scalp dances.

Only a few coaches ventured across the plains without an escort; one carried three veterans of the Third Regiment, on their way to the States. A band of Cheyennes overtook the coach. The passengers surrendered and pleaded for mercy. A year earlier, it might have been granted. But one of the braves, in searching through the luggage, came upon a small scalp. Entwined in its braids he found a shell that he had woven into his son's hair.

Save for this one incident, the innocent died for the guilty. Chivington had punished the Southern Cheyennes for the transgressions of the Northern Arapahoes—and for no reason save that they were the same color. So, by his law, from Larned to Laramie, and from the Arkansas to the Rosebud, white settlers paid with their lives for Chivington's treachery.

In those months, no Indian could approach a white settlement and no white man could ride near an Indian camp. But one man was able, at great risk, to cross from one side to the other.

Jim Beckwourth was an outcast in the white society of Denver. As a one-time chief of the Crows, he was an enemy of the Cheyennes. He was a liar and a thief; he boasted of the number of men that he had knifed to death. Yet he was outraged by the killing of women and children at Sand Creek.

In the seclusion of his cabin, Beckwourth brooded over his role in acting as a guide for Chivington. He did not read the papers, but he listened as men around him discussed the reports of the Indian raids that were published in the *News*. He was close to seventy; his joints were stiff, and his sight was dimming. Still, he saw what he had to do. He picked up his buckskin jacket and his butcher knife; he slipped out of Denver and rode alone, across the frozen plains, to the camp of the Cheyennes.

The Cheyennes knew Beckwourth as an enemy. Yet they suffered his presence. On his plea, they called in their Council to hear him. The chiefs took their places around Beckwourth in one of the lodges; the last to enter the circle was Black Kettle.

"Why do you disturb us?" Black Kettle asked. "Have you not harmed us enough?"

"The harm is done," Beckwourth answered. "Your friends among the whites are sorry."

"We have no friends among the whites," Black Kettle said. "They lied to us. They came in stealth to murder us. We curse them all."

"Not all of them," Backwourth said. "Curse Chivington all you want; but leave Wynkoop out."

"The Tall Chief sent us to Sand Creek," Black Kettle said. "He told us we would be safe there. We believed him, and we did as he said. We loved him, and he betrayed us."

"No," Beckwourth said, "he was betrayed."

"By his own people?" Black Kettle shook his head. "He must have known."

"He knew nothing."

The chiefs were silent for some time. Then Black Kettle spoke. "Our wives and our children are lying along Sand Creek," he said. "They cry out to us for revenge, and we must obey them."

"You'll get your revenge," Beckwourth said. "The whites killed your women and children, so you'll kill their women and children. . . . And then?" he said to the chiefs. "And then?"

"It will be as it was," a young chief said.

"Are you going to kill all the whites that come onto the plains? They come from all over the earth," Beckwourth said, "and from across the seas. There's no end to them. So there's no use in killing them."

"We shall kill them nonetheless," the young chief said.

The others were silent. After a time, Black Kettle spoke again. "We are hunters and we are warriors," he said. "Would you have us live as paupers and as prisoners? Even as prisoners," he added, "we were not protected; we were attacked and slaughtered."

"We will not live as prisoners," the young chief said.

"Why should you?" Beckwourth asked. "I lived as an

Indian for many years. You can live with the whites, as I do."

"We cannot," Black Kettle answered. "Even if they wanted it, we could not trust them."

"You think I trust them?" Beckwourth laughed.

"We can never be friends with them again."

"You think I'm their friend? I'm a nigger," Beckwourth said. "They're whites. I used to be a slave to whites," he added. "I've got cuts across my shoulders and a brand on my hip to prove it."

"You offer that," Black Kettle asked, "to us?"

Beckwourth shook his head. "The man that branded me is dead, in the white man's war. I'm free, and my sons are free. I lay down and get up when I please to. I own my cabin—the prettiest cabin you could put your eyes on. And some of the whites call me Mister.

"Do as I do," Beckwourth told the chiefs. "I live with the whites, in their country; and I get along."

Black Kettle shook his head. "Our land is taken from us," he said; "our game is gone. Our families are dead; we want to rejoin them. We have nothing left to do but to die well, as our fathers died."

"There's room on the plains . . ." Beckwourth began.

Black Kettle cut him short. "No peace," he said, and the other chiefs in the circle echoed his words: "No peace."

Beckwourth tightened the thongs of his jacket against the wind; he climbed onto his pony and rode back to Denver. He was certain that his journey had been useless, and before long his view seemed to be confirmed. For news reached Denver that war parties were raiding our settlements, and that, among the raiders, were some young braves of Black Kettle's band. Later we learned that they were renegades. A month or so after Beckwourth's visit, Black Kettle broke away from the Sioux and the other warring tribes. He led his people—or all that would follow him—eastward into Kansas. There, although the game was sparse and the streams were dry, he stayed through the spring and summer, waiting.

The fighting continued. The battleground shifted to the north, where the Sioux and some Cheyennes whipped Connor and Cole along the Powder River. It shifted back, and a Kansas regiment took a thrashing in its turn, in the Platte Bridge fight.

The Indians won in every encounter; yet, when the summer came, new armies of immigrants pressed across the plains. They demanded protection, and the War Department did its best.

A new commander, General Sanborn, was sent out to Kansas with orders to punish the Indians. It seemed unlikely that Sanborn would distinguish between the warlike and the peaceful. His troops were poorly armed and thinly clothed; Black Kettle's band was the nearest to Leavenworth, and the easiest to attack.

Still, other influences were at work through the spring and summer of 1865. The Army was shrinking as the soldiers headed home; the country was weary of war. Within the War Department and the White House, the volumes of our Sand Creek Inquiry were read and understood. James Harlan, the best friend we had in the Senate, became Secretary of the Interior, in charge of the Bureau of Indian Affairs. Senator Doolittle journeyed with me to the battlefield of Sand Creek, and then returned to Washington to tell the Senate and the President all that he had learned. Still more important, Doolittle persuaded the two great men of the West, Kit Carson and William Bent, to write to the Government pleading for peace. The two men granted that we could, at great cost, defeat the Indians. But, they added, "humanity shudders at the picture presented by the destruction of hundreds of thousands of our fellow creatures until every effort shall have been tried for their redemption and found useless. By dispossessing them of their country we have assumed their stewardship. And the manner in which this duty is performed will add a glorious record to all American history, or a damning blot and reproach, for all future time."

This was the view that won out in Washington in the summer. So it was that in September the President named a Commission to negotiate a new peace.

Carson, Bent, and Sanborn were members of the Commission. So was General Harney, the victor of Ash Hollow, whom Chivington had set out to surpass.

All four men were experienced in warfare; yet they possessed qualities that Chivington wholly lacked. Sanborn was trained in conciliation; Bent was a wise man; in Carson, gentleness was one aspect of courage, true courage in contrast to Chivington's outward bravery. As for Harney, he had presided over the killing of Indian women at Ash Hollow. Then, almost at once, he had been humbled by remorse. Now, white-haired and soft-spoken, he was an ardent supporter of Indian rights.

All this I learned at first hand in October. For a military escort was appointed to lead the Commissioners to the camp of the Cheyennes. And the commander of the escort was myself.

29

The place chosen for the meeting was east of Larned, where the Little Arkansas flows into the Arkansas River. It was far from our forts and our trade routes. And it was far from the hunting grounds of the Cheyennes. The rivers offered a defense against surprise attack; the escape roads were open to the north and the west in case the conference should fail.

I learned from scouts that Black Kettle and his band were moving down the Little Arkansas. I rode to Larned with my own men and worked there, organizing our column, so that it would be ready to leave when the Commissioners arrived.

Dr. Taylor, the Indian Agent at Larned, told me how to proceed. "I know these Cheyennes," he said. "They're treacherous, and they hate us. But they're scared. Take three hundred men out there," he went on, "and they won't stay to parley. Take one hundred, and you won't come back. So do as I say, Wynkoop; take two hundred men."

I paused long enough in my work to tell him that sixty troopers would make up the escort. He shook a bony finger in my face. "I'm warning you, Wynkoop! I won't be responsible for them! You won't come back!" he cried. "You least of all. There are braves in that band that lost their fathers at Sand Creek. They hold you responsible. And they've taken a blood oath to kill you.

"I'm warning you, Wynkoop!" he shouted as I walked off. "I'm their Agent now; I ought to know!"

The Commissioners rode in from Leavenworth in early October. We set out along the lowlands of the Arkansas. The tamarisk and the osier were rusty on the banks of the river; the aspen had turned to pale yellow; the cottonwoods were still green, dark green and deep, in the long slant of the sun. The days were clear and dry, the nights were chill. The passenger pigeons were gathering for their flight south. It all reminded me of another journey—it was just a year since Soule and Cramer and I had led the chiefs home from Denver.

I set a slow pace in order to reassure Black Kettle. I was certain that his scouts were watching us, but I sent my own runners on ahead to inform him of our approach. They returned on our third day out; they reported that Cheyennes in great numbers were settled in a grove of cottonwoods five miles down the river.

I led my column into camp, on high ground. I posted a heavy guard; I kept our horses picketed. Then, when our tents were raised and our fires lit, I went to the Commissioners. I told them that they were to stay in camp, while I rode on, alone.

Carson reminded me of my part in bringing about Sand Creek. Bent held that, by the ancient law of the Cheyennes, the young braves would be compelled to take my scalp. Sanborn added that, if I were killed, there would be no meeting.

I knew the force of those arguments; I set, against them, my own blind sense of what was right: we had come full circle from the day when One Eye had entrusted his life to me; and, if we were going to start over, it would have to be in the same way.

It was late in the day when I set out. The light was failing when I came to the camp of the Cheyennes. Their lodges rose gray and dim among the cottonwoods; the smoke from their fires drifted off into the dusk.

I rode in slowly. I came first upon two children playing in the dirt. They must have thought that I was a brave returning from a day of hunting, for they paid no attention to me. They glanced up when I spoke; then, swiftly and soundlessly, they vanished into the shadows. Their dog lingered on to gnaw on a bone. At the strange scent of my horse, he gripped the bone and fled.

I came upon an old woman, raking the ashes of a smoldering fire. From under a ragged shawl, she looked up at me. She recognized me; she raised her chin, like a dog, and cried out in a high, thin wail. The sound brought other women hurrying from their lodges; they saw me, and took up the cry. So I rode into the camp to the sound of keening; I had raised the dead.

I rode among the lodges; the cry cut into me. Young men turned swiftly from me, as if in search of weapons. Old men bowed their heads, as if the sight of me was more than they could bear. Some of them I knew. I pulled up my horse, and in the Cheyenne tongue, asked one old man where I might find his chief. He shook his head and would not speak to me.

I halted in the center of the village, on open ground. I thought: if you want to shoot, then *now*.

There was no sound, save the cry of grief echoing among the cottonwoods. I rode on and came to a lodge, off by itself. At its entrance, Black Kettle stood, waiting.

We did not shake hands. He turned as I dismounted and led the way into his lodge. He said nothing, but he saw the weariness in my face. He dipped a tin cup into a jug of spring water. He handed it to me, and watched me as I drank.

I had, long since, prepared my opening lines; I knew them by heart. I spoke each phrase and waited; he did not answer. Soon I had said all that I had to say about the Commissioners. We sat in silence.

"We are to trust you," he said at last.

I nodded.

"We trusted you before," he said. "Do you trust us? You come with soldiers."

"Not enough," I said; "not enough to fight."

"That is true," he said.

For the first time, I felt able to look at him. I saw that he was no longer wearing his necklace of eagle bones, and that his gray braids were shorn. I remembered Beckwourth's story: that Black Kettle had hacked off his hair after Sand Creek and thrown away all his medals and marks of bravery. He had humiliated himself before the Council of the Cheyennes, begging to be sent off with the young boys, so that he might learn again the meaning of manhood.

Still, he was well. Stupidly I said: "You're alive then."

He nodded.

"They claimed they had killed you."

He shook his head. "Not yet."

"But your wife?"

"She was shot; many times. . . . I found her in the creek," he added. "I carried her away."

"And One Eye?"

"He is at Sand Creek."

"And your brother, White Antelope?"

"He was the first to die. He would not fight."

"Soule also," I said. "He refused to fight, and later, because he testified . . . because he . . ." I gave up, realizing that I could not convey to him all that had happened.

". . . They killed him," I said.

Black Kettle looked at me steadily, with his grave, sad air. After a time he asked: "Is it true?"

"What?"

"What Beckwourth said. Is it true that you did not know?"

"I knew nothing," I said. "And, like a fool, I suspected nothing; nothing at all."

"I believed it," he said. "I did not want to believe it at first, when we had to revenge our dead. I could not speak of it then. Still I believed it. And after Beckwourth came to us I spoke of it in our Council. I told them: 'Not all are guilty.'

"The Sioux called me a coward," he said. "Our young men mutter against me. They say our ancestors would curse me.

"They will, if I am wrong again in trusting," he added. Half to himself he said: "What if I am wrong?"

30

The Council met beneath the cottonwoods. There were handshakes, and embraces in the Indian style. The Commissioners took their places on folding chairs; the chiefs, in a crescent, faced them, some sitting on logs, some on old robes laid on the sandy ground. The recorder wrote at a table placed in the center. John Smith, the interpreter for the meeting, stood at his side.

The peace pipe moved without haste, for Bent and Carson were masters of all ceremony. Then Sanborn rose and made his opening speech. He spoke quietly; he paused after each phrase so that Smith might translate. The chiefs nodded, and the long shafts of sunlight moved slowly across the scene.

"I greet you in the name of the President of the United States," Sanborn said. "He is filled with sorrow. He has heard that you were attacked by his soldiers while you were at peace with him. He has heard that you suffered great loss of life and property, and that you were forced to make war.

"All this grieves the President and his people.

"We have become a great people. We have vanquished our enemies and restored our Union. Our people are as numerous as the stars. We feel disgraced and ashamed, when we see our officers and our soldiers oppressing those who are weak, and making war on those who want peace.

"The President believes that a great wrong was done. He has sent us to make reparation, and to establish the terms by which we can live in peace.

"We are willing to restore all of the property lost at Sand Creek, or its value.

"So heartily do we repudiate the actions of our soldiers that we are willing to give to the chiefs, in their own right, 320 acres apiece, to hold forever, and to each of their children and squaws we will give 160 acres for their own.

"We will pay all monies and annuities that are due.

"We will recognize Black Kettle as chief of the Cheyennes. And we will support him and protect him in everything that he does for the nation.

"We ask him only to take his people away from the lines of travel, so that we may avoid fighting. We ask him to go south of the Arkansas, or north of the North Platte. If he will do that, we will protect and help him and his people, for as long as they live in peace."

Sanborn turned and took, from one of his secretaries, a copy, handsomely bound, of the transcript of our Inquiry. He held it out to Black Kettle. "I give you this book," he said. "When it is read to you, you will see that there are men among the whites who keep the faith and who tell the truth."

Black Kettle accepted the volume. "I take it, crying," he said.

The two men returned to their places. The first Indian to speak was Little Raven, chief of the Arapahoes.

"It will be hard for us," he said, "to leave the country of our ancestors on the Arkansas. It will be hard to live. There are no buffalo south of the river, or north of the Platte. Still, I and my people will try to settle. We will try to grow corn, and cultivate the land.

"I am a warrior," he said. "I have lived by hunting. It will be hard for me to change. Perhaps my children will change. We will need time, and help."

"We will give you time," Sanborn answered. "And we will give you all the help we can."

Little Raven nodded. "Also," he said, "we will need friends among the whites; honest men."

"We are all your friends."

Little Raven shook his head. "We need them close by us, as our Agents. We have been cheated by our Agents."

At that, Thomas Murphy, the Superintendent of Indian

Affairs for Kansas, jumped up. "Who cheated you?" he shouted. "Name them! Name just one of them!" He looked around for support. "By God, he'd better name them," he muttered. "I'm sick of these insinuations!"

Little Raven did not raise his voice. "There have been many Agents," he said. "There was only one who was honest—Major Fitzpatrick—and he is dead. Give us a good man, and an honest man, as Agent," Little Raven said. "We will need him in the winter, when our young men will be hungry, and when the whites will trouble us. Give us one such as Major Wynkoop."

There were many more speeches that day and on the following day. Black Kettle, as always, waited until the end.

He rose and went to the Commissioners. He shook hands with each of them in turn.

"Is it true that you come for peace?" he asked. "I believe it is true. Once before I believed it. I was mistaken, and my people died. Now that we are together again my shame is as great as the earth.

"Many wrongs have been done; I try to forget them. I live on hopes. I call our young braves into my lodge. I tell them to live on hope as I do. They listen to me now, but they will not listen for long.

"We have lost our way. We need one who can teach us, and protect us, so that we will not be blamed when others do wrong. Give us one such as Colonel Bent was, when he was young; one such as Major Wynkoop. He does not cheat us; he speaks the truth."

The conference ended on the afternoon of the second day. The Commissioners produced, and signed, a treaty of lasting peace. The chiefs listened as Smith read it to them. Then, one by one, they took their places at the recorder's table, gripped the quill pen, and made their marks. Within an hour, the supply wagons were driven into the camp, and sacks of coffee, flour, and bacon were handed out to the Indians. For the first time in a year, they had enough to eat.

Early the next day, we started back to Larned. Everyone felt that we were, once again, within reach of peace.

We moved slowly up the river; the news that a treaty had been signed had traveled ahead of us. As we came to the fort, I saw two of Dr. Taylor's men loading barrels of whiskey onto a wagon, to trade with the Cheyennes.

That night, when my work was over, I went to the sutler's store for a drink. It was crowded as always; contractors and officers leaned across the bar; a gang of railway workers were gathered around a girl whom Taylor had bought from the Indians and then sold, into another kind of slavery. A few Indians were there, the broken-down Agency Indians that Taylor kept on his post.

I wedged my way to the bar, at a point as far as possible from Taylor and his friends. As I waited for a whiskey, someone called my name. I turned and saw General Sanborn, drinking by himself at a corner table. He beckoned to me.

"Sit down, Wynkoop," he said. "I've been wanting to talk to you."

I took my place beside him. Close by, on a bench, an old Indian gripped a glass. He had been a hunter in his day; a necklace of bear claws still hung on his neck. Now he was a beggar, a squalid ruin. He raised his head for a moment; he looked at me sightlessly. He opened his mouth in an effort to speak; he dribbled. His head slumped onto his chest.

"Wynkoop," Sanborn began, "I've been writing my report for the War Department. I think it will interest you.

"I'm going to say," he continued, "that the conference was a notable step forward for the United States. And that the principal credit belongs to you."

I thanked him. I shifted my position, for the old man had sunk until his bare feet were resting on my cavalry boots. Next to him, I saw an Indian woman, stupefied with raw liquor. Her eyes were closed; her mouth was agape. A baby writhed in her arms. It clutched at her dress of sackcloth, and bared a dry breast. It tugged upon it, and drew no nourishment.

"You know, Wynkoop," Sanborn said, "you are regarded as a comer in the Department. General Curtis may have had some reservations about you, but he's out now. General Dodge thinks highly of you. So does General Pope. And they're not the only ones. You may not know it, but you made a great impression upon Senator Doolittle. He swears by you. When he went back to Washington, he spoke to the President and to General Grant about you. . . ." He broke off, sensing that I was not listening. "Perhaps you already know all this?" he said.

"No, sir, I don't." I was watching the woman; she had slid halfway to the floor.

"Well, then," Sanborn said, "Senator Doolittle went so far as to propose you for a colonelcy in the Regular Army. A full colonelcy, Wynkoop! The President was receptive. So were Grant and Sherman. The Department is waiting on my report."

He gripped my arm. "I have been watching you, Wynkoop," he said, "and I like you. I am going to recommend that you be made a colonel."

The woman was flat on the floor—insensible of the crowd around her. The baby, dislodged by her fall, crawled over her, and made its way back to her breast.

"You understand, Wynkoop," Sanborn said, "I'm speaking of the Regular Army, not of the volunteers. The appointment of a colonel in the Regular Army is an event of national importance, particularly in the West. You'll have a regiment, a major post. And remember this: there are only a few generals left. Most of them are looking forward to retirement, Wynkoop; in no time, you'll be moving up to general rank.

"Do you hear me, Wynkoop?" he asked. "You seem to be far away."

He was right. I was thinking of Louisa, living in our crowded quarters at Lyon with our boy and our baby. I was wondering how I would explain to her what I had to do.

31

I stretched out in a chair while she worked at the sink. "Louisa," I began, "I've been thinking . . ."

She laid down the dish that she was drying and waited.

". . . I've been thinking that we've stayed on long enough at Lyon."

She came to the doorway of our sitting room, still holding a dishcloth. She looked intently at me.

"You've been offered a new post," she said.

I denied it, but I couldn't help grinning, flattered as I was by all that General Sanborn had said.

Eagerly she came toward me. "You've been promised a

promotion! You've been recognized, at last!" She stood close by me, ready to rejoice, and fearful lest she be disappointed once again.

"It's true," I admitted. "Doolittle put me up for a colonelcy and General Sanborn is backing me."

"It will come through soon then? . . . We'll be moving out at last!" she went on, when I failed to answer. "But not to Denver?"

"No, never again to Denver."

"To St. Louis then." She turned to a small mirror that hung on the wall. She brushed a strand of hair back from her face. Shy, and pleased, she glanced at me. "I'll have to buy new clothes if we're going to be stationed in St. Louis. I'll have to learn all the new steps, before we go dancing."

"We won't be going to St. Louis."

"To Leavenworth then . . . To Omaha? . . . Where then?"

"To Larned."

"But—Larned's no bigger than Lyon! Why, if you're going to be a colonel, would they send you . . . ?"

"I'm not going to be a colonel."

"But—you said that General Sanborn . . ."

"I said that he offered me a colonelcy. I'm not going to take it."

She stood, crushed. I was angry with myself for hurting her, and angry with her, for being hurt.

"I'm not going to take it!" I cried.

"I thought you—why would we go to Larned then, when the regiment is stationed . . . ?"

"I'm leaving the regiment. I'm resigning from the Army."

"Resigning?" She was lost, and forlorn. "You said we were going to Larned. . . ."

"To take Taylor's place, after he's thrown out. And I'll get him thrown out, before he ruins every chance of peace with his crooked, drunken . . ."

"He means well; he . . ." She stopped short. "You're going to be an Indian Agent? After all you said about . . ."

"Yes, after all I said!"

"But Agents are despised by everyone; they . . ."

"I know that!"

"They get almost no pay!"

"I know that too!"

"They live on what they steal from the Indians. But, you won't steal."

"No, I won't."

"Then, why would you give up all you have for . . . ?"

"Why? Because of Soule. And Pierce. Because of One Eye, and White Antelope, and all the Indians who were killed because they trusted me—can't you see that?"

"I can see that we're . . ."

"I started it all, and I have to finish it. They need me, and there's no one else."

"What about your family? Doesn't your family need you?"

"You'll have a home; you'll get as much as most wives get. . . . What else do you expect," I went on, "when the . . ."

"What else! We need money, to feed the children, and to clothe them! They haven't any warm clothes!"

"Is that my fault?"

"Don't you see how your own children are dressed? Don't you care for your own son?"

"Of course I care for him! I . . ."

"He doesn't know what it means to be with other children! He's never had a home."

"I'm a soldier! I've been . . ."

"You're a father, with two children who . . ."

"Did I want them? Did I say: 'Let's have . . .'?"

I broke off; roused by my shouts, Frank was standing in the doorway, still dazed and half asleep. She gathered him up and laid him back in his bed. She stayed with him, whispering to him. By the time she came back, my anger had passed and I was sorry.

"I didn't mean to wake him."

"He's asleep again."

"If I'd known he was awake, I wouldn't have said what I did."

"He didn't hear."

There was no rancor in her voice; no resentment; only a sadness that drew me to her.

"I didn't mean what I said."

"I know you didn't."

"I wanted our children; at least, I was glad when they came."

"I know."

"I've been a poor father, and a worse husband. . . ."

"I never said that!"

"I've been away most of the time."

"You had no choice."

"That's true. And I have none. It's not that I don't think of you and the children. But I . . ."

"I know. You have to go to Larned. And where you go, we go."

"Louisa . . ." Words welled up in me, suddenly, that I had never spoken before; never felt. I blurted out that I loved her, because she had come to me when I needed her, and stayed with me; because she had given everything and taken nothing; because she had never tried to make me over; because she had never demanded more of me than I could give. I stumbled to a halt, and she said nothing. An hour later I remembered Soule's prophecy at the wedding and I smiled. But at the time we were not smiling. We could not speak; we clung to each other.

PART FIVE

32

I am at Larned now, as Agent for the Arapahoes and Cheyennes. I have been here, with my family, for almost three years. I think we will not be here much longer.

It's not that we want to leave. We have a house on the post; we have enough to live on—when I am paid.

The climate, of course, is harsh. The baby spits up sour milk in the heat of the summer; for the winter, both of our children lack warm clothes. Still, they are content, playing in the dirt outside my door. The air is damp here as it was at Lyon; but I gather enough driftwood from the river to keep our rooms dry. They are small rooms, but well kept, by Louisa. Her own lace collars and cuffs are frayed now, her cheeks are hollow. But she has never complained.

If we leave Larned, it will not be because of Louisa. And it will not be because I choose to desert my post. I may be accused of desertion—no voice will be louder than that of my own conscience, from now on. But if I leave it will be because I have no choice; I have done all that I can do.

The control of my territory has passed back to the Army. And what influence I once had with the Army is gone. To the military, all civilians are suspect if they work for the Department of the Interior. I am no exception to that rule. General Hancock, the new military commander, dismisses me as a special pleader for the Indians. General Grant, I understand, has come around to Hancock's view. Even General Sherman believes that I have carried charity too far. As for George Armstrong Custer—he declared recently that I was a plunderer, enriching myself at the taxpayers' expense. I read the story in a newspaper in the house next to ours—I went there to borrow a can of coffee.

I have no right to expect the Army to defer to me. I would stay on if my own Department would give me support. But Murphy is against me now, for his own reasons. And Secretary Harlan, who might listen to me, is beyond my reach.

My friends out here who helped me once are scattered now; or else they are dead. Cramer is in California, I believe; John Smith is somewhere north of the Platte. Bent is on his deathbed. Carson is dead; the news of his death reached us from Santa Fe a few weeks ago. And Jim Beckwourth is dead. He went with Carrington and the Eighteenth Infantry to the Big Horns, to guard the Bozeman Road. And Carrington sent him out to pacify the Crows. They welcomed him back; they begged him to be their chief again, but Jim refused. So they held a feast in his honor, and stuffed him full of his favorite dish—dog meat. It was poisoned of course—the Crows had concluded that, if they could not have Jim alive, they could, at least, guard his bones.

There are no men here like Beckwourth to whom I can turn. I would stay on nonetheless, if I could talk to the Indians. But even Black Kettle has moved beyond my reach. The sad truth is, I have lost touch with the people I am supposed to protect.

For a time, after we returned from the Little Arkansas, I had great hopes for peace. The treaty that we concluded was ratified by the Senate—after a delay, to be sure, and with many amendments. I was appointed by the President to take it to the Indians for their final approval. And they approved it. One young chief swore that he would kill me rather than make his mark upon my paper. I respected his stand, for the treaty required the Indians to surrender their historic hunting grounds along the Smoky Hill. But I stood fast—I had to. When the young chief's turn came, he could not bring himself to kill me; he signed the treaty with the rest.

The renegade Indians gave us trouble of course. So did the renegade whites. Dr. Taylor, for one, hung on to the Agency at Larned, trading whiskey that made killers of the Indians, for the buffaloes that were their clothing, their shelter, and their food.

It took a full year for the Secretary of the Interior to catch up with Taylor; then he resigned to avoid a term in prison. In due course, a handsome scroll arrived from Washington: Andrew Johnson, President of the United States, sent greetings, and wished it to be known that, reposing special trust and confidence in the integrity, ability, and discretion of Edward Wanshear Wynkoop, he was appointing me Agent for the Indians of the upper Arkansas.

I did all I could to justify the President's confidence; I soon found that Taylor was not alone in betraying the President's trust. The Senate might declare that the Indians were to be clothed and fed, in return for taking their lands; the House of Representatives might vote the necessary funds. But from then on, the supplies of bacon and coffee and flour dwindled, as each official took his share from the train, on its long journey from Washington to Larned.

Had we delivered to the Indians the reparations and annuities that were promised to them, we could have held their allegiance, and started them on the road towards a settled life. Or, if we had promised them nothing, they would have tried to provide for themselves. We promised them help, and, since they believed in our promises, they gave up hunting. They waited for supplies that failed to come.

Each winter has been worse than the last, for the buffalo

are vanishing. The Indians have had to steal cattle or else starve.

The young braves chose to steal. The ranchers, of course, raised a howl; the government gave in. It set aside its plans to provide for the Indians of the Arkansas Agency. It turned over the territory to young generals, fresh from victory over the Confederacy. They are not treacherous, fanatical men, like Chivington. They are impatient, self-confident men who know nothing but war.

In the spring of 1867, when the cattle were stolen, I rode out to meet Black Kettle. I told him that the thieves would have to be delivered up to me, for punishment. He had already placed his life in jeopardy by seeking to restrain his warriors. Yet he promised to do as I asked.

He needed time; Hancock and Custer would not wait. They rode into my territory with their troops; they required me to go along with them, so that the Indians might learn that white men stand together.

I went along. I was able to see that no one was killed, but I could not prevent the generals from burning Black Kettle's village. So the fear of another Sand Creek was revived among the Indians, and their destitution was deepened. When I rode out in January to visit them, I found them close to starvation.

I tried to secure the annuities that were owed to the Indians. The Army, of course, opposed me; so did Murphy and his friends; they won.

The result was predictable: two months ago, in August, a band of young warriors broke loose from Black Kettle's control. They burned ranches along the Saline and Solomon rivers; they killed ten white settlers.

I set out from Larned an hour after I heard the news. I knew that I had only a short time.

I crossed the Arkansas and rode southwest. All the country around me, to the farthest horizon, was deserted. I saw no buffalo, no horsemen; no smoke rising; nothing but the grass and the sky.

On the third day out, I came to the camp site where I had last met Black Kettle. Nothing was left there, save the black ashes of a few dead fires.

The Indians had broken camp and fled. The trail led south, away from any white settlement or road.

For the rest of that day I followed the trail. There's a faint chance, I told myself, that Black Kettle will expect me to follow him, and that he will leave scouts, to watch for me. I looked ahead, as far as I could, in the fading light. I saw nothing but the tracks beneath me: the hoofprints of the ponies; the marks of the moccasins; the lines of the travois, scraping over the bare earth. The trail led on toward the southwest; then it broke up into many trails. They would converge, I guessed, on the banks of the Washita River, a hundred miles on. I could not ride that far alone.

So I am leaving Larned. I cannot bring in the guilty Indians; I will not stand by here while Custer rides out to punish the innocent. I have written out my letter of resignation; I shall send it to Washington by tomorrow's coach. We shall be gone by the time the answer comes.

Where we shall go, and what I shall do, I do not know.

We could go on West, to Santa Fe; but Carson will not be there to welcome us. We could go home to Pennsylvania, but that would be an admission of lasting defeat. Tappan wants me to tour the States with him, speaking on justice for the Indians. But I am no orator. I am not certain any longer where justice lies. I am not certain of anything, save my own uncertainty.

For some time now, I have known that I could not stay on here. I should, I suppose, have spent my evenings canvassing the country for another job. Instead, I have been writing.

It was Tappan who persuaded me to write this story. He came through Larned three months ago, on his way to a conference with the Sioux. He brought with him a copy of the transcript of our Inquiry which had been published by a Senate committee. He looked on as I glanced over the testimony, taken at so great a cost.

"We can be proud of it, Ned," he said, "but it's not the whole story."

He drew a pencil from his pocket and handed it to me. "Soule was our first witness," he said. "You should be the last. For you alone know the whole story, from beginning to end."

So I have written out these pages. I have set down each day's events as I remember them. It is on the larger questions that I am unsure.

We were threatened by Chivington—I am certain of that. The threat was overcome because a brave man held his own life cheap.

Thanks to Soule, the plains will not be fashioned in Chivington's image. But, have we laid the foundations of a decent civilization here, in the West? The test of a civilization, so Tappan says, lies in its treatment of the less civilized. By that standard, we have failed.

Was our failure certain, from the start? I was mistaken, I know, in persuading the Indians that they could place their trust in us. And I was mistaken later on, in thinking that we would honor the commitments that we made.

Would it have been better for both sides if we had hoped for nothing and attempted nothing? Would it have been better, for the Cheyennes and for us, if I had never stirred from my sleep on that September afternoon when the trooper came knocking on my door?

Last night I worked late, to finish up these pages. When I lay down in the darkness, at Louisa's side, I could not sleep. Many questions gathered around me, and demanded answers. I had none.

I am thirty-two, I thought; I still have time. But what am I to do?

> *Failing to fetch me at first, keep encouraged.*
> *Missing me one place, search another.*

I remembered those lines from Soule's volume. And the last line: *I stop somewhere, waiting for you.*

Where, I wondered, where?

Except the Lord of hosts had left unto us a very small remnant, we should have been as Sodom, and we should have been like unto Gomorrah.

Isaiah 1:10

7 - wants to "finish dying"
8 - forgot Mother, son, lover
here's the beginning (= end); R
0 - all people look alike;
2 men encounter image
2 - overtaken by (whose?) anxiety? *
14 - "the less I think of it, the more..."
6 - being alone; silence *
alive b/c hat still exists
9-19 - A + C image
20 - tooting the horn; pluperfect
21 - becoming your parents
22 - four knocks for $
24 - knowing where you're going
25 - "being ingenious" = crutches/bike
- 33 - arrested by policeman
28 - can't bear violence
29 - remembers name is Molloy
30 - charity
33 - only thinks on life b/c dying
34 - easy to speak in present tense
35 - didn't do in end what wanted in begin.
39 - facts, mathematics + knowl.
40 - never left town, doesn't know name
41 - nameless things, thingless names
47 - tesitudes; tense of language
48 - we are not free?
42-80 - story of Lousse
52 - Molloy's studies; tried everything
55 - what counts is to be done
65 - forgot who he was + that he was
72 - nothing to be done
74 - eudemonism
76 - Molloy's 1st sex w/ Ruth/Edith
75-79 - story of
80 - study got him nowhere (stars)
82 - suicide attempt?
84 - returns to his "project"
86 - the peace of the "incurious seeker"
87 - loses interest in his project
91 - ideas about death
92 - "blackening pages" w/ story of seaside
92-100 - stone-sucking
104 - other leg starts to hurt
106 - thought of suicide vs. nausea
107 - thoughts on the human anus
109 - how did he live this long?
113 - Molloy kills someone
118 - purpose in life meaningless
121 - horn growing fainter
122-124 - Molloy crawls forest → ditch

125 - calm, but M. still sleepless
M. + son = reflection
126 - anti-church atti...
- 127 - 137 ← 176 -
127 - last moments of peace...
129 - M. fated for Molloy case
130 - cycle of M.'s parenting
134 - grasps Molloy affair → confuse
should he take autocycle
139 - unchanged by communion
141 - M. bad teeth ... Molloy? *
142 - M. not worthy of son;
143 - present/past tense
144 - M. hates dogs, men, god
145 - gets messages from unknown
146 - only ones - Anti-Kant?
150 - if he's a good parent
151 - seeking phenomena meaning
152-3 - M invented Molloy?
156 - M contrived
157 - 5 Molloys
159 - all language an excess of
166 - universe made of silence
180 - voice in M.'s head
183 - Molloy North of M
187 - what is M. looking for?
189-192 - M.'s leg goes bad
202 - growing accustomed to leg
205-208 - M. kills somebody
212 - reflection on himself
213-216 - bicycles into Bally
216 - intention/desire dead
219-21 - son abandons M.
222 - hoping to find/befriend Molloy
223-226 - Gaber - real? or not
227 - cleverer than things, God
228-229 - theological musings
233 - first hears the voice *
234 - Molloyish shirt wearing
237 - Q. of what am I doing ← Molloy

molloy

Works by Samuel Beckett published by Grove Press

Collected Poems in English and French

Collected Shorter Plays
(All That Fall, Act Without Words I, Act Without Words II, Krapp's Last Tape, Rough for Theatre I, Rough For Theatre II, Embers, Rough for Radio I, Rough for Radio II, Words and Music, Cascando, Play, Film, The Old Tune, Come and Go, Eh Joe, Breath, Not I, That Time, Footfalls, Ghost Trio, . . . but the clouds . . . , A Piece of Monologue, Rockaby, Ohio Impromptu, Quad, Catastrophe, Nacht and Träume, What Where)

Complete Short Prose: 1929–1989
(Assumption, Sedendo et Quiescendo, Text, A Case in a Thousand, First Love, The Expelled, The Calmative, The End, Texts for Nothing 1–13, From an Abandoned Work, The Image, All Strange Away, Imagination Dead Imagine, Enough, Ping, Lessness, The Lost Ones, Fizzles 1–8, Heard in the Dark 1, Heard in the Dark 2, One Evening, As the story was told, The Cliff, neither, Stirrings Still, Variations on a "Still" Point, *Faux Départs*, The Capital of the Ruins)

Disjecta:
Miscellaneous Writings and a Dramatic Fragment

Endgame and Act Without Words

Happy Days

How It Is

I Can't Go On, I'll Go On:
A Samuel Beckett Reader

Krapp's Last Tape (All That Fall, Embers, Act Without Words I, Act Without Words II)

Mercier and Camier

Molloy

More Pricks than Kicks
(Dante and the Lobster, Fingal, Ding-Dong, A Wet Night, Love and Lethe, Walking Out, What a Misfortune, The Smeraldina's Billet Doux, Yellow, Draff)

Murphy

Nohow On (Company, Ill Seen Ill Said, Worstward Ho)

Proust

Stories and Texts for Nothing
(The Expelled, The Calmative, The End, Texts for Nothing 1–13)

Three Novels (Molloy, Malone Dies, The Unnamable)

Waiting For Godot

Watt

Happy Days:
Production Notebooks

Waiting for Godot:
Theatrical Notebooks

SAMUEL BECKETT

MOLLOY

a novel

translated from the French
by Patrick Bowles
in collaboration with the Author

GROVE PRESS
NEW YORK

Published simultaneously in Canada
Printed in the United States of America

Library of Congress Catalog Card Number: 55-5113

ISBN-13: 978-0-8021-5136-0

Grove Press
an imprint of Grove/Atlantic, Inc.
841 Broadway
New York, NY 10003

Distributed by Publishers Group West

www.groveatlantic.com

10 11 12 13 14 18 17 16 15 14 13 12

molloy

I

I am in my mother's room. It's I who live there now. I don't know how I got there. Perhaps in an ambulance, certainly a vehicle of some kind. I was helped. I'd never have got there alone. There's this man who comes every week. Perhaps I got here thanks to him. He says not. He gives me money and takes away the pages. So many pages, so much money. Yes, I work now, a little like I used to, except that I don't know how to work any more. That doesn't matter apparently. What I'd like now is to speak of the things that are left, say my good-byes, finish dying. They don't want that. Yes, there is more than one, apparently. But it's always the same one that comes. You'll do that later, he says. Good. The truth is I haven't much will left. When he comes for the fresh pages he brings back the previous week's. They are marked with signs I don't understand. Anyway I don't read them. When I've done nothing he gives me nothing, he scolds me. Yet I don't work for money. For what then? I don't know. The truth is I don't know much. For example my mother's death. Was she already dead when I came? Or did she only die later? I mean enough to bury. I don't know. Perhaps they haven't buried her yet. In any case I have her room. I sleep in her bed. I piss and shit in her pot. I have taken her place. I must resemble her more and more. All I need now is a son. Perhaps I have one somewhere. But I think not. He would be old now, nearly as old as myself. It was a little chambermaid. It wasn't true love. The true love was in another. We'll come to that. Her name? I've forgotten it again. It seems to me sometimes that I even knew my son, that I helped him. Then I tell myself it's impossible. It's impossible I could ever have helped anyone. I've forgotten how to spell too, and half the words. That doesn't matter apparently. Good. He's a queer one the one who comes to see me. He comes every Sunday apparently. The other days he isn't free. He's always thirsty. It was he told me I'd begun all wrong, that I should have begun differently. He must be right. I began at the beginning, like an old ballocks, can you imagine that? Here's my beginning. Because they're keeping it apparently. I took a lot of trouble with it. Here it is. It gave me a lot of trouble. It was the beginning, do you understand? Whereas now it's nearly the end. Is what I do now any better? I don't know. That's beside the point. Here's my beginning. It must mean something, or they wouldn't keep it. Here it is.

This time, then once more I think, then perhaps a last time, then I think it'll be over, with that world too. Premonition of the last but one but one. All grows dim. A little more and you'll go blind. It's in the head. It doesn't work any more, it says, I don't work any more. You go dumb as well and sounds fade. The threshold scarcely crossed that's how it is. It's the head. It must have had enough. So that you say, I'll manage this time, then perhaps once more, then perhaps a last time, then nothing more. You are hard set to formulate this thought, for it is one, in a sense. Then you try to pay attention, to consider with attention all those dim things, saying to yourself, laboriously, It's my fault. Fault? That was the word. But what fault? It's not goodbye, and what magic in those dim things to which it will be time enough, when next they pass, to say goodbye. For you must say goodbye, it would be madness not to say goodbye, when the time comes. If you think of the forms and light of other days it is without regret. But you seldom think of them, with what would you think of them? I don't know. People pass too, hard to distinguish from yourself. That is discouraging. So I saw A and C going slowly towards each other, unconscious of what they were doing. It was on a road remarkably bare, I mean without hedges or ditches or any kind of edge, in the country, for cows were chewing in enormous fields, lying and standing, in the evening silence. Perhaps I'm inventing a little, perhaps embellishing, but on the whole that's the way it was. They chew, swallow, then after a short pause effortlessly bring up the next mouthful. A neck muscle stirs and the jaws begin to grind again. But perhaps I'm remembering things. The road, hard and white, seared the tender pastures, rose and fell at the whim of hills and hollows. The town was not far. It was two men, unmistakably, one small and one tall. They had left the town, first one, then the other, and then the first, weary or remembering a duty, had retraced his steps. The air was sharp for they wore greatcoats. They looked alike, but no more than others do. At first a wide space lay between them. They couldn't have seen each other, even had they raised their heads and looked about, because of this wide space, and then because of the undulating land, which caused the road to be in waves, not high, but high enough, high enough. But the moment came when together they went down into the same trough and in this trough finally met. To say they knew each other, no, nothing warrants it. But perhaps at the sound of their steps, or warned by some obscure instinct, they raised their heads and observed each other, for a good fifteen paces, before they stopped, breast to breast. Yes, they did not pass each other by, but halted, face to face, as in the country, of an evening, on a deserted road, two wayfaring strangers will, without there being anything extraordinary about it. But they knew each other perhaps. Now in any case they do, now I think they will know each other, greet each other, even in the depths of the town. They turned towards the sea which, far in the east, beyond the fields, loomed high in the waning sky, and exchanged a few words. Then each went on his way. Each went on his way, A back towards the town, C on by ways he seemed hardly to know, or not at all, for he went with uncertain step and often stopped to look about him, like someone trying to fix landmarks in his mind, for one day perhaps he may have to retrace his steps, you never know. The treacherous hills where fearfully he ventured were no doubt only known to him from afar, seen perhaps from his bedroom window or from the summit of a monument which, one black day, having nothing in particular to do and turning to height for solace, he had paid his few coppers to climb, slower and slower, up the winding stones. From there he must have seen it all, the plain, the sea, and then these selfsame hills that some call mountains, indigo in places in the evening light, their serried ranges crowding to the sky-line, cloven with hidden valleys that the eye divines from sudden shifts of colour and then from other signs for which there are no words, nor even thoughts. But all are not divined, even from that height, and often where only one escarpment is discerned, and one crest, in reality there are two, two escarpments, two crests, riven by a valley. But now he knows these hills, that is to say he knows them better, and if ever again he sees them from afar it will be I think with other eyes, and not only that but the within, all that inner space one never sees, the brain and heart and other caverns where thought and feeling dance their sabbath, all that too quite differently disposed. He looks old and it is a sorry sight to see him solitary after so many years, so many days and nights unthinkingly given to that rumour rising at birth and even earlier, What shall I do ? What shall I do? now low, a murmur, now precise as the headwaiter's And to follow? and often rising to a scream. And in the end, or almost, to be abroad alone, by unknown ways, in the gathering night, with a stick. It was a stout stick, he used it to thrust himself onward, or as a defence, when the time came, against dogs and marauders. Yes, night was gathering, but the man was innocent, greatly innocent, he had nothing to fear, though he went in fear, he had nothing to fear, there was nothing they could do to him, or very little. But he can't have known it. I wouldn't know it myself, if I thought about it. Yes, he saw himself threatened, his body threatened, his reason threatened, and perhaps he was, perhaps they were, in spite of his innocence. What business has innocence here? What relation to the innumerable spirits of darkness? It's not clear. It seemed to me he wore a cocked hat. I remember being struck by it, as I wouldn't have been for example by a cap or by a bowler. I watched him recede, overtaken (myself) by his anxiety, at least by an anxiety which was not necessarily his, but of which as it were he partook. Who knows if it wasn't my own anxiety overtaking him. He hadn't seen me. I was perched higher than the road's highest point and flattened what is more against a rock the same colour as myself, that is grey. The rock he probably saw. He gazed around as if to engrave the landmarks on his memory and must have seen the rock in the shadow of which I crouched like Belacqua, or Sordello, I forget. But a man, a fortiori myself, isn't exactly a landmark, because. I mean if by some strange chance he were to pass that way again, after a long lapse of time, vanquished, or to look for some lost thing, or to destroy something, his eyes would search out the rock, not the haphazard in its shadow of that unstable fugitive thing, still living flesh. No, he certainly didn't see me, for the reasons I've given and then because he was in no humour for that, that evening, no humour for the living, but rather for all that doesn't stir, or stirs so slowly that a child would scorn it, let alone an old man. However that may be, I mean whether he saw me or whether he didn't, I repeat I watched him recede, at grips (myself) with the temptation to get up and follow him, perhaps even to catch up with him one day, so as to know him better, be myself less lonely. But in spite of my soul's leap out to him, at the end of its elastic, I saw him only darkly, because of the dark and then because of the terrain, in the folds of which he disappeared from time to time, to re-emerge further on, but most of all I think because of other things calling me and towards which too one after the other my soul was straining, wildly. I mean of course the fields, whitening under the dew, and the animals, ceasing from wandering and settling for the night, and the sea, of which nothing, and the sharpening line of crests, and the sky where without seeing them I felt the first stars tremble, and my hand on my knee and above all the other wayfarer, A or C, I don't remember, going resignedly home. Yes, towards my hand also, which my knee felt tremble and of which my eyes saw the wrist only, the heavily veined back, the pallid rows of knuckles. But that is not, I mean my hand, what I wish to speak of now, everything in due course, but A or C returning to the town he had just left. But after all what was there particularly urban in his aspect? He was bare-headed, wore sand-shoes, smoked a cigar. He moved with a kind of loitering indolence which rightly or wrongly seemed to me expressive. But all that proved nothing, refuted nothing. Perhaps he had come from afar, from the other end of the island even, and was approaching the town for the first time or returning to it after a long absence. A little dog followed him, a pomeranien I think, but I don't think so. I wasn't sure at the time and I'm still not sure, though I've hardly thought about it. The little dog followed wretchedly, after the fashion of pomeranians, stopping, turning in slow circles, giving up and then, a little further on, beginning all over again. Constipation is a sign of good health in pomeranians. At a given moment, pre-established if you like, I don't much mind, the gentleman turned back, took the little creature in his arms, drew the cigar from his lips and buried his face in the orange fleece, for it was a gentleman, that was obvious. Yes, it was an orange pomeranian, the less I think of it the more certain I am. And yet. But would he have come from afar, bare-headed, in sand-shoes, smoking a cigar, followed by a pomeranian? Did, he not seem rather to have issued from the ramparts, after a good dinner, to take his dog and himself for a walk, like so many citizens, dreaming and farting, when the weather is fine? But was not perhaps in reality the cigar a cutty, and were not the sand-shoes boots, hobnailed, dust-whitened, and what prevented the dog from being one of those stray dogs that you pick up and take in your arms, from compassion or because you have long been straying with no other company than the endless roads, sands, shingle, bogs and heather, than this nature answerable to another court, than at long intervals the fellow-convict you long to stop, embrace, suck, suckle and whom you pass by, with hostile eyes, for fear of his familiarities? Until the day when, your endurance gone, in this world for you without arms, you catch up in yours the first mangy cur you meet, carry it the time needed for it to love you and you it, then throw it away. Perhaps he had come to that, in spite of appearances. He disappeared, his head on his chest, the smoking object in his hand. Let me try and explain. From things about to disappear I turn away in time. To watch them out of sight, no, I can't do it. It was in this sense he disappeared. Looking away I thought of him, saying, He is dwindling, dwindling. I knew what I meant. I knew I could catch him, lame as I was. I had only to want to. And yet no, for I did want to. To get up, to get down on the road, to set off hobbling in pursuit of him, to hail him, what could be easier? He hears my cries, turns, waits for me. I am up against him, up against the dog, gasping, between my crutches. He is a little frightened of me, a little sorry for me, I disgust him not a little. I am not a pretty sight, I don't smell good. What is it I want? Ah that tone I know, compounded of pity, of fear, of disgust. I want to see the dog, see the man, at close quarters, know what smokes, inspect the shoes, find out other things. He is kind, tells me of this and that and other things, whence he comes, whither he goes. I believe him, I know it's my only chance to — my only chance, I believe all I'm told, I've disbelieved only too much in my long life, now I swallow everything, greedily. What I need now is stories, it took me a long time to know that, and I'm not sure of it. There I am then, informed as to certain things, knowing certain things about him, things I didn't know, things I had craved to know, things I had never thought of. What rigmarole. I am even capable of having learnt what his profession is, I who am so interested in professions. And to think I try my best not to talk about myself. In a moment I shall talk about the cows, about the sky, if I can. There I am then, he leaves me, he's in a hurry. He didn't seem to be in a hurry, he was loitering, I've already said so, but after three minutes of me he is in a hurry, he has to hurry. I believe him. And once again I am I will not say alone, no, that's not like me, but, how shall I say, I don't know, restored to myself, no, I never left myself, free, yes, I don't know what that means but it's the word I mean to use, free to do what, to do nothing, to know, but what, the laws of the mind perhaps, of my mind, that for example water rises in proportion as it drowns you and that you would do better, at least no worse, to obliterate texts than to blacken margins, to fill in the holes of words till all is blank and flat and the whole ghastly business looks like what it is, senseless, speechless, issueless misery. So I doubtless did better, at least no worse, not to stir from my observation post. But instead of observing I had the weakness to return in spirit to the other, the man with the stick. Then the murmurs began again. To restore silence is the role of objects. I said, Who knows if he hasn't simply come out to take the air, relax, stretch his legs, cool his brain by stamping the blood down to his feet, so as to make sure of a good night, a joyous awakening, an enchanted morrow. Was he carrying so much as a scrip? But the way of walking, the anxious looks, the club, could these be reconciled with one's conception of what is called a little turn? But the hat, a town hat, an old-fashioned town hat, which the least gust would carry far away. Unless it was attached under the chin, by means of a string or an elastic. I took off my hat and looked at it. It is fastened, it has always been fastened, to my buttonhole, always the same buttonhole, at all seasons, by a long lace. I am still alive then. That may come in useful. The hand that held the hat I thrust as far as possible from me and moved in an arc, to and fro. As I did so, I watched the lapel of my greatcoat and saw it open and close. I understand now why I never wore a flower in my buttonhole, though it was large enough to hold a whole nosegay. My buttonhole was set aside for my hat. It was my hat that I beflowered. But it is neither of my hat nor of my greatcoat that I hope to speak at present, it would be premature. Doubtless I shall speak of them later, when the time comes to draw up the inventory of my goods and possessions. Unless I lose them between now and then. But even lost they will have their place, in the inventory of my possessions. But I am easy in my mind, I shall not lose them. Nor my crutches, I shall not lose my crutches either. But I shall perhaps one day throw them away. I must have been on the top, or on the slopes, of some considerable eminence, for otherwise how could I have seen, so far away, so near at hand, so far beneath, so many things, fixed and moving. But what was an eminence doing in this land with hardly a ripple? And I, what was I doing there, and why come? These are things that we shall try and discover. But these are things we must not take seriously. There is a little of everything, apparently, in nature, and freaks are common. And I am perhaps confusing several different occasions, and different times, deep down, and deep down is my dwelling, oh not deepest down, somewhere between the mud and the scum. And perhaps it was A one day at one place, then C another at another, then a third the rock and I, and so on for the other components, the cows, the sky, the sea, the mountains. I can't believe it. No, I will not lie, I can easily conceive it. No matter, no matter, let us go on, as if all arose from one and the same weariness, on and on heaping up and up, until there is no room, no light, for any more. What is certain is that the man with the stick did not pass by again that night, because I would have heard him, if he had. I don't say I would have seen him, I say I would have heard him. I sleep little and that little by day. Oh not systematically, in my life without end I have dabbled with every kind of sleep, but at the time now coming back to me I took my doze in the daytime and, what is more, in the morning. Let me hear nothing of the moon, in my night there is no moon, and if it happens that I speak of the stars it is by mistake. Now of all the noises that night not one was of those heavy uncertain steps, or of that club with which he sometimes smote the earth until it quaked. How agreeable it is to be confirmed, after a more or less long period of vacillation, in one's first impressions. Perhaps that is what tempers the pangs of death. Not that I was so conclusively, I mean confirmed, in my first impressions with regard to — wait — C. For the wagons and carts which a little before dawn went thundering by, on their way to market with fruit, eggs, butter and perhaps cheese, in one of these perhaps he would have been found, overcome by fatigue or discouragement, perhaps even dead. Or he might have gone back to the town by another way too far away for me to hear its sounds, or by little paths through the fields, crushing the silent grass, pounding the silent ground. And so at last I came out of that distant night, divided between the murmurs of my little world, its dutiful confusions, and those so different (so different?) of all that between two suns abides and passes away. Never once a human voice. But the cows, when the peasants passed, crying in vain to be milked. A and

C I never saw again. But perhaps I shall see them again. But shall I be able to recognise them? And am I sure I never saw them again? And what do I mean by seeing and seeing again? An instant of silence, as when the conductor taps on his stand, raises his arms, before the unanswerable clamour. Smoke, sticks, flesh, hair, at evening, afar, flung about the craving for a fellow. I know how to summon these rags to cover my shame. I wonder what that means. But I shall not always be in need. But talking of the craving for a fellow let me observe that having waked between eleven o'clock and midday (I heard the angelus, recalling the incarnation, shortly after) I resolved to go and see my mother. I needed, before I could resolve to go and see that woman, reasons of an urgent nature, and with such reasons, since I did not know what to do, or where to go, it was child's play for me, the play of an only child, to fill my mind until it was rid of all other preoccupation and I seized with a trembling at the mere idea of being hindered from going there, I mean to my mother, there and then. So I got up, adjusted my crutches and went down to the road, where I found my bicycle (I didn't know I had one) in the same place I must have left it. Which enables me to remark that, crippled though I was, I was no mean cyclist, at that period. This is how I went about it. I fastened my crutches to the cross-bar, one on either side, I propped the foot of my stiff leg (I forget which, now they're both stiff) on the projecting front axle, and I pedalled with the other. It was a chainless bicycle, with a free-wheel, if such a bicycle exists. Dear bicycle, I shall not call you bike, you were green, like so many of your generation, I don't know why. It is a pleasure to meet it again. To describe it at length would be a pleasure. It had a little red horn instead of the bell fashionable in your days. To blow this horn was for me a real pleasure, almost a vice. I will go further and declare that if I were obliged to record, in a roll of honour, those activities which in the course of my interminable existence have given me only a mild pain in the balls, the blowing of a rubber horn—toot!—would figure among the first. And when I had to part from my bicycle I took off the horn and kept it about me. I believe I have it still, somewhere, and if I blow it no more it is because it has gone dumb. Even motor-cars have no horns nowadays, as I understand the thing, or rarely. When I see one, through the lowered window of a stationary car, I often stop and blow it. This should all be re-written in the pluperfect. What a rest to speak of bicycles and horns. Unfortunately it is not of them I have to speak, but of her who brought me into the world, through the hole in her arse if my memory is correct. First taste of the shit. So I shall only add that every hundred yards or so I stopped to rest my legs, the good one as well as the bad, and not only my legs, not only my legs. I didn't properly speaking get down off the machine, I remained astride it, my feet on the ground, my arms on the handle-bars, my head on my arms, and I waited until I felt better. But before I leave this earthly paradise, suspended between the mountains and the sea, sheltered from certain winds and exposed to all that Auster vents, in the way of scents and langours, on this accursed country, it would ill become me not to mention the awful cries of the corncrakes that run in the corn, in the meadows, all the short summer night long, dinning their rattles.

And this enables me, what is more, to know when that unreal journey began, the second last but one of a form fading among fading forms, and which I here declare without further ado to have begun in the second or third week of June, at the moment that is to say most painful of all when over what is called our hemisphere the sun is at its pitilessmost and the arctic radiance comes pissing on our midnights. It is then the corncrakes are heard. My mother never refused to see me, that is she never refused to receive me, for it was many a long day since she had seen anything at all. I shall try and speak calmly. We were so old, she and I, she had had me so young, that we were like a couple of old cronies, sexless, unrelated, with the same memories, the same rancours, the same expectations. She never called me son, fortunately, I couldn't have borne it, but Dan, I don't know why, my name is not Dan. Dan was my father's name perhaps, yes, perhaps she took me for my father. I took her for my mother and she took me for my father. Dan, you remember the day I saved the swallow. Dan, you remember the day you buried the ring. I remembered, I remembered, I mean I knew more or less what she was talking about, and if I hadn't always taken part personally in the scenes she evoked, it was just as if I had. I called her Mag, when I had to call her something. And I called her Mag because for me, without my knowing why, the letter g abolished the syllable Ma, and as it were spat on it, better than any other letter would have done. And at the same time I satisfied a deep and doubtless unacknowledged need, the need to have a Ma, that is a mother, and to proclaim it, audibly. For before you say mag you say ma, inevitably. And da, in my part of the world, means father. Besides for me the question did not arise, at the period I'm worming into now, I mean the question of whether to call her Ma, Mag or the Countess Caca, she having for countless years been as deaf as a post. I think she was quite incontinent, both of faeces and water, but a kind of prudishness made us avoid the subject when we met, and I could never be certain of it. In any case it can't have amounted to much, a few niggardly wetted goat-droppings every two or three days. The room smelt of ammonia, oh not merely of ammonia, but of ammonia, ammonia. She knew it was me, by my smell. Her shrunken hairy old face lit up, she was happy to smell me. She jabbered away with a rattle of dentures and most of the time didn't realize what she was saying. Anyone but myself would have been lost in this clattering gabble, which can only have stopped during her brief instants of unconsciousness. In any case I didn't come to listen to her. I got into communication with her by knocking on her skull. One knock meant yes, two no, three I don't know, four money, five goodbye. I was hard put to ram this code into her ruined and frantic understanding, but I did it, in the end. That she should confuse yes, no, I don't know and goodbye, was all the same to me, I confused them myself. But that she should associate the four knocks with anything but money was something to be avoided at all costs. During the period of training therefore, at the same time as I administered the four knocks on her skull, I stuck a bank-note under her nose or in her mouth. In the innocence of my heart! For she seemed to have lost, if not absolutely all notion of mensuration, at least the faculty of counting beyond two. It was too far for her, yes, the distance was too great, from one to four. By the time she came to the fourth knock she imagined she was only at the second, the first two having been erased from her memory as completely as if they had never been felt, though I don't quite see how something never felt can be erased from the memory, and yet it is a common occurrence. She must have thought I was saying no to her all the time, whereas nothing was further from my purpose. Enlightened by these considerations I looked for and finally found a more effective means of putting the idea of money into her head. This consisted in replacing the four knocks of my index-knuckle by one or more (according to my needs) thumps of the fist, on her skull. That she understood. In any case I didn't come for money. I took her money, but I didn't come for that. My mother. I don't think too harshly of her. I know she did all she could not to have me, except of course the one thing, and if she never succeeded in getting me unstuck, it was that fate had earmarked me for less compassionate sewers. But it was well-meant and that's enough for me. No it is not enough for me, but I give her credit, though she is my mother, for what she tried to do for me. And I forgive her for having jostled me a little in the first months and spoiled the only endurable, just endurable, period of my enormous history. And I also give her credit for not having done it again, thanks to me, or for having stopped in time, when she did. And if ever I'm reduced to looking for a meaning to my life, you never can tell, it's in that old mess I'll stick my nose to begin with, the mess of that poor old uniparous whore and myself the last of my foul brood, neither man nor beast. I should add, before I get down to the facts, you'd swear they were facts, of that distant summer afternoon, that with this deaf blind impotent mad old woman, who called me Dan and whom I called Mag, and with her alone, I—no, I can't say it. That is to say I could say it but I won't say it, yes, I could say it easily, because it wouldn't be true. What did I see of her? A head always, the hands sometimes, the arms rarely. A head always. Veiled with hair, wrinkles, filth, slobber. A head that darkened the air. Not that seeing matters, but it's something to go on with. It was I who took the key from under the pillow, who took the money out of the drawer, who put the key back under the pillow. But I didn't come for money. I think there was a woman who came each week. Once I touched with my lips, vaguely, hastily, that little grey wizened pear. Pah. Did that please her? I don't know. Her babble stopped for a second, then began again. Perhaps she said to herself, Pah. I smelt a terrible smell. It must have come from the bowels. Odour of antiquity. Oh I'm not criticizing her, I don't diffuse the perfumes of Araby myself. Shall I describe the room? No. I shall have occasion to do so later perhaps. When I seek refuge there, bet to the world, all shame drunk, my prick in my rectum, who knows. Good. Now that we know where we're going, let's go there. It's so nice to know where you're going, in the early stages. It almost rids you of the wish to go there. I was distraught, who am so seldom distraught, from what should I be distraught, and as to my motions even more uncertain than usual. The night must have tired me, at least weakened me, and the sun, hoisting itself higher and higher in the east, had poisoned me, while I slept.

I ought to have put the bulk of the rock between it and me before closing my eyes. I confuse east and west, the poles too, I invert them readily. I was out of sorts. They are deep, my sorts, a deep ditch, and I am not often out of them. That's why I mention it. Nevertheless I covered several miles and found myself under the ramparts. There I dismounted in compliance with the regulations. Yes, cyclists entering and leaving town are required by the police to dismount, cars to go into bottom gear and horsedrawn vehicles to slow down to a walk. The reason for this regulation is I think this, that the ways into and of course out of this town are narrow and darkened by enormous vaults, without exception. It is a good rule and I observe it religiously, in spite of the difficulty I have in advancing on my crutches pushing my bicycle at the same time. I managed somehow. Being ingenious. Thus we cleared these difficult straits, my bicycle and I, together. But a little further on I heard myself hailed. I raised my head and saw a policeman. Elliptically speaking, for it was only later, by way of induction, or deduction, I forget which, that I knew what it was. What are you doing there? he said. I'm used to that question, I understood it immediately. Resting, I said. Resting, he said. Resting, I said. Will you answer my question? he cried. So it always is when I'm reduced to confabulation, I honestly believe I have answered the question I am asked and in reality I do nothing of the kind. I won't reconstruct the conversation in all its meanderings. It ended in my understanding that my way of resting, my attitude when at rest, astride my bicycle, my arms on the handlebars, my head on my arms, was a violation of I don't know what, public order, public decency. Modestly I pointed to my crutches and ventured one or two noises regarding my infirmity, which obliged me to rest as I could, rather than as I should. But there are not two laws, that was the next thing I thought I understood, not two laws, one for the healthy, another for the sick, but one only to which all must bow, rich and poor, young and old, happy and sad. He was eloquent. I pointed out that I was not sad. That was a mistake. Your papers, he said, I knew it a moment later. Not at all, I said, not at all. Your papers! he cried. Ah my papers. Now the only papers I carry with me are bits of newspaper, to wipe myself, you understand, when I have a stool. Oh I don't say I wipe myself every time I have a stool, no, but I like to be in a position to do so, if I have to. Nothing strange about that, it seems to me. In a panic I took this paper from my pocket and thrust it under his nose. The weather was fine. We took the little side streets, quiet, sunlit, I springing along between my crutches, he pushing my bicycle, with the tips of his white-gloved fingers. I wasn't—I didn't feel unhappy. I stopped a moment, I made so bold, to lift my hand and touch the crown of my hat. It was scorching. I felt the faces turning to look after us, calm faces and joyful faces, faces of men, of women and of children. I seemed to hear, at a certain moment, a distant music. I stopped, the better to listen. Go on, he said. Listen, I said. Get on, he said. I wasn't allowed to listen to the music. It might have drawn a crowd. He gave me a shove. I had been touched, oh not my skin, but none the less my skin had felt it, it had felt a man's hard fist, through its coverings. While still putting my best foot foremost

I gave myself up to that golden moment, as if I had been someone else. It was the hour of rest, the forenoon's toil ended, the afternoon's to come. The wisest perhaps, lying in the squares or sitting on their doorsteps, were savouring its languid ending, forgetful of recent cares, indifferent to those at hand. Others on the contrary were using it to hatch their plans, their heads in their hands. Was there one among them to put himself in my place, to feel how removed I was then from him I seemed to be, and in that remove what strain, as of hawsers about to snap? It's possible. Yes, I was straining towards those spurious deeps, their lying promise of gravity and peace, from all my old poisons I struggled towards them, safely bound. Under the blue sky, under the watchful gaze. Forgetful of my mother, set free from the act, merged in this alien hour, saying, Respite, respite. At the police station I was haled before a very strange official. Dressed in plain-clothes, in his shirt-sleeves, he was sprawling in an arm-chair, his feet on his desk, a straw hat on his head and protruding from his mouth a thin flexible object I could not identify. I had time to become aware of these details before he dismissed me. He listened to his subordinate's report and then began to interrogate me in a tone which, from the point of view of civility, left increasingly to be desired, in my opinion. Between his questions and my answers, I mean those deserving of consideration, the intervals were more or less long and turbulent. I am so little used to being asked anything that when I am asked something I take some time to know what. And the mistake I make then is this, that instead of quietly reflecting on what I have just heard, and heard distinctly, not being hard of hearing, in spite of all I have heard, I hasten to answer blindly, fearing perhaps lest my silence fan their anger to fury. I am full of fear, I have gone in fear all my life, in fear of blows. Insults, abuse, these I can easily bear, but I could never get used to blows. It's strange. Even spits still pain me. But they have only to be a little gentle, I mean refrain from hitting me, and I seldom fail to give satisfaction, in the long run. Now the sergeant, content to threaten me with a cylindrical ruler, was little by little rewarded for his pains by the discovery that I had no papers in the sense this word had a sense for him, nor any occupation, nor any domicile, that my surname escaped me for the moment and that I was on my way to my mother, whose charity kept me dying. As to her address, I was in the dark, but knew how to get there, even in the dark. The district? By the shambles your honour, for from my mother's room, through the closed windows, I had heard, stilling her chatter, the bellowing of the cattle, that violent raucous tremulous bellowing not of the pastures but of the towns, their shambles and cattle-markets. Yes, after all, I had perhaps gone too far in saying that my mother lived near the shambles, it could equally well have been the cattle-market, near which she lived. Never mind, said the sergeant, it's the same district. I took advantage of the silence which followed these kind words to turn towards the window, blindly or nearly, for I had closed my eyes, proffering to that blandness of blue and gold my face and neck alone, and my mind empty too, or nearly, for I must have been wondering if I did not feel like sitting down, after such a long time standing, and remembering what I had learnt in that connexion, namely that the sitting posture was not for me any more, because of my short stiff leg, and that there were only two postures for me any more, the vertical, drooping between my crutches, sleeping on my feet, and the horizontal, down on the ground. And yet the desire to sit down came upon me from time to time, back upon me from a vanished world. And I did not always resist it, forewarned though I was. Yes, my mind felt it surely, this tiny sediment, incomprehensibly stirring like grit at the bottom of a puddle, while on my face and great big Adam's apple the air of summer weighed and the splendid summer sky. And suddenly I remembered my name, Molloy. My name is Molloy, I cried, all of a sudden, now I remember. Nothing compelled me to give this information, but I gave it, hoping to please I suppose. They let me keep my hat on, I don't know why. Is it your mother's name? said the sergeant, it must have been a sergeant. Molloy, I cried, my name is Molloy. Is that your mother's name? said the sergeant. What? I said. Your name is Molloy, said the sergeant. Yes, I said, now I remember. And your mother? said the sergeant. I didn't follow. Is your mother's name Molloy too? said the sergeant. I thought it over. Your mother, said the sergeant, is your mother's—Let me think! I cried. At least I imagine that's how it was. Take your time, said the sergeant. Was mother's name Molloy? Very likely. Her name must be Molloy too, I said. They took me away, to the guardroom I suppose, and there I was told to sit down. I must have tried to explain. I won't go into it. I obtained permission, if not to lie down on a bench, at least to remain standing, propped against the wall. The room was dark and full of people hastening to and fro, malefactors, policemen, lawyers, priests and journalists I suppose. All that made a dark, dark forms crowding in a dark place. They paid no attention to me and I repaid the compliment. Then how could I know they were paying no attention to me, and how could I repay the compliment, since they were paying no attention to me? I don't know. I knew it and I did it, that's all I know. But suddenly a woman rose up before me, a big fat woman dressed in black, or rather in mauve. I still wonder today if it wasn't the social worker. She was holding out to me, on an odd saucer, a mug full of a greyish concoction which must have been green tea with saccharine and powdered milk. Nor was that all, for between mug and saucer a thick slab of dry bread was precariously lodged, so that I began to say, in a kind of anguish, It's going to fall, it's going to fall, as if it mattered whether it fell or not. A moment later I myself was holding, in my trembling hands, this little pile of tottering disparates, in which the hard, the liquid and the soft were joined, without understanding how the transfer had been effected. Let me tell you this, when social workers offer you, free, gratis and for nothing, something to hinder you from swooning, which with them is an obsession, it is useless to recoil, they will pursue you to the ends of the earth, the vomitory in their hands. The Salvation Army is no better. Against the charitable gesture there is no defence, that I know of. You sink your head, you put out your hands all trembling and twined together and you say, Thank you, thank you lady, thank you kind lady. To him who has nothing it is forbidden not to relish filth. The liquid overflowed, the mug rocked with a noise of chattering teeth, not mine, I had none, and the sodden bread sagged more and more. Until, panicstricken, I flung it all far from me. I did not let it fall, no, but with a convulsive thrust of both my hands I threw it to the ground, where it smashed to smithereens, or against the wall, far from me, with all my strength. I will not tell what followed, for I am weary of this place, I want to go. It was late afternoon when they told me I could go. I was advised to behave better in future. Conscious of my wrongs, knowing now the reasons for my arrest, alive to my irregular situation as revealed by the enquiry, I was surprised to find myself so soon at freedom once again, if that is what it was, unpenalised. Had I, without my knowledge, a friend at court? Had I, without knowing it, favourably impressed the sergeant? Had they succeeded in finding my mother and obtaining from her, or from the neighbours, partial confirmation of my statements? Were they of the opinion that it was useless to prosecute me? To apply the letter of the law to a creature like me is not an easy matter. It can be done, but reason is against it. It is better to leave things to the police. I don't know. If it is unlawful to be without papers, why did they not insist on my getting them. Because that costs money and I had none? But in that case could they not have appropriated my bicycle? Probably not, without a court order. All that is incomprehensible. What is certain is this, that I never rested in that way again, my feet obscenely resting on the earth, my arms on the handlebars and on my arms my head, rocking and abandoned. It is indeed a deplorable sight, a deplorable example, for the people, who so need to be encouraged, in their bitter toil, and to have before their eyes manifestations of strength only, of courage and of joy, without which they might collapse, at the end of the day, and roll on the ground. I have only to be told what good behaviour is and I am well-behaved, within the limits of my physical possibilities. And so I have never ceased to improve, from this point of view, for I—I used to be intelligent and quick. And as far as good-will is concerned, I had it to overflowing, the exasperated good-will of the overanxious. So that my repertory of permitted attitudes has never ceased to grow, from my first steps until my last, executed last year. And if I have always behaved like a pig, the fault lies not with me but with my superiors, who corrected me only on points of detail instead of showing me the essence of the system, after the manner of the great English schools, and the guiding principles of good manners, and how to proceed, without going wrong, from the former to the latter, and how to trace back to its ultimate source a given comportment. For that would have allowed me, before parading in public certain habits such as the finger in the nose, the scratching of the balls, digital emunction and the peripatetic piss, to refer them to the first rules of a reasoned theory. On this subject I had only negative and empirical notions, which means that I was in the dark, most of the time, and all the more completely as a lifetime of observations had left me doubting the possibility of systematic decorum, even within a limited area. But it is only since I have ceased to live that I think of these things and the other things. It is in the tranquillity of decomposition that I remember the long confused emotion which was my life, and that I judge it, as it is said that God will judge me, and with no less impertinence. To decompose is to live too, I know, I know, don't torment me, but one sometimes forgets. And of that life too I shall tell you perhaps one day, the day I know that when I thought I knew I was merely existing and that passion without form or stations will have devoured me down to the rotting flesh itself and that when I know that I know nothing, am only crying out as I have always cried out, more or less piercingly, more or less openly. Let me cry out then, it's said to be good for you. Yes, let me cry out, this time, then another time perhaps, then perhaps a last time. Cry out that the declining sun fell full on the white wall of the barracks. It was like being in China. A confused shadow was cast. It was I and my bicycle. I began to play, gesticulating, waving my hat, moving my bicycle to and fro before me, blowing the horn, watching the wall. They were watching me through the bars, I felt their eyes upon me. The policeman on guard at the door told me to go away. He needn't have, I was calm again. The shadow in the end is no better than the substance. I asked the man to help me, to have pity on me. He didn't understand. I thought of the food I had refused. I took a pebble from my pocket and sucked it. It was smooth, from having been sucked so long, by me, and beaten by the storm. A little pebble in your mouth, round and smooth, appeases, soothes, makes you forget your hunger, forget your thirst. The man came towards me, angered by my slowness. Him too they were watching, through the windows. Somewhere someone laughed. Inside me too someone was laughing. I took my sick leg in my hands and passed it over the frame. I went. I had forgotten where I was going.

I stopped to think. It is difficult to think riding, for me. When I try and think riding I lose my balance and fall. I speak in the present tense, it is so easy to speak in the present tense, when speaking of the past. It is the mythological present, don't mind it. I was already settling in my raglimp stasis when I remembered it wasn't done. I went on my way, that way of which I knew nothing, qua way, which was nothing more than a surface, bright or dark, smooth or rough, and always dear to me, in spite of all, and the dear sound of that which goes and is gone, with a brief dust, when the weather is dry. There I am then, before I knew I had left the town, on the canal-bank. The canal goes through the town, I know I know, there are even two. But then these hedges, these fields? Don't torment yourself, Molloy. Suddenly I see, it was my right leg the stiff one, then. Toiling towards me along the tow-path I saw a team of little grey donkeys, on the far bank, and I heard angry cries and dull blows. I got down. I put my foot to the ground the better to see the approaching barge, so gently approaching that the water was unruffled. It was a cargo of nails and timber, on its way to some carpenter I suppose. My eyes caught a donkey's eyes, they fell to his little feet, their brave fastidious tread. The boatman rested his elbow on his knee, his head on his hand. He had a long white beard. Every three or four puffs, without taking his pipe from his mouth, he spat into the water. I could not see his eyes. The horizon was burning with sulphur and phosphorus, it was there I was bound. At last I got right down, hobbled down to the ditch and lay down, beside my bicycle. I lay at full stretch, with outspread arms. The white hawthorn stooped towards me, unfortunately I don't like the smell of hawthorn. In the ditch the grass was thick and high, I took off my hat and pressed about my face the long leafy stalks. Then I could smell the earth, the smell of the earth was in the grass that my hands wove round my face till I was blinded. I ate a little too, a little grass. It came back to my mind, from nowhere, as a moment before my name, that I had set out to see my mother, at the beginning of this ending day. My reasons? I had forgotten them. But I knew them, I must have known them, I had only to find them again and I would sweep, with the clipped wings of necessity, to my mother. Yes, it's all easy when you know why, a mere matter of magic. Yes, the whole thing is to know what saint to implore, any fool can implore him. For the particulars, if you are interested in particulars, there is no need to despair, you may scrabble on the right door, in the right way, in the end. It's for the whole there seems to be no spell. Perhaps there is no whole, before you're dead. An opiate for the life of the dead, that should be easy. What am I waiting for then, to exorcize mine? It's coming, it's coming. I hear from here the howl resolving all, even if it is not mine. Meanwhile there's no use knowing you are gone, you are not, you are writhing yet, the hair is growing, the nails are growing, the entrails emptying, all the morticians are dead. Someone has drawn the blinds, you perhaps. Not the faintest sound. Where are the famous flies? Yes, there is no denying it, any longer, it is not you who are dead, but all the others. So you get up and go to your mother, who thinks she is alive. That's my impression. But now I shall have to get myself out of this ditch. How joyfully I would vanish there, sinking deeper and deeper under the rains. No doubt I'll come back some day, here, or to a similar slough, I can trust my feet for that, as no doubt some day I'll meet again the sergeant and his merry men. And if, too changed to know it is they, I do not say it is they, make no mistake, it will be they, though changed. For to contrive a being, a place, I nearly said an hour, but I would not hurt anyone's feelings, and then to use them no more, that would be, how shall I say, I don't know. Not to want to say, not to know what you want to say, not to be able to say what you think you want to say, and never to stop saying, or hardly ever, that is the thing to keep in mind, even in the heat of composition. That night was not like the other night, if it had been I would have known. For when I try and think of that night, on the canal-bank, I find nothing, no night properly speaking, nothing but Molloy in the ditch, and perfect silence, and behind my closed lids the little night and its little lights, faint at first, then flaming and extinguished, now ravening, now fed, as fire by filth and martyrs. I say that night, but there was more than one perhaps. The lie, the lie, to lying thought. But I find the morning, a morning, and the sun already high, and the little sleep I had then, according to my custom, and space with its sounds again, and the shepherd watching me sleep and under whose eyes I opened my eyes. Beside him a panting dog, watching me too, but less closely than his master, for from time to time he stopped watching me to gnaw at his flesh, furiously, where the ticks were in him I suppose. Did he take me for a black sheep entangled in the brambles and was he waiting for an order from his master to drag me out? I don't think so. I don't smell like a sheep, I wish I smelt like a sheep, or a buck-goat. When I wake I see the first things quite clearly, the first things that offer, and I understand them, when they are not too difficult. Then in my eyes and in my head a fine rain begins to fall, as from a rose, highly important. So I knew at once it was a shepherd and his dog I had before me, above me rather, for they had not left the path. And I identified the bleating too, without any trouble, the anxious bleating of the sheep, missing the dog at their heels. It is then too that the meaning of words is least obscure to me, so that I said, with tranquil assurance, Where are you taking them, to the fields or to the shambles? I must have completely lost my sense of direction, as if direction had anything to do with the matter. For even if he was going towards the town, what prevented him from skirting it, or from leaving it again by another gate, on his way to new pastures, and if he was going away from it that meant nothing either, for slaughter-houses are not confined to towns, no, they are everywhere, the country is full of them, every butcher has his slaughter-house and the right to slaughter, according to his lights. But whether it was he didn't understand, or didn't want to reply, he didn't reply, but went on his way without a word, without a word for me I mean, for he spoke to his dog who listened attentively, cocking his ears. I got to my knees, no, that doesn't work, I got up and watched the little procession recede. I heard the shepherd whistle, and I saw him flourishing his crook, and the dog bustling about the herd, which but for him would no doubt have fallen into the canal. All that through a glittering dust, and soon through that mist too which rises in me every day and veils the world from me and veils me from myself. The bleating grew faint, because the sheep were less anxious, or because they were further away, or because my hearing was worse than a moment before, which would surprise me, for my hearing is still very good, scarcely blunted coming up to dawn, and if I sometimes hear nothing for hours on end it is for reasons of which I know nothing, or because about me all goes really silent, from time to time, whereas for the righteous the tumult of the world never stops. That then is how that second day began, unless it was the third, or the fourth, and it was a bad beginning, because it left me with persisting doubts, as to the destination of those sheep, among which there were lambs, and often wondering if they had safely reached some commonage or fallen, their skulls shattered, their thin legs crumpling, first to their knees, then over on their fleecy sides, under the pole-axe, though that is not the way they slaughter sheep, but with a knife, so that they bleed to death. But there is much to be said too for these little doubts. Good God, what a land of breeders, you see quadrupeds everywhere. And it's not over yet, there are still horses and goats, to mention only them, I feel them watching out for me, to get in my path. I have no need of that. But I did not lose sight of my immediate goal, which was to get to my mother as quickly as possible, and standing in the ditch I summoned to my aid the good reasons I had for going there, without a moment's delay. And though there were many things I could do without thinking, not knowing what I was going to do until it was done, and not even then, going to my mother was not one of them. My feet, you see, never took me to my mother unless they received a definite order to do so. The glorious, the truly glorious weather would have gladdened any other heart than mine. But I have no reason to be gladdened by the sun and I take good care not to be. The Aegean, thirsting for heat and light, him I killed, he killed himself, early on, in me. The pale gloom of rainy days was better fitted to my taste, no, that's not it, to my humour, no, that's not it either, I had neither taste nor humour, I lost them early on. Perhaps what I mean is that the pale gloom etc., hid me better, without its being on that account particularly pleasing to me. Chameleon in spite of himself, there you have Molloy, viewed from a certain angle. And in winter, under my greatcoat, I wrapped myself in swathes of newspaper, and did not shed them until the earth awoke, for good, in April. The Times Literary Supplement was admirably adapted to this purpose, of a neverfailing toughness and impermeability. Even farts made no impression on it. I can't help it, gas escapes from my fundament on the least pretext, it's hard not to mention it now and then, however great my distaste. One day I counted them. Three hundred and fifteen farts in nineteen hours, or an average of over sixteen farts an hour. After all it's not excessive. Four farts every fifteen minutes. It's nothing. Not even one fart every four minutes. It's unbelievable. Damn it, I hardly fart at all, I should never have mentioned it. Extraordinary how mathematics help you to know yourself. In any case this whole question of climate left me cold, I could stomach any mess. So I will only add that the mornings were often sunny, in that part of the world, until ten o'clock or coming up to eleven, and that then the sky darkened and the rain fell, fell till evening.

Then the sun came out and went down, the drenched earth sparkled an instant, then went out, bereft of light. There I am then back in the saddle, in my numbed heart a prick of misgiving, like one dying of cancer obliged to consult his dentist. For I did not know if it was the right road. All roads were right for me, a wrong road was an event, for me. But when I was on my way to my mother only one road was right, the one that led to her, or one of those that led to her, for all did not lead to her. I did not know if I was on one of those right roads and that disturbed me, like all recall to life. Judge then of my relief when I saw, ahead of me, the familiar ramparts loom. I passed beyond them, into a district I did not know. And yet I knew the town well, for I was born there and had never succeeded in putting between it and me more than ten or fifteen miles, such was its grasp on me, I don't know why. So that I came near to wondering if I was in the right town, where I first saw the murk of day and which still harboured my mother, somewhere or other, or if I had not stumbled, as a result of a wrong turn, on a town whose very name I did not know. For my native town was the only one I knew, having never set foot in any other. But I had read with care, while I still could read, accounts of travellers more fortunate than myself, telling of other towns as beautiful as mine, and even more beautiful, though with a different beauty. And now it was a name I sought, in my memory, the name of the only town it had been given me to know, with the intention, as soon as I had found it, of stopping, and saying to a passer-by, doffing my hat, I beg your pardon, Sir, this *is* X, is it not?, X being the name of my town. And this name that I sought, I felt sure that it began with a B or with a P, but in spite of this clue, or perhaps because of its falsity, the other letters continued to escape me. I had been living so far from words so long, you understand, that it was enough for me to see my town, since we're talking of my town, to be unable, you understand. It's too difficult to say, for me. And even my sense of identity was wrapped in a namelessness often hard to penetrate, as we have just seen I think. And so on for all the other things which made merry with my senses. Yes, even then, when already all was fading, waves and particles, there could be no things but nameless things, no names but thingless names. I say that now, but after all what do I know now about then, now when the icy words hail down upon me, the icy meanings, and the world dies too, foully named. All I know is what the words know, and the dead things, and that makes a handsome little sum, with a beginning, a middle and an end as in the well-built phrase and the long sonata of the dead. And truly it little matters what I say, this or that or any other thing. Saying is inventing. Wrong, very rightly wrong. You invent nothing, you think you are inventing, you think you are escaping, and all you do is stammer out your lesson, the remnants of a pensum one day got by heart and long forgotten, life without tears, as it is wept. To hell with it anyway. Where was I. Unable to remember the name of my town I resolved to stop by the kerb, to wait for a passer-by with a friendly and intelligent air and then to whip off my hat and say, with my smile, I beg your pardon Sir, excuse me Sir, what is the name of this town, if you please? For the word once let fall I would know if it was the right word the one I was seeking, in my memory, or another, and so where I stood. This resolution, actually formed as I rode along, was never to be carried out, an absurd mishap prevented it. Yes, my resolutions were remarkable in this, that they were no sooner formed than something always happened to prevent their execution. That must be why I am even less resolute now than then, just as then I was even less so than I once had been. But to tell the truth (to tell the truth!) I have never been particularly resolute, I mean given to resolutions, but rather inclined to plunge headlong into the shit, without knowing who was shitting against whom or on which side I had the better chance of skulking with success. But from this leaning too I derived scant satisfaction and if I have never quite got rid of it it is not for want of trying. The fact is, it seems, that the most you can hope is to be a little less, in the end, the creature you were in the beginning, and the middle. For I had hardly perfected my plan, in my head, when my bicycle ran over a dog, as subsequently appeared, and fell to the ground, an ineptness all the more unpardonable as the dog, duly leashed, was not out on the road, but in on the pavement, docile at its mistress's heels. Precautions are like resolutions, to be taken with precaution. The lady must have thought she had left nothing to chance, so far as the safety of her dog was concerned, whereas in reality she was setting the whole system of nature at naught, no less surely than I myself with my insane demands for more light. But instead of grovelling in my turn, invoking my great age and infirmities, I made things worse by trying to run away. I was soon overtaken, by a bloodthirsty mob of both sexes and all ages, for I caught a glimpse of white beards and little almost angelfaces, and they were preparing to tear me to pieces when the lady intervened. She said in effect, she told me so later on and I believed her, Leave this poor old man alone. He has killed Teddy, I grant you that, Teddy whom I loved like my own child, but it is not so serious as it seems, for as it happens I was taking him to the veterinary surgeon, to have him put out of his misery. For Teddy was old, blind, deaf, crippled with rheumatism and perpetually incontinent, night and day, indoors and out of doors. Thanks then to this poor old man I have been spared a painful task, not to mention the expense which I am ill able to afford, having no other means of support than the pension of my dear departed, fallen in defence of a country that called itself his and from which in his lifetime he never derived the smallest benefit, but only insults and vexations. The crowd was beginning to disperse, the danger was past, but the lady in her stride. You may say, she said, that he did wrong to run away, that he should have explained, asked to be forgiven. Granted. But it is clear he has not all his wits about him, that he is beside himself, for reasons of which we know nothing and which might put us all to shame, if we did know them. I even wonder if he knows what he has done. There emanated such tedium from this droning voice that I was making ready to move on when the unavoidable police constable rose up before me. He brought down heavily on my handlebars his big red hairy paw, I noticed it myself, and had it appears with the lady the following conversation. Is this the man who ran over your dog, Madam? He is, sergeant, and what of it? No, I can't record this fatuous colloquy. So I will merely observe that finally in his turn the constable too dispersed, the word is not too strong, grumbling and growling, followed by the last idlers who had given up all hope of my coming to a bad end. But he turned back and said, Remove that dog. Free at last to go I began to do so. But the lady, a Mrs Loy, I might as well say it now and be done with it, or Lousse, I forget, Christian name something like Sophie, held me back, by the tail of my coat, and said, assuming the words were the same when I heard them as when first spoken, Sir, I need you. And seeing I suppose from my expression, which frequently betrays me, that she had made herself understood, she must have said, If he understands that he can understand anything. And she was not mistaken, for after some time I found myself in possession of certain ideas or points of view which could only have come to me from her, namely that having killed her dog I was morally obliged to help her carry it home and bury it, that she did not wish to prosecute me for what I had done, but that it was not always possible to do as one did not wish, that she found me likeable enough in spite of my hideous appearance and would be happy to hold out to me a helping hand, and so on, I've forgotten the half of it. Ah yes, I too needed her, it seemed. She needed me to help her get rid of her dog, and I needed her, I've forgotten for what. She must have told me, for that was an insinuation I could not decently pass over in silence as I had the rest, and I made no bones about telling her I needed neither her nor anyone else, which was perhaps a slight exaggeration, for I must have needed my mother, otherwise why this frenzy of wanting to get to her? That is one of the many reasons why I avoid speaking as much as possible. For I always say either too much or too little, which is a terrible thing for a man with a passion for truth like mine. And I shall not abandon this subject, to which I shall probably never have occasion to return, with such a storm blowing up, without making this curious observation, that it often happened to me, before I gave up speaking for good, to think I had said too little when in fact I had said too much and in fact to have said too little when I thought I had said too much. I mean that on reflexion, in the long run rather, my verbal profusion turned out to be penury, and inversely. So time sometimes turns the tables. In other words, or perhaps another thing, whatever I said it was never enough and always too much. Yes, I was never silent, whatever I said I was never silent. Divine analysis that conduces thus to knowledge of yourself, and of your fellow-men, if you happen to have any. For to say I needed no one was not to say too much, but an infinitesimal part of what I should have said, could not have said, should never have said. Need of my mother! No, there were no words for the want of need in which I was perishing. So that she, I mean Sophie, must have told me the reasons why I needed her, since I had dared to disagree. And perhaps if I took the trouble I might find them again, but trouble, many thanks, some other time. And now enough of this boulevard, it must have been a boulevard, of all these righteous ones, these guardians of the peace, all these feet and hands, stamping, clutching, clenched in vain, these bawling mouths that never bawl out of season, this sky beginning to drip, enough of being abroad, trapped, visible. Someone was poking the dog, with a malacca. The dog was uniformly yellow, a mongrel I suppose, or a pedigree, I can never tell the difference. His death must have hurt him less than my fall me. And he at least was dead. We slung him across the saddle and set off like an army in retreat, helping each other I suppose, to keep the corpse from falling, to keep the bicycle moving, to keep ourselves moving, through the jeering crowd. The house where Sophie—no, I can't call her that any more, I'll try calling her Lousse, without the Mrs—the house where Lousse lived was not far away. Oh it was not nearby either, I had my bellyful by the time I got there. That is to say I didn't have it really. You think you have your bellyful but you seldom have it really. It was because I knew I was there that I had my bellyful, a mile more to go and I would only have had my bellyful an hour later. Human nature. Marvellous thing. The house where Lousse lived. Must I describe it? I don't think so. I won't, that's all I know, for the moment. Perhaps later on, if I get to know it. And Lousse? Must I describe her? I suppose so. Let's first bury the dog. It was she dug the hole, under a tree. You always bury your dog under a tree, I don't know why. But I have my suspicions. It was she dug the hole because I couldn't, though I was the gentleman, because of my leg. That is to say I could have dug with a trowel, but not with a spade. For when you dig a grave one leg supports the weight of the body while the other, flexing and unflexing, drives the spade into the earth. Now my sick leg, I forget which, it's immaterial here, was in a condition neither to dig, because it was rigid, nor alone to support me, because it would have collapsed. I had so to speak only one leg at my disposal, I was virtually onelegged, and I would have been happier, livelier, amputated at the groin. And if they had removed a few testicles into the bargain I wouldn't have objected. For from such testicles as mine, dangling at mid-thigh at the end of a meagre cord, there was nothing more to be squeezed, not a drop. So that non che la speme il desiderio, and I longed to see them gone, from the old stand where they bore false witness, for and against, in the lifelong charge against me. For if they accused me of having made a balls of it, of me, of them, they thanked me for it too, from the depths of their rotten bag, the right lower than the left, or inversely, I forget, decaying circus clowns. And, worse still, they got in my way when I tried to walk, when I tried to sit down, as if my sick leg was not enough, and when I rode my bicycle they bounced up and down. So the best thing for me would have been for them to go, and I would have seen to it myself, with a knife or secateurs, but for my terror of physical pain and festered wounds, so that I shook. Yes, all my life I have gone in terror of festered wounds, I who never festered, I was so acid. My life, my life, now I speak of it as of something over, now as of a joke which still goes on, and it is neither, for at the same time it is over and it goes on, and is there any tense for that? Watch wound and buried by the watchmaker, before he died, whose ruined works will one day speak of God, to the worms. But those cullions, I must be attached to them after all, cherish them as others do their scars, or the family album. In any case it wasn't their fault I couldn't dig, but my leg's. It was Lousse dug the hole while I held the dog in my arms. He was heavy already and cold, but he had not yet begun to stink. He smelt bad, if you like, but bad like an old dog, not like a dead dog. He too had dug holes, perhaps at this very spot. We buried him as he was, no box or wrapping of any kind, like a Carthusian monk, but with his collar and lead. It was she put him in the hole, though I was the gentleman. For I cannot stoop, neither can I kneel, because of my infirmity, and if ever I stoop, forgetting who I am, or kneel, make no mistake, it will not be me, but another. To throw him in the hole was all I could have done, and I would have done it gladly. And yet I did not do it. All the things you would do gladly, oh without enthusiasm, but gladly, all the things there seems no reason for your not doing, and that you do not do! Can it be we are not free? It might be worth looking into. But what was my contribution to this burial? It was she dug the hole, put in the dog, filled up the hole. On the whole I was a mere spectator, I contributed my presence. As if it had been my own burial. And it was. It was a larch. It is the only tree I can identify, with certainty. Funny she should have chosen, to bury her dog beneath, the only tree I can identify, with certainty. The sea-green needles are like silk and speckled, it always seemed to me, with little red, how shall I say, with little red specks. The dog had ticks in his ears, I have an eye for such things, they were buried with him. When she had finished her grave she handed me the spade and began to muse, or brood. I thought she was going to cry, it was the thing to do, but on the contrary she laughed. It was perhaps her way of crying. Or perhaps I was mistaken and she was really crying, with the noise of laughter. Tears and laughter, they are so much Gaelic to me. She would see him no more, her Teddy she had loved like an only child. I wonder why, since she had obviously made up her mind to bury the dog at home, she had not asked the vet to call and destroy the brute on the premises. Was she really on her way to the vet at the moment her path crossed mine? Or had she said so solely in order to attenuate my guilt? Private calls are naturally more expensive. She ushered me into the drawing-room and gave me food and drink, good things without a doubt. Unfortunately I didn't much care for good things to eat. But I quite liked getting drunk. If she lived in embarrassed circumstances there was no sign of it. That kind of embarrassment I feel at once. Seeing how painful the sitting posture was for me she fetched a chair for my stiff leg. Without ceasing to ply me with delicacies she kept up a chatter of which I did not understand the hundredth part. With her own hand she took off my hat, and carried it away, to hang it up somewhere, on a hat-rack I suppose, and seemed surprised when the lace pulled her up in her stride. She had a parrot, very pretty, all the most approved colours. I understood him better than his mistress. I don't mean I understood him better than she understood him, I mean I understood him better than I understood her. He exclaimed from time to time, Fuck the son of a bitch, fuck the son of a bitch. He must have belonged to an American sailor, before he belonged to Lousse. Pets often change masters. He didn't say much else. No, I'm wrong, he also said, Putain de merde! He must have belonged to a French sailor before he belonged to the American sailor. Putain de merde!

Unless he had hit on it alone, it wouldn't surprise me. Lousse tried to make him say, Pretty Polly! I think it was too late. He listened, his head on one side, pondered, then said, Fuck the son of a bitch. It was clear he was doing his best. Him too one day she would bury. In his cage probably. Me too, if I had stayed, she would have buried. If I had her address I'd write to her, to come and bury me. I fell asleep. I woke up in a bed, in my skin. They had carried their impertinence to the point of washing me, to judge by the smell I gave off, no longer gave off. I went to the door. Locked. To the window. Barred. It was not yet quite dark. What is there left to try when you have tried the door and the window? The chimney perhaps. I looked for my clothes. I found a light switch and switched it on. No result. What a story! All that left me cold, or nearly. I found my crutches, against an easy chair. It may seem strange that I was able to go through the motions I have described without their help. I find it strange. You don't remember immediately who you are, when you wake. On a chair I found a white chamber pot with a roll of toilet-paper in it. Nothing was being left to chance. I recount these moments with a certain minuteness, it is a relief from what I feel coming. I set a pouffe against the easy chair, sat down in the latter and on the former laid my stiff leg. The room was chock-full of pouffes and easy chairs, they thronged all about me, in the gloom. There were also occasional tables, footstools, tallboys, etc., in abundance. Strange feeling of congestion that the night dispersed, though it lit the chandelier, which I had left turned on. My beard was missing, when I felt for it with anguished hand. They had shaved me, they had shorn me of my scant beard. How had my sleep withstood such liberties? My sleep as a rule so uneasy. To this question I found a number of replies. But I did not know which of them was right. Perhaps they were all wrong. My beard grows properly only on my chin and dewlap. Where the pretty bristles grow on other faces, on mine there are none. But such as it was they had docked my beard. Perhaps they had dyed it too, I had no proof they had not. I thought I was naked, in the easy chair, but I finally realized I was wearing a nightdress, very flimsy. If they had come and told me I was to be sacrificed at sunrise I would not have been taken aback. How foolish one can be. It seemed to me too that I had been perfumed, lavender perhaps. I said, If only your poor mother could see you now. I am no enemy of the commonplace. She seemed far away, my mother, far away from me, and yet I was a little closer to her than the night before, if my reckoning was accurate. But was it? If I was in the right town, I had made progress. But was I? If on the other hand I was in the wrong town, from which my mother would necessarily be absent, then I had lost ground. I must have fallen asleep, for all of a sudden there was the moon, a huge moon framed in the window. Two bars divided it in three segments, of which the middle remained constant, while little by little the right gained what the left lost. For the moon was moving from left to right, or the room was moving from right to left, or both together perhaps, or both were moving from left to right, but the room not so fast as the moon, or from right to left, but the moon not so fast as the room. But can one speak of right and left in such circumstances?

That movements of an extreme complexity were taking place seemed certain, and yet what a simple thing it seemed, that vast yellow light sailing slowly behind my bars and which little by little the dense wall devoured, and finally eclipsed. And now its tranquil course was written on the walls, a radiance scored with shadow, then a brief quivering of leaves, if they were leaves, then that too went out, leaving me in the dark. How difficult it is to speak of the moon and not lose one's head, the witless moon. It must be her arse she shows us always. Yes, I once took an interest in astronomy, I don't deny it. Then it was geology that killed a few years for me. The next pain in the balls was anthropology and the other disciplines, such as psychiatry, that are connected with it, disconnected, then connected again, according to the latest discoveries. What I liked in anthropology was its inexhaustible faculty of negation, its relentless definition of man, as though he were no better than God, in terms of what he is not, But my ideas on this subject were always horribly confused, for my knowledge of men was scant and the meaning of being beyond me. Oh I've tried everything. In the end it was magic that had the honour of my ruins, and still today, when I walk there, I find its vestiges. But mostly they are a place with neither plan nor bounds and of which I understand nothing, not even of what it is made, still less into what. And the thing in ruins. I don't know what it is, what it was, nor whether it is not less a question of ruins than the indestructible chaos of timeless things, if that is the right expression. It is in any case a place devoid of mystery, deserted by magic, because devoid of mystery. And if I do not go there gladly, I go perhaps more gladly there than anywhere else, astonished and at peace, I nearly said as in a dream, but no, no. But it is not the kind of place where you go, but where you find yourself, sometimes, not knowing how, and which you cannot leave at will, and where you find yourself without any pleasure, but with more perhaps than in those places you can escape from, by making an effort, places full of mystery, full of the familiar mysteries. I listen and the voice is of a world collapsing endlessly, a frozen world, under a faint untroubled sky, enough to see by, yes, and frozen too. And I hear it murmur that all wilts and yields, as if loaded down, but here there are no loads, and the ground too, unfit for loads, and the light too, down towards an end it seems can never come. For what possible end to these wastes where true light never was, nor any upright thing, nor any true foundation, but only these leaning things, forever lapsing and crumbling away, beneath a sky without memory of morning or hope of night. These things, what things, come from where, made of what? And it says that here nothing stirs, has never stirred, will never stir, except myself, who do not stir either, when I am there, but see and am seen. Yes, a world at an end, in spite of appearances, its end brought it forth, ending it began, is it clear enough? And I too am at an end, when I am there, my eyes close, my sufferings cease and I end, I wither as the living can not. And if I went on listening to that far whisper, silent long since and which I still hear, I would learn still more, about this. But I will listen no longer, for the time being, to that far whisper, for I do not like it, I fear it. But it is not a sound like the other sounds, that you listen to, when you choose, and can sometimes silence, by going away or stopping your ears, no, but it is a sound which begins to rustle in your head, without your knowing how, or why. It's with your head you hear it, not your ears, you can't stop it, but it stops itself, when it chooses. It makes no difference therefore whether I listen to it or not, I shall hear it always, no thunder can deliver me, until it stops. But nothing compels me to speak of it, when it doesn't suit me. And it doesn't suit me, at the moment. No, what suits me, at the moment, is to be done with this business of the moon which was left unfinished, by me, for me. And if I get done with it less successfully than if I had all my wits about me, I shall none the less get done with it, as best I can, at least I think so. That moon then, all things considered, filled me suddenly with amaze, with surprise, perhaps better. Yes, I was considering it, after my fashion, with indifference, seeing it again, in a way, in my head, when a great fright came suddenly upon me. And deeming this deserved to be looked into I looked into it and quickly made the following discovery, among others, but I confine myself to the following, that this moon which had just sailed gallant and full past my window had appeared to me the night before, or the night before that, yes, more likely, all young and slender, on her back, a shaving. And then I had said, Now I see, he has waited for the new moon before launching forth on unknown ways, leading south. And then a little later, Perhaps I should go to mother tomorrow. For all things hang together, by the operation of the Holy Ghost, as the saying is. And if I failed to mention this detail in its proper place, it is because you cannot mention everything in its proper place, you must choose, between the things not worth mentioning and those even less so. For if you set out to mention everything you would never be done, and that's what counts, to be done, to have done. Oh I know, even when you mention only a few of the things there are, you do not get done either, I know, I know. But it's a change of muck. And if all muck is the same muck that doesn't matter, it's good to have a change of muck, to move from one heap to another a little further on, from time to time, fluttering you might say, like a butterfly, as if you were ephemeral. And if you are wrong, and you are wrong, I mean when you record circumstances better left unspoken, and leave unspoken others, rightly, if you like, but how shall I say, for no good reason, yes, rightly, but for no good reason, as for example that new moon, it is often in good faith, excellent faith. Had there then elapsed, between that night on the mountain, that night when I saw A and C and then made up my mind to go and see my mother, and this other night, more time than I had thought, namely fourteen full days, or nearly? And if so, what had happened to those fourteen days, or nearly, and where had they flown? And what possible chance was there of finding a place for them, no matter what their burden, in the so rigorous chain of events I had just undergone? Was it not wiser to suppose either that the moon seen two nights before, far from being new as I had thought, was on the eve of being full, or else that the moon seen from Lousse's house, far from being full, as it had appeared to me, was in fact merely entering on its first quarter, or else finally that here I had to do with two moons, as far from the new as from the full and so alike in outline that the naked eye could hardly tell between them, and that whatever was at variance with these hypotheses was so much smoke and delusion. It was at all events with the aid of these considerations that I grew calm again and was restored, in the face of nature's pranks, to my old ataraxy, for what it was worth. And it came back also to my mind, as sleep stole over it again, that my nights were moonless and the moon foreign, to my nights, so that I had never seen, drifting past the window, carrying me back to other nights, other moons, this moon I had just seen, I had forgotten who I was (excusably) and spoken of myself as I would have of another, if I had been compelled to speak of another. Yes it sometimes happens and will sometimes happen again that I forget who I am and strut before my eyes, like a stranger. Then I see the sky different from what it is and the earth too takes on false colours. It looks like rest, it is not, I vanish happy in that alien light, which must have once been mine, I am willing to believe it, then the anguish of return, I won't say where, I can't, to absence perhaps, you must return, that's all I know, it's misery to stay, misery to go. The next day I demanded my clothes. The valet went to find out. He came back with the news they had been burnt. I continued my inspection of the room. It was at first sight a perfect cube. Through the lofty window I saw boughs. They rocked gently, but not all the time, shaken now and then by sudden spasms. I noticed the chandelier was burning. My clothes, I said, my crutches, forgetting my crutches were there, against the chair. He left me alone again, leaving the door open. Through the door I saw a big window, bigger than the door which it overlapped entirely, and opaque. The valet came back with the news my clothes had been sent to the dyers, to have the shine taken off. He held my crutches, which should have seemed strange to me, but seemed natural to me, on the contrary. I took hold of one and began to strike the pieces of furniture with it, not very hard, just hard enough to overturn them, without breaking them. They were fewer than in the night. To tell the truth I pushed them rather than struck them, I thrust at them, I lunged, and that is not pushing either, but it's more like pushing than striking. But recalling who I was I soon threw away my crutch and came to a standstill in the middle of the room, determined to stop asking for things, to stop pretending to be angry. For to want my clothes, and I thought I wanted them, was no reason for pretending be to angry, when they were refused. And alone once more I resumed my inspection of the room and was on the point of endowing it with other properties when the valet came back with the news my clothes had been sent for and I would have them soon. Then he began to straighten the tables and chairs I had overturned and to put them back into place, dusting them as he did so with a feather duster which suddenly appeared in his hand. And so I began to help him as best I could, by way of proving that I bore no grudge against anyone. And though I could not do much, because of my stiff leg, yet I did what I could, that is to say I took each object as he straightened it and proceeded with excruciating meticulousness to restore it to its proper place, stepping back with raised arms the better to assess the result and then springing forward to effect minute improvements. And with the tail of my nightdress as with a duster I petulantly flicked them one by one. But of this little game too I soon wearied and suddenly stood stock still in the middle of the room. But seeing him ready to go I took a step forward and said, My bicycle. And I said it again, and again, the same words, until he appeared to understand. I don't know to what race he belonged, he was so tiny and ageless, assuredly not to mine. He was an oriental perhaps, a vague oriental, a child of the Rising Sun. He wore white trousers, a white shirt and a yellow waistcoat, like a chamois he was, with brass buttons and sandals. It is not often that I take cognizance so clearly of the clothes that people wear and I am happy to give you the benefit of it. The reason for that was perhaps this, that all morning the talk had been of clothes, of mine. And perhaps I had been saying, to myself, words to this effect, Look at him, peaceful in his own clothes, and look at me, floating about inside another man's nightdress, another woman's probably, for it was pink and transparent and adorned with ribands and frills and lace. Whereas the room, I saw the room but darkly, at each fresh inspection it seemed changed, and that is known as seeing darkly, in the present state of our knowledge. The boughs themselves seemed to shift, as though endowed with an orbital velocity of their own, and in the big frosted window the door was no longer inscribed, but had slightly shifted to the right, or to the left, I forget, so that there now appeared within its frame a panel of white wall, on which I succeeded in casting faint shadows when I moved. But that there were natural causes to all these things I am willing to concede, for the resources of nature are infinite apparently. It was I who was not natural enough to enter into that order of things, and appreciate its niceties. But I was used to seeing the sun rise in the south, used to not knowing where I was going, what I was leaving, what was going with me, all things turning and twisting confusedly about me. It is difficult, is it not, to go to one's mother with things in such a state, more difficult than to the Lousses of this world, or to its police-stations, or to the other places that are waiting for me, I know. But the valet having brought my clothes, in a paper which he unwrapped in front of me, I saw that my hat was not among them, so that I said, My hat. And when he finally understood what I wanted he went away and came back a little later with my hat. Nothing was missing then except the lace to fasten my hat to my buttonhole, but that was something I could not hope to make him understand, and so I did not mention it. An old lace, you can always find an old lace, no lace lasts for ever, the way clothes do, real clothes. As for the bicycle, I had hopes that it was waiting for me somewhere below stairs, perhaps even before the front door, ready to carry me away from these horrible scenes. And I did not see what good it would do to ask for it again, to submit him and myself to this fresh ordeal, when it could be avoided. These considerations crossed my mind with a certain rapidity. Now with regard to the pockets, four in all, of my clothes, I verified their contents in front of the valet and discovered that certain things were missing. My sucking-stone in particular was no longer there. But sucking-stones abound on our beaches, when you know where to look for them, and I deemed it wiser to say nothing about it, all the more so as he would have been capable, after an hour's argument, of going and fetching me from the garden a completely unsuckable stone. This was a decision too which I took almost instantaneously. But of the other objects which had disappeared why speak, since I did not know exactly what they were. And perhaps they had been taken from me at the police-station, without my knowing it, or scattered and lost, when I fell, or at some other time, or thrown away, for I would sometimes throw away all I had about me, in a burst of irritation. So why speak of them? I resolved nevertheless to declare loudly that a knife was missing, a noble knife, and I did so to such effect that I soon received a very fine vegetable knife, so-called stainless, but it didn't take me long to stain it, and which opened and shut into the bargain, unlike all the vegetable knives I had ever known, and which had a safety catch, highly dangerous as soon appeared and the cause of innumerable cuts, all over my fingers caught between the handle of so-called genuine Irish horn and the blade red with rust and so blunted that it was less a matter of cuts than of contusions. And if I deal at such length with this knife it is because I have it somewhere still I think, among my possessions, and because having dealt with it here at such length I shall not have to deal with it again, when the moment comes, if it ever comes, to draw up the list of my possessions, and that will be a relief, a welcome relief, when that moment comes, I know. For it is natural I should dilate at lesser length on what I lost than on what I could not lose, that goes without saying. And if I do not always appear to observe this principle it is because it escapes me, from time to time, and vanishes, as utterly as if I had never educed it. Mad words, no matter. For I no longer know what I am doing, nor why, those are things I understand less and less, I don't deny it, for why deny it, and to whom, to you, to whom nothing is denied? And then doing fills me with such a, I don't know, impossible to express, for me, now, after so long, yes, that I don't stop to enquire in virtue of what principle. And all the less so as whatever I do, that is to say whatever I say, it will always as it were be the same thing, yes, as it were. And if I speak of principles, when there are none, I can't help it, there must be some somewhere. And if always doing the same thing as it were is not the same as observing the same principle, I can't help it either. And then how can you know whether you are observing it or not? And how can you want to know? No, all that is not worth while, not worth while bothering about, and yet you do bother about it, your sense of values gone. And the things that are worth while you do not bother about, you let them be, for the same reason, or wisely, knowing that all these questions of worth and value have nothing to do with you, who don't know what you're doing, nor why, and must go on not knowing it, on pain of, I wonder what, yes, I wonder. For anything worse than what I do, without knowing what, or why, I have never been able to conceive, and that doesn't surprise me, for I never tried. For had I been able to conceive something worse than what I had I would have known no peace until I got it, if I know anything about myself. And what I have, what I am, is enough, was always enough for me, and as far as my dear little sweet little future is concerned I have no qualms, I have a good time coming. So I put on my clothes, having first made sure they had not been tampered with that is to say I put on my trousers, my great coat, my hat and my boots. My boots. They came up to where my calves would have been if I had had calves, and partly they buttoned, or would have buttoned, if they had had buttons, and partly they laced, and I have them still, I think, somewhere. Then I took my crutches and left the room. The whole day had gone in this tomfoolery and it was dusk again. Going down the stairs I inspected the window I had seen through the door. It lit the staircase with its wild tawny light. Lousse was in the garden, fussing around the grave. She was sowing grass on it, as if grass wouldn't have sown itself on it. She was taking advantage of the cool of evening. Seeing me, she came warmly towards me and gave me food and drink. I ate and drank standing, casting about me in search of my bicycle. She talked and talked. Soon sated, I began the search for my bicycle. She followed me. In the end I found it, half buried in a soft bush. I threw aside my crutches and took it in my hands, by the saddle and the handlebars, intending to wheel it a little, back and forth, before getting on and leaving for ever this accursed place. But I pushed and pulled in vain, the wheels would not turn. It was as though the brakes were jammed, and heaven knows they were not, for my bicycle had no brakes. And suddenly overcome by a great weariness, in spite of the dying day when I always felt most alive, I threw the bicycle back in the bush and lay down on the ground, on the grass, careless of the dew, I never feared the dew. It was then that Lousse, taking advantage of my weakness, squatted down beside me and began to make me propositions, to which I must confess I listened, absent-mindedly, I had nothing else to do, I could do nothing else, and doubtless she had poisoned my beer with something intended to mollify me, to mollify Molloy, with the result that I was nothing more than a lump of melting wax, so to speak. And from these propositions, which she enunciated slowly and distinctly, repeating each clause several times, I finally elicited the following, or gist. I could not prevent her having a weakness for me, neither could she. I would live in her home, as though it were my own. I would have plenty to eat and drink, to smoke too if I smoked, for nothing, and my remaining days would glide away without a care. I would as it were take the place of the dog I had killed, as it for her had taken the place of a child. I would help in the garden, in the house, when I wished, if I wished. I would not go out on the street, for once out I would never find my way in again. I would adopt the rhythm of life which best suited me, getting up, going to bed and taking my meals at whatsoever hours I pleased. If I did not choose to be clean, to wear nice clothes, to wash and so on, I need not. She would be grieved, but what was her grief, compared to my grief? All she asked was to feel me near her, with her, and the right to contemplate from time to time this extraordinary body both at rest and in motion. Every now and then I interrupted her, to ask what town I was in. But either because she did not understand me, or because she preferred to leave me in ignorance, she did not reply to my question, but went on with her soliloquy, reiterating tirelessly each new proposition, then expounding further, slowly, gently, the benefits for both of us if I would make my home with her. Till nothing was left but this monotonous voice, in the deepening night and the smell of the damp earth and of a strongly scented flower which at the time I could not identify, but which later I identified as spike-lavender. There were beds of it everywhere, in this garden, for Lousse loved spike, she must have told me herself, otherwise I would not have known, she loved it above all other herbs and flowers, because of its smell, and then also because of its spikes, and its colour. And if I had not lost my sense of smell the smell of lavender would always make me think of Lousse, in accordance with the well-known mechanism of association. And she gathered this lavender when it bloomed I presume, left it to dry and then made it up into lavender-bags that she put in her cupboards to perfume her handkerchiefs, her underclothing and house-linen. But none the less from time to time I heard the chiming of the hours, from the clocks and belfries, chiming out longer and longer, then suddenly briefly, then longer and longer again. This will give some idea of the time she took to cozen me, of her patience and physical endurance, for all the time she was squatting or kneeling beside me, whereas I was stretched out at my ease on the grass, now on my back, now on my stomach, now on one side, now on the other. And all the time she never stopped talking, whereas I only opened my mouth to ask, at long intervals, more and more feebly, what town we were in. And sure of her victory at last, or simply feeling she had done all she could and that further insistence was useless, she got up and went away, I don't know where, for I stayed where I was, with regret, mild regret. For in me there have always been two fools, among others, one asking nothing better than to stay where he is and the other imagining that life might be slightly less horrible a little further on. So that I was never disappointed, so to speak, whatever I did, in this domain. And these inseparable fools I indulged turn about, that they might understand their foolishness. And that night there was no question of moon, nor any other light, but it was a night of listening, a night given to the faint soughing and sighing stirring at night in little pleasure gardens, the shy sabbath of leaves and petals and the air that eddies there as it does not in other places, where there is less constraint, and as it does not during the day, when there is more vigilance, and then something else that is not clear, being neither the air nor what it moves, perhaps the far unchanging noise the earth makes and which other noises cover, but not for long. For they do not account for that noise you hear when you really listen, when all seems hushed. And there was another noise, that of my life become the life of this garden as it rode the earth of deeps and wildernesses. Yes, there were times when I forgot not only who I was, but that I was, forgot to be. Then I was no longer that sealed jar to which I owed my being so well preserved, but a wall gave way and I filled with roots and tame stems for example, stakes long since dead and ready for burning, the recess of night and the imminence of dawn, and then the labour of the planet rolling eager into winter, winter would rid it of these contemptible scabs. Or of that winter I was the precarious calm, the thaw of the snows which make no difference and all the horrors of it all all over again. But that did not happen to me often, mostly I stayed in my jar which knew neither seasons nor gardens. And a good thing too. But in there you have to be careful, ask yourself questions, as for example whether you still are, and if no when it stopped, and if yes how long it will still go on, anything at all to keep you from losing the thread of the dream. For my part I willingly asked myself questions, one after the other, just for the sake of looking at them. No, not willingly, wisely, so that I might believe I was still there. And yet it mean. nothing to me to be still there. I called that thinking. I thought almost without stopping, I did not dare stop Perhaps that was the cause of my innocence. It was a little the worse for wear, a little threadbare perhaps, but I was glad to have it, yes, I suppose. Thanks I suppose, as the urchin said when I picked up his marble, I don't know why, I didn't have to, and I suppose he would have preferred to pick it up himself. Or perhaps it wasn't to be picked up. And the effort it cost me, with my stiff leg. The words engraved themselves for ever on my memory, perhaps because I understood them at once, a thing I didn't often do. Not that I was hard of hearing, for I had quite a sensitive ear, and sounds unencumbered with precise meaning were registered perhaps better by me than by most. What was it then? A defect of the understanding perhaps, which only began to vibrate on repeated solicitations, or which did vibrate, if you like, but at a lower frequency, or a higher, than that of ratiocination, if such a thing is conceivable, and such a thing is conceivable, since I conceive it. Yes, the words I heard, and heard distinctly, having quite a sensitive ear, were heard a first time, then a second, and often even a third, as pure sounds, free of all meaning, and this is probably one of the reasons why conversation was unspeakably painful to me. And the words I uttered myself, and which must nearly always have gone with an effort of the intelligence, were often to me as the buzzing of an insect. And this is perhaps one of the reasons I was so untalkative, I mean this trouble I had in understanding not only what others said to me, but also what I said to them. It is true that in the end, by dint of patience, we made ourselves understood, but understood with regard to what, I ask of you, and to what purpose? And to the noises of nature too, and of the works of men, I reacted I think in my own way and without desire of enlightenment. And my eye too, the seeing one, must have been ill-connected with the spider, for I found it hard to name what was mirrored there, often quite distinctly. And without going so far as to say that I saw the world upside down (that would have been too easy) it is certain I saw it in a way inordinately formal, though I was far from being an aesthete, or an artist. And of my two eyes only one functioning more or less correctly, I misjudged the distance separating me from the other world, and often I stretched out my hand for what was far beyond my reach, and often I knocked against obstacles scarcely visible on the horizon. But I was like that even when I had my two eyes, it seems to me, but perhaps not, for it is long since that era of my life, and my recollection of it is more than imperfect. And now I come to think of it, my attempts at taste and smell were scarcely more fortunate, I smelt and tasted without knowing exactly what, nor whether it was good, nor whether it was bad, and seldom twice running the same thing. I would have been I think an excellent husband, incapable of wearying of my wife and committing adultery only from absent-mindedness. Now as to telling you why I stayed a good while with Lousse, no,

I cannot. That is to say I could I suppose, if I took the trouble. But why should I? In order to establish beyond all question that I could not do otherwise? For that is the conclusion I would come to, fatally. I who had loved the image of old Geulincx, dead young, who left me free, on the black boat of Ulysses, to crawl towards the East, along the deck. That is a great measure of freedom, for him who has not the pioneering spirit. And from the poop, poring upon the wave, a sadly rejoicing slave, I follow with my eyes the proud and futile wake. Which, as it bears me from no fatherland away, bears me onward to no shipwreck. A good while then with Lousse. It's vague, a good while, a few months perhaps, a year perhaps. I know it was warm again the day I left, but that meant nothing, in my part of the world, where it seemed to be warm or cold or merely mild at any moment of the year and where the days did not run gently up and down, no, not gently. Perhaps things have changed since. So all I know is that it was much the same weather when I left as when I came, so far as I was capable of knowing what the weather was. And I had been under the weather so long, under all weathers, that I could tell quite well between them, my body could tell between them and seemed even to have its likes, its dislikes. I think I stayed in several rooms one after the other, or alternately, I don't know. In my head there are several windows, that I do know, but perhaps it is always the same one, open variously on the parading universe. The house was fixed, that is perhaps what I mean by these different rooms. House and garden were fixed, thanks to some unknown mechanism of compensation, and I, when I stayed still, as I did most of the time, was fixed too, and when I moved, from place to place, it was very slowly, as in a cage out of time, as the saying is, in the jargon of the schools, and out of space too to be sure. For to be out of one and not out of the other was for cleverer than me, who was not clever, but foolish. But I may be quite wrong. And these different windows that open in my head, when I grope again among those days, really existed perhaps and perhaps do still, in spite of my being no longer there, I mean there looking at them, opening them and shutting them, or crouched in a corner of the room marvelling at the things they framed. But I will not dwell on this episode, so ludicrously brief when you think of it and so poor in substance. For I helped neither in the house nor the garden and knew nothing of what work was going forward, day and night, nothing save the sounds that came to me, dull sounds and sharp ones too, and then often the roar of air being vigorously churned, it seemed to me, and which perhaps was nothing more than the sound of burning. I preferred the garden to the house, to judge by the long hours I spent there, for I spent there the greater part of the day and of the night, whether it was wet or whether it was fine. Men were always busy there, working at I know not what. For the garden seemed hardly to change, from day to day, apart from the tiny changes due to the customary cycle of birth, life and death. And in the midst of those men I drifted like a dead leaf on springs, or else I lay down on the ground, and then they stepped gingerly over me as though I had been a bed of rare flowers. Yes, it was doubtless in order to preserve the garden from apparent change that they laboured at it thus.

My bicycle had disappeared again. Sometimes I felt the wish to look for it again, to find it again and find out what was wrong with it or even go for a little ride on the walks and paths connecting the different parts of the garden. But instead of trying to satisfy this wish I stayed where I was looking at it, if I may say so, looking at it as it shrivelled up and finally disappeared, like the famous fatal skin, only much quicker. For there seem to be two ways of behaving in the presence of wishes, the active and the contemplative, and though they both give the same result it was the latter I preferred, matter of temperament I presume. The garden was surrounded with a high wall, its top bristling with broken glass like fins. But what must have been absolutely unexpected was this, that this wall was broken by a wicket-gate giving free access to the road, for it was never locked, of that I was all but convinced, having opened and closed it without the least trouble on more than one occasion, both by day and by night, and seen it used by others than myself, for the purpose as well of entrance as of exit. I would stick out my nose, then hastily call it in again. A few further remarks. Never did I see a woman within these precincts, and by precincts I do not merely mean the garden, as I probably should, but the house too, but only men, with the obvious exception of Lousse. What I saw and did not see did not matter much admittedly, but I mention it all the same. Lousse herself I saw but little, she seldom showed herself, to me, out of tact perhaps, fearing to alarm me. But I think she spied on me a great deal, hiding behind the bushes, or the curtains, or skulking in the shadows of a first-floor room, with a spy-glass perhaps. For had she not said she desired above all to see me, both coming and going and rooted to the spot. And to get a good view you need the keyhole, the little chink among the leaves, and so on, whatever prevents you from being seen and from seeing more than a little at a time. No? I don't know. Yes, she inspected me, little by little, and even in my very going to bed, my sleeping and my getting up, the mornings that I went to bed. For in this matter I remained faithful to my custom, which was to sleep in the morning, when I slept at all. For it sometimes happened that I did not sleep at all, for several days, without feeling at all the worse for it. For my waking was a kind of sleeping. And I did not always sleep in the same place, but now I slept in the garden, which was large, and now I slept in the house, which was large too, really extremely spacious. And this uncertainty as to the hour and place of my sleeping must have entranced her, I imagine, and made the time pass pleasantly. But it is useless to dwell on this period of my life. If I go on long enough calling that my life I'll end up by believing it. It's the principle of advertising. This period of my life. It reminds me, when I think of it, of air in a water-pipe. So I will only add that this woman went on giving me slow poison, slipping I know not what poisons into the drink she gave me, or into the food she gave me, or both, or one day one, the next the other. That is a grave charge to bring and I do not bring it lightly. And I bring it without ill-feeling, yes, I accuse her without ill-feeling of having drugged my food and drink with noxious and insipid powders and potions. But even sipid they would have made no difference, I would have swallowed it all down with the same whole-heartedness. That celebrated whiff of almonds for example would never have taken away my appetite. My appetite! What a subject. For conversation. I had hardly any. I ate like a thrush. But the little I did eat I devoured with a voracity usually attributed to heavy eaters, and wrongly, for heavy eaters as a rule eat ponderously and with method, that follows from the very notion of heavy eating. Whereas I flung myself at the mess, gulped down the half or the quarter of it in two mouthfuls without chewing (with what would I have chewed?), then pushed it from me with loathing. One would have thought I ate to live! Similarly I would engulf five or six mugs of beer with one swig, then drink nothing for a week. What do you expect, one is what one is, partly at least. Nothing or little to be done. Now as to the substances she insinuated thus into my various systems, I could not say whether they were stimulants or whether they were not rather depressants. The truth is, coenaesthetically speaking of course, I felt more or less the same as usual, that is to say, if I may give myself away, so terror-stricken that I was virtually bereft of feeling, not to say of consciousness, and drowned in a deep and merciful torpor shot with brief abominable gleams, I give you my word. Against such harmony of what avail the miserable molys of Lousse, administered in infinitesimal doses probably, to draw the pleasure out. Not that they remained entirely without effect, no, that would be an exaggeration. For from time to time I caught myself making a little bound in the air, two or three feet off the ground at least, at least, I who never bounded. It looked like levitation. And it happened too, less surprisingly, when I was walking, or even propped up against something, that I suddenly collapsed, like a puppet when its strings are dropped, and lay long where I fell, literally boneless. Yes, that struck me as less strange, for I was used to collapsing thus, but with this difference, that I felt it coming, and prepared myself accordingly, as an epileptic does when he feels the fit coming. I mean that knowing I was going to fall I lay down, or I wedged myself where I stood so firmly that nothing short of an earthquake could have dislodged me, and I waited. But these were precautions I did not always take, preferring the fall to the trouble of having to lie down or stand fast. Whereas the falls I suffered when with Lousse did not give me a chance to circumvent them. But all the same they surprised me less, they were more in keeping with me, than the little bounds. For even as a child I do not remember ever having bounded, neither rage nor pain ever made me bound, even as a child, however ill-qualified I am to speak of that time. Now with regard to my food, it seems to me I ate it as, when and where it best suited me. I never had to call for it. It was brought to me, wherever I happened to be, on a tray. I can still see the tray, almost at will, it was round, with a low rim, to keep the things from falling off, and coated with red lacquer, cracking here and there. It was small too, as became a tray having to hold a single dish and one slab of bread For the little I ate I crammed into my mouth with my hands, and the bottles I drank from the bottle were brought to me separately, in a basket. But this basket made no impression on me, good or bad, and I could not tell you what it was like. And many a time, having strayed for one reason or another from the place where the meal had been brought to me, I couldn't find it again, when I felt the desire to eat. Then I searched high and low, often with success, being fairly familiar with the places where I was likely to have been, but often too in vain. Or I did not search at all, preferring hunger and thirst to the trouble of having to search without being sure of finding, or of having to ask for another tray to be brought, and another basket, or the same, to the place where I was. It was then I regretted my sucking-stone. And when I talk of preferring, for example, or regretting, it must not be supposed that I opted for the least evil, and adopted it, for that would be wrong. But not knowing exactly what I was doing or avoiding, I did it and avoided it all unsuspecting that one day, much later, I would have to go back over all these acts and omissions, dimmed and mellowed by age, and drag them into the eudemonistic slop. But I must say that with Lousse my health got no worse, or scarcely. By which I mean that what was already wrong with me got worse and worse, little by little, as was only to be expected. But there was kindled no new seat of suffering or infection, except of course those arising from the spread of existing plethoras and deficiencies. But I may very well be wrong. For of the disorders to come, as for example the loss of the toes of my left foot, no, I am wrong, my right foot, who can say exactly when on my helpless clay the fatal seeds were sown. So all I can say, and I do my best to say no more, is that during my stay with Lousse no more new symptoms appeared, of a pathological nature, I mean nothing new or strange, nothing I could not have foreseen if I could have, nothing at all comparable to the sudden loss of half my toes. For that is something I could never have foreseen and the meaning of which I have never fathomed, I mean its connexion with my other discomforts, from my ignorance of medical matters, I suppose. For all things run together, in the body's long madness, I feel it. But it is useless to drag out this chapter of my, how shall I say, my existence, for it has no sense, to my mind. It is a dug at which I tug in vain, it yields nothing but wind and spatter. So I will confine myself to the following brief additional remarks, and the first of which is this, that Lousse was a woman of an extraordinary flatness, physically speaking of course, to such a point that I am still wondering this evening, in the comparative silence of my last abode, if she was not a man rather or at least an androgyne. She had a somewhat hairy face, or am I imagining it, in the interests of the narrative? The poor woman, I saw her so little, so little looked at her. And was not her voice suspiciously deep? So she appears to me today. Don't be tormenting yourself, Molloy, man or woman, what does it matter? But I cannot help asking myself the following question. Could a woman have stopped me as I swept towards mother? Probably. Better still, was such an encounter possible, I mean between me and a woman? Now men, I have rubbed up against a few men in my time, but women? Oh well, I may as well confess it now, yes, I once rubbed up against one. I don't mean my mother, I did more than rub up against her. And if you don't mind we'll leave my mother out of all this. But another who might have been my mother, and even I think my grandmother, if chance had not willed otherwise. Listen to him now talking about chance. It was she made me acquainted with love. She went by the peaceful name of Ruth I think, but I can't say for certain. Perhaps the name was Edith. She had a hole between her legs, oh not the bunghole I had always imagined, but a slit, and in this I put, or rather she put, my so-called virile member, not without difficulty, and I toiled and moiled until I discharged or gave up trying or was begged by her to stop. A mug's game in my opinion and tiring on top of that, in the long run. But I lent myself to it with a good enough grace, knowing it was love, for she had told me so. She bent over the couch, because of her rheumatism, and in I went from behind. It was the only position she could bear, because of her lumbago. It seemed all right to me for I had seen dogs, and I was astonished when she confided that you could go about it differently. I wonder what she meant exactly. Perhaps after all she put me in her rectum. A matter of complete indifference to me, I needn't tell you. But is it true love, in the rectum? That's what bothers me sometimes. Have I never known true love, after all? She too was an eminently flat woman and she moved with short stiff steps, leaning on an ebony stick. Perhaps she too was a man, yet another of them. But in that case surely our testicles would have collided, while we writhed. Perhaps she held hers tight in her hand, on purpose to avoid it. She favoured voluminous tempestuous shifts and petticoats and other undergarments whose names I forget. They welled up all frothing and swishing and then, congress achieved, broke over us in slow cascades. And all I could see was her taut yellow nape which every now and then I set my teeth in, forgetting I had none, such is the power of instinct. We met in a rubbish dump, unlike any other, and yet they are all alike, rubbish dumps. I don't know what she was doing there. I was limply poking about in the garbage saying probably, for at that age I must still have been capable of general ideas, This is life. She had no time to lose, I had nothing to lose, I would have made love with a goat, to know what love was She had a dainty flat, no, not dainty, it made you want to lie down in a corner and never get up again. I liked it. It was full of dainty furniture, under our desperate strokes the couch moved forward on its castors, the whole place fell about our ears, it was pandemonium. Our commerce was not without tenderness, with trembling hands she cut my toe-nails and I rubbed her rump with winter cream. This idyll was of short duration. Poor Edith, I hastened her end perhaps. Anyway it was she who started it, in the rubbish dump, when she laid her hand upon my fly. More precisely, I was bent double over a heap of muck, in the hope of finding something to disgust me for ever with eating, when she, undertaking me from behind, thrust her stick between my legs and began to titillate my privates. She gave me money after each session, to me who would have consented to know love, and probe it to the bottom, without charge. But she was an idealist. I would have preferred it seems to me an orifice less arid and roomy, that would have given me a higher opinion of love it seems to me. However. Twixt finger and thumb tis heaven in comparison. But love is no doubt above such base contingencies. And not when you are comfortable, but when your frantic member casts about for a rubbing-place, and the unction of a little mucous membrane, and meeting with none does not beat in retreat, but retains its tumefaction, it is then no doubt that true love comes to pass, and wings away, high above the tight fit and the loose. And when you add a little pedicure and massage, having nothing to do with the instant of bliss strictly speaking, then I feel no further doubt is justified, in this connexion. The other thing that bothers me, in this connexion, is the indifference with which I learnt of her death, one black night I was crawling towards her, an indifference softened indeed by the pain of losing a source of revenue. She died taking a warm tub, as her custom was before receiving me. It limbered her up. When I think she might have expired in my arms! The tub overturned and the dirty water spilt all over the floor and down on top of the lodger below, who gave the alarm. Well, well, I didn't think I knew this story so well. She must have been a woman after all, if she hadn't been it would have got around, in the neighbourhood. It is true they were extraordinarily reserved, in my part of the world, about everything connected with sexual matters. But things have perhaps changed since my time. And it is quite possible that the fact of having found a man when they should have found a woman was immediately repressed and forgotten, by the few unfortunate enough to know about it. As it is quite possible that everybody knew about it, and spoke about it, with the sole exception of myself. But there is one thing that torments me, when I delve into all this, and that is to know whether all my life has been devoid of love or whether I really met with it, in Ruth. What I do know for certain is that I never sought to repeat the experience, having I suppose the intuition that it had been unique and perfect, of its kind, achieved and inimitable, and that it behoved me to preserve its memory, pure of all pastiche, in my heart, even if it meant my resorting from time to time to the alleged joys of so-called self-abuse. Don't talk to me about the chambermaid, I should never have mentioned her, she was long before, I was sick, perhaps there was no chambermaid, ever, in my life. Molloy, or life without a chambermaid. All of which goes to demonstrate that the fact of having met Lousse and even frequented her, in a way, proved nothing as to her sex. And I am quite willing to go on thinking of her as an old woman, widowed and withered, and of Ruth as another, for she too used to speak of her defunct husband and of his inability to satisfy her legitimate cravings. And there are days, like this evening, when my memory confuses them and I am tempted to think of them as one and the same old hag, flattened and crazed by life. And God forgive me, to tell you the horrible truth, my mother's image sometimes mingles with theirs, which is literally unendurable, like being crucified, I don't know why and I don't want to. But I left Lousse at last, one warm airless night, without saying goodbye, as I might at least have done, and without her trying to hold me back, except perhaps by spells. But she must have seen me go, get up, take my crutches and go away, springing on them through the air. And she must have seen the wicket close behind me, for it closed by itself, with the help of a spring, and known me gone, for ever. For she knew the way I had of going to the wicket and peeping out, then quickly drawing back. And she did not try and hold me back but she went and sat down on her dog's grave, perhaps, which was mine too in a way, and which by the way she had not sown with grass, as I had thought, but with all kinds of little many-coloured flowers and herbacious plants, selected I imagine in such a way that when some went out others lit up. I left her my bicycle which I had taken a dislike to, suspecting it to be the vehicle of some malignant agency and perhaps the cause of my recent misfortunes. But all the same I would have taken it with me if I had known where it was and that it was in running order. But I did not. And I was afraid, if I tried to find out, of wearing out the small voice saying, Get out of here, Molloy, take your crutches and get out of here and which I had taken so long to understand, for I had been hearing it for a long time. And perhaps I understood it all wrong, but I understood it and that was the novelty. And it seemed to me I was not necessarily going for good and that I might come back one day, by devious winding ways, to the place I was leaving. And perhaps my course is not yet fully run. Outside in the road the wind was blowing, it was another world. Not knowing where I was nor consequently what way I ought to go I went with the wind. And when, well slung between my crutches, I took off, then I felt it helping me, that little wind blowing from what quarter I could not tell. And don't come talking at me of the stars, they look all the same to me, yes, I cannot read the stars, in spite of my astronomical studies. But I entered the first shelter I came to and stayed there till dawn, for I knew I was bound to be stopped by the first policeman and asked what I was doing, a question to which I have never been able to find the correct reply. But it cannot have been a real shelter and I did not stay till dawn, for a man came in soon after me and drove me out. And yet there was room for two. I think he was a kind of nightwatchman, a man of some kind certainly, he must have been employed to watch over some kind of public works, digging I suppose. I see a brazier. There must have been a touch of autumn in the air, as the saying is. I therefore moved on and ensconced myself on a flight of stairs, in a mean lodging-house, because there was no door or it didn't shut, I don't know. Long before dawn this lodging-house began to empty. People came down the stairs, men and women. I glued myself against the wall. They paid no heed to me, nobody interfered with me. In the end I too went away, when I deemed it prudent, and wandered about the town in search of a familiar monument, so that I might say, I am in my town, after all, I have been there all the time. The town was waking, doors opening and shutting, soon the noise would be deafening. But espying a narrow alley between two high buildings I looked about me, then slipped into it. Little windows overlooked it, on either side, on every floor, facing one another. Lavatory lights I suppose. There are things from time to time, in spite of everything, that impose themselves on the understanding with the force of axioms, for unknown reasons. There was no way out of the alley, it was not so much an alley as a blind alley. At the end there were two recesses, no, that's not the word, opposite each other, littered with miscellaneous rubbish and with excrements, of dogs and masters, some dry and odourless, others still moist. Ah those papers never to be read again, perhaps never read. Here lovers must have lain at night and exchanged their vows. I entered one of the alcoves, wrong again, and leaned against the wall. I would have preferred to lie down and there was no proof that I would not. But for the moment I was content to lean against the wall, my feet far from the wall, on the verge of slipping, but I had other props, the tips of my crutches. But a few minutes later I crossed the alley into the other chapel, that's the word, where I felt I might feel better, and settled myself in the same hypotenusal posture. And at first I did actually seem to feel a little better, but little by little I acquired the conviction that such was not the case. A fine rain was falling and I took off my hat to give my skull the benefit of it, my skull all cracked and furrowed and on fire, on fire. But I also took it off because it was digging into my neck, because of the thrust of the wall. So I had two good reasons for taking it off and they were none too many, neither alone would ever have prevailed I feel. I threw it from me with a careless lavish gesture and back it came, at the end of its string or lace, and after a few throes came to rest against my side. At last I began to think, that is to say to listen harder. Little chance of my being found there, I was in peace for as long as I could endure peace. For the space of an instant I considered settling down there, making it my lair and sanctuary, for the space of an instant. I took the vegetable knife from my pocket and set about opening my wrist. But pain soon got the better of me. First I cried out, then I gave up, closed the knife and put it back in my pocket. I wasn't particularly disappointed, in my heart of hearts I had not hoped for anything better. So much for that. And backsliding has always depressed me, but life seems made up of backsliding, and death itself must be a kind of backsliding, I wouldn't be surprised. Did I say the wind had fallen? A fine rain falling, somehow that seems to exclude all idea of wind.

My knees are enormous, I have just caught a glimpse of them, when I got up for a second. My two legs are as stiff as a life-sentence and yet I sometimes get up. What can you expect? Thus from time to time I shall recall my present existence compared to which this is a nursery tale. But only from time to time, so that it may be said, if necessary, whenever necessary, Is it possible that thing is still alive? Or again, Oh it's only a diary, it'll soon be over. That my knees are enormous, that I still get up from time to time, these are things that do not seem at first sight to signify anything in particular. I record them all the more willingly. In the end I left the impasse, where half-standing half-lying I may have had a little sleep, my little morning sleep, and I set off, believe it or not, towards the sun, why not, the wind having fallen. Or rather towards the least gloomy quarter of the heavens which a vast cloud was shrouding from the zenith to the skylines. It was from this cloud the above rain was falling. See how all things hang together. And as to making up my mind which quarter of the heavens was the least gloomy, it was no easy matter. For at first sight the heavens seemed uniformly gloomy. But by taking a little pains, for there were moments in my life when I took a little pains, I obtained a result, that is to say I came to a decision, in this matter. So I was able to continue on my way, saying, I am going towards the sun, that is to say in theory towards the East, or perhaps the South-East, for I am no longer with Lousse, but out in the heart again of the pre-established harmony, which makes so sweet a music, which is so sweet a music, for one who has an ear for music. People were hastening angrily to and fro, most of them, some in the shelter of the umbrella, others in that perhaps a little less effective of the rainproof coat. A few had taken refuge under trees and archways. And among those who, more courageous or less delicate, came and went, and among those who had stopped, to avoid getting wet, many a one must have said, They are right, I am wrong, meaning by they the category to which he did not belong, or so I imagine. As many a one too must have said, I am right, they are wrong, while continuing to storm against the foul weather that was the occasion of his superiority. But at the sight of a young old man of wretched aspect, shivering all alone in a narrow doorway, I suddenly remembered the project conceived the day of my encounter with Lousse and her dog and which this encounter had prevented me from carrying out. So I went and stood beside him, with the air I hoped of one who says, Here's a clever fellow, let me follow his example. But before I should make my little speech, which I wished to seem spontaneous and so did not make at once, he went out into the rain and away. For this speech was one liable, in virtue of its content, if not to offend at least to astonish. And that was why it was important to deliver it at the right moment and in the right tone. I apologize for these details, in a moment we'll go faster, much faster. And then perhaps relapse again into a wealth of filthy circumstance. But which in its turn again will give way to vast frescoes, dashed off with loathing. Homo mensura can't do without staffage. There I am then in my turn alone, in the doorway. I could not hope for anyone to come and stand beside me, and yet it was a possibility I did not exclude. That's a fairly good caricature of my state of mind at that instant. Net result, I stayed where

I was. I had stolen from Lousse a little silver, oh nothing much, massive teaspoons for the most part, and other small objects whose utility I did not grasp but which seemed as if they might have some value. Among these latter there was one which haunts me still, from time to time. It consisted of two crosses joined, at their points of intersection, by a bar, and resembled a tiny sawing-horse, with this difference however, that the crosses of the true sawing-horse are not perfect crosses, but truncated at the top, whereas the crosses of the little object I am referring to were perfect, that is to say composed each of two identical V's, one upper with its opening above, like all V's for that matter, and the other lower with its opening below, or more precisely of four rigorously identical V's, the two I have just named and then two more, one on the right hand, the other on the left, having their openings on the right and the left respectively. But perhaps it is out of place to speak here of right and left, of upper and lower. For this little object did not seem to have any base properly so-called, but stood with equal stability on any one of its four bases, and without any change of appearance, which is not true of the sawing-horse. This strange instrument I think I still have somewhere, for I could never bring myself to sell it, even in my worst need, for I could never understand what possible purpose it could serve, nor even contrive the faintest hypothesis on the subject. And from time to time I took it from my pocket and gazed upon it, with an astonished and affectionate gaze, if I had not been incapable of affection. But for a certain time I think it inspired me with a kind of veneration, for there was no doubt in my mind that it was not an object of virtu, but that it had a most specific function always to be hidden from me. I could therefore puzzle over it endlessly without the least risk. For to know nothing is nothing, not to want to know anything likewise, but to be beyond knowing anything, to know you are beyond knowing anything, that is when peace enters in, to the soul of the incurious seeker. It is then the true division begins, of twenty-two by seven for example, and the pages fill with the true ciphers at last. But I would rather not affirm anything on this subject. What does seem undeniable to me on the contrary is this, that giving in to the evidence, to a very strong probability rather, I left the shelter of the doorway and began levering myself forward, swinging slowly through the sullen air. There is rapture, or there should be, in the motion crutches give. It is a series of little flights, skimming the ground. You take off, you land, through the thronging sound in wind and limb, who have to fasten one foot to the ground before they dare lift up the other. And even their most joyous hastening is less aerial than my hobble. But these are reasonings, based on analysis. And though my mind was still taken up with my mother, and with the desire to know if I was near her, it was gradually less so, perhaps because of the silver in my pockets, but I think not, and then too because these were ancient cares and the mind cannot always brood on the same cares, but needs fresh cares from time to time, so as to revert with renewed vigour, when the time comes, to ancient cares. But can one speak here of fresh and ancient cares? I think not. But it would be hard for me to prove it. What I can assert, without fear of—without fear, is that I gradually lost interest in knowing, among other things, what town I was in and if I should soon find my mother and settle the matter between us. And even the nature of that matter grew dim, for me, without however vanishing completely. For it was no small matter and I was bent on it. All my life, I think, I had been bent on it. Yes, so far as I was capable of being bent on anything all a lifetime long, and what a lifetime, I had been bent on settling this matter between my mother and me, but had never succeeded. And while saying to myself that time was running out, and that soon it would be too late, was perhaps too late already, to settle the matter in question, I felt myself drifting towards other cares, other phantoms. And far more than to know what town I was in, my haste was now to leave it, even were it the right one, where my mother had waited so long and perhaps was waiting still. And it seemed to me that if I kept on in a straight line I was bound to leave it, sooner or later. So I set myself to this as best I could, making allowance for the drift to the right of the feeble light that was my guide. And my pertinacity was such that I did indeed come to the ramparts as night was falling, having described a good quarter of a circle, through bad navigation. It is true I stopped many times, to rest, but not for long, for I felt harried, wrongly perhaps. But in the country there is another justice, other judges, at first. And having cleared the ramparts I had to confess the sky was clearing, prior to its winding in the other shroud, night. Yes, the great cloud was ravelling, discovering here and there a pale and dying sky, and the sun, already down, was manifest in the livid tongues of fire darting towards the zenith, falling and darting again, ever more pale and languid, and doomed no sooner lit to be extinguished. This phenomenon, if I remember rightly, was characteristic of my region. Things are perhaps different today. Though I fail to see, never having left my region, what right I have to speak of its characteristics. No, I never escaped, and even the limits of my region were unknown to me. But I felt they were far away. But this feeling was based on nothing serious, it was a simple feeling. For if my region had ended no further than my feet could carry me, surely I would have felt it changing slowly. For regions do not suddenly end, as far as I know, but gradually merge into one another. And I never noticed anything of the kind, but however far I went, and in no matter what direction, it was always the same sky, always the same earth, precisely, day after day and night after night. On the other hand, if it is true that regions gradually merge into one another, and this remains to be proved, then I may well have left mine many times, thinking I was still within it. But I preferred to abide by my simple feeling and its voice that said, Molloy, your region is vast, you have never left it and you never shall. And wheresoever you wander, within its distant limits, things will always be the same, precisely. It would thus appear, if this is so, that my movements owed nothing to the places they caused to vanish, but were due to something else, to the buckled wheel that carried me, in unforeseeable jerks, from fatigue to rest, and inversely, for example. But now I do not wander any more, anywhere any more, and indeed I scarcely stir at all, and yet nothing is changed. And the confines of my room, of my bed, of my body, are as remote from me as were those of my region, in the days of my splendour.

And the cycle continues, joltingly, of flight and bivouac, in an Egypt without bounds, without infant, without mother. And when I see my hands, on the sheet, which they love to floccillate already, they are not mine, less than ever mine, I have no arms, they are a couple, they play with the sheet, love-play perhaps, trying to get up perhaps, one on top of the other. But it doesn't last, I bring them back, little by little, towards me, it's resting time. And with my feet it's the same, sometimes, when I see them at the foot of the bed, one with toes, the other without. And that is more deserving of mention. For my legs, corresponding here to my arms of a moment ago, are both stiff now and very sore, and I shouldn't be able to forget them as I can my arms, which are more or less sound and well. And yet I do forget them and I watch the couple as they watch each other, a great way off. But my feet are not like my hands, I do not bring them back to me, when they become my feet again, for I cannot, but they stay there, far from me, but not so far as before. End of the recall. But you'd think that once well clear of the town, and having turned round to look at it, what there was to see of it, you'd think that then I should have realized whether it was really my town or not. But no, I looked at it in vain, and perhaps unquestioningly, and simply to give the gods a chance, by turning round. Perhaps I only made a show of looking at it. I didn't feel I missed my bicycle, no, not really, I didn't mind going on my way the way I said, swinging low in the dark over the earth, along the little empty country roads. And I said there was little likelihood of my being molested and that it was more likely I should molest them, if they saw me.

Morning is the time to hide. They wake up, hale and hearty, their tongues hanging out for order, beauty and justice, baying for their due. Yes, from eight or nine till noon is the dangerous time. But towards noon things quiet down, the most implacable are sated, they go home, it might have been better but they've done a good job, there have been a few survivors but they'll give no more trouble, each man counts his rats. It may begin again in the early afternoon, after the banquet, the celebrations, the congratulations, the orations, but it's nothing compared to the morning, mere fun. Coming up to four or five of course there is the night-shift, the watchmen, beginning to bestir themselves. But already the day is over, the shadows lengthen, the walls multiply, you hug the walls, bowed down like a good boy, oozing with obsequiousness, having nothing to hide, hiding from mere terror, looking neither right nor left, hiding but not provocatively, ready to come out, to smile, to listen, to crawl, nauseating but not pestilent, less rat than toad. Then the true night, perilous too but sweet to him who knows it, who can open to it like the flower to the sun, who himself is night, day and night. No there is not much to be said for the night either, but compared to the day there is much to be said for it, and notably compared to the morning there is everything to be said for it. For the night purge is in the hands of technicians, for the most part. They do nothing else, the bulk of the population have no part in it, preferring their warm beds, all things considered. Day is the time for lynching, for sleep is sacred, and especially the morning, between breakfast and lunch. My first care then, after a few miles in the desert dawn, was to look for a place to sleep, for sleep too is a kind of protection, strange as it may seem. For sleep, if it excites the lust to capture, seems to appease the lust to kill, there and then and bloodily, any hunter will tell you that. For the monster on the move, or on the watch, lurking in his lair, there is no mercy, whereas he taken unawares, in his sleep, may sometimes get the benefit of milder feelings, which deflect the barrel, sheathe the kris. For the hunter is weak at heart and sentimental, overflowing with repressed treasures of gentleness and compassion. And it is thanks to this sweet sleep of terror or exhaustion that many a foul beast, and worthy of extermination, can live on till he dies in the peace and quiet of our zoological gardens, broken only by the innocent laughter, the knowing laughter, of children and their elders, on Sundays and Bank Holidays. And I for my part have always preferred slavery to death, I mean being put to death. For death is a condition I have never been able to conceive to my satisfaction and which therefore cannot go down in the ledger of weal and woe. Whereas my notions on being put to death inspired me with confidence, rightly or wrongly, and I felt I was entitled to act on them, in certain emergencies. Oh they weren't notions like yours, they were notions like mine, all spasm, sweat and trembling, without an atom of common sense or lucidity. But they were the best I had. Yes, the confusion of my ideas on the subject of death was such that I sometimes wondered, believe me or not, if it wasn't a state of being even worse than life. So I found it natural not to rush into it and, when I forgot myself to the point of trying, to stop in time. It's my only excuse. So I crawled into some hole somewhere I suppose and waited, half sleeping, half sighing, groaning and laughing, or feeling my body, to see if anything had changed, for the morning frenzy to abate. Then I resumed my spirals. And as to saying what became of me, and where I went, in the months and perhaps the years that followed, no. For I weary of these inventions and others beckon to me. But in order to blacken a few more pages may I say I spent some time at the seaside, without incident. There are people the sea doesn't suit, who prefer the mountains or the plain. Personally I feel no worse there than anywhere else. Much of my life has ebbed away before this shivering expanse, to the sound of the waves in storm and calm, and the claws of the surf. Before, no, more than before, one with, spread on the sand, or in a cave. In the sand I was in my element, letting it trickle between my fingers, scooping holes that I filled in a moment later or that filled themselves in, flinging it in the air by handfuls, rolling in it. And in the cave, lit by the beacons at night, I knew what to do in order to be no worse off than elsewhere. And that my land went no further, in one direction at least, did not displease me. And to feel there was one direction at least in which I could go no further, without first getting wet, then drowned, was a blessing. For I have always said, First learn to walk, then you can take swimming lessons. But don't imagine my region ended at the coast, that would be a grave mistake. For it was this sea too, its reefs and distant islands, and its hidden depths. And I too once went forth on it, in a sort of oarless skiff, but I paddled with an old bit of driftwood. And I sometimes wonder if I ever came back, from that voyage. For if I see myself putting to sea, and the long hours without landfall, I do not see the return, the tossing on the breakers, and I do not hear the frail keel grating on the shore. I took advantage of being at the seaside to lay in a store of sucking stones. They were pebbles but I call them stones. Yes, on this occasion I laid in a considerable store. I distributed them equally between my four pockets, and sucked them turn and turn about. This raised a problem which I first solved in the following way. I had say sixteen stones, four in each of my four pockets these being the two pockets of my trousers and the two pockets of my greatcoat. Taking a stone from the right pocket of my greatcoat, and putting it in my mouth, I replaced it in the right pocket of my greatcoat by a stone from the right pocket of my trousers, which I replaced by a stone from the left pocket of my trousers, which I replaced by a stone from the left pocket of my greatcoat, which I replaced by the stone which was in my mouth, as soon as I had finished sucking it. Thus there were still four stones in each of my four pockets, but not quite the same stones. And when the desire to suck took hold of me again, I drew again on the right pocket of my greatcoat, certain of not taking the same stone as the last time. And while I sucked it I rearranged the other stones in the way I have just described. And so on. But this solution did not satisfy me fully. For it did not escape me that, by an extraordinary hazard, the four stones circulating thus might always be the same four. In which case, far from sucking the sixteen stones turn and turn about, I was really only sucking four, always the same, turn and turn about. But I shuffled them well in my pockets, before I began to suck, and again, while I sucked, before transferring them, in the hope of obtaining a more general circulation of the stones from pocket to pocket. But this was only a makeshift that could not long content a man like me. So I began to look for something else. And the first thing I hit upon was that I might do better to transfer the stones four by four, instead of one by one, that is to say, during the sucking, to take the three stones remaining in the right pocket of my greatcoat and replace them by the four in the right pocket of my trousers, and these by the four in the left pocket of my trousers, and these by the four in the left pocket of my greatcoat, and finally these by the three from the right pocket of my greatcoat, plus the one, as soon as I had finished sucking it, which was in my mouth. Yes, it seemed to me at first that by so doing I would arrive at a better result. But on further reflection I had to change my mind and confess that the circulation of the stones four by four came to exactly the same thing as their circulation one by one. For if I was certain of finding each time, in the right pocket of my greatcoat, four stones totally different from their immediate predecessors, the possibility nevertheless remained of my always chancing on the same stone, within each group of four, and consequently of my sucking, not the sixteen turn and turn about as I wished, but in fact four only, always the same, turn and turn about. So I had to seek elsewhere than in the mode of circulation. For no matter how I caused the stones to circulate, I always ran the same risk. It was obvious that by increasing the number of my pockets I was bound to increase my chances of enjoying my stones in the way I planned, that is to say one after the other until their number was exhausted. Had I had eight pockets, for example, instead of the four I did have, then even the most diabolical hazard could not have prevented me from sucking at least eight of my sixteen stones, turn and turn about. The truth is I should have needed sixteen pockets in order to be quite easy in my mind. And for a long time I could see no other conclusion than this, that short of having sixteen pockets, each with its stone, I could never reach the goal I had set myself, short of an extraordinary hazard. And if at a pinch I could double the number of my pockets, were it only by dividing each pocket in two, with the help of a few safety-pins let us say, to quadruple them seemed to be more than I could manage. And I did not feel inclined to take all that trouble for a half-measure. For I was beginning to lose all sense of measure, after all this wrestling and wrangling, and to say, All or nothing. And if I was tempted for an instant to establish a more equitable proportion between my stones and my pockets, by reducing the former to the number of the latter, it was only for an instant. For it would have been an admission of defeat. And sitting on the shore, before the sea, the sixteen stones spread out before my eyes, I gazed at them in anger and perplexity. For just as I had difficulty in sitting on a chair, or in an arm-chair, because of my stiff leg you understand, so I had none in sitting on the ground, because of my stiff leg and my stiffening leg, for it was about this time that my good leg, good in the sense that it was not stiff, began to stiffen. I needed a prop under the ham you understand, and even under the whole length of the leg, the prop of the earth. And while I gazed thus at my stones, revolving interminable martingales all equally defective, and crushing handfuls of sand, so that the sand ran through my fingers and fell back on the strand, yes, while thus I lulled my mind and part of my body, one day suddenly it dawned on the former, dimly, that I might perhaps achieve my purpose without increasing the number of my pockets, or reducing the number of my stones, but simply by sacrificing the principle of trim. The meaning of this illumination, which suddenly began to sing within me, like a verse of Isaiah, or of Jeremiah, I did not penetrate at once, and notably the word trim, which I had never met with, in this sense, long remained obscure. Finally I seemed to grasp that this word trim could not here mean anything else, anything better, than the distribution of the sixteen stones in four groups of four, one group in each pocket, and that it was my refusal to consider any distribution other than this that had vitiated my calculations until then and rendered the problem literally insoluble. And it was on the basis of this interpretation, whether right or wrong, that I finally reached a solution, inelegant assuredly, but sound, sound. Now I am willing to believe, indeed I firmly believe, that other solutions to this problem might have been found, and indeed may still be found, no less sound, but much more elegant, than the one I shall now describe, if I can. And I believe too that had I been a little more insistent, a little more resistant, I could have found them myself. But I was tired, but I was tired, and I contented myself ingloriously with the first solution that was a solution, to this problem. But not to go over the heartbreaking stages through which I passed before I came to it, here it is, in all its hideousness. All (all !) that was necessary was to put for example, to begin with, six stones in the right pocket of my greatcoat, or supply-pocket, five in the right pocket of my trousers, and five in the left pocket of my trousers, that makes the lot, twice five ten plus six sixteen, and none, for none remained, in the left pocket of my greatcoat, which for the time being remained empty, empty of stones that is, for its usual contents remained, as well as occasional objects. For where do you think I hid my vegetable knife, my silver, my horn and the other things that I have not yet named, perhaps shall never name. Good. Now I can begin to suck. Watch me closely. I take a stone from the right pocket of my greatcoat, suck it, stop sucking it, put it in the left pocket of my greatcoat, the one empty (of stones). I take a second stone from the right pocket of my greatcoat, suck it, put it in the left pocket of my greatcoat. And so on until the right pocket of my greatcoat is empty (apart from its usual and casual contents) and the six stones I have just sucked, one after the other, are all in the left pocket of my greatcoat. Pausing then, and concentrating, so as not to make a balls of it, I transfer to the right pocket of my greatcoat, in which there are no stones left, the five stones in the right pocket of my trousers, which I replace by the five stones in the left pocket of my trousers, which I replace by the six stones in the left pocket of my greatcoat. At this stage then the left pocket of my greatcoat is again empty of stones, while the right pocket of my greatcoat is again supplied, and in the right way, that is to say with other stones than those I have just sucked. These other stones I then begin to suck, one after the other, and to transfer as I go along to the left pocket of my greatcoat, being absolutely certain, as far as one can be in an affair of this kind, that I am not sucking the same stones as a moment before, but others. And when the right pocket of my greatcoat is again empty (of stones), and the five I have just sucked are all without exception in the left pocket of my greatcoat, then I proceed to the same redistribution as a moment before, or a similar redestribution, that is to say I transfer to the right pocket of my greatcoat, now again available, the five stones in the right pocket of my trousers, which I replace by the six stones in the left pocket of my trousers, which I replace by the five stones in the left pocket of my greatcoat. And there I am ready to begin again. Do I have to go on? No, for it is clear that after the next series, of sucks and transfers, I shall be back where I started, that is to say with the first six stones back in the supply pocket, the next five in the right pocket of my stinking old trousers and finally the last five in left pocket of same, and my sixteen stones will have been sucked once at least in impeccable succession, not one sucked twice, not one left unsucked. It is true that the next time I could scarcely hope to suck my stones in the same order as the first time and that the first, seventh and twelfth for example of the first cycle might very well be the sixth, eleventh and sixteenth respectively of the second, if the worst came to the worst. But that was a drawback I could not avoid. And if in the cycles taken together utter confusion was bound to reign, at least within each cycle taken separately I could be easy in my mind, at least as easy as one can be, in a proceeding of this kind. For in order for each cycle to be identical, as to the succession of stones in my mouth, and God knows I had set my heart on it, the only means were numbered stones or sixteen pockets. And rather than make twelve more pockets or number my stones, I preferred to make the best of the comparative peace of mind

I enjoyed within each cycle taken separately. For it was not enough to number the stones, but I would have had to remember, every time I put a stone in my mouth, the number I needed and look for it in my pocket. Which would have put me off stone for ever, in a very short time. For I would never have been sure of not making a mistake, unless of course I had kept a kind of register, in which to tick off the stones one by one, as I sucked them. And of this I believed myself incapable. No, the only perfect solution would have been the sixteen pockets, symmetrically disposed, each one with its stone. Then I would have needed neither to number nor to think, but merely, as I sucked a given stone, to move on the fifteen others, each to the next pocket, a delicate business admittedly, but within my power, and to call always on the same pocket when I felt like a suck. This would have freed me from all anxiety, not only within each cycle taken separately, but also for the sum of all cycles, though they went on forever. But however imperfect my own solution was, I was pleased at having found it all alone, yes, quite pleased. And if it was perhaps less sound than I had thought in the first flush of discovery, its inelegance never diminished. And it was above all inelegant in this, to my mind, that the uneven distribution was painful to me, bodily. It is true that a kind of equilibrium was reached, at a given moment, in the early stages of each cycle, namely after the third suck and before the fourth, but it did not last long, and the rest of the time I felt the weight of the stones dragging me now to one side, now to the other. So it was something more than a principle I abandoned, when I abandoned the equal distribution, it was a bodily need. But to suck the stones in the way I have described, not haphazard, but with method, was also I think a bodily need. Here then were two incompatible bodily needs, at loggerheads. Such things happen. But deep down I didn't give a tinker's curse about being off my balance, dragged to the right hand and the left, backwards and forwards. And deep down it was all the same to me whether I sucked a different stone each time or always the same stone, until the end of time. For they all tasted exactly the same. And if I had collected sixteen, it was not in order to ballast myself in such and such a way, or to suck them turn about, but simply to have a little store, so as never to be without. But deep down I didn't give a fiddler's curse about being without, when they were all gone they would be all gone, I wouldn't be any the worse off, or hardly any. And the solution to which I rallied in the end was to throw away all the stones but one, which I kept now in one pocket, now in another, and which of course I soon lost, or threw away, or gave away, or swallowed. It was a wild part of the coast. I don't remember having been seriously molested. The black speck I was, in the great pale stretch of sand, who could wish it harm? Some came near, to see what it was, whether it wasn't something of value from a wreck, washed up by the storm. But when they saw the jetsam was alive, decently if wretchedly clothed, they turned away. Old women and young ones, yes, too, come to gather wood, came and stared, in the early days. But they were always the same and it was in vain I moved from one place to another, in the end they all knew what I was and kept their distance. I think one of them one day, detaching herself from her companions, came and offered me something to eat and that I looked at her in silence, until she went away. Yes, it seems to me some such incident occurred about this time. But perhaps I am thinking of another stay, at an earlier time, for this will be my last, my last but one, or two, there is never a last, by the sea. However that may be I see a young woman coming towards me and stopping from time to time to look back at her companions. Huddled together like sheep they watch her recede, urging her on, and laughing no doubt, I seem to hear laughter, far away. Then it is her back I see, as she goes away, now it is towards me she looks back, but without stopping. But perhaps I am merging two times in one, and two women, one coming towards me, shyly, urged on by the cries and laughter of her companions, and the other going away from me, unhesitatingly. For those who came towards me I saw coming from afar, most of the time, that is one of the advantages of the seaside. Black specks in the distance I saw them coming, I could follow all their manœuvres, saying, It's getting smaller, or, it's getting bigger. Yes, to be taken unawares was so to speak impossible, for I turned often towards the land too. Let me tell you something, my sight was better at the seaside ! Yes, ranging far and wide over these vast flats, where nothing lay, nothing stood, my good eye saw more clearly and there were even days when the bad one too had to look away. And not only did I see more clearly, but I had less difficulty in saddling with a name the rare things I saw. These are some of the advantages and disadvantages of the seaside. Or perhaps it was I who was changing, why not ? And in the morning, in my cave, and even sometimes at night, when the storm raged, I felt reasonably secure from the elements and mankind. But there too there is a price to pay. In your box, in your caves, there too there is a price to pay. And which you pay willingly, for a time, but which you cannot go on paying forever. For you cannot go on buying the same thing forever, with your little pittance. And unfortunately there are other needs than that of rotting in peace, it's not the word, I mean of course my mother whose image, blunted for some time past, was beginning now to harrow me again. So I went back inland, for my town was not strictly speaking on the sea, whatever may have been said to the contrary. And to get to it you had to go inland, I at least knew of no other way. For between my town and the sea there was a kind of swamp which, as far back as I can remember, and some of my memories have their roots deep in the immediate past, there was always talk of draining, by means of canals I suppose, or of transforming into a vast port and docks, or into a city on piles for the workers, in a word of redeeming somehow or other. And with the same stone they would have killed the scandal, at the gates of their metropolis, of a stinking steaming swamp in which an incalculable number of human lives were yearly engulfed, the statistics escape me for the moment and doubtless always will, so complete is my indifference to this aspect of the question. It is true they actually began to work and that work is still going on in certain areas in the teeth of adversity, setbacks, epidemics and the apathy of the Public Works Department, far from me to deny it. But from this to proclaiming that the sea came lapping at the ramparts of my town, there was a far cry. And I for my part will never lend myself to such a perversion (of the truth), until such time as I am compelled or find it convenient to do so. And I knew this swamp a little, having risked my life in it, cautiously, on several occasions, at a period of my life richer in illusions than the one I am trying to patch together here, I mean richer in certain illusions, in others poorer. So there was no way of coming at my town directly, by sea, but you had to disembark well to the north or the south and take to the roads, just imagine that, for they had never heard of Watt, just imagine that too. And now my progress, slow and painful at all times, was more so than ever, because of my short stiff leg, the same which I thought had long been as stiff as a leg could be, but damn the bit of it, for it was growing stiffer than ever, a thing I would not have thought possible, and at the same time shorter every day, but above all because of the other leg, supple hitherto and now growing rapidly stiff in its turn but not yet shortening, unhappily. For when the two legs shorten at the same time, and at the same speed, then all is not lost, no. But when one shortens, and the other not, then you begin to be worried. Oh not that I was exactly worried, but it was a nuisance, yes, a nuisance. For I didn't know which foot to land on, when I came down. Let us try and get this dilemma clear. Follow me carefully. The stiff leg hurt me, admittedly, I mean the old stiff leg, and it was the other which I normally used as a pivot, or prop. But now this latter, as a result of its stiffening I suppose, and the ensuing commotion among nerves and sinews, was beginning to hurt me even more than the other. What a story, God send I don't make a balls of it. For the old pain, do you follow me, I had got used to it, in a way, yes, in a kind of way. Whereas to the new pain, though of the same family exactly, I had not yet had time to adjust myself. Nor should it be forgotten that having one bad leg plus another more or less good, I was able to nurse the former, and reduce its sufferings to the minimum, to the maximum, by using the former exclusively, with the help of my crutches. But I no longer had this resource ! For I no longer had one bad leg plus another more or less good, but now both were equally bad. And the worse, to my mind, was that which till now had been good, at least comparatively good, and whose change for the worse I had not yet got used to. So in a way, if you like, I still had one bad leg and one good, or rather less bad, with this difference however, that the less bad now was the less good of heretofore. It was therefore on the old bad leg that I often longed to lean, between one crutchstroke and the next. For while still extremely sensitive, it was less so than the other, or it was equally so, if you like, but it did not seem so, to me, because of its seniority. But I couldn't ! What ? Lean on it. For it was shortening, don't forget, whereas the other, though stiffening, was not yet shortening, or so far behind its fellow that to all intents and purposes, intents and purposes, I'm lost, no matter. If I could even have bent it, at the knee, or even at the hip, I could have made it seem as short as the other, long enough to land on the true short one, before taking off again. But I couldn't. What? Bend it. For how could I bend it, when it was stiff? I was therefore compelled to work the same old leg as heretofore, in spite of its having become, at least as far as the pain was concerned, the worse of the two and the more in need of nursing. Sometimes to be sure, when I was lucky enough to chance on a road conveniently cambered, or by taking advantage of a not too deep ditch or any other breach of surface, I managed to lengthen my short leg, for a short time. But it had done no work for so long that it did not know how to go about it. And I think a pile of dishes would have better supported me than it, which had so well supported me, when I was a tiny tot. And another factor of disequilibrium was here involved, I mean when I thus made the best of the lie of the land, I mean my crutches, which would have needed to be unequal, one short and one long, if I was to remain vertical. No? I don't know. In any case the ways I went were for the most part little forest paths, that's understandable, where differences of level, though abounding, were too confused and too erratic to be of any help to me. But did it make such a difference after all, as far as the pain was concerned, whether my leg was free to rest or whether it had to work? I think not. For the suffering of the leg at rest was constant and monotonous. Whereas the leg condemned to the increase of pain inflicted by work knew the decrease of pain dispensed by work suspended, the space of an instant. But I am human, I fancy, and my progress suffered, from this state of affairs, and from the slow and painful progress it had always been, whatever may have been said to the contrary, was changed, saving your presence, to a veritable calvary, with no limit to its stations and no hope of crucifixion, though I say it myself, and no Simon, and reduced me to frequent halts. Yes, my progress reduced me to stopping more and more often, it was the only way to progress, to stop. And though it is no part of my tottering intentions to treat here in full, as they deserve, these brief moments of the immemorial expiation, I shall nevertheless deal with them briefly, out of the goodness of my heart, so that my story, so clear till now, may not end in darkness, the darkness of these towering forests, these giant fronds, where I hobble, listen, fall, rise, listen and hobble on, wondering sometimes, need I say, if I shall ever see again the hated light, at least unloved, stretched palely between the last boles, and my mother, to settle with her, and if I would not do better, at least just as well, to hang myself from a bough, with a liane. For frankly light meant nothing to me now, and my mother could scarcely be waiting for me still, after so long. And my leg, my legs. But the thought of suicide had little hold on me, I don't know why, I thought I did, but I see I don't. The idea of strangulation in particular, however tempting, I always overcame, after a short struggle. And between you and me there was never anything wrong with my respiratory tracts, apart of course from the agonies intrinsic to that system. Yes, I could count the days when I could neither breathe in the blessed air with its life-giving oxygen nor, when I had breathed it in, breathe out the bloody stuff, I could have counted them. Ah yes, my asthma, how often I was tempted to put an end to it, by cutting my throat. But I never succumbed. The noise betrayed me, I turned purple. It came on mostly at night, fortunately, or unfortunately, I could never make up my mind. For if sudden changes of colour matter less at night, the least unusual noise is then more noticeable, because of the silence of the night. But these were mere crises, and what are crises compared to all that never stops, knows neither ebb nor flow, its surface leaden above infernal depths. Not a word, not a word against the crises that seized me, wrung me, and finally threw me away, mercifully, safe from help. And I wrapped my head in my coat, to stifle the obscene noise of choking, or I disguised it as a fit of coughing, universally accepted and approved and whose only disadvantage is this, that it is liable to let you in for pity. And this is perhaps the moment to observe, better late than never, that when I speak of my progress being slowed down, consequent on the defection of my good leg, I express only an infinitesimal part of the truth. For the truth is I had other weak points, here and there, and they too were growing weaker and weaker, as was only to be expected. But what was not to be expected was the speed at which their weakness had increased, since my departure from the seaside. For as long as I had remained at the seaside my weak points, while admittedly increasing in weakness, as was only to be expected, only increased imperceptibly, in weakness I mean. So that I would have hesitated to exclaim, with my finger up my arse-hole for example, Jesus-Christ, it's much worse than yesterday, I can hardly believe it is the same hole. I apologise for having to revert to this lewd orifice, 'tis my muse will have it so. Perhaps it is less to be thought of as the eyesore here called by its name than as the symbol of those passed over in silence, a distinction due perhaps to its centrality and its air of being a link between me and the other excrement. We underestimate this little hole, it seems to me, we call it the arse-hole and affect to despise it. But is it not rather the true portal of our being and the celebrated mouth no more than the kitchen-door. Nothing goes in, or so little, that is not rejected on the spot, or very nearly. Almost everything revolts it that comes from without and what comes from within does not seem to receive a very warm welcome either. Are not these significant facts. Time will tell. But I shall do my utmost none the less to keep it in the background, in the future. And that will be easy, for the future is by no means uncertain, the unspeakable future. And when it comes to neglecting fundamentals, I think I have nothing to learn, and indeed I confuse them with accidentals. But to return to my weak points, let me say again that at the seaside they had developed normally, yes, I had noticed nothing abnormal. Either because I did not pay enough attention to them, absorbed as I was in the metamorphosis of my excellent leg, or because there was in fact nothing special to report, in this connection. But I had hardly left the shore, harried by the dread of waking one fine day, far from my mother, with my two legs as stiff as my crutches, when they suddenly began to gallop, my weak points did, and their weakness became literally the weakness of death, with all the disadvantages that this entails, when they are not vital points. I fix at this period the dastardly desertion of my toes, so to speak in the thick of the fray. You may object that this is covered by the business of my legs, that it has no importance, since in any case I could not put to the ground the foot in question. Quite, quite. But do you as much as know what foot we're talking about? No. Nor I. Wait till I think. But you are right, that wasn't a weak point properly speaking, I mean my toes, I thought they were in excellent fettle, apart from a few corns, bunions, ingrowing nails and a tendency to cramp. No, my true weak points were elsewhere. And if I do not draw up here and now the impressive list of them it is because I shall never draw it up. No, I shall never draw it up, yes, perhaps I shall. And then I should be sorry to give a wrong idea of my health which, if it was not exactly rude, to the extent of my bursting with it, was at bottom of an incredible robustness. For otherwise how could I have reached the enormous age I have reached. Thanks to moral qualities? Hygienic habits? Fresh air? Starvation? Lack of sleep? Solitude? Persecution? The long silent screams (dangerous to scream)? The daily longing for the earth to swallow me up? Come come. Fate is rancorous, but not to that extent. Look at Mammy. What rid me of her, in the end? I sometimes wonder. Perhaps they buried her alive, it wouldn't surprise me. Ah the old bitch, a nice dose she gave me, she and her lousy unconquerable genes. Bristling with boils ever since I was a brat, a fat lot of good that ever did me. The heart beats, and what a beat. That my ureters—no, not a word on that subject. And the capsules. And the bladder. And the urethra. And the glans. Santa Maria. I give you my word, I cannot piss, my word of honour, as a gentleman. But my prepuce, sat verbum, oozes urine, day and night, at least I think it's urine, it smells of kidney. What's all this, I thought I had lost the sense of smell. Can one speak of pissing, under these conditions? Rubbish! My sweat too, and God knows I sweat, has a queer smell. I think it's in my dribble as well, and heaven knows I dribble. How I eliminate, to be sure, uremia will never be the death of me. Me too they would bury alive, in despair, if there was any justice in the world. And this list of my weak points I shall never draw up, for fear of its finishing me, I shall perhaps, one day, when the time comes for the inventory of my goods and chattels. For that day, if it ever dawns, I shall be less afraid, of being finished, than I am today. For today, if I do not feel precisely at the beginning of my career, I have not the presumption either to think I am near the end. So I husband my strength, for the spurt. For to be unable to spurt, when the hour strikes, no, you might as well give up. But it is forbidden to give up and even to stop an instant. So I wait, jogging along, for the bell to say, Molloy, one last effort, it's the end. That's how I reason, with the help of images little suited to my situation. And I can't shake off the feeling, I don't know why, that the day will come for me to say what is left of all I had. But I must first wait, to be sure there is nothing more I can acquire, or lose, or throw away, or give away. Then I can say, without fear of error, what is left, in the end, of my possessions. For it will be the end. And between now and then I may get poorer, or richer, oh not to the extent of being any better off, or any worse off, but sufficiently to preclude me from announcing, here and now, what is left of all I had, for I have not yet had all. But I can make no sense of this presentiment, and that I understand is very often the case with the best presentiments, that you can make no sense of them. So perhaps it is a true presentiment, apt to be borne out. But can any more sense be made of false presentiments? I think so, yes, I think that all that is false may more readily be reduced, to notions clear and distinct, distinct from all other notions. But I may be wrong. But I was not given to presentiments, but to sentiments sweet and simple, to episentiments rather, if I may venture to say so. For I knew in advance, which made all presentiment superfluous. I will even go further (what can I lose?), I knew only in advance, for when the time came I knew no longer, you may have noticed it, or only when I made a superhuman effort, and when the time was past I no longer knew either, I regained my ignorance. And all that taken together, if that is possible, should serve to explain many things, and notably my astonishing old age, still green in places, assuming the state of my health, in spite of all I have said about it, is insufficient to account for it. Simple supposition, committing me to nothing. But I was saying that if my progress, at this stage, was becoming more and more slow and painful, this was not due solely to my legs, but also to innumerable so-called weak points, having nothing to do with my legs. Unless one is to suppose, gratuitously, that they and my legs were part of the same syndrome, which in that case would have been of a diabolical complexity. The fact is, and I deplore it, but it is too late now to do anything about it, that I have laid too much stress on my legs, throughout these wanderings, to the detriment of the rest. For I was no ordinary cripple, far from it, and there were days when my legs were the best part of me, with the exception of the brain capable of forming such a judgement. I was therefore obliged to stop more and more often, I shall never weary of repeating it, and to lie down, in defiance of the rules, now prone, now supine, now on one side, now on the other, and as much as possible with the feet higher than the head, to dislodge the clots. And to lie with the feet higher than the head, when your legs are stiff, is no easy matter. But don't worry, I did it. When my comfort was at stake there was no trouble I would not go to. The forest was all about me and the boughs, twining together at a prodigious height, compared to mine, sheltered me from the light and the elements. Some days I advanced no more than thirty or forty paces, I give you my oath. To say I stumbled in impenetrable darkness, no, I cannot. I stumbled, but the darkness was not impenetrable. For there reigned a kind of blue gloom, more than sufficient for my visual needs. I was astonished this gloom was not green, rather than blue, but I saw it blue and perhaps it was. The red of the sun, mingling with the green of the leaves, gave a blue result, that is how I reasoned. But from time to time. From time to time. What tenderness in these little words, what savagery. But from time to time I came on a kind of crossroads, you know, a star, or circus, of the kind to be found in even the most unexplored of forests. And turning then methodically to face the radiating paths in turn, hoping for I know not what, I described a complete circle, or less than a circle, or more than a circle, so great was the resemblance between them. Here the gloom was not so thick and I made haste to leave it. I don't like gloom to lighten, there's something shady about it. I had a certain number of encounters in this forest, naturally, where does one not, but nothing to signify. I notably encountered a charcoal-burner. I might have loved him, I think, if I had been seventy years younger. But it's not certain. For then he too would have been younger by as much, oh not quite as much, but much younger. I never really had much love to spare, but all the same I had my little quota, when I was small, and it went to the old men, when it could. And I even think I had time to love one or two, oh not with true love, no, nothing like the old woman, I've lost her name again, Rose, no, anyway you see who I mean, but all the same, how shall I say, tenderly, as those on the brink of a better earth. Ah I was a precocious child, and then I was a precocious man. Now they all give me the shits, the ripe, the unripe and the rotting from the bough. He was all over me, begging me to share his hut, believe it or not. A total stranger. Sick with solitude probably. I say charcoal-burner, but I really don't know. I see smoke somewhere. That's something that never escapes me, smoke. A long dialogue ensued, interspersed with groans. I could not ask him the way to my town, the name of which escaped me still. I asked him the way to the nearest town, I found the neccessary words, and accents. He did not know. He was born in the forest probably and had spent his whole life there. I asked him to show me the nearest way out of the forest. I grew eloquent. His reply was exceedingly confused. Either I didn't understand a word he said, or he didn't understand a word I said, or he knew nothing, or he wanted to keep me near him. It was towards this fourth hypothesis that in all modesty I leaned, for when I made to go, he held me back by the sleeve. So I smartly freed a crutch and dealt him a good dint on the skull. That calmed him. The dirty old brute. I got up and went on. But I hadn't gone more than a few paces, and for me at this time a few paces meant something, when I turned and went back to where he lay, to examine him. Seeing he had not ceased to breathe I contented myself with giving him a few warm kicks in the ribs, with my heels. This is how I went about it. I carefully chose the most favourable position, a few paces from the body, with my back of course turned to it. Then, nicely balanced on my crutches, I began to swing, backwards, forwards, feet pressed together, or rather legs pressed together, for how could I press my feet together, with my legs in the state they were? But how could I press my legs together, in the state they were? I pressed them together, that's all I can tell you. Take it or leave it. Or I didn't press them together. What can that possibly matter? I swung, that's all that matters, in an ever-widening arc, until I decided the moment had come and launched myself forward with all my strength and consequently, a moment later, backward, which gave the desired result. Where did I get this access of vigour? From my weakness perhaps. The shock knocked me down. Naturally. I came a cropper. You can't have everything, I've often noticed it. I rested a moment, then got up, picked up my crutches, took up my position on the other side of the body and applied myself with method to the same exercise. I always had a mania for symmetry. But I must have aimed a little low and one of my heels sank in something soft. However. For if I had missed the ribs, with that heel, I had no doubt landed in the kidney, oh not hard enough to burst it, no, I fancy not. People imagine, because you are old, poor, crippled, terrified, that you can't stand up for yourself, and generally speaking that is so. But given favourable conditions, a feeble and awkward assailant, in your own class what, and a lonely place, and you have a good chance of showing what stuff you are made of. And it is doubtless in order to revive interest in this possibility, too often forgotten, that I have delayed over an incident of no interest in itself, like all that has a moral. But did I at least eat, from time to time? Perforce, perforce, roots, berries, sometimes a little mulberry, a mushroom from time to time, trembling, knowing nothing about mushrooms. What else, ah yes, carobs, so dear to goats. In a word whatever I could find, forests abound in good things. And having heard, or more probably read somewhere, in the days when I thought I would be well advised to educate myself, or amuse myself, or stupefy myself, or kill time, that when a man in a forest thinks he is going forward in a straight line, in reality he is going in a circle, I did my best to go in a circle, hoping in this way to go in a straight line. For I stopped being half-witted and became sly, whenever I took the trouble. And my head was a storehouse of useful knowledge. And if I did not go in a rigorously straight line, with my system of going in a circle, at least I did not go in a circle, and that was something. And by going on doing this, day after day, and night after night, I looked forward to getting out of the forest, some day. For my region was not all forest, far from it. But there were plains too, mountains and sea, and some towns and villages, connected by highways and byways. And I was all the more convinced that I would get out of the forest some day as I had already got out of it, more than once, and I knew how difficult it was not to do again what you have done before. But things had been rather different then. And yet I did not despair of seeing the light tremble, some day, through the still boughs, the strange light of the plain, its pale wild eddies, through the bronze-still boughs, which no breath ever stirred. But it was a day I dreaded too. So that I was sure it would come sooner or later. For it was not so bad being in the forest, I could imagine worse, and I could have stayed there till I died, unrepining, yes, without pining for the light and the plain and the other amenities of my region. For I knew them well, the amenities of my region, and I considered that the forest was no worse. And it was not only no worse, to my mind, but it was better, in this sense, that I was there. That is a strange way, is it not, of looking at things. Perhaps less strange than it seems. For being in the forest, a place neither worse nor better than the others, and being free to stay there, was it not natural I should think highly of it, not because of what it was, but because I was there. For I was there. And being there I did not have to go there, and that was not to be despised, seeing the state of my legs and my body in general. That is all I wished to say, and if I did not say it at the outset it is simply that something was against it. But I could not, stay in the forest I mean, I was not free to. That is to say I could have, physically nothing could have been easier, but I was not purely physical, I lacked something, and I would have had the feeling, if I had stayed in the forest, of going against an imperative, at least I had that impression. But perhaps I was mistaken, perhaps I would have been better advised to stay in the forest, perhaps I could have stayed there, without remorse, without the painful impression of committing a fault, almost a sin. For I have greatly sinned, at all times, greatly sinned against my prompters. And if I cannot decently be proud of this I see no reason either to be sorry. But imperatives are a little different, and I have always been inclined to submit to them, I don't know why. For they never led me anywhere, but tore me from places where, if all was not well, all was no worse than anywhere else, and then went silent, leaving me stranded. So I knew my imperatives well, and yet I submitted to them. It had become a habit. It is true they nearly all bore on the same question, that of my relations with my mother, and on the importance of bringing as soon as possible some light to bear on these and even on the kind of light that should be brought to bear and the most effective means of doing so. Yes, these imperatives were quite explicit and even detailed until, having set me in motion at last, they began to falter, then went silent, leaving me there like a fool who neither knows where he is going nor why he is going there. And they nearly all bore, as I may have said already, on the same painful and thorny question. And I do not think I could mention even one having a different purport. And the one enjoining me then to leave the forest without delay was in no way different from those I was used to, as to its meaning. For in its framing I thought I noticed something new. For after the usual blarney there followed this solemn warning, Perhaps it is already too late. It was in Latin, nimis sero, I think that's Latin. Charming things, hypothetical imperatives. But if I had never succeeded in liquidating this matter of my mother, the fault must not be imputed solely to that voice which deserted me, prematurely. It was partly to blame, that's all it can be reproached with. For the outer world opposed my succeeding too, with its wiles, I have given some examples. And even if the voice could have harried me to the very scene of action, even then I might well have succeeded no better, because of the other obstacles barring my way. And in this command which faltered, then died, it was hard not to hear the unspoken entreaty, Don't do it, Molloy. In forever reminding me thus of my duty was its purpose to show me the folly of it? Perhaps. Fortunately it did no more than stress, the better to mock if you like, an innate velleity. And of myself, all my life, I think I had been going to my mother, with the purpose of establishing our relations on a less precarious footing. And when I was with her, and I often succeeded, I left her without having done anything. And when I was no longer with her I was again on my way to her, hoping to do better the next time. And when I appeared to give up and to busy myself with something else, or with nothing at all any more, in reality I was hatching my plans and seeking the way to her house. This is taking a queer turn. So even without this so-called imperative I impugn, it would have been difficult for me to stay in the forest, since I was forced to assume my mother was not there. And yet it might have been better for me to try and stay. But I also said, Yet a little while, at the rate things are going, and I won't be able to move, but will have to stay, where I happen to be, unless someone comes and carries me. Oh I did not say it in such limpid language. And when I say I said, etc., all I mean is that I knew confusedly things were so, without knowing exactly what it was all about. And every time I say, I said this, or, I said that, or speak of a voice saying, far away inside me, Molloy, and then a fine phrase more or less clear and simple, or find myself compelled to attribute to others intelligible words, or hear my own voice uttering to others more or less articulate sounds, I am merely complying with the convention that demands you either lie or hold your peace. For what really happened was quite different. And I did not say, Yet a little while, at the rate things are going, etc., but that resembled perhaps what I would have said, if I had been able. In reality I said nothing at all, but I heard a murmur, something gone wrong with the silence, and I pricked up my ears, like an animal I imagine, which gives a start and pretends to be dead. And then sometimes there arose within me, confusedly, a kind of consciousness, which I express by saying, I said, etc., or, Don't do it Molloy, or, Is that your mother's name? said the sergeant, I quote from memory. Or which I express without sinking to the level of oratio recta, but by means of other figures quite as deceitful, as for example, It seemed to me that, etc., or, I had the impression that, etc., for it seemed to me nothing at all, and I had no impression of any kind, but simply somewhere something had changed, so that I too had to change, or the world too had to change, in order for nothing to be changed. And it was these little adjustments, as between Galileo's vessels, that I can only express by saying, I feared that, or, I hoped that, or, Is that your mother's name? said the sergeant, for example, and that I might doubtless have expressed otherwise and better, if I had gone to the trouble. And so I shall perhaps some day when I have less horror of trouble than today. But I think not. So I said, Yet a little while, at the rate things are going, and I won't be able to move, but will have to stay, where I happen to be, unless some kind person comes and carries me. For my marches got shorter and shorter and my halts in consequence more and more frequent and I may add prolonged. For the notion of the long halt does not necessarily follow from that of the short march, nor that of the frequent halt either, when you come to think of it, unless you give frequent a meaning it does not possess, and I could never bring myself to do a thing like that. And it seemed to me all the more important to get out of this forest with all possible speed as I would very soon be powerless to get out of anything whatsoever, were it but a bower. It was winter, it must have been winter, and not only many trees had lost their leaves, but these lost leaves had gone all black and spongy and my crutches sank into them, in places right up to the fork. Strange to say I felt no colder than usual. Perhaps it was only autumn. But I was never very sensitive to changes of temperature. And the gloom, if it seemed less blue than before, was as thick as ever. Which made me say in the end, It is less blue because there is less green, but it is no less thick thanks to the leaden winter sky. Then something about the black dripping from the black boughs, something in that line. The black slush of leaves slowed me down even more. But leaves or no leaves I would have abandoned erect motion, that of man. And I still remember the day when, flat on my face by way of rest, in defiance of the rules, I suddenly cried, striking my brow, Christ, there's crawling, I never thought of that. But could I crawl, with my legs in such a state, and my trunk? And my head. But before I go on, a word about the forest murmurs. It was in vain I listened, I could hear nothing of the kind. But rather, with much goodwill and a little imagination, at long intervals a distant gong. A horn goes well with the forest, you expect it. It is the huntsman. But a gong! Even a tom-tom, at a pinch, would not have shocked me. But a gong! It was mortifying, to have been looking forward to the celebrated murmurs if to nothing else, and to succeed only in hearing, at long intervals, in the far distance, a gong. For a moment I dared hope it was only my heart, still beating. But only for a moment. For it does not beat, not my heart, I'd have to refer you to hydraulics for the squelch that old pump makes. To the leaves too I listened, before their fall, attentively in vain. They made no sound, motionless and rigid, like brass, have I said that before? So much for the forest murmurs. From time to time I blew my horn, through the cloth of my pocket. Its hoot was fainter every time. I had taken it off my bicycle. When? I don't know. And now, let us have done. Flat on my belly, using my crutches like grapnels, I plunged them ahead of me into the undergrowth, and when I felt they had a hold, I pulled myself forward, with an effort of the wrists. For my wrists were still quite strong, fortunately, in spite of my decrepitude, though all swollen and racked by a kind of chronic arthritis probably. That then briefly is how I went about it. The advantage of this mode of locomotion compared to others, I mean those I have tried, is this, that when you want to rest you stop and rest, without further ado. For standing there is no rest, nor sitting either. And there are men who move about sitting, and even kneeling, hauling themselves to right and left, forward and backward, with the help of hooks. But he who moves in this way, crawling on his belly, like a reptile, no sooner comes to rest than he begins to rest, and even the very movement is a kind of rest, compared to other movements, I mean those that have worn me out. And in this way I moved onward in the forest, slowly, but with a certain regularity, and I covered my fifteen paces, day in, day out, without killing myself. And I even crawled on my back, plunging my crutches blindly behind me into the thickets, and with the black boughs for sky to my closing eyes. I was on my way to mother. And from time to time I said, Mother, to encourage me I suppose. I kept losing my hat, the lace had broken long ago, until in a fit of temper I banged it down on my skull with such violence that I couldn't get it off again. And if I had met any lady friends, if I had had any lady friends, I would have been powerless to salute them correctly. But there was always present to my mind, which was still working, if laboriously, the need to turn, to keep on turning, and every three or four jerks I altered course, which permitted me to describe, if not a circle, at least a great polygon, perfection is not of this world, and to hope that I was going forward in a straight line, in spite of everything, day and night, towards my mother. And true enough the day came when the forest ended and I saw the light, the light of the plain, exactly as I had foreseen. But I did not see it from afar, trembling beyong the harsh trunks, as I had foreseen, but suddenly I was in it, I opened my eyes and saw I had arrived. And the reason for that was probably this, that for some time past I had not opened my eyes, or seldom. And even my little changes of course were made blindly, in the dark. The forest ended in a ditch, I don't know why, and it was in this ditch that I became aware of what had happened to me. I suppose it was the fall into the ditch that opened my eyes, for why would they have opened otherwise? I looked at the plain rolling away as far as the eye could see. No, not quite so far as that. For my eyes having got used to the light I fancied I saw, faintly outlined against the horizon, the towers and steeples of a town, which of course I could not assume was mine, on such slight evidence. It is true the plain seemed familiar, but in my region all the plains looked alike, when you knew one you knew them all. In any case, whether it was my town or not, whether somewhere under that faint haze my mother panted on or whether she poisoned the air a hundred miles away, were ludicrously idle questions for a man in my position, though of undeniable interest on the plane of pure knowledge. For how could I drag myself over that vast moor, where my crutches would fumble in vain. Rolling perhaps. And then? Would they let me roll on to my mother's door? Fortunately for me at this painful juncture, which I had vaguely foreseen, but not in all its bitterness, I heard a voice telling me not to fret, that help was coming. Literally. These words struck it is not too much to say as clearly on my ear, and on my understanding, as the urchin's thanks I suppose when I stooped and picked up his marble. Don't fret Molloy, we're coming. Well, I suppose you have to try everything once, succour included, to get a complete picture of the resources of their planet. I lapsed down to the bottom of the ditch. It must have been spring, a morning in spring. I thought I heard birds, skylarks perhaps. I had not heard a bird for a long time. How was it I had not heard any in the forest? Nor seen any. It had not seemed strange to me. Had I heard any at the seaside? Mews? I could not remember. I remembered the corn-crakes.

The two travellers came back to my memory. One had a club. I had forgotten them. I saw the sheep again. Or so I say now. I did not fret, other scenes of my life came back to me. There seemed to be rain, then sunshine, turn about. Real spring weather. I longed to go back into the forest. Oh not a real longing. Molloy could stay, where he happened to be.

II

It is midnight. The rain is beating on the windows. I am calm. All is sleeping. Nevertheless I get up and go to my desk. I can't sleep. My lamp sheds a soft and steady light. I have trimmed it. It will last till morning. I hear the eagle-owl. What a terrible battle-cry! Once I listened to it unmoved. My son is sleeping. Let him sleep. The night will come when he too, unable to sleep, will get up and go to his desk. I shall be forgotten.

My report will be long. Perhaps I shall not finish it. My name is Moran, Jacques. That is the name I am known by. I am done for. My son too. All unsuspecting. He must think he's on the threshold of life, of real life. He's right there. His name is Jacques, like mine. This cannot lead to confusion.

I remember the day I received the order to see about Molloy. It was a Sunday in summer. I was sitting in my little garden, in a wicker chair, a black book closed on my knees. It must have been about eleven o'clock, still too early to go to church. I was savouring the day of rest, while deploring the importance attached to it, in certain parishes. To work, even to play on Sunday, was not of necessity reprehensible, in my opinion. It all depended on the state of mind of him who worked, or played, and on the nature of his work, of his play, in my opinion. I was reflecting with satisfaction on this, that this slightly libertarian view was gaining ground, even among the clergy, more and more disposed to admit that the sabbath, so long as you go to mass and contribute to the collection, may be considered a day like any other, in certain respects. This did not affect me personally, I've always loved doing nothing. And I would gladly have rested on weekdays too, if I could have afforded it. Not that I was positively lazy. It was something else Seeing something done which I could have done better myself, if I had wished, and which I did do better whenever I put my mind to it, I had the impression of discharging a function to which no form of activity could have exalted me. But this was a joy in which, during the week, I could seldom indulge.

The weather was fine. I watched absently the coming and going of my bees. I heard on the gravel the scampering steps of my son, caught up in I know not what fantasy of flight and pursuit. I called to him not to dirty himself. He did not answer.

All was still. Not a breath. From my neighbours' chimneys the smoke rose straight and blue. None but tranquil sounds, the clicking of mallet and ball, a rake on pebbles, a distant lawn-mower, the bell of my beloved church. And birds of course, blackbird and thrush, their song sadly dying, vanquished by the heat, and leaving dawn's high boughs for the bushes' gloom. Contentedly I inhaled the scent of my lemon-verbena.

In such surroundings slipped away my last moments of peace and happiness.

A man came into the garden and walked swiftly towards me. I knew him well. Now I have no insuperable objection to a neighbour's dropping in, on a Sunday, to pay his respects, if he feels the need, though I much prefer to see nobody. But this man was not a neighbour. Our dealings were strictly of a business nature and he had journeyed from afar, on purpose to disturb me. So I was disposed to receive him frostily enough, all the more so as he had the impertinence to come straight to where I was sitting, under my Beauty of Bath. With people who took this liberty I had no patience. If they wished to speak to me they had only to ring at the door of my house. Martha had her instructions. I thought I was hidden from anybody coming into my grounds and following the short path which led from the garden-gate to the front door, and in fact I must have been. But at the noise of the gate being slammed I turned angrily and saw, blurred by the leaves, this high mass bearing down on me, across the lawn. I neither got up nor invited him to sit down. He stopped in front of me and we stared at each other in silence. He was dressed in his heavy, sombre Sunday best, and at this my displeasure knew no bounds. This gross external observance, while the soul exults in its rags, has always appeared to me an abomination. I watched the enormous feet crushing my daisies. I would gladly have driven him away, with a knout. Unfortunately it was not he who mattered. Sit down, I said, mollified by the reflection that after all he was only acting his part of go-between. Yes, suddenly I had pity on him, pity on myself. He sat down and mopped his forehead. I caught a glimpse of my son spying on us from behind a bush. My son was thirteen or fourteen at the time. He was big and strong for his age. His intelligence seemed at times little short of average. My son, in fact. I called him and ordered him to go and fetch some beer. Peeping and prying were part of my profession. My son imitated me instinctively. He returned after a remarkably short interval with two glasses and a quart bottle of beer. He uncorked the bottle and served us. He was very fond of uncorking bottles. I told him to go and wash himself, to straighten his clothes, in a word to get ready to appear in public, for it would soon be time for mass. He can stay, said Gaber. I don't wish him to stay, I said. And turning to my son I told him again to go and get ready. If there was one thing displeased me, at that time, it was being late for the last mass. Please yourself, said Gaber. Jacques went away grumbling with his finger in his mouth, a detestable and unhygienic habit, but preferable all things considered to that of the finger in the nose, in my opinion. If putting his finger in his mouth prevented my son from putting it in his nose, or elsewhere, he was right to do it, in a sense.

Here are your instructions, said Gaber. He took a notebook from his pocket and began to read. Every now and then he closed the notebook, taking care to leave his finger in it as a marker, and indulged in comments and observations of which I had no need, for I knew my business. When at last he had finished I told him the job did not interest me and that the chief would do better to call on another agent. He wants it to be you, God knows why, said Gaber. I presume he told you why, I said, scenting flattery, for which I had a weakness. He said, replied Gaber, that no one could do it but you. This was more or less what I wanted to hear. And yet, I said, the affair seems childishly simple. Gaber began bitterly to inveigh against our employer, who had made him get up in the middle of the night, just as he was getting into position to make love to his wife. For this kind of nonsense, he added. And he said he had confidence in no one but me? I said. He doesn't know what he says, said Gaber. He added, Nor what he does. He wiped the lining of his bowler, peering inside as if in search of something. In that case it's hard for me to refuse, I said, knowing perfectly well that in any case it was impossible for me to refuse. Refuse! But we agents often amused ourselves with grumbling among ourselves and giving ourselves the airs of free men. You leave today, said Gaber. Today! I cried, but he's out of his mind! Your son goes with you, said Gaber. I said no more. When it came to the point we said no more. Gaber buttoned his notebook and put it back in his pocket, which he also buttoned. He stood up, rubbing his hands over his chest. I could do with another beer, he said. Go to the kitchen, I said, the maid will serve you. Goodbye, Moran, he said.

It was too late for mass. I did not need to consult my watch to know, I could feel mass had begun without me. I who never missed mass, to have missed it on that Sunday of all Sundays! When I so needed it! To buck me up! I decided to ask for a private communion, in the course of the afternoon. I would go without lunch. Father Ambrose was always very kind and accommodating.

I called Jacques. Without result. I said, Seeing me still in conference he has gone to mass alone. This explanation turned out subsequently to be the correct one. But I added, He might have come and seen me, before leaving. I liked thinking in monologue and then my lips moved visibly. But no doubt he was afraid of disturbing me and of being reprimanded. For I was sometimes inclined to go too far when I reprimanded my son, who was consequently a little afraid of me. I myself had never been sufficiently chastened. Oh I had not been spoiled either, merely neglected. Whence bad habits ingrained beyond remedy and of which even the most meticulous piety has never been able to break me. I hoped to spare my son this misfortune, by giving him a good clout from time to time, together with my reasons for doing so. Then I said, Is he barefaced enough to tell me, on his return, that he has been to mass if he has not, if for example he has merely run off to join his little friends, behind the slaughter-house? And I determined to get the truth out of Father Ambrose, on this subject. For it was imperative my son should not imagine he was capable of lying to me with impunity. And if Father Ambrose could not enlighten me, I would apply to the verger, whose vigilance it was inconceivable that the presence of my son at twelve o'clock mass had escaped. For I knew for a fact that the verger had a list of the faithful and that, from his place beside the font, he ticked us off when it came to the absolution. It is only fair to say that Father Ambrose knew nothing of these manœuvres, yes, anything in the nature of surveillance was hateful to the good Father Ambrose. And he would have sent the verger flying about his business if he had suspected him of such a work of supererogation. It must have been for his own edification that the verger kept this register, with such assiduity. Admittedly I knew only what went on at the last mass, having no experience personally of the other offices, for the good reason that I never went within a mile of them. But I had heard it said that they were the occasion of exactly the same supervision, at the hands either of the verger himself or, when his duties called him elsewhere, of one of his sons. A strange parish whose flock knew more than its pastor of a circumstance which seemed rather in his province than in theirs.

Such were my thoughts as I waited for my son to come back and Gaber, whom I had not yet heard leave, to go. And tonight I find it strange I could have thought of such things, I mean my son, my lack of breeding, Father Ambrose, Verger Joly with his register, at such a time. Had I not something better to do, after what I had just heard? The fact is I had not yet begun to take the matter seriously. And I am all the more surprised as such light-mindedness was not like me. Or was it in order to win a few more moments of peace that I instinctively avoided giving my mind to it? Even if, as set forth in Gaber's report, the affair had seemed unworthy of me, the chief's insistence on having me, me Moran, rather than anybody else, ought to have warned me that it was no ordinary one. And instead of bringing to bear upon it without delay all the resources of my mind and of my experience, I sat dreaming of my breed's infirmities and the singularities of those about me. And yet the poison was already acting on me, the poison I had just been given. I stirred restlessly in my arm-chair, ran my hands over my face, crossed and uncrossed my legs, and so on. The colour and weight of the world were changing already, soon I would have to admit I was anxious.

I remembered with annoyance the lager I had just absorbed. Would I be granted the body of Christ after a pint of Wallenstein? And if I said nothing? Have you come fasting, my son? He would not ask. But God would know, sooner or later. Perhaps he would pardon me. But would the eucharist produce the same effect, taken on top of beer, however light? I could always try. What was the teaching of the Church on the matter? What if I were about to commit sacrilege? I decided to suck a few peppermints on the way to the presbytery.

I got up and went to the kitchen. I asked if Jacques was back. I haven't seen him, said Martha. She seemed in bad humour. And the man? I said. What man? she said. The man who came for a glass of beer, I said. No one came for anything, said Martha. By the way, I said, unperturbed apparently, I shall not eat lunch today. She asked if I were ill. For I was naturally a rather heavy eater. And my Sunday midday meal especially I always liked extremely copious. It smelt good in the kitchen. I shall lunch a little later today, that's all, I said. Martha looked at me furiously. Say four o'clock, I said. In that wizened, grey skull what raging and rampaging then, I knew. You will not go out today, I said coldly, I regret. She flung herself at her pots and pans, dumb with anger. You will keep all that hot for me, I said, as best you can. And knowing her capable of poisoning me I added, You can have the whole day off tomorrow, if that is any good to you.

I left her and went out on the road. So Gaber had gone without his beer. And yet he had wanted it badly. It was a good brand, Wallenstein. I stood there on the watch for Jacques. Coming from church he would appear on my right, on my left if he came from the slaughter-house. A neighbour passed. A free-thinker. Well well, he said, no worship today? He knew my habits, my Sunday habits I mean. Everyone knew them and the chief perhaps better than any, in spite of his remoteness. You look as if you had seen a ghost, said the neighbour. Worse than that, I said, you. I went in, at my back the dutifully hideous smile. I could see him running to his concubine with the news, You know that poor bastard Moran, you should have heard me, I had him lepping! Couldn't speak! Took to his heels!

Jacques came back soon afterwards. No trace of frolic. He said he had been to church alone. I asked him a few pertinent questions concerning the march of the ceremony. His answers were plausible. I told him to wash his hands and sit down to his lunch. I went back to the kitchen. I did nothing but go to and fro. You may dish up, I said. She had wept. I peered into the pots. Irish stew. A nourishing and economical dish, if a little indigestible. All honour to the land it has brought before the world. I shall sit down at four o'clock, I said. I did not need to add sharp. I liked punctuality, all those whom my roof sheltered had to like it too. I went up to my room. And there, stretched on my bed, the curtains drawn, I made a first attempt to grasp the Molloy affair.

My concern at first was only with its immediate vexations and the preparations they demanded of me. The kernel of the affair I continued to shirk. I felt a great confusion coming over me.

Should I set out on my autocycle? This was the question with which I began. I had a methodical mind and never set out on a mission without prolonged reflection as to the best way of setting out. It was the first problem to solve, at the outset of each enquiry, and I never moved until I had solved it, to my satisfaction. Sometimes I took my autocycle, sometimes the train, sometimes the motor-coach, just as sometimes too I left on foot, or on my bicycle, silently, in the night. For when you are beset with enemies, as I am, you cannot leave on your autocycle, even in the night, without being noticed, unless you employ it as an ordinary bicycle, which is absurd. But if I was in the habit of first settling this delicate question of transport, it was never without having, if not fully sifted, at least taken into account the factors on which it depended. For how can you decide on the way of setting out if you do not first know where you are going, or at least with what purpose you are going there? But in the present case I was tackling the problem of transport with no other preparation than the languid cognizance I had taken of Gaber's report. I would be able to recover the minutest details of this report when I wished. But I had not yet troubled to do so, I had avoided doing so, saying, The affair is banal. To try and solve the problem of transport under such conditions was madness. Yet that was what I was doing. I was losing my head already.

I liked leaving on my autocycle, I was partial to this way of getting about. And in my ignorance of the reasons against it I decided to leave on my autocycle. Thus was inscribed, on the threshold of the Molloy affair, the fatal pleasure principle.

The sun's beams shone through the rift in the curtains and made visible the sabbath of the motes. I concluded from this that the weather was still fine and rejoiced. When you leave on your autocycle fine weather is to be preferred. I was wrong, the weather was fine no longer, the sky was clouding over, soon it would rain. But for the moment the sun was still shining. It was on this that I went, with inconceivable levity, having nothing else to go on.

Next I attacked, according to my custom, the capital question of the effects to take with me. And on this subject too I should have come to a quite otiose decision but for my son, who burst in wanting to know if he might go out. I controlled myself. He was wiping his mouth with the back of his hand, a thing I do not like to see. But there are nastier gestures, I speak from experience.

Out? I said. Where? Out! Vagueness I abhor. I was beginning to feel hungry. To the Elms, he replied. So we call our little public park. And yet there is not an elm to be seen in it, I have been told. What for? I said. To go over my botany, he replied. There were times I suspected my son of deceit. This was one. I would almost have preferred him to say, For a walk, or, To look at the tarts. The trouble was he knew far more than I, about botany. Otherwise I could have set him a few teasers, on his return. Personally I just liked plants, in all innocence and simplicity. I even saw in them at times a superfetatory proof of the existence of God. Go, I said, but be back at half-past four, I want to talk to you. Yes papa, he said. Yes papa! Ah!

I slept a little. Faster, faster. Passing the church, something made me stop. I looked at the door, baroque, very fine. I found it hideous. I hastened on to the presbytery. The Father is sleeping, said the servant. I can wait, I said. Is it urgent? she said. Yes and no, I said. She showed me into the sitting-room, bare and bleak, dreadful. Father Ambrose came in, rubbing his eyes. I disturb you, Father, I said. He clicked his tongue against the roof of his mouth, protestingly. I shall not describe our attitudes, characteristic his of him, mine of me. He offered me a cigar which I accepted with good grace and put in my pocket, between my fountain-pen and my propelling-pencil. He flattered himself, Father Ambrose, with being a man of the world and knowing its ways, he who never smoked. And everyone said he was most broad. I asked him if he had noticed my son at the last mass. Certainly, he said, we even spoke together. I must have looked surprised. Yes, he said, not seeing you at your place, in the front row, I feared you were ill. So I called for the dear child, who reassured me. A most untimely visitor, I said, whom I could not shake off in time. So your son explained to me, he said. He added, But let us sit down, we have no train to catch. He laughed and sat down, hitching up his heavy cassock. May I offer you a little glass of something? he said. I was in a quandary. Had Jacques let slip an allusion to the lager. He was quite capable of it. I came to ask you a favour, I said. Granted, he said. We observed each other. It's this, I said,

Sunday for me without the Body and Blood is like—. He raised his hand. Above all no profane comparisons, he said. Perhaps he was thinking of the kiss without a moustache or beef without mustard. I dislike being interrupted. I sulked. Say no more, he said, a wink is as good as a nod, you want communion. I bowed my head. It's a little unusual, he said. I wondered if he had fed. I knew he was given to prolonged fasts, by way of mortification certainly, and then because his doctor advised it. Thus he killed two birds with one stone. Not a word to a soul, he said, let it remain between us and—. He broke off, raising a finger, and his eyes, to the ceiling. Heavens, he said, what is that stain? I looked in turn at the ceiling. Damp, I said. Tut tut, he said, how annoying. The words tut tut seemed to me the maddest I had heard. There are times, he said, when one feels like weeping. He got up. I'll go and get my kit, he said. He called that his kit. Alone, my hands clasped until it seemed my knuckles would crack, I asked the Lord for guidance. Without result. That was some consolation. As for Father Ambrose, in view of his alacrity to fetch his kit, it seemed evident to me he suspected nothing. Or did it amuse him to see how far I would go? Or did it tickle him to have me commit a sin? I summarised the situation briefly as follows. If knowing I have beer taken he gives me the sacrament, his sin, if sin there be, is as great as mine. I was therefore risking little. He came back with a kind of portable pyx, opened it and dispatched me without an instant's hesitation. I rose and thanked him warmly. Pah! he said, it's nothing. Now we can talk.

I had nothing else to say to him. All I wanted was to return home as quickly as possible and stuff myself with stew. My soul appeased, I was ravenous. But being slightly in advance of my schedule I resigned myself to allowing him eight minutes. They seemed endless. He informed me that Mrs Clement, the chemist's wife and herself a highly qualified chemist, had fallen, in her laboratory, from the top of a ladder, and broken the neck—. The neck! I cried. Of her femur, he said, can't you let me finish. He added that it was bound to happen. And I, not to be outdone, told him how worried I was about my hens, particularly my grey hen, which would neither brood nor lay and for the past month and more had done nothing but sit with her arse in the dust, from morning to night. Like Job, haha, he said. I too said haha. What a joy it is to laugh, from time to time, he said. Is it not? I said. It is peculiar to man, he said. So I have noticed, I said. A brief silence ensued. What do you feed her on? he said. Corn chiefly, I said. Cooked or raw? he said. Both, I said. I added that she ate nothing any more. Nothing! he cried. Next to nothing, I said. Animals never laugh, he said. It takes us to find that funny, I said. What? he said. It takes us to find that funny, I said loudly. He mused. Christ never laughed either, he said, so far as we know. He looked at me. Can you wonder? I said. There it is, he said. He smiled sadly. She has not the pip, I hope, he said. I said she had not, certainly not, anything he liked, but not the pip. He meditated. Have you tried bicarbonate? he said. I beg your pardon? I said. Bicarbonate of soda, he said, have you tried it? Why no, I said. Try it! he cried, flushing with pleasure, have her swallow a few dessertspoonfuls, several times a day, for a few months. You'll see, you won't know her. A powder? I said. Bless my heart to be sure, he said. Many thanks, I said, I'll begin today. Such a fine hen, he said, such a good layer. Or rather tomorrow, I said. I had forgotten the chemist was closed. Except in case of emergency. And now that little cordial, he said. I declined.

This interview with Father Ambrose left me with a painful impression. He was still the same dear man, and yet not. I seemed to have surprised, on his face, a lack, how shall I say, a lack of nobility. The host, it is only fair to say, was lying heavy on my stomach. And as I made my way home I felt like one who, having swallowed a pain-killer, is first astonished, then indignant, on obtaining no relief. And I was almost ready to suspect Father Ambrose, alive to my excesses of the forenoon, of having fobbed me off with unconsecrated bread. Or of mental reservation as he pronounced the magic words. And it was in vile humour that I arrived home, in the pelting rain.

The stew was a great disappointment. Where are the onions? I cried. Gone to nothing, replied Martha. I rushed into the kitchen, to look for the onions I suspected her of having removed from the pot, because she knew how much I liked them. I even rummaged in the bin. Nothing. She watched me mockingly.

I went up to my room again, drew back the curtains on a calamitous sky and lay down. I could not understand what was happening to me. I found it painful at that period not to understand. I tried to pull myself together. In vain. I might have known. My life was running out, I knew not through what breach. I succeeded however in dozing off, which is not so easy, when pain is speculative. And I was marvelling, in that half-sleep, at my half sleeping, when my son came in, without knocking. Now if there is one thing I abhor, it is someone coming into my room, without knocking. I might just happen to be masturbating, before my cheval-glass. Father with yawning fly and starting eyes, toiling to scatter on the ground his joyless seed, that was no sight for a small boy. Harshly I recalled him to the proprieties. He protested he had knocked twice. If you had knocked a hundred times, I replied, it would not give you the right to come in without being invited. But, he said. But what? I said. You told me to be here at half-past four, he said. There is something, I said, more important in life than punctuality, and that is decorum. Repeat. In that disdainful mouth my phrase put me to shame. He was soaked. What have you been looking at? I said. The liliaceae, papa, he answered. The liliaceae papa! My son had a way of saying papa, when he wanted to hurt me, that was very special. Now listen to me, I said. His face took on an expression of anguished attention. We leave this evening, I said in substance, on a journey. Put on your school suit, the green—. But it's blue, papa, he said. Blue or green, put it on, I said violently. I went on. Put in your little knapsack, the one I gave you for your birthday, your toilet things, one shirt, one pair of socks and seven pairs of drawers. Do you understand? Which shirt, papa? he said. It doesn't matter which shirt, I cried, any shirt! Which shoes am I to wear? he said. You have two pairs of shoes, I said, one for Sundays and one for weekdays, and you ask me which you are to wear. I sat up. I want none of your lip, I said.

Thus to my son I gave precise instructions. But were they the right ones? Would they stand the test of second thoughts? Would I not be impelled, in a very short time, to cancel them? I who never changed my mind before my son. The worst was to be feared.

Where are we going, papa? he said. How often had I told him not to ask me questions. And where were we going, in point of fact. Do as you're told, I said. I have an appointment with Mr Py tomorrow, he said. You'll see him another day, I said. But I have an ache, he said. There exist other dentists, I said, Mr Py is not the unique dentist of the northern hemisphere. I added rashly, We are not going into the wilderness. But he's a very good dentist, he said. All dentists are alike, I said. I could have told him to get to hell out of that with his dentist, but no, I reasoned gently with him, I spoke with him as with an equal. I could furthermore have pointed out to him that he was lying when he said he had an ache. He did have an ache, in a bicuspid I believe, but it was over. Py himself had told me so. I have dressed the tooth, he said, your son cannot possibly feel any more pain. I remembered this conversation well. He has naturally very bad teeth, said Py. Naturally, I said, what do you mean, naturally? What are you insinuating? He was born with bad teeth, said Py, and all his life he will have bad teeth. Naturally I shall do what I can. Meaning, I was born with the disposition to do all I can, all my life I shall do all I can, necessarily. Born with bad teeth! As for me, I was down to my incisors, the nippers.

Is it still raining? I said. My son had drawn a small glass from his pocket and was examining the inside of his mouth, prising away his upper lip with his finger. Aaw, he said, without interrupting his inspection. Stop messing about with your mouth! I cried. Go to the window and tell me if it's still raining. He went to the window and told me it was still raining. Is the sky completely overcast? I said. Yes, he said. Not the least rift? I said. No, he said. Draw the curtains, I said. Delicious instants, before one's eyes get used to the dark. Are you still there? I said. He was still there. I asked him what he was waiting for to do as I had told him. If I had been my son I would have left me long ago. He was not worthy of me, not in the same class at all. I could not escape this conclusion. Cold comfort that is, to feel superior to one's son, and hardly sufficient to calm the remorse of having begotten him. May I bring my stamps? he said. My son had two albums, a big one for his collection properly speaking and a small one for the duplicates. I authorised him to bring the latter. When I can give pleasure, without doing violence to my principles, I do so gladly. He withdrew.

I got up and went to the window. I could not keep still. I passed my head between the curtains. Fine rain, lowering sky. He had not lied to me. Likely to lift round about eight. Fine sunset, twilight, night. Waning moon, rising towards midnight. I rang for Martha and lay down again. We shall dine at home, I said. She looked at me in astonishment. Did we not always dine at home? I had not yet told her we were leaving. I would not tell her till the last moment, one foot in the stirrup as the saying is. I did not wholly trust her. I would call her at the last moment and say, Martha, we're leaving, for one day, two days, three days, a week, two weeks, God knows, goodbye. It was important to leave her in the dark. Then why had I called her? She would have served us dinner in any case, as she did every day. I had made the mistake of putting myself in her place. That was understandable. But to tell her we would dine at home, what a blunder. For she knew it already, thought she knew, did know. And as a result of this useless reminder she would sense that something was afoot and spy on us, in the hope of learning what it was. First mistake. The second, first in time, was my not having enjoined my son to keep what I had told him to himself. Not that this would have served any purpose. Nevertheless I should have insisted on it, as due to myself. I was floundering. I so sly as a rule. I tried to mend matters, saying, A little later than usual, not before nine. She turned to go, her simple mind already in a turmoil. I am at home to no one, I said. I knew what she would do, she would throw a sack over her shoulders and slip off to the bottom of the garden. There she would call Hannah, the old cook of the Elsner sisters, and they would whisper together for a long time, through the railings. Hannah never went out, she did not like going out. The Elsner sisters were not bad neighbours, as neighbours go. They made a little too much music, that was the only fault I could find with them. If there is one thing gets on my nerves it is music. What I assert, deny, question, in the present, I still can. But mostly I shall use the various tenses of the past. For mostly I do not know, it is perhaps no longer so, it is too soon to know, I simply do not know, perhaps shall never know. I thought a little of the Elsner sisters. Everything remained to be planned and there I was thinking of the Elsner sisters. They had an aberdeen called Zulu. People called it Zulu. Sometimes, when I was in a good humour, I called, Zulu! Little Zulu! and he would come and talk to me, through the railings. But I had to be feeling gay. I don't like animals. It's a strange thing, I don't like men and I don't like animals. As for God, he is beginning to disgust me. Crouching down I would stroke his ears, through the railings, and utter wheedling words. He did not realize he disgusted me. He reared up on his hind legs and pressed his chest against the bars. Then I could see his little black penis ending in a thin wisp of wetted hair. He felt insecure, his hams trembled, his little paws fumbled for purchase, one after the other. I too wobbled, squatting on my heels. With my free hand I held on to the railings. Perhaps I disgusted him too. I found it hard to tear myself away from these vain thoughts.

I wondered, suddenly rebellious, what compelled me to accept this commission. But I had already accepted it, I had given my word. Too late. Honour. It did not take me long to gild my impotence.

But could I not postpone our departure to the following day? Or leave alone? Ah shilly-shally. But we would wait till the very last moment, a little before midnight. This decision is irrevocable, I said. It was justified moreover by the state of the moon.

I did as when I could not sleep. I wandered in my mind, slowly, noting every detail of the labyrinth, its paths as familiar as those of my garden and yet ever new, as empty as the heart could wish or alive with strange encounters. And I heard the distant cymbals, There is still time, still time. But there was not, for I ceased, all vanished and I tried once more to turn my thoughts to the Molloy affair. Unfathomable mind, now beacon, now sea.

The agent and the messenger. We agents never took anything in writing. Gaber was not an agent in the sense I was. Gaber was a messenger. He was therefore entitled to a notebook. A messenger had to be possessed of singular qualities, good messengers were even more rare than good agents. I who was an excellent agent would have made but a sorry messenger. I often regretted it. Gaber was protected in numerous ways. He used a code incomprehensible to all but himself. Each messenger, before being appointed, had to submit his code to the directorate. Gaber understood nothing about the messages he carried. Reflecting on them he arrived at the most extravagantly false conclusions. Yes, it was not enough for him to understand nothing about them, he had also to believe he understood everything about them. This was not all. His memory was so bad that his messages had no existence in his head, but only in his notebook. He had only to close his notebook to become, a moment later, perfectly innocent as to its contents. And when I say that he reflected on his messages and drew conclusions from them, it was not as we would have reflected on them, you and I, the book closed and probably the eyes too, but little by little as he read. And when he raised his head and indulged in his commentaries, it was without losing a second, for if he had lost a second he would have forgotten everything, both text and gloss. I have often wondered if the messengers were not compelled to undergo a surgical operation, to induce in them such a degree of amnesia. But I think not. For otherwise their memory was good enough. And I have heard Gaber speak of his childhood, and of his family, in extremely plausible terms. To be undecipherable to all but oneself, dead without knowing it to the meaning of one's instructions and incapable of remembering them for more than a few seconds, these are capacities rarely united in the same individual. No less however was demanded of our messengers. And that they were more highly esteemed than the agents, whose qualities were sound rather than brilliant, is shown by the fact that they received a weekly wage of eight pounds as against ours of six pounds ten only, these figures being exclusive of bonuses and travelling expenses. And when I speak of agents and of messengers in the plural, it is with no guarantee of truth. For I had never seen any other messenger than Gaber nor any other agent than myself. But I supposed we were not the only ones and Gaber must have supposed the same. For the feeling that we were the only ones of our kind would, I believe, have been more than we could have borne. And it must have appeared natural, to me that each agent had his own particular messenger, and to Gaber that each messenger had his own particular agent. Thus I was able to say to Gaber, Let him give this job to someone else, I don't want it, and Gaber was able to reply, He wants it to be you. And these last words, assuming Gaber had not invented them especially to annoy me, had perhaps been uttered by the chief with the sole purpose of fostering our illusion, if it was one. All this is not very clear.

That we thought of ourselves as members of a vast organization was doubtless also due to the all too human feeling that trouble shared, or is it sorrow, is trouble something, I forget the word. But to me at least, who knew how to listen to the falsetto of reason, it was obvious that we were perhaps alone in doing what we did. Yes, in my moments of lucidity I thought it possible. And, to keep nothing from you, this lucidity was so acute at times that I came even to doubt the existence of Gaber himself. And if I had not hastily sunk back into my darkness I might have gone to the extreme of conjuring away the chief too and regarding myself as solely responsible for my wretched existence. For I knew I was wretched, at six pounds ten a week plus bonuses and expenses. And having made away with Gaber and the chief (one Youdi), could I have denied myself the pleasure of—you know. But I was not made for the great light that devours, a dim lamp was all I had been given, and patience without end, to shine it on the empty shadows. I was a solid in the midst of other solids.

I went down to the kitchen. I did not expect to find Martha there, but I found her there. She was sitting in her rocking-chair, in the chimney-corner, rocking herself moodily. This rocking-chair, she would have you believe, was the only possession to which she clung and she would not have parted with it for an empire. It is interesting to note that she had installed it not in her room, but in the kitchen, in the chimney-corner. Late to bed and early to rise, it was in the kitchen that she benefited by it most. The wage-payers are numerous, and I was one of them, who do not like to see, in the place set aside for toil, the furniture of reclining and repose.

The servant wishes to rest? Let her retire to her room. In the kitchen all must be of wood, white and rigid. I should mention that Martha had insisted, before entering my service, that I permit her to keep her rocking-chair in the kitchen. I had refused, indignantly. Then, seeing she was inflexible, I had yielded. I was too kind-hearted.

My weekly supply of lager, half-a-dozen quart bottles, was delivered every Saturday. I never touched them until the next day, for lager must be left to settle after the least disturbance. Of these six bottles Gaber and I, together, had emptied one. There should therefore be five left, plus the remains of a bottle from the previous week. I went into the pantry. The five bottles were there, corked and sealed, and one open bottle three quarters empty. Martha followed me with her eyes. I left without a word to her and went upstairs. I did nothing but go to and fro. I went into my son's room. Sitting at his little desk he was admiring his stamps, the two albums, large and small, open before him. On my approach he shut them hastily. I saw at once what he was up to. But first I said, Have you got your things ready? He stood up, got his pack and gave it to me. I looked inside. I put my hand inside and felt through the contents, staring vacantly before me. Everything was in. I gave it back to him. What are you doing? I said. Looking at my stamps, he said. You call that looking at your stamps? I said. Yes papa, he said, with unimaginable effrontery. Silence, you little liar! I cried. Do you know what he was doing? Transferring to the album of duplicates, from his good collection properly so-called, certain rare and valuable stamps which he was in the habit of gloating over daily and could not bring himself to leave, even for a few days. Show me your new Timor, the five reis orange, I said. He hesitated. Show it to me! I cried. I had given it to him myself, it had cost me a florin. A bargain, at the time. I've put it in here, he said piteously, picking up the album of duplicates. That was all I wanted to know, to hear him say rather, for I knew it already. Very good, I said. I went to the door. You leave both your albums at home, I said, the small one as well as the large one. Not a word of reproach, a simple prophetic present, on the model of those employed by Youdi. Your son goes with you. I went out. But as with delicate steps, almost mincing, congratulating myself as usual on the resilience of my Wilton, I followed the corridor towards my room, I was struck by a thought which made me go back to my son's room. He was sitting in the same place, but in a slightly different attitude, his arms on the table and his head on his arms. This sight went straight to my heart, but nevertheless I did my duty. He did not move. To make assurance doubly sure, I said, we shall put the albums in the safe, until our return. He still did not move. Do you hear me? I said. He rose with a bound that knocked over his chair and uttered the furious words, Do what you like with them! I never want to see them again! Anger should be left to cool, in my opinion, crisis to pass, before one operates. I took the albums and withdrew, without a word. He had been lacking in respect, but this was not the moment to have him admit it. Motionless in the corridor I heard sounds of falling and collision. Another, less master of himself than I of myself, would have intervened. But it did not positively displease me that my son should give free vent to his grief. It purges. Sorrow does more harm when dumb, to my mind.

The albums under my arm, I returned to my room. I had spared my son a grave temptation, that of putting in his pocket his most cherished stamps, in order to gloat on them, during our journey. Not that his having one or two stamps about him was reprehensible in itself. But it would have been an act of disobedience. To look at them he would have had to hide from his father. And when he had lost them, as he inevitably would, he would have been driven to lie, to account for their disappearance. No, if he could not really bear to be parted from the gems of his collection, it would have been better for him to take the entire album. For an album is less readily lost than a stamp. But I was a better judge than he of what he could and could not. For I knew what he did not yet know, among other things that this ordeal would be of profit to him. *Sollst entbehren*, that was the lesson I desired to impress upon him, while he was still young and tender. Magic words which I had never dreamt, until my fifteenth year, could be coupled together. And should this undertaking make me odious in his eyes and not only me, but the very idea of fatherhood, I would pursue it none the less, with everything in my power. The thought that between my death and his own, ceasing for an instant from heaping curses on my memory, he might wonder, in a flash, whether I had not been right, that was enough for me, that repaid me for all the trouble I had taken and was still to take. He would answer in the negative, the first time, and resume his execrations. But the doubt would be sown. He would go back to it. That was how I reasoned.

I still had a few hours left before dinner. I decided to make the most of them. Because after dinner I drowse. I took off my coat and shoes, opened my trousers and got in between the sheets. It is lying down, in the warmth, in the gloom, that I best pierce the outer turmoil's veil, discern my quarry, sense what course to follow, find peace in another's ludicrous distress. Far from the world, its clamours, frenzies, bitterness and dingy light, I pass judgement on it and on those, like me, who are plunged in it beyond recall, and on him who has need of me to be delivered, who cannot deliver myself. All is dark, but with that simple darkness that follows like a balm upon the great dismemberings. From their places masses move, stark as laws. Masses of what? One does not ask. There somewhere man is too, vast conglomerate of all of nature's kingdoms, as lonely and as bound. And in that block the prey is lodged and thinks himself a being apart. Anyone would serve. But I am paid to seek. I arrive, he comes away. His life has been nothing but a waiting for this, to see himself preferred, to fancy himself damned, blessed, to fancy himself everyman, above all others. Warmth, gloom, smells of my bed, such is the effect they sometimes have on me. I get up, go out, and everything is changed. The blood drains from my head, the noise of things bursting, merging, avoiding one another, assails me on all sides, my eyes search in vain for two things alike, each pinpoint of skin screams a different message, I drown in the spray of phenomena. It is at the mercy of these sensations, which happily I know to be illusory, that I have to live and work. It is thanks to them I find myself a meaning. So he whom a sudden pain awakes. He stiffens, ceases to breathe, waits, says, It's a bad dream, or, It's a touch of neuralgia, breathes again, sleeps again, still trembling. And yet it is not unpleasant, before setting to work, to steep oneself again in this slow and massive world, where all things move with the ponderous sullenness of oxen, patiently through the immemorial ways, and where of course no investigation would be possible. But on this occasion, I repeat, on this occasion, my reasons for doing so were I trust more serious and imputable less to pleasure than to business. For it was only by transferring it to this atmosphere, how shall I say, of finality without end, why not, that I could venture to consider the work I had on hand. For where Molloy could not be, nor Moran either for that matter, there Moran could bend over Molloy. And though this examination prove unprofitable and of no utility for the execution of my orders, I should nevertheless have established a kind of connexion, and one not necessarily false. For the falsity of the terms does not necessarily imply that of the relation, so far as I know. And not only this, but I should have invested my man, from the outset, with the air of a fabulous being, which something told me could not fail to help me later on. So I took off my coat and my shoes, I opened my trousers and I slipped in between the sheets, with an easy conscience, knowing only too well what I was doing.

Molloy, or Mollose, was no stranger to me. If I had had colleagues, I might have suspected I had spoken of him to them, as of one destined to occupy us, sooner or later. But I had no colleagues and knew nothing of the circumstances in which I had learnt of his existence. Perhaps I had invented him, I mean found him ready made in my head. There is no doubt one sometimes meets with strangers who are not entire strangers, through their having played a part in certain cerebral reels. This had never happened to me, I considered myself immune from such experiences, and even the simple *déjà vu* seemed infinitely beyond my reach. But it was happening to me then, or I was greatly mistaken. For who could have spoken to me of Molloy if not myself and to whom if not to myself could I have spoken of him? I racked my mind in vain. For in my rare conversations with men I avoided such subjects. If anyone else had spoken to me of Molloy I would have requested him to stop and I myself would not have confided his existence to a living soul for anything in the world. If I had had colleagues things would naturally have been different. Among colleagues one says things which in any other company one keeps to oneself. But I had no colleagues. And perhaps this accounts for the immense uneasiness I had been feeling ever since the beginning of this affair. For it is no small matter, for a grown man thinking he is done with surprises, to see himself the theatre of such ignominy. I had really good cause to be alarmed.

Mother Molloy, or Mollose, was not completely foreign to me either, it seemed. But she was much less alive than her son, who God knows was far from being so. After all perhaps I knew nothing of mother Molloy, or Mollose, save in so far as such a son might bear, like a scurf of placenta, her stamp.

Of these two names, Molloy and Mollose, the second seemed to me perhaps the more correct. But barely. What I heard, in my soul I suppose, where the acoustics are so bad, was a first syllable, Mol, very clear, followed almost at once by a second, very thick, as though gobbled by the first, and which might have been oy as it might have been ose, or one, or even oc. And if I inclined towards ose, it was doubtless that my mind had a weakness for this ending, whereas the others left it cold. But since Gaber had said Molloy, not once but several times, and each time with equal incisiveness, I was compelled to admit that I too should have said Molloy and that in saying Mollose I was at fault. And henceforward, unmindful of my preferences, I shall force myself to say Molloy, like Gaber. That there may have been two different persons involved, one my own Mollose, the other the Molloy of the enquiry, was a thought which did not so much as cross my mind, and if it had I should have driven it away, as one drives away a fly, or a hornet. How little one is at one with oneself, good God. I who prided myself on being a sensible man, cold as crystal and as free from spurious depth.

I knew then about Molloy, without however knowing much about him. I shall say briefly what little I did know about him. I shall also draw attention, in my knowledge of Molloy, to the most striking lacunae.

He had very little room. His time too was limited. He hastened incessantly on, as if in despair, towards extremely close objectives. Now, a prisoner, he hurled himself at I know not what narrow confines, and now, hunted, he sought refuge near the centre.

He panted. He had only to rise up within me for me to be filled with panting.

Even in open country he seemed to be crashing through jungle. He did not so much walk as charge.

In spite of this he advanced but slowly. He swayed, to and fro, like a bear.

He rolled his head, uttering incomprehensible words.

He was massive and hulking, to the point of misshapenness. And, without being black, of a dark colour.

He was forever on the move. I had never seen him rest. Occasionally he stopped and glared furiously about him.

This was how he came to me, at long intervals. Then I was nothing but uproar, bulk, rage, suffocation, effort unceasing, frenzied and vain. Just the opposite of myself, in fact. It was a change. And when I saw him disappear, his whole body a vociferation, I was almost sorry.

What it was all about I had not the slightest idea.

I had no clue to his age. As he appeared to me, so I felt he must have always appeared and would continue to appear until the end, an end indeed which I was hard put to imagine. For being unable to conceive what had brought him to such a pass, I was no better able to conceive how, left to his own resources, he could put an end to it. A natural end seemed unlikely to me, I don't know why. But then my own natural end, and I was resolved to have no other, would it not at the same time be his? Modest, I had my doubts. And then again, what end is not natural, are they not all by the grace of nature, the undeniably good and the so-called bad? Idle conjectures.

I had no information as to his face. I assumed it was hirsute, craggy and grimacing. Nothing justified my doing so.

That a man like me, so meticulous and calm in the main, so patiently turned towards the outer world as towards the lesser evil, creature of his house, of his garden, of his few poor possessions, discharging faithfully and ably a revolting function, reining back his thoughts within the limits of the calculable so great is his horror of fancy, that a man so contrived, for I was a contrivance, should let himself be haunted and possessed by chimeras, this ought to have seemed strange to me and been a warning to me to have a care, in my own interest. Nothing of the kind. I saw it only as the weakness of a solitary, a weakness admittedly to be deplored, but which had to be indulged in if I wished to remain a solitary, and I did, I clung to that, with as little enthusiasm as to my hens or to my faith, but no less lucidly. Besides this took up very little room in the inenarrable contraption I called my life, jeopardized it as little as my dreams and was as soon forgotten. Don't wait to be hunted to hide, that was always my motto. And if I had to tell the story of my life I should not so much as allude to these apparitions, and least of all to that of the unfortunate Molloy. For his was a poor thing, compared to others.

But images of this kind the will cannot revive without doing them violence. Much of what they had it takes away, much they never had it foists upon them. And the Molloy I brought to light, that memorable August Sunday, was certainly not the true denizen of my dark places, for it was not his hour. But so far as the essential features were concerned, I was easy in my mind, the likeness was there. And the discrepancy could have been still greater for all I cared. For what I was doing I was doing neither for Molloy, who mattered nothing to me, nor for myself, of whom I despaired, but on behalf of a cause which, while having need of us to be accomplished, was in its essence anonymous, and would subsist, haunting the minds of men, when its miserable artisans should be no more. It will not be said, I think, that I did not take my work to heart. But rather, tenderly, Ah those old craftsmen, their race is extinct and the mould broken.

Two remarks.

Between the Molloy I stalked within me thus and the true Molloy, after whom I was so soon to be in full cry, over hill and dale, the resemblance cannot have been great.

I was annexing perhaps already, without my knowing it, to my private Molloy, elements of the Molloy described by Gaber.

The fact was there were three, no, four Molloys. He that inhabited me, my caricature of same, Gaber's and the man of flesh and blood somewhere awaiting me. To these I would add Youdi's were it not for Gaber's corpse fidelity to the letter of his messages. Bad reasoning. For could it seriously be supposed that Youdi had confided to Gaber all he knew, or thought he knew (all one to Youdi) about his protégé? Assuredly not. He had only revealed what he deemed of relevance for the prompt and proper execution of his orders. I will therefore add a fifth Molloy, that of Youdi. But would not this fifth Molloy necessarily coincide with the fourth, the real one as the saying is, him dogged by his shadow? I would have given a lot to know. There were others too, of course. But let us leave it at that, if you don't mind, the party is big enough. And let us not meddle either with the question as to how far these five Molloys were constant and how far subject to variation. For there was this about Youdi, that he changed his mind with great facility.

That makes three remarks. I had only anticipated two.

The ice thus broken, I felt equal to facing Gaber's report and getting down to the official facts. It seemed as if the enquiry were about to start at last.

It was then that the sound of a gong, struck with violence, filled the house. True enough, it was nine o'clock. I got up, adjusted my clothes and hurried down. To give notice that the soup was in, nay, that it had begun to coagulate, was always for Martha a little triumph and a great satisfaction. For as a rule I was at table, my napkin tucked into my collar, crumbling the bread, fiddling with the cover, playing with the knife-rest, waiting to be served, a few minutes before the appointed hour. I attacked the soup. Where is Jacques? I said. She shrugged her shoulders. Detestable slavish gesture. Tell him to come down at once, I said. The soup before me had stopped steaming. Had it ever steamed? She came back. He won't come down, she said. I laid down my spoon. Tell me, Martha, I said, what is this preparation? She named it. Have I had it before? I said. She assured me I had. I then made a joke which pleased me enormously, I laughed so much I began to hiccup. It was lost on Martha who stared at me dazedly. Tell him to come down, I said at last. What? said Martha. I repeated my phrase. She still looked genuinely perplexed. There are three of us in this charming home, I said, you, my son and finally myself.

What I said was, Tell him to come down. But he's sick, said Martha. Were he dying, I said, down he must come. Anger led me sometimes to slight excesses of language. I could not regret them. It seemed to me that all language was an excess of language. Naturally I confessed them. I was short of sins.

Jacques was scarlet in the face. Eat your soup, I said, and tell me what you think of it. I'm not hungry, he said. Eat your soup, I said. I saw he would not eat it. What ails you? I said. I don't feel well, he said. What an abominable thing is youth. Try and be more explicit, I said. I was at pains to use this term, a little difficult for juveniles, having explained its meaning and application to him a few days before. So I had high hopes of his telling me he didn't understand. But he was a cunning little fellow, in his way. Martha! I bellowed. She appeared. The sequel, I said. I looked more attentively out of the window. Not only had the rain stopped, that I knew already, but in the west scarves of fine red sheen were mounting in the sky. I felt them rather than saw them, through my little wood. A great joy, it is hardly too much to say, surged over me at the sight of so much beauty, so much promise. I turned away with a sigh, for the joy inspired by beauty is often not unmixed, and saw in front of me what with good reason I had called the sequel. Now what have we here? I said. Usually on Sunday evening we had the cold remains of a fowl, chicken, duck, goose, turkey, I can think of no other fowl, from Saturday evening. I have always had great success with my turkeys, they are a better proposition than ducks, in my opinion, for rearing purposes. More delicate, possibly, but more remunerative, for one who knows and caters for their little ways, who likes them in a word and is liked by them in return. Shepherd's pie, said Martha. I tasted it, from the dish. And what have you done with yesterday's bird? I said. Martha's face took on an expression of triumph. She was waiting for this question, that was obvious, she was counting on it. I thought, she said, you ought to eat something hot, before you left. And who told you I was leaving? I said. She went to the door, a sure sign she was about to launch a shaft. She could only be insulting when in flight. I'm not blind, she said. She opened the door. More's the pity, she said. She closed the door behind her.

I looked at my son. He had his mouth open and his eyes closed. Was it you blabbed on us? I said. He pretended not to know what I was talking about. Did you tell Martha we were leaving? I said. He said he had not. And why not? I said. I didn't see her, he said brazenly. But she has just been up to your room, I said. The pie was already made, he said. At times he was almost worthy of me. But he was wrong to invoke the pie. But he was still young and inexperienced and I refrained from humbling him. Try and tell me, I said, a little more precisely, what it is you feel. I've a stomach-ache, he said. A stomach-ache! Have you a temperature? I said. I don't know, he said. Find out, I said. He was looking more and more stupefied. Fortunately I rather enjoyed dotting my i's. Go and get the minute-thermometer, I said, out of the second right-hand drawer of my desk, counting from the top, take your temperature and bring me the thermometer. I let a few minutes go by and then, without being asked, repeated slowly, word for word, this rather long and difficult sentence, which contained no fewer than three or four imperatives. As he went out, having presumably understood the gist of it, I added jocosely, You know which mouth to put it in? I was not averse, in conversation with my son, to jests of doubtful taste, in the interests of his education. Those whose pungency he could not fully savour at the time, and they must have been many, he could reflect on at his leisure or seek in company with his little friends to interpret as best he might. Which was in itself an excellent exercise. And at the same time I inclined his young mind towards that most fruitful of dispositions, horror of the body and its functions. But I had turned my phrase badly, mouth was not the word I should have used. It was while examining the shepherd's pie more narrowly that I had this afterthought. I lifted the crust with my spoon and looked inside. I probed it with my fork. I called Martha and said, His dog wouldn't touch it. I thought with a smile of my desk which had only six drawers in all and for all, three on each side of the space where I put my legs. Since your dinner is uneatable, I said, be good enough to prepare a packet of sandwiches, with the chicken you couldn't finish. My son came back at last. That's all the thanks you get for having a minute-thermometer. He handed it to me. Did you have time to wipe it? I said. Seeing me squint at the mercury he went to the door and switched on the light. How remote Youdi was at that instant. Sometimes in the winter, coming home harassed and weary after a day of fruitless errands, I would find my slippers warming in front of the fire, the uppers turned to the flame. He had a temperature. There's nothing wrong with you, I said. May I go up? he said. What for? I said. To lie down, he said. Was not this the providential hindrance for which I could not be held responsible? Doubtless, but I would never dare invoke it. I was not going to expose myself to thunderbolts which might be fatal, simply because my son had the gripes. If he fell seriously ill on the way, it would be another matter. It was not for nothing I had studied the old testament. Have you shat, my child, I said gently. I've tried, he said. Do you want to, I said. Yes, he said. But nothing comes, I said. No, he said. A little wind, I said. Yes, he said. Suddenly I remembered Father Ambrose's cigar. I lit it. We'll see what we can do, I said, getting up. We went upstairs. I gave him an enema, with salt water. He struggled, but not for long. I withdrew the nozzle. Try and hold it, I said, don't stay sitting on the pot, lie flat on your stomach. We were in the bathroom. He lay down on the tiles, his big fat bottom sticking up. Let it soak well in, I said. What a day. I looked at the ash on my cigar. It was firm and blue. I sat down on the edge of the bath. The porcelain, the mirrors, the chromium, instilled a great peace within me. At least I suppose it was they. It wasn't a great peace in any case. I got up, laid down my cigar and brushed my incisors. I also brushed the back gums. I looked at myself, puffing out my lips which normally recede into my mouth. What do I look like? I said. The sight of my moustache, as always, annoyed me. It wasn't quite right. It suited me, without a moustache I was inconceivable. But it ought to have suited me better. A slight change in the cut would have sufficed. But what change? Was there too much of it, not enough? Now, I said, without ceasing to inspect myself, get back on the pot and strain. Was it not rather the colour? A noise as of a waste recalled me to less elevated preoccupations. He stood up trembling all over. We bent together over the pot which at length I took by the handle and tilted from side to side. A few fibrous shreds floated in the yellow liquid. How can you hope to shit, I said, when you've nothing in your stomach? He protested he had had his lunch. You ate nothing, I said. He said no more. I had scored a hit. You forget we are leaving in an hour or so, I said. I can't, he said. So that, I pursued, you will have to eat something. An acute pain shot through my knee. What's the matter, papa? he said. I let myself fall on the stool, pulled up the leg of my trousers and examined my knee, flexing and unflexing it. Quick the iodex, I said. You're sitting on it, he said. I stood up and the leg of my trousers fell down over my ankle. This inertia of things is enough to drive one literally insane. I let out a bellow which must have been heard by the Elsner sisters. They stop reading, raise their heads, look at each other, listen. Nothing more. Just another cry in the night. Two old hands, veined, ringed, seek each other, clasp. I pulled up the leg of my trousers again, rolled it in a fury round my thigh, raised the lid of the stool, took out the iodex and rubbed it into my knee. The knee is full of little loose bones. Let it soak well in, said my son. He would pay for that later on. When I had finished I put everything back in place, rolled down the leg of my trousers, sat down on the stool again and listened. Nothing more. Unless you'd like to try a real emetic, I said, as if nothing had happened.

I'm tired, he said. You go and lie down, I said, I'll bring you something nice and light in bed, you'll have a little sleep and then we'll leave together. I drew him to me. What do you say to that? I said. He said to it, Yes papa. Did he love me then as much as I loved him? You could never be sure with that little hypocrite. Be off with you now, I said, cover yourself up well, I won't be long. I went down to the kitchen, prepared and set out on my handsome lacquer tray a bowl of hot milk and a slice of bread and jam. He asked for a report he'll get his report. Martha watched me in silence, lolling in her rocking-chair. Like a Fate who had run out of thread. I cleaned up everything after me and turned to the door. May I go to bed? she said. She had waited till I was standing up, the laden tray in my hands, to ask me this question. I went out, set down the tray on the chair at the foot of the stairs and went back to the kitchen. Have you made the sandwiches? I said. Meanwhile the milk was getting cold and forming a revolting skin. She had made them. I'm going to bed, she said. Everyone was going to bed. You will have to get up in an hour or so, I said, to lock up. I was for her to decide if it was worth while going to bed, under these conditions. She asked me how long I expected to be away. Did she realize I was not setting out alone? I suppose so. When she went up to tell my son to come down, even if he had told her nothing, she must have noticed the knapsack. I have no idea, I said. Then almost in the same breath, seeing her so old, worse than old, aging, so sad and solitary in her everlasting corner, There, there, it won't be long. And I advised her, in terms for me warm, to have a good rest while I was away and a good time visiting her friends and receiving them. Stint neither tea nor sugar, I said, and if by any chance you should happen to need money, apply to Mr Savory. I carried this sudden cordiality so far as to shake her by the hand, which she hastily wiped, as soon as she grasped my intention, on her apron. When I had finished shaking it, that flabby red hand, I did not let it go. But I took one finger between the tips of mine, drew it towards me and gazed at it. And had I had any tears to shed I should have shed them then, in torrents, for hours. She must have wondered if I was not on the point of making an attempt on her virtue. I gave her back her hand, took the sandwiches and left her.

Martha had been a long time in my service. I was often away from home. I had never taken leave of her in this way, but always offhandedly, even when a prolonged absence was to be feared, which was not the case on this occasion. Sometimes I departed without a word to her.

Before going into my son's room I went into my own. I still had the cigar in my mouth, but the pretty ash had fallen off. I reproached myself with this negligence. I dissolved a sleeping-powder in the milk. He asked for a report, he'll get his report. I was going out with the tray when my eyes fell on the two albums lying on my desk. I wondered if I might not relent, at any rate so far as the album of duplicates was concerned. A little while ago he had come here to fetch the thermometer. He had been a long time. Had he taken advantage of the opportunity to secure some of his favourite stamps? I had not time to check them all. I put down the tray and looked for a few stamps at random, the Togo one mark carmine with the pretty boat, the Nyassa 1901 ten reis, and several others. I was very fond of the Nyassa. It was green and showed a giraffe grazing off the top of a palm-tree. They were all there. That proved nothing. It only proved that those particular stamps were there. I finally decided that to go back on my decision, freely taken and clearly stated, would deal a blow to my authority which it was in no condition to sustain. I did so with sorrow. My son was already sleeping. I woke him. He ate and drank, grimacing in disgust. That was all the thanks I got. I waited until the last drop, the last crumb, had disappeared. He turned to the wall and I tucked him in. I was within a hair's breadth of kissing him. Neither he nor I had uttered a word. We had no further need of words, for the time being. Besides my son rarely spoke to me unless I spoke to him. And when I did so he answered but lamely and as it were with reluctance. And yet with his little friends, when he thought I was out of the way, he was incredibly voluble. That my presence had the effect of dampening this disposition was far from displeasing me. Not one person in a hundred knows how to be silent and listen, no, nor even to conceive what such a thing means. Yet only then can you detect, beyond the fatuous clamour, the silence of which the universe is made. I desired this advantage for my son. And that he should hold aloof from those who pride themselves on their eagle gaze. I had not struggled, toiled, suffered, made good, lived like a Hottentot, so that my son should do the same. I tiptoed out. I quite enjoyed playing my parts through the bitter end.

Since in this way I shirked the issue, have I to apologise for saying so? I let fall this suggestion for what it is worth. And perfunctorily. For in describing this day I am once more he who suffered it, who crammed it full of futile anxious life, with no other purpose than his own stultification and the means of not doing what he had to do. And as then my thoughts would have none of Molloy, so tonight my pen. This confession has been preying on my mind for some time past. To have made it gives me no relief.

I reflected with bitter satisfaction that if my son lay down and died by the wayside, it would be none of my doing. To every man his own responsibilities. I know of some they do not keep awake.

I said, There is something in this house tying my hands. A man like me cannot forget, in his evasions, what it is he evades. I went down to the garden and moved about in the almost total darkness. If I had not known my garden so well I would have blundered into my shrubberies, or my bee-hives. My cigar had gone out unnoticed. I shook it and put it in my pocket, intending to discard it in the ash-tray, or in the waste-paper basket, later on. But the next day, far from Turdy, I found it in my pocket and indeed not without satisfaction. For I was able to get a few more puffs out of it. To discover the cold cigar between my teeth, to spit it out, to search for it in the dark, to pick it up, to wonder what I should do with it, to shake it needlessly and put it in my pocket, to conjure up the ash-tray and the waste-paper basket, these were merely the principal stages of a sequence which I spun out for a quarter of an hour at least. Others concerned the dog Zulu, the perfumes sharpened tenfold by the rain and whose sources I amused myself exploring, in my head and with my hands, a neighbour's light, another's noise, and so on. My son's window was faintly lit. He liked sleeping with a night-light beside him. I sometimes felt it was wrong of me to let him humour this weakness. Until quite recently he could not sleep unless he had his woolly bear to hug. When he had forgotten the bear (Baby Jack) I would forbid the night-light. What would I have done that day without my son to distract me? My duty perhaps.

Finding my spirits as low in the garden as in the house, I turned to go in, saying to myself it was one of two things, either my house had nothing to do with the kind of nothingness in the midst of which I stumbled or else the whole of my little property was to blame. To adopt this latter hypothesis was to condone what I had done and, in advance, what I was to do, pending my departure. It brought me a semblance of pardon and a brief moment of factitious freedom. I therefore adopted it.

From a distance the kitchen had seemed to be in darkness. And in a sense it was. But in another sense it was not. For gluing my eyes to the window-pane I discerned a faint reddish glow which could not have come from the oven, for I had no oven, but a simple gas-stove. An oven if you like, but a gas-oven. That is to say there was a real oven too in the kitchen, but out of service. I'm sorry, but there it is, in a house without a gas-oven I would not have felt easy. In the night, interrupting my prowl, I like to go up to a window, lit or unlit, and look into the room, to see what is going on. I cover my face with my hands and peer through my fingers. I have terrified more than one neighbour in this way. He rushes outside, finds no one. For me then from their darkness the darkest rooms emerge, as if still instant with the vanished day or with the light turned out a moment before, for reasons perhaps of which less said the better. But the gloaming in the kitchen was of another kind and came from the night-light with the red chimney which, in Martha's room, adjoining the kitchen, burned eternally at the feet of a little Virgin carved in wood, hanging on the wall. Weary of rocking herself she had gone in and lain down on her bed, leaving the door of her room open so as to miss none of the sounds in the house. But perhaps she had gone to sleep.

I went upstairs again. I stopped at my son's door. I stooped and applied my ear to the keyhole. Some apply the eye, I the ear, to keyholes. I heard nothing, to my great surprise. For my son slept noisily, with open mouth. I took good care not to open the door. For this silence was of a nature to occupy my mind, for some little time. I went to my room.

It was then the unheard of sight was to be seen of Moran making ready to go without knowing where he was going, having consulted neither map nor time-table, considered neither itinerary nor halts, heedless of the weather outlook, with only the vaguest notion of the outfit he would need, the time the expedition was likely to take, the money he would require and even the very nature of the work to be done and consequently the means to be employed. And yet there I was whistling away while I stuffed into my haversack a minimum of effects, similar to those I had recommended to my son. I put on my old pepper-and-salt shooting-suit with the knee-breeches, stockings to match and a pair of stout black boots. I bent down, my hands on my buttocks, and looked at my legs. Knock-kneed and skeleton thin they made a poor show in this accoutrement, unknown locally I may add. But when I left at night, for a distant place, I wore it with pleasure, for the sake of comfort, though I looked a sight. All I needed was a butterfly-net to have vaguely the air of a country schoolmaster on convalescent leave. The heavy glittering black boots, which seemed to implore a pair of navy-blue serge trousers, gave the finishing blow to this get-up which otherwise might have appeared, to the uninformed, an example of well-bred bad taste. On my head, after mature hesitation, I decided to wear my straw boater, yellowed by the rain. It had lost its band, which gave it an appearance of inordinate height. I was tempted to take my black cloak, but finally rejected it in favour of a heavy massive-handled winter umbrella. The cloak is a serviceable garment and I had more than one. It leaves great freedom of movement to the arms and at the same time conceals them. And there are times when a cloak is so to speak indispensable. But the umbrella too has great merits. And if it had been winter, or even autumn, instead of summer, I might have taken both. I had already done so, with most gratifying results.

Dressed thus I could hardly hope to pass unseen. I did not wish to. Conspicuousness is the A B C of my profession. To call forth feelings of pity and indulgence, to be the butt of jeers and hilarity, is indispensable. So many vent-holes in the cask of secrets. On condition you cannot feel, nor denigrate, nor laugh. This state was mine at will. And then there was night.

My son could only embarrass me. He was like a

thousand other boys of his age and condition. There is something about a father that discourages derision. Even grotesque he commands a certain respect. And when he is seen out with his young hopeful, whose face grows longer and longer and longer with every step, then no further work is possible. He is taken for a widower, the gaudiest colours are of no avail, rather make things worse, he finds himself saddled with a wife long since deceased, in child-bed as likely as not. And my antics would be viewed as the harmless effect of my widowhood, presumed to have unhinged my mind. I boiled with anger at the thought of him who had shackled me thus. If he had desired my failure he could not have devised a better means to it. If I could have reflected with my usual calm on the work I was required to do, it would perhaps have seemed of a nature more likely to benefit than to suffer by the presence of my son. But let us not go back on that. Perhaps I could pass him off as my assistant, or a mere nephew. I would forbid him to call me papa, or show me any sign of affection, in public, if he did not want to get one of those clouts he so dreaded.

And if I whistled fitfully while revolving these lugubrious thoughts, I suppose it was because I was happy at heart to leave my house, my garden, my village, I who usually left them with regret. Some people whistle for no reason at all. Not I. And while I came and went in my room, tidying up, putting back my clothes in the wardrobe and my hats in the boxes from which I had taken them the better to make my choice, locking the various drawers, while thus employed I had the joyful vision of myself far from home, from the familiar faces, from all my sheet-anchors, sitting on a milestone in the dark, my legs crossed, one hand on my thigh, my elbow in that hand, my chin cupped in the other, my eyes fixed on the earth as on a chessboard, coldly hatching my plans, for the next day, for the day after, creating time to come. And then I forgot that my son would be at my side, restless, plaintive, whinging for food, whinging for sleep, dirtying his drawers. I opened the drawer of my night-table and took out a full tube of morphine tablets, my favourite sedative.

I have a huge bunch of keys, it weighs over a pound. Not a door, not a drawer in my house but the key to it goes with me, wherever I go. I carry them in the right-hand pocket of my trousers, of my breeches in this case. A massive chain, attached to my braces, prevents me from losing them. This chain, four or five times longer than necessary, lies, coiled, on the bunch, in my pocket. Its weight gives me a list to the right, when I am tired, or when I forget to counteract it, by a muscular effort.

I looked round for the last time, saw that I had neglected certain precautions, rectified this, took up my haversack, I nearly wrote my bagpipes, my boater, my umbrella, I hope I'm not forgetting anything, switched off the light, went out into the passage and locked my door. That at least is clear. Immediately I heard a strangling noise. It was my son, sleeping. I woke him. We haven't a moment to lose, I said. Desperately he clung to his sleep. That was natural. A few hours sleep however deep are not enough for an organism in the first stages of puberty suffering from stomach trouble. And when I began to shake him and help him out of bed, pulling him first by the arms, then by the hair, he turned away from me in fury, to the wall, and dug his nails into the mattress. I had to muster all my strength to overcome his resistance. But I had hardly freed him from the bed when he broke from my hold, threw himself down on the floor and rolled about, screaming with anger and defiance. The fun was beginning already. This disgusting exhibition left me no choice but to use my umbrella, holding it by the end with both hands. But a word on the subject of my boater, before I forget. Two holes were bored in the brim, one on either side of course, I had bored them myself, with my little gimlet. And in these holes I had secured the ends of an elastic long enough to pass under my chin, under my jaws rather, but not too long, for it had to hold fast, under my jaws rather. In this way, however great my exertions, my boater stayed in its place, which was on my head. Shame on you, I cried, you ill-bred little pig! I would get angry if I were not careful. And anger is a luxury I cannot afford. For then I go blind, blood veils my eyes and I hear what the great Gustave heard, the benches creaking in the court of assizes. Oh it is not without scathe that one is gentle, courteous, reasonable, patient, day after day, year after year. I threw down my umbrella and ran from the room. On the stairs I met Martha coming up, capless, dishevelled, her clothes in disorder. What's going on? she cried. I looked at her. She went back to her kitchen. Trembling I hastened to the shed, seized my axe, went into the yard and began hacking madly at an old chopping-block that lay there and on which in winter, tranquilly, I split my logs. Finally the blade sank into it so deeply that I could not get it out. The efforts I made to do so brought me, with exhaustion, calm. I went upstairs again. My son was dressing. He was crying. Everybody was crying. I helped him put on his knapsack. I told him not to forget his raincoat. He began to put it in his knapsack. I told him to carry it over his arm, for the moment. It was nearly midnight. I picked up my umbrella. Intact. Get on, I said. He went out of the room which I paused for a moment to survey, before I followed him. It was a shambles. The night was fine, in my humble opinion. Scents filled the air. The gravel crunched under our feet. No, I said, this way. I entered the little wood. My son floundered behind me, bumping into the trees. He did not know how to find his way in the dark. He was still young, the words of reproach died on my lips. I stopped. Take my hand, I said. I might have said, Give me your hand. I said, Take my hand. Strange. But the path was too narrow for us to walk abreast. So I put my hand behind me and my son grasped it, gratefully I fancied. So we came to the little wicket-gate. It was locked. I unlocked it and stood aside, to let my son precede me. I turned back to look at my house. It was partly hidden by the little wood. The roof's serrated ridge, the single chimney-stack with its four flues, stood out faintly against the sky spattered with a few dim stars. I offered my face to the black mass of fragrant vegetation that was mine and with which I could do as I pleased and never be gainsaid. It was full of songbirds, their heads under their wings, fearing nothing, for they knew me. My trees, my bushes, my flower-beds, my tiny lawns, I used to think I loved them. If I sometimes cut a branch, a flower, it was solely for their good, that they might increase in strength and happiness. And I never did it without a pang. Indeed if the truth were known, I did not do it at all, I got Christy to do it. I grew no vegetables. Not far off was the hen-house. When I said I had turkeys, and so on, I lied. All I had was a few hens. My grey hen was there, not on the perch with the others, but on the ground, in a corner, in the dust, at the mercy of the rats. The cock no longer sought her out to tread her angrily. The day was at hand, if she did not take a turn for the better, when the other hens would join forces and tear her to pieces, with their beaks and claws. All was silent. I have an extremely sensitive ear. Yet I have no ear for music. I could just hear that adorable murmur of tiny feet, of quivering feathers and feeble, smothered clucking that hen-houses make at night and that dies down long before dawn. How often I had listened to it, entranced, in the evening, saying, Tomorrow I am free. And so I turned again a last time towards my little all, before I left it, in the hope of keeping it.

In the lane, having locked the wicket-gate, I said to my son, Left. I had long since given up going for walks with my son, though I sometimes longed to do so. The least outing with him was torture, he lost his way so easily. Yet when alone he seemed to know all the short cuts. When I sent him to the grocer's, or to Mrs Clement's, or even further afield, on the road to V for grain, he was back in half the time I would have taken for the journey myself, and without having run. For I did not want my son to be seen capering in the streets like the little hooligans he frequented on the sly. No, I wanted him to walk like his father, with little rapid steps, his head up, his breathing even and economical, his arms swinging, looking neither to left nor right, apparently oblivious to everything and in reality missing nothing. But with me he invariably took the wrong turn, a crossing or a simple corner was all he needed to stray from the right road, it of my election. I do not think he did this on purpose. But leaving everything to me he did not heed what he was doing, or look where he was going, and went on mechanically plunged in a kind of dream. It was as though he let himself be sucked in out of sight by every opening that offered. So that we had got into the habit of taking our walks separately. And the only walk we regularly took together was that which led us, every Sunday, from home to church and, mass over, from church to home. Caught up then in the slow tide of the faithful my son was not alone with me. But he was part of that docile herd going yet again to thank God for his goodness and to implore his mercy and forgiveness, and then returning, their souls made easy, to other gratifications.

I waited for him to come back, then spoke the words calculated to settle this matter once and for all. Get behind me, I said, and keep behind me. This solution had its points, from several points of view. But was he capable of keeping behind me? Would not the time be bound to come when he would raise his head and find himself alone, in a strange place, and when I, waking from my reverie, would turn and find him gone? I toyed briefly with the idea of attaching him to me by means of a long rope, its two ends tied about our waists. There are various ways of attracting attention and I was not sure that this was one of the good ones. And he might have undone his knots in silence and escaped, leaving me to go on my way alone, followed by a long rope trailing in the dust, like a burgess of Calais. Until such time as the rope, catching on some fixed or heavy object, should stop me dead in my stride. We should have needed, not the soft and silent rope, but a chain, which was not to be dreamt of. And yet I did dream of it, for an instant I amused myself dreaming of it, imagining myself in a world less ill contrived and wondering how, having nothing more than a simple chain, without collar or band or gyves or fetters of any kind, I could chain my son to me in such a way as to prevent him from ever shaking me off again. It was a simple problem of toils and knots and I could have solved it at a pinch. But already I was called elsewhere by the image of my son no longer behind me, but before me. Thus in the rear I could keep my eye on him and intervene, at the least false movement he might make. But apart from having other parts to play, during this expedition, than those of keeper and sick-nurse, the prospect was more than I could bear of being unable to move a step without having before my eyes my son's little sullen plump body. Come here! I cried. For on hearing me say we were to go to the left he had gone to the left, as if his dearest wish was to infuriate me. Slumped over my umbrella, my head sunk as beneath a malediction, the fingers of my free hand between two slats of the wicket, I no more stirred than if I had been of stone. So he came back a second time. I tell you to keep behind me and you go before me, I said.

It was the summer holidays. His school cap was green with initials and a boar's head, or a deer's, in gold braid on the front. It lay plumb on his big blond skull as precise as a lid on a pot. There is something about this strict sit of hats and caps that never fails to exasperate me. As for his raincoat, instead of carrying it folded over his arm, or flung across his shoulder, as I had told him, he had rolled it in a ball and was holding it with both hands, on his belly. There he was before me, his big feet splayed, his knees sagging, his stomach sticking out, his chest sunk, his chin in the air, his mouth open, in the attitude of a veritable half-wit. I myself must have looked as if only the support of my umbrella and the wicket were keeping me from falling. I managed finally to articulate, Are you capable of following me? He did not answer. But I seized his thoughts as clearly as if he had spoken them, namely, And you, are you capable of leading me? Midnight struck, from the steeple of my beloved church. It did not matter. I was gone from home. I sought in my mind, where all I need is to be found, what treasured possession he was likely to have about him. I hope, I said, you have not forgotten your scout-knife, we might need it. This knife comprised, apart from the five or six indispensable blades, a cork-screw, a tin-opener, a punch, a screw-driver, a claw, a gouge for removing stones from hooves and I know not what other futilities besides. I had given it to him myself, on the occasion of his first first prize for history and geography, subjects which, at the school he attended, were for obscure reasons regarded as inseparable. The veriest dunce when it came to literature and the so-called exact sciences, he had no equal for the dates of battles, revolutions, restorations and other exploits of the human race, in its slow ascension towards the light, and for the configuration of frontiers and the heights of mountain peaks. He deserved his scout-knife. Don't tell me you've left it behind, I said. Not likely, he said, with pride and satisfaction, tapping his pocket. Then give it to me, I said. Naturally he did not answer. Prompt obedience was contrary to his habits. Give me that knife! I cried. He gave it to me. What could he do, alone with me in the night that tells no tales? It was for his own good, to save him from getting lost. For where a scout's knife is, there will his heart be also, unless he can afford to buy another, which was not the case with my son. For he never had any money in his pocket, not needing it. But every penny he received, and he did not receive many, he deposited first in his savings-box, then in the savings-bank, where they were entered in a book that remained in my possession. He would doubtless at that moment with pleasure have cut my throat, with that selfsame knife I was putting so placidly in my pocket. But he was still a little on the young side, my son, a little on the soft side, for the great deeds of vengeance. But time was on his side and he consoled himself perhaps with that thought, foolish though he was. Be that as it may, he kept back his tears, for which I was obliged to him. I straightened myself and laid my hand on his shoulder, saying, Patience, my child, patience. The awful thing in affairs of this kind is that when you have the will you do not have the way, and vice versa. But of that my unfortunate son could as yet have no suspicion, he must have thought that the rage which distorted his features and made him tremble would never leave him till the day he could vent it as it deserved. And not even then. Yes, he must have felt his soul the soul of a pocket Monte Cristo, with whose antics as adumbrated in the Schoolboys' Classics he was needless to say familiar. Then with a good clap on that impotent back I said, Off we go. And off indeed I did go, what is more, and my son drew out behind me. I had left, accompanied by my son, in accordance with instructions received.

I have no intention of relating the various adventures which befell us, me and my son, together and singly, before we came to the Molloy country. It would be tedious. But that is not what stops me. All is tedious, in this relation that is forced upon me. But I shall conduct it in my own way, up to a point. And if it has not the good fortune to give satisfaction, to my employer, if there are passages that give offence to him and to his colleagues, then so much the worse for us all, for them all, for there is no worse for me. That is to say, I have not enough imagination to imagine it. And yet I have more than before. And if I submit to this paltry scrivening which is not of my province, it is for reasons very different from those that might be supposed. I am still obeying orders, if you like, but no longer out of fear. No, I am still afraid, but simply from force of habit. And the voice I listen to needs no Gaber to make it heard. For it is within me and exhorts me to continue to the end the faithful servant I have always been, of a cause that is not mine, and patiently fulfil in all its bitterness my calamitous part, as it was my will, when I had a will, that others should. And this with hatred in my heart, and scorn, of my master and his designs. Yes, it is rather an ambiguous voice and not always easy to follow, in its reasonings and decrees. But I follow it none the less, more or less, I follow it in this sense, that I know what it means, and in this sense, that I do what it tells me. And I do not think there are many voices of which as much may be said. And I feel I shall follow it from this day forth, no matter what it commands. And when it ceases, leaving me in doubt and darkness, I shall wait for it to come back, and do nothing, even though the whole world, through the channel of its innumerable authorities speaking with one accord, should enjoin upon me this and that, under pain of unspeakable punishments. But this evening, this morning, I have drunk a little more than usual and tomorrow I may be of a different mind. It also tells me, this voice I am only just beginning to know, that the memory of this work brought scrupulously to a close will help me to endure the long anguish of vagrancy and freedom. Does this mean I shall one day be banished from my house, from my garden, lose my trees, my lawns, my birds of which the least is known to me and the way all its own it has of singing, of flying, of coming up to me or fleeing at my coming, lose and be banished from the absurd comforts of my home where all is snug and neat and all those things at hand without which I could not bear being a man, where my enemies cannot reach me, which it was my life's work to build, to adorn, to perfect, to keep? I am too old to lose all this, and begin again, I am too old! Quiet, Moran, quiet. No emotion, please.

I was saying I would not relate all the vicissitudes of the journey from my country to Molloy's, for the simple reason that I do not intend to. And in writing these lines I know in what danger I am of offending him whose favour I know I should court, now more than ever. But I write them all the same, and with a firm hand weaving inexorably back and forth and devouring my page with the indifference of a shuttle. But some I shall relate briefly, because that seems to me desirable, and in order to give some idea of the methods of my full maturity. But before coming to that I shall say what little I knew, on leaving my home, about the Molloy country, so different from my own. For it is one of the features of this penance that I may not pass over what is over and straightway come to the heart of the matter. But that must again be unknown to me which is no longer so and that again fondly believed which then I fondly believed, at my setting out. And if I occasionally break this rule, it is only over details of little importance. And in the main I observe it. And with such zeal that I am far more he who finds than he who tells what he has found, now as then, most of the time, I do not exaggerate. And in the silence of my room, and all over as far as I am concerned, I know scarcely any better where I am going and what awaits me than the night I clung to the wicket, beside my idiot of a son, in the lane. And it would not surprise me if I deviated, in the pages to follow, from the true and exact succession of events. But I do not think even Sisyphus is required to scratch himself, or to groan, or to rejoice, as the fashion is now, always at the same appointed places. And it may even be they are not too particular about the route he takes provided it gets him to his destination safely and on time. And perhaps he thinks each journey is the first. This would keep hope alive, would it not, hellish hope. Whereas to see yourself doing the same thing endlessly over and over again fills you with satisfaction.

By the Molloy country I mean that narrow region

whose administrative limits he had never crossed and presumably never would, either because he was forbidden to, or because he had no wish to, or of course because of some extraordinary fortuitous conjunction of circumstances. This region was situated in the north, I mean in relation to mine, less bleak, and comprised a settlement, dignified by some with the name of market-town, by others regarded as no more than a village, and the surrounding country. This market-town, or village, was, I hasten to say, called Bally, and represented, with its dependent lands, a surface area of five or six square miles at the most. In modern countries this is what I think is called a commune, or a canton, I forget, but there exists with us no abstract and generic term for such territorial subdivisions. And to express them we have another system, of singular beauty and simplicity, which consists in saying Bally (since we are talking of Bally) when you mean Bally and Ballyba when you mean Bally plus its domains and Ballybaba when you mean the domains exclusive of Bally itself. I myself for example lived, and come to think of it still live, in Turdy, hub of Turdyba. And in the evening, when I went for a stroll, in the country outside Turdy, to get a breath of fresh air, it was the fresh air of Turdybaba that I got, and no other.

Ballybaba, in spite of its limited range, could boast of a certain diversity. Pastures so-called, a little bogland, a few copses and, as you neared its confines, undulating and almost smiling aspects, as if Ballybaba was glad to go no further.

But the principal beauty of this region was a kind of strangled creek which the slow grey tides emptied and filled, emptied and filled. And the people came flocking from the town, unromantic people, to admire this spectacle. Some said, There is nothing more beautiful than these wet sands. Others, High tide is the best time to see the creek of Ballyba. How lovely then that leaden water, you would swear it was stagnant, if you did not know it was not. And yet others held it was like an underground lake. But all were agreed, like the inhabitants of Blackpool, that their town was on the sea. And they had Bally-on-Sea printed on their notepaper.

The population of Ballyba was small. I confess this thought gave me great satisfaction. The land did not lend itself to cultivation. No sooner did a tilth, or a meadow, begin to be sizeable than it fell foul of a sacred grove or a stretch of marsh from which nothing could be obtained beyond a little inferior turf or scraps of bogoak used for making amulets, paper-knives, napkin-rings, rosaries and other knick-knacks. Martha's madonna, for example, came from Ballyba. The pastures, in spite of the torrential rains, were exceedingly meagre and strewn with boulders. Here only quitchweed grew in abundance, and a curious bitter blue grass fatal to cows and horses, though tolerated apparently by the ass, the goat and the black sheep. What then was the source of Ballyba's prosperity? I'll tell you. No, I'll tell you nothing. Nothing.

That then is a part of what I thought I knew about Ballyba when I left home. I wonder if I was not confusing it with some other place.

Some twenty paces from my wicket-gate the lane skirts the graveyard wall. The lane descends, the wall rises, higher and higher. Soon you are faring below the dead. It is there I have my plot in perpetuity. As long as the earth endures that spot is mine, in theory. Sometimes I went and looked at my grave. The stone was up already. It was a simple Latin cross, white. I wanted to have my name put on it, with the here lies and the date of my birth. Then all it would have wanted was the date of my death. They would not let me. Sometimes I smiled, as if I were dead already.

We walked for several days, by sequestered ways. I did not want to be seen on the highways.

The first day I found the butt of Father Ambrose's cigar. Not only had I not thrown it away, in the ash-tray, in the waste-paper basket, but I had put it in my pocket, when changing my suit. That had happened unbeknown to me. I looked at it in astonishment, lit it, took a few puffs, threw it away. This was the outstanding event of the first day.

I showed my son how to use his pocket-compass. This gave him great pleasure. He was behaving well, better than I had hoped. On the third day I gave him back his knife.

The weather was kind. We easily managed our ten miles a day. We slept in the open. Safety first.

I showed my son how to make a shelter out of branches. He was in the scouts, but knew nothing. Yes, he knew how to make a camp fire. At every halt he implored me to let him exercise this talent. I saw no point in doing so.

We lived on tinned food which I sent him to get in the villages. He was that much use to me. We drank the water to the streams.

All these precautions were assuredly useless. One day in a field I saw a farmer I knew. He was coming towards us. I turned immediately, took my son by the arm and led him away in the direction we were coming from. The farmer overtook us, as I had foreseen. Having greeted me, he asked where we were going. It must have been his field. I replied that we were going home. Fortunately we had not yet left it far behind. Then he asked me where we had been. Perhaps one of his cows had been stolen, or one of his pigs. Out walking, I said. I'd give you a lift and welcome, he said, but I won't be leaving till night. Oh how very unfortunate, I said. If you care to wait, he said, you're very welcome. I declined with thanks. Fortunately it was not yet midday. There was nothing strange in not wanting to wait till night. Well, safe home, he said. We made a wide detour and turned our faces to the north again.

These precautions were doubtless exaggerated. The right thing would have been to travel by night and hide during the day, at least in the early stages. But the weather was so fine I could not bring myself to do it. My pleasure was not my sole consideration, but it was a consideration! Such a thing had never happened to me before, in the course of my work. And our snail's pace! I cannot have been in a hurry to arrive.

I gave fitful thought, while basking in the balm of the warm summer days, to Gaber's instructions. I could not reconstruct them to my entire satisfaction. In the night, under the boughs, screened from the charms of nature, I devoted myself to this problem. The sounds my son made during his sleep hindered me considerably. Sometimes I went out of the shelter and walked up and down, in the dark. Or I sat down with my back against a trunk, drew my feet up under me, took my legs in my arms and rested my chin on my knee. Even in this posture I could throw no light on the matter. What was I looking for exactly? It is hard to say. I was looking for what was wanting to make Gaber's statement complete. I felt he must have told me what to do with Molloy once he was found. My particular duties never terminated with the running to earth. That would have been too easy. But I had always to deal with the client in one way or another, according to instructions. Such operations took on a multitude of forms, from the most vigorous to the most discreet. The Yerk affair, which took me nearly three months to conclude successfully, was over on the day I succeeded in possessing myself of his tiepin and destroying it. Establishing contact was the least important part of my work. I found Yerk on the third day. I was never required to prove I had succeeded, my word was enough. Youdi must have had some way of verifying. Sometimes I was asked for a report.

On another occasion my mission consisted in bringing the person to a certain place at a certain time. A most delicate affair, for the person concerned was not a woman. I have never had to deal with a woman. I regret it. I don't think Youdi had much interest in them. That reminds me of the old joke about the female soul. Question, Have women a soul? Answer, Yes. Question, Why? Answer, In order that they may be damned. Very witty. Fortunately I had been allowed considerable licence as to the day. The hour was the important thing, not the date. He came to the appointed place and there I left him, on some pretext or other. He was a nice youth, rather sad and silent. I vaguely remember having invented some story about a woman. Wait, it's coming back. Yes, I told him she had been in love with him for six months and greatly desired to meet him in some secluded place. I even gave her name. Quite a well-known actress. Having brought him to the place appointed by her, it was only natural I should withdraw, out of delicacy. I can see him still, looking after me. I fancy he would have liked me for a friend. I don't know what became of him. I lost interest in my patients, once I had finished with them. I may even truthfully say I never saw one of them again, subsequently, not a single one. No conclusions need be drawn from this. Oh the stories I could tell you, if I were easy. What a rabble in my head, what a gallery of moribunds. Murphy, Watt, Yerk, Mercier and all the others. I would never have believed that—yes, I believe it willingly. Stories, stories. I have not been able to tell them. I shall not be able to tell this one.

I could not determine therefore how I was to deal with Molloy, once I had found him. The directions which Gaber must certainly have given me with reference to this had gone clean out of my head. That is what came of wasting the whole of that Sunday on stupidities. There was no good my saying, Let me see now, what is the usual thing? There were no usual things, in my instructions. Admittedly there was one particular operation that recurred from time to time, but not often enough to be, with any degree of probability, the one I was looking for. But even if it had always figured in my instructions, except on one single occasion, then that single occasion would have been enough to tie my hands, I was so scrupulous.

I told myself I had better give it no more thought, that the first thing to do was to find Molloy, that then I would devise something, that there was no hurry, that the thing would come back to me when I least expected it and that if, having found Molloy, I still did not know what to do with him, I could always manage to get in touch with Gaber without Youdi's knowing. I had his address just as he had mine. I would send him a telegram, How deal with M? To give me an explicit reply, though in terms if necessary veiled, was not beyond his powers. But was there a telegraph in Ballyba? But I also told myself, being only human, that the longer I took to find Molloy the greater my chances of remembering what I was to do with him. And we would have peacably pursued our way on foot, but for the following incident.

One night, having finally succeeded in falling asleep beside my son as usual, I woke with a start, feeling as if I had just been dealt a violent blow. It's all right, I am not going to tell you a dream properly so called. It was pitch dark in the shelter. I listened attentively without moving. I heard nothing save the snoring and gasping of my son. I was about to conclude as usual that it was just another bad dream when a fulgurating pain went through my knee. This then was the explanation of my sudden awakening. The sensation could indeed well be compared to that of a blow, such as I fancy a horse's hoof might give. I waited anxiously for it to recur, motionless and hardly breathing, and of course sweating. I acted in a word precisely as one does, if my information was correct, at such a juncture. And sure enough the pain did recur a few minutes later, but not so bad as the first time, as the second rather. Or did it only seem less bad to me because I was expecting it? Or because I was getting used to it already? I think not. For it recurred again, several times, and each time less bad than the time before, and finally subsided altogether so that I was able to get to sleep again more or less reassured. But before getting to sleep again I had time to remember that the pain in question was not altogether new to me. For I had felt it before, in my bathroom, when giving my son his enema. But then it had only attacked me once and never recurred, till now. And I went to sleep again wondering, by way of lullaby, whether it had been the same knee then as the one which had just excruciated me, or the other. And that is a thing I have never been able to determine. And my son too, when asked, was incapable of telling me which of my two knees I had rubbed in front of him, with iodex, the night we left. And I went to sleep again a little reassured, saying, It's a touch of neuralgia brought on by all the tramping and trudging and the chill damp nights, and promising myself to procure a packet of thermogene wool, with the pretty demon on the outside, at the first opportunity. Such is the rapidity of thought. But there was more to come. For waking again towards dawn, this time in consequence of a natural need, and with a mild erection, to make things more lifelike, I was unable to get up. That is to say I did get up finally to be sure, I simply had to, but by dint of what exertions! Unable, unable, it's easy to talk about being unable, whereas in reality nothing is more difficult. Because of the will I suppose, which the least opposition seems to lash into a fury. And this explains no doubt how it was I despaired at first of ever bending my leg again and then, a little later, through sheer determination, did succeed in bending it, slightly. The anchylosis was not total! I am still talking about my knee. But was it the same one that had waked me early in the night? I could not have sworn it was. It was not painful. It simply refused to bend. The pain, having warned me several times in vain, had no more to say. That is how I saw it. It would have been impossible for me to kneel, for example, for no matter how you kneel you must always bend both knees, unless you adopt an attitude frankly grotesque and impossible to maintain for more than a few seconds, I mean with the bad leg stretched out before you, like a Caucasian dancer. I examined the bad knee in the light of my torch. It was neither red nor swollen. I fiddled with the knee-cap. It felt like a clitoris. All this time my son was puffing like a grampus. He had no suspicion of what life could do to you. I too was innocent. But I knew it.

The sky was that horrible colour which heralds dawn. Things steal back into position for the day, take their stand, sham dead. I sat down cautiously, and I must say with a certain curiosity, on the ground. Anyone else would have tried to sit down as usual, off-handedly. Not I. New as this new cross was I at once found the most comfortable way of being crushed. But when you sit down on the ground you must sit down tailor-wise, or like a foetus, these are so to speak the only possible positions, for a beginner. So that I was not long in letting myself fall back flat on my back. And I was not long either in making the following addition to the sum of my knowledge, that when of the innumerable attitudes adopted unthinkingly by the normal man all are precluded but two or three, then these are enhanced. I would have sworn just the opposite, but for this experience. Yes, when you can neither stand nor sit with comfort, you take refuge in the horizontal, like a child in its mother's lap. You explore it as never before and find it possessed of unsuspected delights. In short it becomes infinite. And if in spite of all you come to tire of it in the end, you have only to stand up, or indeed sit up, for a few seconds. Such are the advantages of a local and painless paralysis. And it would not surprise me if the great classical paralyses were to offer analogous and perhaps even still more unspeakable satisfactions. To be literally incapable of motion at last, that must be something! My mind swoons when I think of it. And mute into the bargain! And perhaps as deaf as a post! And who knows as blind as a bat! And as likely as not your memory a blank! And just enough brain intact to allow you to exult! And to dread death like a regeneration.

I considered the problem of what I should do if my leg did not get better or got worse. I watched, through the branches, the sky sinking. The sky sinks in the morning, this fact has been insufficiently observed. It stoops, as if to get a better look. Unless it is the earth that lifts itself up, to be approved, before it sets out.

I shall not expound my reasoning. I could do so easily, so easily. Its conclusion made possible the composition of the following passage.

Did you have a good night? I said, as soon as my son opened his eyes. I could have waked him, but no, I let him wake naturally. Finally he told me he did not feel well. My son's replies were often beside the point.

Where are we, I said, and what is the nearest village? He named it. I knew it, I had been there, it was a small town, luck was on our side. I even had a few acquaintances, among its inhabitants. What day is it? I said. He specified the day without a moment's hesitation. And he had only just regained consciousness! I told you he had a genius for history and geography. It was from him I learned that Condom is on the Baise. Good, I said, off you go now to Hole, it'll take you—I worked it out—at the most three hours. He stared at me in astonishment. There, I said, buy a bicycle to fit you, second-hand for preference. You can go up to five pounds. I gave him five pounds, in ten-shilling notes. It must have a very strong carrier, I said, if it isn't very strong get it changed, for a very strong one. I was trying to be clear. I asked him if he was pleased. He did not look pleased. I repeated these instructions and asked him again if he was pleased. He looked if anything stupefied. A consequence perhaps of the great joy he felt. Perhaps he could not believe his ears. Do you understand if nothing else? I said. What a boon it is from time to time, a little real conversation. Tell me what you are to do, I said. It was the only way of knowing if he understood. Go to Hole, he said, fifteen miles away. Fifteen miles! I cried. Yes, he said. All right, I said, go on. And buy a bicycle, he said. I waited. Silence. A bicycle! I cried. But there are millions of bicycles in Hole! What kind of bicycle? He reflected. Second-hand, he said, at a venture. And if you can't find one second-hand? I said. You told me second-hand, he said. I remained silent for some time. And if you can't find one second-hand, I said at last, what will you do? You didn't tell me, he said. What a restful change it is from time to time, a little dialogue. How much money did I give you? I said. He counted the notes. Four pounds ten, he said. Count them again, I said. He counted them again. Four pounds ten, he said. Give it to me, I said. He gave me the notes and I counted them. Four pounds ten. I gave you five, I said. He did not answer, he let the figures speak for themselves. Had he stolen ten shillings and hidden them on his person? Empty your pockets, I said. He began to empty them. It must not be forgotten that all this time I was lying down. He did not know I was ill. Besides I was not ill. I looked vaguely at the objects he was spreading out before me. He took them out of his pockets one by one, held them up delicately between finger and thumb, turned them this way and that before my eyes and laid them finally on the ground beside me. When a pocket was emptied he pulled out its lining and shook it. Then a little cloud of dust arose. I was very soon overcome by the absurdity of this verification. I told him to stop. Perhaps he was hiding the ten shillings up his sleeve, or in his mouth. I should have had to get up and search him myself, inch by inch. But then he would have seen I was ill. Not that I was exactly ill. And why did I not want him to know I was ill? I don't know. I could have counted the money I had left. But what use would that have been? Did I even know the amount I had brought with me? No. To me too I cheerfully applied the maieutic method. Did I know how much I had spent? No. Usually I kept the most rigorous accounts when away on business and was in a position to justify my expenditure down to the last penny

This time no. For I was throwing my money away with as little concern as if I had been travelling for my pleasure. Let us suppose I am wrong, I said, and that I only gave you four pounds ten. He was calmly picking up the objects littered on the ground and putting them back in his pockets. How could he be made to understand? Stop that and listen, I said. I gave him the notes. Count them, I said. He counted them. How much? I said. Four pounds ten, he said. Ten what? I said. Ten shillings, he said. You have four pounds ten shillings? I said. Yes, he said. It was not true, I had given him five. You agree, I said. Yes, he said. And why do you think I have given you all that money? I said. His face brightened. To buy a bicycle, he said, without hesitation. Do you imagine a second-hand bicycle costs four pounds ten shillings? I said. I don't know, he said. I did not know either. But that was not the point. What did I tell you exactly? I said. We racked our brains together. Second-hand for preference, I said finally, that's what I told you. Ah, he said. I am not giving this duet in full. Just the main themes. I didn't tell you second-hand, I said, I told you second-hand for preference. He had started picking up his things again. Will you stop that, I cried, and pay attention to what I am saying. He ostentatiously let fall a big ball of tangled string. The ten shillings were perhaps inside it. You see no difference between second-hand and second-hand for preference, I said, do you? I looked at my watch. It was ten o'clock. I was only making our ideas more confused. Stop trying to understand, I said, just listen to what I am going to say, because I shall not say it twice. He came over to me and knelt down. You would have thought I was about to breathe my last. Do you know what a new bicycle is? I said. Yes papa, he said. Very well, I said, if you can't find a second-hand bicycle buy a new bicycle. I repeat. I repeated. I who had said I would not repeat. Now tell me what you are to do, I said. I added, Take your face away, your breath stinks. I almost added, You don't brush your teeth and you complain of having abscesses, but I stopped myself in time. It was not the moment to introduce another theme. I repeated, Tell me what you are to do. He pondered. Go to Hole, he said, fifteen miles away—.Don't worry about the miles, I said. You're in Hole. What for? No, I can't. Finally he understood. Who is this bicycle for, I said, Goering? He had not yet grasped that the bicycle was for him. Admittedly he was nearly my size already. As for the carrier, I might just as well not have mentioned it. But in the end he had the whole thing off pat. So much so that he actually asked me what he was to do if he had not enough money. Come back here and ask me, I said. I had naturally foreseen, while reflecting on all these matters before my son woke, that he might have trouble with people asking him how he came by so much money and he so young. And I knew what he was to do in that event, namely go and see, or send for, the police-sergeant, give his name and say it was I, Jacques Moran, ostensibly at home in Turdy, who had sent him to buy a bicycle in Hole. Here obviously two distinct operations were involved, the first consisting in foreseeing the difficulty (before my son woke), the second in overcoming it (at the news that Hole was the nearest locality). But there was no question of my conveying instructions of such complexity. But don't worry, I said, you've enough and to spare to buy yourself a good bicycle. I added, And bring it back here as fast as you can. You had to allow for everything with my son. He could never have guessed what to do with the bicycle once he had it. He was capable of hanging about Hole, under God knows what conditions, waiting for further instructions. He asked me what was wrong. I must have winced. I'm sick of the sight of you, I said, that's what's wrong. And I asked him what he was waiting for. I don't feel well, he said. When he asked me how I was I said nothing, and when no one asked him anything he announced he was not feeling well. Are you not pleased, I said, to have a nice brand-new bicycle, all your own? I was decidedly set on hearing him say he was pleased. But I regretted my phrase, it could only add to his confusion. But perhaps this family chat has lasted long enough. He left the shelter and when I judged he was at a safe distance I left it too, painfully. He had gone about twenty paces. Leaning nonchalantly against a tree-trunk, my good leg boldly folded across the other, I tried to look light-hearted. I hailed him. He turned. I waved my hand. He stared at me an instant, then turned away and went on. I shouted his name. He turned again. A lamp! I cried. A good lamp! He did not understand. How could he have understood, at twenty paces, he who could not understand at one. He came back towards me. I waved him away, crying, Go on! Go on! He stopped and stared at me, his head on one side like a parrot, utterly bewildered apparently. Foolishly I made to stoop, to pick up a stone or a piece of wood or a clod, anything in the way of a projectile, and nearly fell. I reached up above my head, broke off a live bough and hurled it violently in his direction. He spun round and took to his heels. Really there were times I could not understand my son. He must have known he was out of range, even of a good stone, and yet he took to his heels. Perhaps he was afraid I would run after him. And indeed, I think there is something terrifying about the way I run, with my head flung back, my teeth clenched, my elbows bent to the full and my knees nearly hitting me in the face. And I have often caught faster runners than myself thanks to this way of running. They stop and wait for me, rather than prolong such a horrible outburst at their heels. As for the lamp, we did not need a lamp. Later, when the bicycle had taken its place in my son's life, in the round of his duties and his innocent games, then a lamp would be indispensable, to light his way in the night. And no doubt it was in anticipation of those happy days that I had thought of the lamp and cried out to my son to buy a good one, that later on his comings and his goings should not be hemmed about with darkness and with dangers. And similarly I might have told him to be careful about the bell, to unscrew the little cap and examine it well inside, so as to make sure it was a good bell and in good working order, before concluding the transaction, and to ring it to hear the ring it made. But we would have time enough, later on, to see to all these things. And it would be my joy to help my son, when the time came, to fit his bicycle with the best lamps, both front and rear, and the best bell and the best brakes that money could buy.

The day seemed very long. I missed my son! I busied myself as best I could. I ate several times. I took advantage of being alone at last, with no other witness than God, to masturbate. My son must have had the same idea, he must have stopped on the way to masturbate. I hope he enjoyed it more than I did. I circled the shelter several times, thinking the exercise would benefit my knee. I moved at quite a good speed and without much pain, but I soon tired. After ten or eleven steps a great weariness seized hold of my leg, a heaviness rather, and I had to stop. It went away at once and I was able to go on. I took a little morphine. I asked myself certain questions. Why had I not told my son to bring me back something for my leg? Why had I hidden my condition from him? Was I secretly glad that this had happened to me, perhaps even to the point of not wanting to get well? I surrendered myself to the beauties of the scene, I gazed at the trees, the fields, the sky, the birds, and I listened attentively to the sounds, faint and clear, borne to me on the air. For an instant I fancied I heard the silence mentioned, if I am not mistaken, above. Stretched out in the shelter, I brooded on the undertaking in which I was embarked. I tried again to remember what I was to do with Molloy, when I found him. I dragged myself down to the stream. I lay down and looked at my reflection, then I washed my face and hands. I waited for my image to come back, I watched it as it trembled towards an ever increasing likeness. Now and then a drop, falling from my face, shattered it again. I did not see a soul all day. But towards evening I heard a prowling about the shelter. I did not move, and the footsteps died away. But a little later, having left the shelter for some reason or other, I saw a man a few paces off, standing motionless. He had his back to me. He wore a coat much too heavy for the time of the year and was leaning on a stick so massive, and so much thicker at the bottom than at the top, that it seemed more like a club. He turned and we looked at each other for some time in silence. That is to say I looked him full in the face, as I always do, to make people think I am not afraid, whereas he merely threw me a rapid glance from time to time, then lowered his eyes, less from timidity apparently than in order quietly to think over what he had just seen, before adding to it. There was a coldness in his stare, and a thrust, the like of which I never saw. His face was pale and noble, I could have done with it. I was thinking he could not be much over fifty-five when he took off his hat, held it for a moment in his hand, then put it back on his head. No resemblance to what is called raising one's hat. But I thought it advisable to nod. The hat was quite extraordinary, in shape and colour. I shall not attempt to describe it, it was like none I had ever seen. He had a huge shock of dirty snow-white hair. I had time, before he squeezed it in back under his hat, to see the way it swelled up on his skull. His face was dirty and hairy, yes, pale, noble, dirty and hairy. He made a curious movement, like a hen that puffs up its feathers and slowly dwindles till it is smaller than before. I thought he was going to depart without a word to me. But suddenly he asked me to give him a piece of bread. He accompanied this humiliating request with a fiery look. His accent was that of a foreigner or of one who had lost the habit of speech. But had I not said already, with relief, at the mere sight of his back, He's a foreigner. Would you like a tin of sardines? I said. He asked for bread and I offered him fish. That is me all over. Bread, he said. I went into the shelter and took the piece of bread I was keeping for my son, who would probably be hungry when he came back. I gave it to him. I expected him to devour it there and then. But he broke it in two and put the pieces in his coat-pockets. Do you mind if I look at your stick? I said. I stretched out my hand. He did not move. I put my hand on the stick, just under his. I could feel his fingers gradually letting go. Now it was I who held the stick. Its lightness astounded me. I put it back in his hand. He threw me a last look and went. It was almost dark. He walked with swift uncertain step, often changing his course, dragging the stick like a hindrance. I wished I could have stood there looking after him, and time at a standstill. I wished I could have been in the middle of a desert, under the midday sun, to look after him till he was only a dot, on the edge of the horizon. I stayed out in the air for a long time. Every now and then I listened. But my son did not come. Beginning to feel cold I went back into the shelter and lay down, under my son's raincoat. But beginning to feel sleepy I went out again and lit a big wood-fire, to guide my son towards me. When the fire had kindled I said, Why of course, now I can warm myself! I warmed myself, rubbing my hands together after having held them to the flame and before holding them to it again, and turning my back to the flame and lifting the tail of my coat, and turning as on a spit. And in the end, overcome with heat and weariness, I lay down on the ground near the fire and fell asleep, saying, Perhaps a spark will set fire to my clothes and I wake a living torch. And saying many other things besides, belonging to separate and apparently unconnected trains of thought. But when I woke it was day again and the fire was out. But the embers were still warm. My leg was no better, but it was no worse either. That is to say it was perhaps a little worse, without my being in a condition to realize it, for the simple reason that this leg was becoming a habit, mercifully. But I think not. For at the same time as I listened to my knee, and then submitted it to various tests, I was on my guard against the effects of this habit and tried to discount them. And it was not so much Moran as another, in the secret of Moran's sensations exclusively, who said, No change, Moran, no change. This may seem impossible. I went into the copse to cut myself a stick. But having finally found a suitable branch, I remembered I had no knife. I went back to the shelter, hoping to find my son's knife among the things he had laid on the ground and neglected to pick up. It was not among them. To make up for this I came across my umbrella and said, Why cut myself a stick when I have my umbrella? And I practised walking with the help of my umbrella. And though in this way I moved no faster and no less painfully, at least I did not tire so quickly. And instead of having to stop every ten steps, to rest, I easily managed fifteen, before having to stop. And even while I rested my umbrella was a help. For I found that when I leaned upon it the heaviness in my leg, due probably to a defect in the bloodstream, disappeared even more quickly than when I stood supported only by my muscles and the tree of life. And thus equipped I no longer confined myself to circling about the shelter, as I had done the previous day, but I radiated from it in every direction. And I even gained a little knoll from which I had a better view of the expanse where my son might suddenly rise into view, at any moment. And in my mind's eye from time to time I saw him, bent over the handlebars or standing on the pedals, drawing near, and I heard him panting and I saw written on the chubby face his joy at being back at last. But at the same time I kept my eye on the shelter, which drew me with an extraordinary pull, so that to cut across from the terminus of one sally to the terminus of the next, and so on, which would have been convenient, was out of the question. But each time I had to retrace my steps, the way I had come, to the shelter, and make sure all was in order, before I sallied forth again. And I consumed the greater part of this second day in these vain comings and goings, these vigils and imaginings, but not all of it. For I also lay down from time to time in the shelter, which I was beginning to think of as my little house, to ruminate in peace on certain things, and notably on my provisions of food which were rapidly running out, so that after a meal devoured at five o'clock I was left with only two tins of sardines, a handful of biscuits and a few apples. But I also tried to remember what I was to do with Molloy, once I had found him. And on myself too I pored, on me so changed from what I was. And I seemed to see myself ageing as swiftly as a day-fly. But the idea of ageing was not exactly the one which offered itself to me. And what I saw was more like a crumbling, a frenzied collapsing of all that had always protected me from all I was always condemned to be. Or it was like a kind of clawing towards a light and countenance I could not name, that I had once known and long denied. But what words can describe this sensation at first all darkness and bulk, with a noise like the grinding of stones, then suddenly as soft as water flowing. And then I saw a little globe swaying up slowly from the depths, through the quiet water, smooth at first, and scarcely paler than its escorting ripples, then little by little a face, with holes for the eyes and mouth and other wounds, and nothing to show if it was a man's face or a woman's face, a young face or an old face, or if its calm too was not an effect of the water trembling between it and the light. But I confess I attended but absently to these poor figures, in which I suppose my sense of disaster sought to contain itself. And that I did not labour at them more diligently was a further index of the great changes I had suffered and of my growing resignation to being dispossessed of self. And doubtless I should have gone from discovery to discovery, concerning myself, if I had persisted. But at the first faint light, I mean in these wild shadows gathering about me, dispensed by a vision or by an effort of thought, at the first light I fled to other cares. And all had been for nothing. And he who acted thus was a stranger to me too. For it was not my nature, I mean it was not my custom, to conduct my calculations simultaneously, but separately and turn about, pushing each one as far as it would go before turning in desperation to another. Similarly the missing instructions concerning Molloy, when I felt them stirring in the depths of my memory, I turned from them in haste towards other unknowns. And I who a fortnight before would joyfully have reckoned how long I could survive on the provisions that remained, probably with reference to the question of calories and vitamins, and established in my head a series of menus asymptotically approaching nutritional zero, was now content to note feebly that I should soon be dead of inanition, if I did not succeed in renewing my provisions. So much for the second day. But one incident remains to be noted, before I go on to the third.

It was evening I had lit my fire and was watching it take when I heard myself hailed. The voice, already so near that I started violently, was that of a man. But after this one violent start I collected myself and continued to busy myself with my fire as if nothing had happened, poking it with a branch I had torn from its tree for the purpose a little earlier and stripped of its twigs and leaves and even part of its bark, with my bare nails. I have always loved skinning branches and laying bare the pretty white glossy shaft of sapwood. But obscure feelings of love and pity for the tree held me back most of the time. And I numbered among my familiars the dragon-tree of Teneriffe that perished at the age of five thousand years, struck by lightning. It was an example of longevity. The branch was thick and full of sap and did not burn when I stuck it in the fire. I held it by the thin end. The crackling of the fire, of the writhing brands rather, for fire triumphant does not crackle, but makes an altogether different noise, had permitted the man to come right up to me, without my knowledge. If there is one thing infuriates me it is being taken myself by surprise. I continued then, in spite of my spasm of fright, hoping it had passed unnoticed, to poke the fire as if I were alone. But at the thump of his hand on my shoulder I had no choice but to do what anyone else would have done in my place, and this I achieved by suddenly spinning round in what I trust was a good imitation of fear and anger. There I was face to face with a dim man, dim of face and dim of body, because of the dark. Put it there, he said. But little by little I formed an idea of the type of individual it was. And indeed there reigned between his various parts great harmony and concord, and it could be truly said that his face was worthy of his body, and vice versa. And if I could have seen his arse, I do not doubt I should have found it on a par with the whole. What are you doing in this God-forsaken place, he said, you unexpected pleasure. And moving aside from the fire which was now burning merrily, so that its light fell full on the intruder, I could see he was precisely the kind of pest I had thought he was, without being sure, because of the dark. Can you tell me, he said. I shall have to describe him briefly, though such a thing is contrary to my principles. He was on the small side, but thick-set. He wore a thick navy-blue suit (double-breasted) of hideous cut and a pair of outrageously wide black shoes, with the toe-caps higher than the uppers. This dreadful shape seems only to occur in black shoes. Do you happen to know, he said. The fringed extremities of a dark muffler, seven feet long at least, wound several times round his neck, hung down his back. He had a narrow-brimmed dark blue felt hat on his head, with a fish-hook and an artificial fly stuck in the band, which produced a highly sporting effect. Do you hear me? he said. But all this was nothing compared to the face which I regret to say vaguely resembled my own, less the refinement of course, same little abortive moustache, same little ferrety eyes, same paraphimosis of the nose, and a thin red mouth that looked as if it was raw from trying to shit its tongue. Hey you! he said. I turned back to my fire. It was doing nicely. I threw more wood on it. Do you hear me talking to you? he said. I went towards the shelter, he barred my way, emboldened by my limp. Have you a tongue in your head? he said. I don't know you, I said. I laughed. I had not intended to be witty. Would you care to see my card? he said. It would mean nothing to me, I said. He came closer to me. Get out of my way, I said. It was his turn no laugh. You refuse to answer? he said. I made a great effort. What do you want to know? I said. He must have thought I was weakening. That's more like it, he said. I called to my aid the image of my son who might arrive at any moment. I've already told you, he said. I was trembling all over. Have the goodness to tell me again, I said. To cut a long story short he wanted to know if I had seen an old man with a stick pass by. He described him. Badly. The voice seemed to come to me from afar. No, I said. What do you mean no? he said. I have seen no one, I said. And yet he passed this way, he said. I said nothing. How long have you been here? he said. His body too grew dim, as if coming asunder. What is your business here? he said. Are you on night patrol? I said. He thrust his hand at me. I have an idea I told him once again to get out of my way. I can still see the hand coming towards me, pallid, opening and closing. As if self-propelled. I do not know what happened then. But a little later, perhaps a long time later, I found him stretched on the ground, his head in a pulp. I am sorry I cannot indicate more clearly how this result was obtained, it would have been something worth reading. But it is not at this late stage of my relation that I intend to give way to literature. I myself was unscathed, except for a few scratches I did not discover till the following day.

I bent over him. As I did so I realized my leg was bending normally. He no longer resembled me. I took him by the ankles and dragged him backwards into the shelter. His shoes shone with highly polished blacking. He wore fancy socks. The trousers slid back, disclosing the white hairless legs. His ankles were bony, like my own. My fingers encircled them nearly. He was wearing suspenders, one of which had come undone and was hanging loose. This detail went to my heart. Already my knee was stiffening again. It no longer required to be supple. I went back to the shelter and took my son's raincoat. I went back to the fire and lay down, with the coat over me. I did not get much sleep, but I got some. I listened to the owls. They were not eagle-owls, it was a cry like the whistle of a locomotive. I listened to a nightingale. And to distant corncrakes. If I had heard of other birds that cry and sing at night, I should have listened to them too. I watched the fire dying, my cheek pillowed on my hands. I watched out for the dawn. It was hardly breaking when I got up and went to the shelter. His legs too were on the stiff side, but there was still some play in the hip joints, fortunately. I dragged him into the copse, with frequent rests on the way, but without letting go his legs, so as not to have to stoop again to pick them up. Then I dismantled the shelter and threw the branches over the body. I packed and shouldered the two bags, took the raincoat and the umbrella. In a word I struck camp. But before leaving I consulted with myself to make sure I was forgetting nothing, and without relying on my intelligence alone, for I felt my pockets and looked around me. And it was while feeling my pockets that I discovered something of which my mind had been powerless to inform me, namely that my keys were no longer there. I was not long in finding them, scattered on the ground, the ring having broken. And to tell the truth first I found the chain, then the keys and last the ring, in two pieces. And since it was out of the question, even with the help of my umbrella, to stoop each time to pick up a key, I put down my bags, my umbrella and the coat and lay down flat on my stomach among the keys which in this way I was able to recover without much difficulty. And when a key was beyond my reach I took hold of the grass and dragged myself over to it. And I wiped each key on the grass, before putting it in my pocket, whether it needed wiping or not. And from time to time I raised myself on my hands, to get a better view. And in this way I located a number of keys at some distance from me, and these I reached by rolling over and over, like a great cylinder. And finding no more keys, I said, There is no use my counting them, for I do not know how many there were. And my eyes resumed their search. But finally I said, Hell to it, I'll do with those I have. And while looking in this way for my keys I found an ear which I threw into the copse. And, to my even greater surprise, I found my straw hat which I thought was on my head! One of the holes for the elastic had expanded to the edge of the rim and consequently was no longer a hole, but a slit. But the other had been spared and the elastic was still in it. And finally I said, I shall rise now and, from my full height, run my eyes over this area for the last time. Which I did. It was then I found the ring, first one piece, then the other. Then, finding nothing more belonging either to me or to my son, I shouldered my bags again, jammed the straw-hat hard down on my skull, folded my son's raincoat over my arm, caught up the umbrella and went.

But I did not go far. For I soon stopped on the crest of a rise from where I could survey, without fatigue, the camp-site and the surrounding country. And I made this curious observation, that the land from where I was, and even the clouds in the sky, were so disposed as to lead the eyes gently to the camp, as in a painting by an old master. I made myself as comfortable as possible I got rid of my various burdens and I ate a whole tin of sardines and one apple. I lay down flat on my stomach on my son's coat. And now I propped my elbows on the ground and my jaws between my hands, which carried my eyes towards the horizon, and now I made a little cushion of my two hands on the ground and laid my cheek upon it, five minutes one, five minutes the other, all the while flat on my stomach. I could have made myself a pillow of the bags, but I did not, it did not occur to me. The day passed tranquilly, without incident And the only thing that relieved the monotony of this third day was a dog. When I first saw him he was sniffing about the remains of my fire, then he went into the copse. But I did not see him come out again, either because my attention was elsewhere, or because he went out the other side, having simply as it were gone straight through it. I mended my hat, that is to say with the tin-opener I pierced a new hole beside the old one and made fast the elastic again. And I also mended the ring, twisting the two pieces together, and I slipped on the keys and made fast the long chain again. And to kill time I asked myself a certain number of questions and tried to answer them. For example.

Question. What had happened to the blue felt hat?

Answer.

Question. Would they not suspect the old man with the stick?

Answer. Very probably.

Question. What were his chances of exonerating himself?

Answer. Slight.

Question. Should I tell my son what had happened?

Answer. No, for then it would be his duty to denounce me.

Question. Would he denounce me?

Answer.

Question. How did I feel?

Answer. Much as usual.

Question. And yet I had changed and was still changing?

Answer. Yes.

Question. And in spite of this I felt much as usual?

Answer. Yes.

Question. How was this to be explained?

Answer.

These questions and others too were separated by more or less prolonged intervals of time not only from one another, but also from the answers appertaining to them. And the answers did not always follow in the order of the questions. But while looking for the answer, or the answers, to a given question, I found the answer, or the answers, to a question I had already asked myself in vain, in the sense that I had not been able to answer it, or I found another question, or other questions, demanding in their turn an immediate answer.

Translating myself now in imagination to the present moment, I declare the foregoing to have been written with a firm and even satisfied hand, and a mind calmer than it has been for a long time. For I shall be far away, before these lines are read, in a place where no one will dream of coming to look for me. And then Youdi will take care of me, he will not let me be punished for a fault committed in the execution of my duty. And they can do nothing to my son, rather they will commiserate with him on having had such a father, and offers of help and expressions of esteem will pour in upon him from every side.

So this third day wore away. And about five o'clock I ate my last tin of sardines and a few biscuits, with a good appetite. This left me with only a few apples and a few biscuits. But about seven o'clock my son arrived. The sun was low in the west. I must have dozed a moment, for I did not see him coming, a speck on the horizon, then rapidly bigger and bigger, as I had foreseen. But he was already between me and the camp, making for the latter, when I saw him. A wave of irritation broke over me, I jumped to my feet and began to vociferate, brandishing my umbrella. He turned and I beckoned him to join me, waving the umbrella as if I wanted to hook something with the handle. I thought for a moment he was going to defy me and continue on his way to the camp, to where the camp had been rather, for it was there no more. But finally he came towards me. He was pushing a bicycle which, when he had joined me, he let fall with a gesture signifying he could bear no more. Pick it up, I said, till I look at it. I had to admit it must once have been quite a good bicycle. I would gladly describe it, I would gladly write four thousand words on it alone. And you call that a bicycle? I said. Only half expecting him to answer me I continued to inspect it. But there was something so strange in his silence that I looked up at him. His eyes were starting out of his head. What's the matter, I said, is my fly open? He let go the bicycle again. Pick it up, I said. He picked it up. What happened to you? he said. I had a fall, I said. A fall? he said. Yes, a fall, I cried, did you never have a fall? I tried to remember the name of the plant that springs from the ejaculations of the hanged and shrieks when plucked. How much did you give for it? I said. Four pounds, he said. Four pounds! I cried. If he had said two pounds or even thirty shillings I should have cried, Two pounds! or, Thirty shillings! the same. They asked four pounds five, he said. Have you the receipt? I said. He did not know what a receipt was. I described one. The money I spent on my son's education and he did not know what a simple receipt was. But I think he knew as well as I. For when I said to him, Now tell me what a receipt is, he told me very prettily. I really did not care in the least whether he had been fooled into paying for the bicycle three or four times what it was worth or whether on the other hand he had appropriated the best part of the purchase money for his own use. The loss would not be mine. Give me the ten shillings, I said. I spent them, he said. Enough, enough. He began explaining that the first day the shops had been closed, that the second— I said, Enough, enough. I looked at the carrier. It was the best thing about that bicycle. It and the pump. Does it go by any chance? I said. I had a puncture two miles from Hole, he said, I walked the rest of the way. I looked at his shoes. Pump it up, I said. I held the bicycle. I forget which wheel it was. As soon as two things are nearly identical I am lost. The dirty little twister was letting the air escape between the valve and the connexion which he had purposely not screwed tight. Hold the bicycle, I said, and give me the pump. The tyre was soon hard. I looked at my son. He began to protest. I soon put a stop to that. Five minutes later I felt the tyre. It was as hard as ever. I cursed him. He took a bar of chocolate from his pocket and offered it to me. I took it. But instead of eating it, as I longed to, and although I have a horror of waste, I cast it from me, after a moment's hesitation, which I trust my son did not notice. Enough. We went down to the road. It was more like a path. I tried to sit down on the carrier. The foot of my stiff leg tried to sink into the ground, into the grave. I propped myself up on one of the bags. Keep her steady, I said. I was still too low. I added the other. Its bulges dug into my buttocks. The more things resist me the more rabid I get. With time, and nothing but my teeth and nails, I would rage up from the bowels of the earth to its crust, knowing full well I had nothing to gain. And when I had no more teeth, no more nails, I would dig through the rock with my bones. Here then in a few words is the solution I arrived at. First the bags, then my son's raincoat folded in four, all lashed to the carrier and the saddle with my son's bits of string. As for the umbrella, I hooked it round my neck, so as to have both hands free to hold on to my son by the waist, under the armpits rather, for by this time my seat was higher than his. Pedal, I said. He made a despairing effort, I can well believe it. We fell. I felt a sharp pain in my shin. I was all tangled up in the back wheel. Help! I cried. My son helped me up. My stocking was torn and my leg bleeding. Happily it was the sick leg. What would I have done, with both legs out of action? I would have found a way. It was even perhaps a blessing in disguise. I was thinking of phlebotomy of course. Are you all right? I said. Yes, he said. He would be. With my umbrella I caught him a smart blow on the hamstrings, gleaming between the leg of his shorts and his stocking. He cried out. Do you want to kill us? I said. I'm not strong enough, he said, I'm not strong enough. The bicycle was all right apparently, the back wheel slightly buckled perhaps. I at once saw the error I had made. It was to have settled down in my seat, with my feet clear of the ground, before we moved off. I reflected. We'll try again, I said. I can't, he said. Don't try me too far, I said. He straddled the frame. Start off gently when I tell you, I said. I got up again behind and settled down in my seat, with my feet clear of the ground. Good. Wait till I tell you, I said. I let myself slide to one side till the foot of my good leg touched the ground. The only weight now on the back wheel was that of my sick leg, cocked up rigid at an excruciating angle. I dug my fingers into my son's jacket. Go easy, I said. The wheels began to turn. I followed, half dragged, half hopping. I trembled for my testicles which swing a little low. Faster! I cried. He bore down on the pedals. I bounded up to my place. The bicycle swayed, righted itself, gained speed. Bravo! I cried, beside myself with joy. Hurrah! cried my son. How I loathe that exclamation! I can hardly set it down. He was as pleased as I, I do believe. His heart was beating under my hand and yet my hand was far from his heart. Happily it was downhill. Happily I had mended my hat, or the wind would have blown it away. Happily the weather was fine and I no longer alone. Happily, happily.

In this way we came to Ballyba. I shall not tell of the obstacles we had to surmount, the fiends we had to circumvent, the misdemeanours of the son, the disintegrations of the father. It was my intention, almost my desire, to tell of all these things, I rejoiced at the thought that the moment would come when I might do so. Now the intention is dead, the moment is come and the desire is gone. My leg was no better. It was no worse either. The skin had healed. I would never have got there alone. It was thanks to my son. What? That I got there. He often complained of his health, his stomach, his teeth. I gave him some morphine. He looked worse and worse. When I asked him what was wrong he could not tell me. We had trouble with the bicycle. But I patched it up. I would not have got there without my son. We were a long time getting there. Weeks. We kept losing our way, taking our time. I still did not know what I was to do with Molloy, when I found him. I thought no more about it. I thought about myself, much, as we went along, sitting behind my son, looking over his head, and in the evening, when we camped, while he made himself useful, and when he went away, leaving me alone. For he often went away, to spy out the lie of the land and to buy provisions. I did practically nothing any more. He took good care of me, I must say. He was clumsy, stupid, slow, dirty, untruthful, deceitful, prodigal, unfilial, but he did not abandon me. I thought much about myself. That is to say I often took a quick look at myself, closed my eyes, forgot, began again. We took a long time getting to Ballyba, we even got there without knowing it. Stop, I said to my son one day. I had just caught sight of a shepherd I liked the look of. He was sitting on the ground stroking his dog. A flock of black shorn sheep strayed about them, unafraid. What a pastoral land, my God. Leaving my son on the side of the road I went towards them, across the grass. I often stopped and rested, leaning on my umbrella. The shepherd watched me as I came, without getting up. The dog too, without barking. The sheep too. Yes, little by little, one by one, they turned and faced me, watching me as I came. Here and there faint movements of recoil, a tiny foot stamping the ground, betrayed their uneasiness. They did not seem timid, as sheep go. And my son of course watched me as I went, I felt his eyes in my back. The silence was absolute. Profound in any case. All things considered it was a solemn moment. The weather was divine. It was the close of day. Each time I stopped I looked about me. I looked at the shepherd, the sheep, the dog and even at the sky. But when I moved I saw nothing but the ground and the play of my feet, the good one springing forward, holding back, setting itself down, waiting for the other to come up. I came finally to a halt about ten paces from the shepherd. There was no use going any further. How I would love to dwell upon him. His dog loved him, his sheep did not fear him. Soon he would rise, feeling the falling dew. The fold was far, far, he would see from afar the light in his cot. Now I was in the midst of the sheep, they made a circle round me, their eyes converged on me. Perhaps I was the butcher come to make his choice. I took off my hat. I saw the dog's eyes following the movement of my hand. I looked about me again incapable of speech. I did not know how I would ever be able to break this silence. I was on the point of turning away without having spoken. Finally I said, Ballyba, hoping it sounded like a question. The shepherd drew the pipe from his mouth and pointed the stem at the ground. I longed to say, Take me with you, I will serve you faithfully, just for a place to lie and a little food. I had understood, but without seeming to I suppose, for he repeated his gesture, pointing the stem of his pipe at the ground, several times. Bally, I said. He raised one hand, it wavered an instant as if over a map, then stiffened. The pipe still smoked faintly, the smoke hung blue in the air an instant, then vanished. I looked in the direction indicated. The dog too. We were all three turned to the north. The sheep were losing interest in me. Perhaps they had understood. I heard them straying about again and grazing. I distinguished at last, at the limit of the plain, a dim glow, the sum of countless points of light blurred by the distance, I thought of Juno's milk. It lay like a faint splash on the sharp dark sweep of the horizon. I gave thanks for evening that brings out the lights, the stars in the sky and on earth the brave little lights of men. By day the shepherd would have raised his pipe in vain, towards the long clear-cut commissure of earth and sky. But now I felt the man turning towards me again, and the dog, and the man drawing on his pipe again, in the hope it had not gone out.

And I knew I was all alone gazing at that distant glow that would get brighter and brighter, I knew that too, then suddenly go out. And I did not like the feeling of being alone, with my son perhaps, no, alone, spellbound. And I was wondering how to depart without self-loathing or sadness, or with as little as possible, when a kind of immense sigh all round me announced it was not I who was departing, but the flock. I watched them move away, the man in front, then the sheep, huddled together, their heads sunk, jostling one another, breaking now and then into a little trot, snatching blindly without stopping a last mouthful from the earth, and last of all the dog, jauntily, waving his long black plumy tail, though there was no one to witness his contentment, if that is what it was. And so in perfect order, the shepherd silent and the dog unneeded, the little flock departed. And so no doubt they would plod on, until they came to the stable or the fold. And there the shepherd stands aside to let them pass and he counts them as they go by, though he knows not one is missing. Then he turns towards his cottage, the kitchen door is open, the lamp is burning, he goes in and sits down at the table, without taking off his hat. But the dog stops at the threshold, not knowing whether he may go in or whether he must stay out, all night.

That night I had a violent scene with my son. I do not remember about what. Wait, it may be important.

No, I don't know. I have had so many scenes with my son. At the time it must have seemed a scene like any other, that's all I know.

I must have got the better of it as I always did, thanks to my infallible technique, and brought him unerringly to a proper sense of his iniquities. But the next day I realized my mistake. For waking early I found myself alone, in the shelter, I who was always the first to wake. And what is more my instinct told me I had been alone for some considerable time, my breath no longer mingling with the breath of my son, in the narrow shelter he had erected, under my supervision. Not that the fact of his having disappeared with the bicycle, during the night or with the first guilty flush of dawn, was in itself a matter for grave anxiety. And I would have found excellent and honourable reasons for this, if this had been all. Unfortunately he had taken his knapsack and his raincoat. And there remained nothing in the shelter, nor outside the shelter, belonging to him absolutely nothing. And this was not yet all, for he had left with a considerable sum of money, he who was only entitled to a few pence from time to time, for his savings-box. For since he had been in charge of everything, under my supervision of course, and notably of the shopping, I was obliged to place a certain reliance on him in the matter of money. And he always had a far greater sum in his pocket than was strictly necessary. And in order to make all this sound more likely I shall add what follows.

1. I desired him to learn double-entry book-keeping and had instructed him in its rudiments.

2. I could no longer be bothered with these wretched trifles which had once been my delight.

3. I had told him to keep an eye out, on his expeditions, for a second bicycle, light and inexpensive. For I was weary of the carrier and I also saw the day approaching when my son would no longer have the

strength to pedal for the two of us. And I believed I was capable, more than that, I knew I was capable, with a little practice, of learning to pedal with one leg. And then I would resume my rightful place, I mean in the van. And my son would follow me. And then the scandal would cease of my son's defying me, and going left when I told him right, or right when I told him left, or straight on when I told him right or left as he had been doing of late, more and more frequently.

That is all I wished to add.

But on examining my pocket-book I found it contained no more than fifteen shillings, which led me to the conclusion that my son had not been content with the sum already in his possession, but had gone through my pockets, before he left, while I slept. And the human breast is so bizarre that my first feeling was of gratitude for his leaving me this little sum, enough to keep me going until help arrived, and I saw in this a kind of delicacy!

I was therefore alone, with my bag, my umbrella (which he might easily have taken too) and fifteen shillings, knowing myself coldly abandoned, with deliberation and no doubt premeditation, in Ballyba it is true, if indeed I was in Ballyba, but still far from Bally. And I remained for several days, I do not know how many, in the place where my son had abandoned me, eating my last provisions (which he might easily have taken too), seeing no living soul, powerless to act, or perhaps strong enough at last to act no more. For I had no illusions, I knew that all was about to end, or to begin again, it little mattered which, and it little mattered how, I had only to wait. And on and off, for fun, and the better to scatter them to the winds, I dallied with the hopes that spring eternal, childish hopes, as for example that my son, his anger spent, would have pity on me and come back to me! Or that Molloy, whose country this was, would come to me, who had not been able to go to him, and grow to be a friend, and like a father to me, and help me do what I had to do, so that Youdi would not be angry with me and would not punish me! Yes, I let them spring within me and grow in strength, brighten and charm me with a thousand fancies, and then I swept them away, with a great disgusted sweep of all my being, I swept myself clean of them and surveyed with satisfaction the void they had polluted. And in the evening I turned to the lights of Bally, I watched them shine brighter and brighter, then all go out together, or nearly all, foul little flickering lights of terrified men. And I said, To think I might be there now, but for my misfortune! And with regard to the Obidil, of whom I have refrained from speaking, until now, and whom I so longed to see face to face, all I can say with regard to him is this, that I never saw him, either face to face or darkly, perhaps there is no such person, that would not greatly surprise me. And at the thought of the punishments Youdi might inflict upon me I was seized by such a mighty fit of laughter that I shook, with mighty silent laughter and my features composed in their wonted sadness and calm. But my whole body shook, and even my legs, so that I had to lean against a tree, or against a bush, when the fit came on me standing, my umbrella being no longer sufficient to keep me from falling. Strange laughter truly, and no doubt misnamed, through indolence perhaps, or ignorance. And as for myself, that unfailing pastime, I must say it was far now from my thoughts. But there were moments when it did not seem so far from me, when I seemed to be drawing towards it as the sands towards the wave, when it crests and whitens, though I must say this image hardly fitted my situation, which was rather that of the turd waiting for the flush. And I note here the little beat my heart once missed, in my home, when a fly, flying low above my ash-tray, raised a little ash, with the breath of its wings. And I grew gradually weaker and weaker and more and more content. For several days I had eaten nothing. I could probably have found blackberries and mushrooms, but I had no wish for them. I remained all day stretched out in the shelter, vaguely regretting my son's raincoat, and I crawled out in the evening to have a good laugh at the lights of Bally. And though suffering a little from wind and cramps in the stomach I felt extraordinarily content, content with myself, almost elated, enchanted with my performance. And I said, I shall soon lose consciousness altogether, it is merely a question of time. But Gaber's arrival put a stop to these frolics.

It was evening. I had just crawled out of the shelter for my evening guffaw and the better to savour my exhaustion. He had already been there for some time. He was sitting on a tree-stump, half asleep. Well Moran, he said. You recognize me? I said. He took out and opened his notebook, licked his finger, turned over the pages till he came to the right page, raised it towards his eyes which at the same time he lowered towards it. I can see nothing, he said. He was dressed as when I had last seen him. My strictures on his Sunday clothes had therefore been unjustified. Unless it was Sunday again. But had I not always seen him dressed in this way? Would you have a match? he said. I did not recognize this far-off voice. Or a torch, he said. He must have seen from my face that I possessed nothing of a luminous nature. He took a small electric torch from his pocket and shone it on his page. He read, Moran, Jacques, home, instanter. He put out his torch, closed his notebook on his finger and looked at me. I can't walk, I said. What? he said. I'm sick, I can't move, I said. I can't hear a word you say, he said. I cried to him that I could not move, that I was sick, that I should have to be carried, that my son had abandoned me, that I could bear no more. He examined me laboriously from head to foot. I executed a few steps leaning on my umbrella to prove to him I could not walk. He opened his notebook again, shone the torch on his page, studied it at length and said, Moran, home, instanter. He closed his notebook, put it back in his pocket, put his lamp back in his pocket, stood up, drew his hands over his chest and announced he was dying of thirst. Not a word on how I was looking. And yet I had not shaved since the day my son brought back the bicycle from Hole, nor combed my hair, nor washed, not to mention all the privations I had suffered and the great inward metamorphoses. Do you recognize me? I cried. Do I recognize you? he said. He reflected. I knew what he was doing, he was searching for the phrase most apt to wound me. Ah Moran, he said, what a man! I was staggering with weakness. If I had dropped dead at his feet he would have said, Ah poor old Moran, that's him all over. It was getting darker and darker. I wondered if it was really Gaber. Is he angry? I said. You wouldn't have a sup of beer by any chance?

he said. I'm asking you if he is angry, I cried. Angry, said Gaber, don't make me laugh, he keeps rubbing his hands from morning to night, I can hear them in the outer room. That means nothing, I said. And chuckling to himself, said Gaber. He must be angry with me, I said. Do you know what he told me the other day? said Gaber. Has he changed? I cried. Changed, said Gaber, no he hasn't changed, why would he have changed, he's getting old, that's all, like the world. You have a queer voice this evening, I said. I do not think he heard me. Well, he said, drawing his hands once more over his chest, downwards, I'll be going, if that's all you have to say to me. He went, without saying goodbye. But I overtook him, in spite of my loathing for him, in spite of my weakness and my sick leg, and held him back by the sleeve. What did he tell you? I said. He stopped. Moran, he said, you are beginning to give me a serious pain in the arse. For pity's sake, I said, tell me what he told you. He gave me a shove. I fell. He had not intended to make me fall, he did not realize the state I was in, he had only wanted to push me away. I did not try to get up. I let a roar. He came and bent over me. He had a walrus moustache, chestnut in colour. I saw it lift, the lips open, and almost at the same time I heard words of solicitude, at a great distance. He was not brutal, Gaber, I knew him well. Gaber, I said, it's not much I'm asking you. I remember this scene well. He wanted to help me up. I pushed him away. I was all right where I was. What did he tell you? I said. I don't understand, said Gaber. You were saying a minute ago that he had told you something, I said, then I cut you short. Short? said Gaber.

Do you know what he told me the other day, I said, those were your very words. His face lit up. The clod was just about as quick as my son. He said to me, said Gaber, Gaber, he said—. Louder! I cried. He said to me, said Gaber, Gaber, he said, life is a thing of beauty, Gaber, and a joy for ever. He brought his face nearer mine. A joy for ever, he said, a thing of beauty, Moran, and a joy for ever. He smiled. I closed my eyes. Smiles are all very nice in their own way, very heartening, but at a reasonable distance. I said, Do you think he meant human life? I listened. Perhaps he didn't mean human life, I said. I opened my eyes. I was alone. My hands were full of grass and earth I had torn up unwittingly, was still tearing up. I was literally uprooting. I desisted, yes, the second I realized what I had done, what I was doing, such a nasty thing, I desisted from it, I opened my hands, they were soon empty.

That night I set out for home. I did not get far. But it was a start. It is the first step that counts. The second counts less. Each day saw me advance a little further. That last sentence is not clear, it does not say what I hoped it would. I counted at first by tens of steps. I stopped when I could go no further and I said, Bravo, that makes so many tens, so many more than yesterday. Then I counted by fifteens, by twenties and finally by fifties. Yes, in the end I could go fifty steps before having to stop, for rest, leaning on my faithful umbrella. In the beginning I must have strayed a little in Ballyba, if I really was in Ballyba. Then I followed more or less the same paths we had taken on the way out. But paths look different, when you go back along them. I ate, in obedience to the voice of reason, all that nature, the woods, the fields, the waters had to offer me in the way of edibles. I finished the morphine.

It was in August, in September at the latest, that I was ordered home. It was Spring when I got there, I will not be more precise. I had therefore been all winter on the way.

Anyone else would have lain down in the snow, firmly resolved never to rise again. Not I. I used to think that men would never get the better of me. I still think I am cleverer than things. There are men and there are things, to hell with animals. And with God. When a thing resists me, even if it is for my own good, it does not resist me long. This snow, for example. Though to tell the truth it lured me more than it resisted me. But in a sense it resisted me. That was enough. I vanquished it, grinding my teeth with joy, it is quite possible to grind one's incisors. I forged my way through it, towards what I would have called my ruin if I could have conceived what I had left to be ruined. Perhaps I have conceived it since, perhaps I have not done conceiving it, it takes time, one is bound to in time, I am bound to. But on the way home, a prey to the malignancy of man and nature and my own failing flesh, I could not conceive it. My knee, allowance made for the dulling effects of habit, was neither more nor less painful than the first day. The disease, whatever it was, was dormant! How can such things be? But to return to the flies, I like to think of those that hatch out at the beginning of winter, within doors, and die shortly after. You see them crawling and fluttering in the warm corners, puny, sluggish, torpid, mute. That is you see an odd one now and then. They must die very young, without having been able to lay. You sweep them away, you push them into the dust-pan with the brush, without knowing. That is a strange race of flies. But I was succumbing to other affections, that is not the word, intestinal for the most part. I would have described them once, not now, I am sorry, it would have been worth reading. I shall merely say that no one else would have surmounted them, without help. But I! Bent double, my free hand pressed to my belly, I advanced, and every now and then I let a roar, of triumph and distress. Certain mosses I consumed must have disagreed with me. I if I once made up my mind not to keep the hangman waiting, the bloody flux itself would not stop me, I would get there on all fours shitting out my entrails and chanting maledictions. Didn't I tell you it's my brethren that have done for me.

But I shall not dwell upon this journey home, its furies and treacheries. And I shall pass over in silence the fiends in human shape and the phantoms of the dead that tried to prevent me from getting home, in obedience to Youdi's command. But one or two words nevertheless, for my own edification and to prepare my soul to make an end. To begin with my rare thoughts.

Certain questions of a theological nature preoccupied me strangely. As for example.

1. What value is to be attached to the theory that Eve sprang, not from Adam's rib, but from a tumour in the fat of his leg (arse?)?

2. Did the serpent crawl or, as Comestor affirms, walk upright?

3. Did Mary conceive through the ear, as Augustine and Adobard assert?

4. How much longer are we to hang about waiting for the antechrist?

5. Does it really matter which hand is employed to absterge the podex?

6. What is one to think of the Irish oath sworn by the natives with the right hand on the relics of the saints and the left on the virile member?

7. Does nature observe the sabbath?

8. Is it true that the devils do not feel the pains of hell?

9. The algebraic theology of Craig. What is one to think of this?

10. Is it true that the infant Saint-Roch refused suck on Wednesdays and Fridays?

11. What is one to think of the excommunication of vermin in the sixteenth century?

12. Is one to approve of the Italian cobbler Lovat who, having cut off his testicles, crucified himself?

13. What was God doing with himself before the creation?

14. Might not the beatific vision become a source of boredom, in the long run?

15. Is it true that Judas' torments are suspended on Saturdays?

16. What if the mass for the dead were read over the living?

And I recited the pretty quietist Pater, Our Father who art no more in heaven than on earth or in hell, I neither want nor desire that thy name be hallowed, thou knowest best what suits thee. Etc. The middle and the end are very pretty.

It was in this frivolous and charming world that I took refuge, when my cup ran over.

But I asked myself other questions concerning me perhaps more closely. As for example.

1. Why had I not borrowed a few shillings from Gaber?

2. Why had I obeyed the order to go home?

3. What had become of Molloy?

4. Same question for me.

5. What would become of me?

6. Same questions for my son.

7. Was his mother in heaven?

8. Same question for my mother.

9. Would I go to heaven?

10. Would we all meet again in heaven one day, I, my mother, my son, his mother, Youdi, Gaber, Molloy, his mother, Yerk, Murphy, Watt, Camier and the rest?

11. What had become of my hens, my bees? Was my grey hen still living?

12. Zulu, the Elsner sisters, were they still living?

13. Was Youdi's business address still 8, Acacia Square? What if I wrote to him? What if I went to see him? I would explain to him. What would I explain to him? I would crave his forgiveness. Forgiveness for what?

14. Was not the winter exceptionally severe?

15. How long had I gone now without either confession or communion?

16. What was the name of the martyr who, being in prison, loaded with chains, covered with wounds and vermin, unable to stir, celebrated the consecration on his stomach and gave himself absolution?

17. What would I do until my death? Was there no means of hastening this, without falling into a state of sin?

But before I launch my body properly so-called across these icy, then, with the thaw, muddy solitudes, I wish to say that I often thought of my bees, more often than of my hens, and God knows I thought often of my hens. And I thought above all of their dance, for my bees danced, oh not as men dance, to amuse themselves, but in a different way. I alone of all mankind knew this, to the best of my belief. I had investigated this phenomenon very fully. The dance was best to be observed among the bees returning to the hive, laden more or less with nectar, and it involved a great variety of figures and rhythms. These evolutions I finally interpreted as a system of signals by means of which the incoming bees, satisfied or dissatisfied with their plunder, informed the outgoing bees in what direction to go, and in what not to go. But the outgoing bees danced too. It was no doubt their way of saying, I understand, or, Don't worry about me. But away from the hive, and busily at work, the bees did not dance. Here their watchword seemed to be, Every man for himself, assuming bees to be capable of such notions. The most striking feature of the dance was its very complicated figures, traced in flight, and I had classified a great number of these, with their probable meanings. But there was also the question of the hum, so various in tone in the vicinity of the hive that this could hardly be an effect of chance. I first concluded that each figure was reinforced by means of a hum peculiar to it. But I was forced to abandon this agreeable hypothesis. For I saw the same figure (at least what I called the same figure) accompanied by very different hums. So that I said, The purpose of the hum is not to emphasize the dance, but on the contrary to vary it. And the same figure exactly differs in meaning according to the hum that goes with it. And I had collected and classified a great number of observations on this subject, with gratifying results. But there was to be considered not only the figure and the hum, but also the height at which the figure was executed. And I acquired the conviction that the selfsame figure, accompanied by the selfsame hum, did not mean at all the same thing at twelve feet from the ground as it did at six. For the bees did not dance at any level, haphazard, but there were three or four levels, always the same, at which they danced. And if I were to tell you what these levels were, and what the relations between them, for I had measured them with care, you would not believe me. And this is not the moment to jeopardize my credit. Sometimes you would think I was writing for the public. And in spite of all the pains I had lavished on these problems, I was more than ever stupefied by the complexity of this innumerable dance, involving doubtless other determinants of which I had not the slightest idea. And I said, with rapture, Here is something I can study all my life, and never understand. And all during this long journey home, when I racked my mind for a little joy in store, the thought of my bees and their dance was the nearest thing to comfort. For I was still eager for my little joy, from time to time! And I admitted with good grace the possibility that this dance was after all no better than the dances of the people of the West, frivolous and meaningless. But for me, sitting near my sun-drenched hives, it would always be a noble thing to contemplate, too noble ever to be sullied by the cogitations of a man like me, exiled in his manhood. And I would never do my bees the wrong I had done my God, to whom I had been taught to ascribe my angers, fears, desires, and even my body.

I have spoken of a voice giving me orders, or rather advice. It was on the way home I heard it for the first time. I paid no attention to it.

Physically speaking it seemed to me I was now becoming rapidly unrecognizable. And when I passed my hands over my face, in a characteristic and now more than ever pardonable gesture, the face my hands felt was not my face any more, and the hands my face felt were my hands no longer. And yet the gist of the sensation was the same as in the far-off days when I was well-shaven and perfumed and proud of my intellectual's soft white hands. And this belly I did not know remained my belly, my old belly, thanks to I know not what intuition. And to tell the truth I not only knew who I was, but I had a sharper and clearer sense of my identity than ever before, in spite of its deep lesions and the wounds with which it was covered. And from this point of view I was less fortunate than my other acquaintances. I am sorry if this last phrase is not so happy as it might be. It deserved, who knows, to be without ambiguity.

Then there are the clothes that cleave so close to the body and are so to speak inseparable from it, in time of peace. Yes, I have always been very sensitive to clothing, though not in the least a dandy. I had not to complain of mine, tough and of good cut. I was of course inadequately covered, but whose fault was that? And I had to part with my straw, not made to resist the rigours of winter, and with my stockings (two pairs) which the cold and damp, the trudging and the lack of laundering facilities had literally annihilated. But I let out my braces to their fullest extent and my knickerbockers, very baggy as the fashion is, came down to my calves. And at the sight of the blue flesh, between the knickerbockers and the tops of my boots, I sometimes thought of my son and the blow I had fetched him, so avid is the mind of the flimsiest analogy. My boots became rigid, from lack of proper care. So skin defends itself, when dead and tanned. The air coursed through them freely, preserving perhaps my feet from freezing. And I had likewise sadly to part with my drawers (two pairs). They had rotted, from constant contact with my incontinences. Then the seat of my breeches, before it too decomposed, sawed my crack from Dan to Beersheba. What else did I have to discard? My shirt? Never! But I often wore it inside out and back to front. Let me see. I had four ways of wearing my shirt. Front to front right side out, front to front inside out, back to front right side out, back to front inside out. And the fifth day I began again. It was in the hope of making it last. Did this make it last? I do not know. It lasted. To major things the surest road is on the minor pains bestowed, if you don't happen to be in a hurry. But what else did I have to discard? My hard collars, yes, I discarded them all, and even before they were quite worn and torn. But I kept my tie, I even wore it, knotted round my bare neck, out of sheer bravado I suppose. It was a spotted tie, but I forget the colour.

When it rained, when it snowed, when it hailed,

then I found myself faced with the following dilemma. Was I to go on leaning on my umbrella and get drenched or was I to stop and take shelter under my open umbrella? It was a false dilemma, as so many dilemmas are. For on the one hand all that remained of the canopy of my umbrella was a few flitters of silk fluttering from the stays and on the other I could have gone on, very slowly, using the umbrella no longer as a support, but as a shelter. But I was so accustomed, on the one hand to the perfect watertightness of my expensive umbrella, and on the other hand to being unable to walk without its support, that the dilemma remained entire, for me. I could of course have made myself a stick, out of a branch, and gone on, in spite of the rain, the snow, the hail, leaning on the stick and the umbrella open above me. But I did not, I do not know why. But when the rain descended, and the other things that descend upon us from above, sometimes I pushed on, leaning on the umbrella, getting drenched, but most often I stopped dead, opened the umbrella above me and waited for it to be over. Then I got equally drenched. But that was not the point. And if it had suddenly begun to rain manna I would have waited, stock still, under my umbrella, for it to be over, before taking advantage of it. And when my arm was weary of holding up the umbrella, then I gave it to the other hand. And with my free hand I slapped and rubbed every part of my body within its reach, in order to keep the blood trickling freely, or I drew it over my face, in a gesture that was characteristic, of me. And the long spike of my umbrella was like a finger. My best thoughts came to me during these halts. But when it was clear that the rain, etc., would not stop all day, or all night, then I did the sensible thing and built myself a proper shelter. But I did not like proper shelters, made of boughs, any more. For soon there were no more leaves, but only the needles of certain conifers. But this was not the real reason why I did not like proper shelters any more, no. But when I was inside them I could think of nothing but my son's raincoat, I literally saw it, I saw nothing else, it filled all space. It was in reality what our English friends call a trench-coat, and I could smell the rubber, though trench-coats are not rubberized as a rule. So I avoided as far as possible having recourse to proper shelters, made of boughs, preferring the shelter of my faithful umbrella, or of a tree, or of a hedge, or of a bush, or of a ruin.

The thought of taking to the road, to try and get a lift, never crossed my mind.

The thought of turning for help to the villages, to the peasants, would have displeased me, if it had occurred to me.

I reached home with my fifteen shillings intact. No, I spent two. This is how.

I had to suffer other molestations than this, other offences, but I shall not record them. Let us be content with paradigms. I may have to suffer others in the future. This is not certain. But they will never be known. This is certain.

It was evening. I was waiting quietly, under my umbrella, for the weather to clear, when I was brutally accosted from behind. I had heard nothing. I had been in a place where I was all alone. A hand turned me about. It was a big ruddy farmer. He was wearing an oilskin, a bowler hat and wellingtons. His chubby cheeks were streaming, the water was dripping from his bushy moustache. But why describe him? We glared at each other with hatred. Perhaps he was the same who had so politely offered to drive us home in his car. I think not. And yet his face was familiar. Not only his face. He held a lantern in his hand. It was not lit. But he might light it at any moment. In the other he held a spade. To bury me with if necessary. He seized me by the jacket, by the lapel. He had not yet begun to shake me exactly, he would shake me in his own good time, not before. He merely cursed me. I wondered what I could have done, to put him in such a state. I must have raised my eyebrows. But I always raise my eyebrows, they are almost in my hair, my brow is nothing but wales and furrows. I understood finally that I did not own the land. It was his land. What was I doing on his land? If there is one question I dread, to which I have never been able to invent a satisfactory reply, it is the question what am I doing. And on someone else's land to make things worse! And at night! And in weather not fit for a dog! But I did not lose my presence of mind. It is a vow. I said. I have a fairly distinguished voice, when I choose. It must have impressed him. He unhanded me. A pilgrimage, I said, following up my advantage. He asked me where to. He was lost. To the Turdy Madonna, I said. The Turdy Madonna? he said, as if he knew Turdy like the back of his hand and there were no Madonna in the length and breadth of it. But where is the place in which there is no Madonna? Herself, I said. The black one? he said, to try me. She is not black that I know of, I said. Another would have lost countenance. Not I. I knew my yokels and their weak points. You'll never get there, he said. It's thanks to her I lost my infant boy, I said, and kept his mamma. Such sentiments could not fail to please a cattle breeder. Had he but known! I told him more fully what alas had never happened. Not that I miss Ninette. But she, at least, who knows, in any case, yes, a pity, no matter. She is the Madonna of pregnant women, I said, of pregnant married women, and I have vowed to drag myself miserably to her niche, and thank her. This incident gives but a feeble idea of my ability, even at this late period. But I had gone a little too far, for the vicious look came back into his eye. May I ask you a favour, I said, God will reward you. I added, God sent you to me, this evening. Humbly to ask a favour of people who are on the point of knocking your brains out sometimes produces good results. A little hot tea, I implored, without sugar or milk, to revive me. To grant such a small favour to a pilgrim on the rocks was frankly a temptation difficult to resist. Oh all right, he said, come back to the house, you can dry yourself, before the fire. But I cannot, I cannot, I cried, I have sworn to make a bee-line to her! And to efface the bad impression created by these words I took a florin from my pocket and gave it to him. For your poor-box, I said. And I added, because of the dark, A florin for your poor-box. It's a long way, he said. God will go with you, I said. He thought it over. Well he might. Above all nothing to eat, I said, no really, I must not eat. Ah Moran, wily as a serpent, there was never the like of old Moran. Of course I would have preferred violence, but I dared not take the risk. Finally he took himself off telling me to stay where I was. I do not know what was in his mind. When I judged him at a safe remove I closed the umbrella and set off in the opposite direction, at right angles to the way I was going, in the driving rain. That was how I spent a florin.

Now I may make an end.

I skirted the graveyard. It was night. Midnight perhaps. The lane is steep, I laboured. A little wind was chasing the clouds over the faint sky. It is a great thing to own a plot in perpetuity, a very great thing indeed. If only that were the only perpetuity. I came to the wicket. It was locked. Very properly. But I could not open it. The key went into the hole, but would not turn. Long disuse? A new lock? I burst it open. I drew back to the other side of the lane and hurled myself at it. I had come home, as Youdi had commanded me. In the end I got to my feet. What smelt so sweet? The lilacs? The primroses perhaps. I went towards my hives. They were there, as I feared. I lifted the top off one and laid it on the ground. It was a little roof, with a sharp ridge, and steep overhanging slopes. I put my hand in the hive, moved it among the empty trays, felt along the bottom. It encountered, in a corner, a dry light ball. It crumbled under my fingers. They had clustered together for a little warmth, to try and sleep. I took out a handful. It was too dark to see, I put it in my pocket. It weighed nothing. They had been left out all winter, their honey taken away, without sugar. Yes, now I may make an end. I did not go to the hen-house. My hens were dead too, I knew they were dead. They had not been killed in the same way, except the grey one perhaps, that was the only difference. My bees, my hens, I had deserted them.

I went towards the house. It was in darkness. The door was locked. I burst it open. Perhaps I could have opened it, with one of my keys. I turned the switch. No light. I went to the kitchen, to Martha's room. No one. There is nothing more to tell. The house was empty. The company had cut off the light. They have offered to let me have it back. But I told them they could keep it. That is the kind of man I have become. I went back to the garden. The next day I looked at my handful of bees. A little dust of annulets and wings. I found some letters, at the foot of the stairs, in the box. A letter from Savory. My son was well. He would be. Let us hear no more about him. He has come back. He is sleeping. A letter from Youdi, in the third person, asking for a report. He will get his report. It is summer again. This time a year ago I was setting out. I am clearing out. One day I received a visit from Gaber. He wanted the report. That's funny, I thought I was done with people and talk. Call back, I said. One day I received a visit from Father Ambrose. Is it possible! he said when he saw me. I think he really liked me, in his own way. I told him not to count on me any more. He began to talk. He was right. Who is not right? I left him. I am clearing out. Perhaps I shall meet Molloy. My knee is no better. It is no worse either. I have crutches now. I shall go faster, all will go faster. They will be happy days. I shall learn. All there was to sell I have sold. But I had heavy debts. I have been a man long enough, I shall not put up with it any more, I shall not try any more. I shall never light this lamp again. I am going to blow it out and go into the garden. I think of the long

May days, June days, when I lived in the garden. One day I talked to Hannah. She gave me news of Zulu, of the Elsner sisters. She knew who I was, she was not afraid of me. She never went out, she disliked going out. She talked to me from her window. The news was bad, but might have been worse. There was a bright side. They were lovely days. The winter had been exceptionally rigorous, everybody said so. We had therefore a right to this superb summer. I do not know if we had a right to it. My birds had not been killed. They were wild birds. And yet quite trusting. I recognized them and they seemed to recognize me. But one never knows. Some were missing and some were new. I tried to understand their language better. Without having recourse to mine. They were the longest, loveliest days of all the year. I lived in the garden. I have spoken of a voice telling me things. I was getting to know it better now, to understand what it wanted. It did not use the words that Moran had been taught when he was little and that he in his turn had taught to his little one. So that at first I did not know what it wanted. But in the end I understood this language. I understood it, I understand it, all wrong perhaps. That is not what matters. It told me to write the report. Does this mean I am freer now than I was? I do not know. I shall learn. Then I went back into the house and wrote, It is midnight. The rain is beating on the windows It was not midnight. It was not raining.